T0363192

Romantic Suspense

Danger. Passion. Drama.

Colton's Last Resort
Amber Leigh Williams

Arctic Pursuit
Anna J. Stewart

MILLS & BOON

Amber Leigh Williams is acknowledged as the author of this work
COLTON'S LAST RESORT
© 2024 by Harlequin Eneterprises ULC
Philippine Copyright 2024
Australian Copyright 2024
New Zealand Copyright 2024

First Published 2024
First Australian Paperback Edition 2024
ISBN 978 1 038 93902 9

ARCTIC PURSUIT
© 2024 by Anna J. Stewart
Philippine Copyright 2024
Australian Copyright 2024
New Zealand Copyright 2024

First Published 2024
First Australian Paperback Edition 2024
ISBN 978 1 038 93902 9

MIX
Paper | Supporting
responsible forestry
FSC® C001695

Published by
Harlequin Mills & Boon
An imprint of Harlequin Enterprises (Australia) Pty Limited
(ABN 47 001 180 918), a subsidiary of HarperCollins
Publishers Australia Pty Limited
(ABN 36 009 913 517)
Level 19, 201 Elizabeth Street
SYDNEY NSW 2000 AUSTRALIA

Cover art used by arrangement with Harlequin Books S.A.. All rights reserved.

Printed and bound in Australia by McPherson's Printing Group

Colton's Last Resort
Amber Leigh Williams

MILLS & BOON

Amber Leigh Williams is an author, wife, mother of two and dog mom. She has been writing sexy small-town romance with memorable characters since 2006. Her Harlequin romance miniseries is set in her charming hometown of Fairhope, Alabama. She lives on the Alabama Gulf Coast, where she loves being outdoors with her family and a good book. Visit her on the web at www.amberleighwilliams.com!

Visit the Author Profile page at
millsandboon.com.au
for more titles.

Dear Reader,

Welcome to Mariposa Resort & Spa, owned and operated by Adam, Laura and Joshua Colton!

I enjoyed writing this first book in The Coltons of Arizona continuity. Red Rock Country is a dream destination and this has been a dream of a project. I loved working with the other authors and our editor to bring Mariposa, the Colton siblings, and their friends, family and staff to life.

Laura and Noah have been so much fun to pit against one another for their common goal of flushing out a killer on the resort. I love an opposites-attract romance—even better that these opposites must engage in a fake relationship in order to catch the bad guy.

Words have never come to the page faster than when Noah and Laura clash for the first time, or when their shared grief over Allison's death binds them together in spite of everything that is so wrong about their relationship (and yet so very right)!

I hope you love The Coltons of Arizona as much as I do. Stay tuned for the second book in the continuity by Patricia Sargeant for Alexis's story.

Happy reading!

Amber

To Beardy and the littles,
I've never written a book faster. It's a testament to
your love and understanding that I was able to do so
during a difficult time. Endless bear hugs and
ice cream kisses for all of you!

And to Patricia, Kacy, Kimberly, Charlene,
Addison and our editor, Emma Cole.

It has been lovely working with all of you.

Prologue

Allison Brewer didn't belong in a morgue. She was a twenty-five-year-old yoga instructor with zero underlying conditions. She never smoked, rarely drank, and was the picture of health and vitality.

Detective Noah Steele sucked in a breath as the coroner, Rod Steinbeck, pulled back the sheet. How many times had he stood over a body at the Yavapai County Coroner's Office? How many times had he stared unflinchingly at death—at what nature did to humans and what human nature did to others?

She looks like she could still be alive, he thought. No cuts or bruises marred her face. There were no ligature marks. She could have been asleep. She looked perfectly at peace. If Noah squinted, he could fool himself into thinking there was a slight smile at the corners of her mouth. Just as there had been when she'd feigned sleep as a girl.

However, an inescapable blue stain spread across her lips. He could deny it all he wanted, but his sister was gone.

"I'm sorry, Noah," Rod said and lifted the sheet over her face again.

"No." The word wasn't soft or hard, loud or quiet. Noah surprised himself by speaking mildly. As if this were any other body…any other case. His mind was somewhere near the ceiling. His gut turned, and his chest ached. But he let that piece of himself float away, detached. He made himself think like he was trained to think. "What're your impressions?"

"Fulton's already been here. It's his case. And for good reason. You're going to need some time to process—"

"Rod." He sounded cold. He was. He was so bitterly cold. And he didn't know how to live with it. He didn't know how to live in a world without Allison. "Next of kin would be informed of any progress made in the investigation. I'm her next of kin. Inform me."

Rod shuffled his feet. Placing his hands at each corner of the head of the steel table, he studied Allison. "I'm not sure I'm comfortable with this."

"She's dead." Noah made himself say it. He needed to hear it, the finality of it. "If Sedona Police wants me to process that, I need to know how and why."

Rod adjusted his glasses. "Look, maybe you should talk to Fulton."

"She was found at the resort," Noah prompted, undeterred, "where she works."

"Mariposa."

"You were on scene there," Noah surmised. "What time did you arrive?"

Rod gave in. "Nine fifteen."

"Where was she?"

"One of the pool cabanas," the coroner explained.

"Tell me what you saw."

"Come on, Noah…"

"Tell me," Noah said. He knew not to raise his voice. If he were hysterical, it would get back to his CO. He'd be put on leave.

He needed to work through this. If he stopped working, stopped thinking objectively, he would lose his mind.

Rod lifted his hands. "She was found face down, but one of the staff performed CPR, so she was on her back when I arrived. Her shoes were missing."

That could've been something, Noah thought, if Allison hadn't had a habit of going around barefoot where she was comfortable, particularly when entering someone's home.

The temperature had dipped into the thirties the night before. *A little cold for no shoes, even for her*, he considered. "What was she wearing?"

"Sport jacket and leggings," Rod explained. "Underneath, she wore a long-sleeved ballet-like top cropped above the navel with crisscrossed bands underneath. It was a matching set, all green."

"What do you figure for time of death?"

"Right now, I'd say she died somewhere between one and two this morning."

She hadn't gone home to bed, Noah mused. "Any cuts, lacerations? Signs of foul play?"

"Some abrasions on the backs of her legs."

"Show me."

Again, Rod paused before he walked to the bottom of the table. Lifting the drape, he revealed one long, pale leg with toes still painted pink. Noah tried not to see the unearthly blue tone of the skin around the nails. He craned his neck when Rod showed him the marks on her calves.

"She was dragged," Noah said as he realized what had happened. Why did the air feel like ice? The cold filled his lungs. They felt wind-burned, and the pain of it made his hands knot into fists.

"That would be my understanding," Rod agreed. He replaced the sheet gingerly.

"Before or after TOD?" Noah asked.

"After."

Noah's brow furrowed. "She was killed somewhere other than the cabana and staged there." His voice had gone rough, but he kept going, searching. "Were there any items with her at the scene?"

"Fulton noted there was no purse, wallet or cell phone. She was identified by members of Mariposa's staff."

"Were her lips blue when you got there?"

"Yes." Rod nodded. "Her fingernails and toes were discolored as well."

Noah scraped his knuckles over the thick growth of beard that covered his jawline. "Who found her?"

"From what I understand," Rod said slowly, "it was a staff member. You'll have to get the name of the person from Fulton."

"Who was there when you arrived on scene?" Noah asked curiously.

"There was a small crowd that had been blocked by officers," Rod told him. "Several members of security, one pool maintenance person and all three of the Coltons."

"Coltons." Noah recognized the name, but he let it hang in the air, waiting for Rod to elaborate.

"The siblings," Rod said. "They own and manage Mariposa. Adam, Laura and Joshua, I believe, are their names."

"What was your impression of them?" Noah asked, homing in.

Rod considered. "The younger one, Joshua, was quiet. Laura didn't say much either. She seemed stricken by the whole thing. The oldest one, Adam…"

When Rod paused, Noah narrowed his eyes. "What about him?"

"He did all the talking," Rod said. "He ordered everyone back and let the uniforms, Fulton, crime scene technicians and myself work. There was no attempt to tamper with the scene. Although I did hear him speaking to Fulton as we readied the body for transport."

"What did he say?" Noah asked, feeling like a dog with a bone.

"He wanted Fulton's word that the investigation would remain discreet," Rod said. "They get some high-profile guests at Mariposa. He didn't want their privacy or, I expect, their experience hindered."

The muscles around Noah's mouth tensed. "A member of their staff is found dead, and the Coltons' first thought is how it's going to affect their clientele? Does that seem right to you?"

"I'm not the detective," Steinbeck noted.

No, Noah considered. *I am.* "You'll do a tox screen?"

"It's routine," Rod replied. "As it stands, I don't have a cause of death for you."

"You'll keep me informed?" Noah asked.

"I'll stay in touch."

Noah forced himself to back away from Allison's body. Deep in some unbottled canyon, he felt himself scream.

"Have your parents been notified?"

The question nearly made him flinch. Rod didn't know. No one did. Not really.

It didn't matter, he told himself. He'd loved her, hadn't he? He'd loved her as his own. "She doesn't have parents," he said. "Neither of us do."

"I'm sorry." Rod placed his hand on Noah's shoulder. "I'll take care of her."

"I know." Noah turned for the door.

"Don't get yourself in trouble over this," Rod warned. "Let Fulton handle it. He'll find out what happened to her."

Noah didn't answer. In seconds, he was out of the autopsy room, down the hall, crossing the lobby. Planting both hands on the glass door, he shoved it open.

Cold air hit him in the face and did nothing for the lethal ice now channeling through his blood.

He thought about stopping, doubling over, bracing his hands on his knees.

He could hear her. Still.

Breathe, Noah. Deep breath in. And let it out.

Noah shook his head firmly, blocking out her voice. He thought of what Rod had said—about the scene and his impressions of the people there.

He took out his keys, walking to the unmarked vehicle that was his. Opening the driver's door, he got behind the wheel and cranked the engine. The sun was sinking swiftly toward the red rock mountains in the distance, but he picked up his phone. Using voice commands, he said, "Hey, Google, set a course for Mariposa Resort & Spa."

He studied the GPS route that popped up on-screen before mounting the phone on the dash. Shifting into Reverse, he cupped the back of the passenger headrest. Turning his head over his shoulder, he backed out of the parking space.

To hell with staying out of Fulton's way. Someone was responsible for Allison's death. He would find out who.

And he was going to nail the Coltons' asses to the floor.

Chapter One

Ten Hours Earlier

"**D**ad wants to meet."

Laura Colton stared at her brother over the rim of her thermos. "You couldn't have let me finish my coffee before dropping that bombshell?"

Her brother Adam raised a brow as he eyed the overlarge bottle. "There are three cups of java in that thing. If that's not enough to prepare you for the day, it's time you rethink some of your life choices."

"I demand coffee before chaos," Laura informed him and took another hit to prove her point. She was no stranger to butting heads with her older brother. They worked closely as owners and managers of Arizona's premier resort and spa.

It was their passion for Mariposa that made them lock horns. The resort wasn't simply the business venture that supported them. Before it was Mariposa, it was the respite their mother had sought when the disappointment of her marriage to Clive Colton had grown to be too much. Laura and her siblings' memories of Annabeth Colton were tied not just to the project she had started shortly after the birth of her third child, Joshua, but the land itself.

The three of them had buried her here at Mariposa after her battle with pancreatic cancer.

Laura loved Mariposa. It was more home than her actual hometown of Los Angeles had ever been. When Adam had asked her and Joshua to join him after he'd taken legal control of the resort at the age of twenty-one, neither of them had hesitated. From there, their management styles had been born out of renovations and the desire to make Mariposa their own.

The Coltons had put the once-small hotel on the map. It had been transformed into a getaway for the rich and famous, with twenty-four acres of spacious grounds northeast of Sedona. It now boasted thirty guest bungalows with stunning views of Red Rock Country, a five-star restaurant named after Annabeth herself, a garden, rock labyrinth, golf course, spa, horse stables and paddocks, and hiking trails.

Laura had learned to work with both of her brothers. They were invested in their shared vision, in this life. She could take their ribbing. Just as she could take the fact that she and Adam were both workaholics whose dedication and zeal left little in the way of private lives.

She drank more coffee and tried not to rue the long chain of failed relationships she'd endured, letting her eyes stray to the view from the conference room windows of L Building.

Shadows were long across the rocky vista with its stunning juxtaposition of blue sky and red geography. From its flat ridge top, Mariposa woke briskly. Staff would be going about preparations for the day. The chef at Annabeth would be arranging its signature champagne breakfast. Below the ridge and the bungalows, the horses would be feeding. The helicopter pilot who transported guests from the airport in Flagstaff would be doing preflight checks.

If she had to scrap her plans to be married with children by her late twenties for this, so be it. *There's plenty of time for all that*, Adam liked to say when anyone commented on his lack of a wife or children.

Plenty of time, she mused. No need to worry about the fact that she was tripping fast toward thirty.

Cautiously, she asked, "What does Clive want?"

Adam chuckled a little as he always did when she called their father by his given name. "He didn't say."

She ran her tongue over her teeth. "Is he bringing Glenna?"

"He didn't mention her," Adam said, referring to their step-mother of four years. Laura imagined it seemed odd to him still, too. Clive's string of mistresses hadn't been a well-kept secret. He'd fathered a fourth child outside of his marriage to Anna-beth. Dani had come to live with Adam, Laura and Joshua in Los Angeles for a time. Laura had been only too happy not to be the only girl, and the four of them had been all too aware of Clive's neglect.

Laura had never forgotten that, and she'd never been able to forgive Clive for his carelessness or whims. She knew his affairs had been one reason Annabeth had escaped time after time to Arizona. She'd loved Clive, despite his faults and mis-handlings. The heartbreak and embarrassment of knowing he had looked for companionship elsewhere...that he had married her for her money...it had been too much for Annabeth to bear.

No, Laura had never forgiven her father, even if Glenna wasn't like the other women. She was close to Clive's age, for one, and beautiful, like his mistresses. Unlike the others, she was mature and independent. She even owned her own busi-ness, and it was a successful one.

It didn't mean Laura's father had turned things around. He'd had little to do with his children's upbringing. Annabeth had raised them practically on her own until the cancer had taken a turn for the worse when Laura was just twelve years old.

"I thought we could arrange Bungalow Twelve for him," Adam continued as he shuffled papers in the file spread on the table in front of him.

Laura pursed her lips. Adam was a businessperson, not a bit-ter man or a hard one. The snub was subtle. Every bungalow at Mariposa was luxurious, but only bungalows one through ten featured a private outdoor pool and were prioritized for VIP guests. She rubbed her lips together, considering. "You don't think he'll notice?"

Adam picked up a pen and made a mark on the latest bud-get report he'd likely stayed up late last night reviewing. "Notice what?"

Adam wasn't petty either. Neither was she, Laura told herself as she made a notation in the notes app on her phone. "Bungalow Twelve," she agreed. "When are we expecting him?"

"The day after tomorrow."

"And when is he departing?"

"He didn't say that either."

"He can't just come and go as he pleases," Laura pointed out. "We have guests coming in after him, and the concierge and Housekeeping require notice."

Adam lifted his eyes briefly to hers. Even sitting, he looked lanky despite his broad shoulders. His blue eyes matched hers, and his medium-blond hair was never not short, trim and stylish, even when the rest of the world was waking up. People liked to think he'd been born in a suit, and if she hadn't grown up with him, she'd wonder, too.

"I'm sure you'll let him know when he arrives. Let's move on."

Laura made another notation about her father's visit and did her best to ignore the unsettled feeling that pricked along her spine.

"The wedding on Valentine's Day weekend," Adam continued. "I'm assuming everything's on schedule?"

"I spoke to the mother of the bride yesterday," she explained. "They've asked for another three bungalows, as the guest list has expanded."

"A little late for that."

"I said we could do it," she admitted, "as long as they agreed to cap the number there."

He let loose a sigh. "I'll have to adjust the price points. How many more plates is that for the reception?"

"Five adults, four children."

He scrawled and started talking numbers.

"We need to talk about this year's anniversary celebration," she interrupted. Mariposa had opened on Valentine's Day almost twenty-two years ago. "Since the wedding is on Valentine's Day, I propose we move the celebration to Wednesday, the eighteenth."

Adam stopped counting to consider. "That works for me."

"We'll have a bandstand, like last year," she said, ticking items off her list. "Live music, hors d'oeuvres, cocktails and fireworks. And you'll make a speech."

He raised his gaze to hers. "Will I?"

"Yes," she said, beaming. "People like to hear you speak."

He waved a hand. "If I must."

"Good man," she praised and put a check mark next to Adam's Speech on her list.

An infinitesimal smile wavered across his lips. "You enjoy painting me into a corner and patting me on the head when I have no choice but to comply."

"I'm sure I don't know what you mean." She tapped the hollow of her collarbone. "Is that the tie I bought you?"

"Yes," he said after a glance at it.

"It looks very nice," she said. "And I was right. It does bring out your eyes."

His smile strengthened. "Clever girl."

The door to the conference room opened. Laura eased back in her chair as Joshua loped in. He smiled distractedly through dark-tinted shades when he saw the two of them seated on either side of the table. "Greetings, siblings."

"You're late," Adam pointed out.

"Oh, you noticed," Joshua said, unfazed as he pulled out a chair and dropped to it. "How thoughtful of you." He caught Laura's look. "You're not going to tell me off, are you?"

He was so charmingly rumpled, any urge to scold him fell long by the wayside. Joshua was twenty-seven. His dirty-blond hair was perpetually shaggy. When he took off his glasses, his eyes laughed in the same shade as hers and Adam's. At six feet, he was trim and muscular. He couldn't claim to eat and sleep work as they did, but he was just as devoted to Mariposa. He was very much at home in his role as the resort's Activities Director.

"No," she replied.

He pecked a kiss on her cheek. "You're my favorite."

"For the moment."

He leaned his chair back and crossed his legs at the ankles. "What's the latest?"

"Clive is coming," she warned, handing over her thermos easily when he held out his hand for it.

He took a long sip. "And how do we feel about that?" he asked, squinting at Adam across the long, flat plane of the table.

Adam answered without inflection. "Indifferent."

"Oh?" Joshua said with a raised brow. He looked at Laura for confirmation.

Laura cleared her throat. "We're placing him in Bungalow Twelve."

Joshua laughed shortly before setting the thermos on the table between him and her. "I approve."

"I thought you might," Adam said, again without looking up.

Joshua had been only ten when their mother had died. His memories of Annabeth were the foggiest—most of them mere reflections through a vintage-cast mirror. Though he remembered well how Clive had abandoned them to their grief. As the youngest, he'd needed the most stability and guidance. It was Adam and Laura who had stepped into that role—not their father.

"Glenna won't stand being demoted to anything below the amenities of Bungalow Ten," he warned.

"We don't know she's coming," Laura revealed.

"I'm just saying," Joshua said, holding up his hands.

None of them had gotten to know their stepmother well. But Joshua was right. Glenna may keep her thoughts to herself, and she could be perfectly cordial. But she also had a discerning eye and was accustomed to a certain type of lifestyle. One reason, no doubt, she had been drawn to Clive Colton. As CEO of Colton Textiles, he lived in a Beverly Hills mansion she had already refined to her tastes.

Laura sighed. "I'll deal with that if it comes."

Joshua sketched a lazy salute. "I'll have Knox loan you a helmet."

"I have one," she reminded him. Not that she'd need it. She could handle Clive, and she could certainly handle Glenna. She shook her head. "Are we being unkind?"

Her brothers exchanged a look. "In what way?" Adam asked.

"He hasn't been well," Laura reminded them. "The ministrokes last year and the rumors about sideline business deals going sideways... We could be losing him."

They lapsed into silence. Joshua reached up to scratch his chin. "Is it not fair to say I feel like I lost him a long time ago?"

She studied him, and she saw the ten-year-old who'd needed a parent. His hand clutched the arm of the swivel chair. She covered it with her own. "It is fair," she assured him.

Adam had shielded his mouth with his writing hand. He dropped it to the table, the ballpoint pen still gripped between his fingers. "Mom left the resort to us in her will not just because she wanted us to have a piece of her and financial security. She left it because she knew the house in Los Angeles wasn't a home. She left us a place we could belong to. Dad never provided that for her or us. She made sure after she was gone we wouldn't need to rely on him, because she knew all he would ever do was disappoint us. Like he disappointed her."

"She left us fifty percent of the shares in Colton Textiles, too," Joshua added. "If it'd been him...if he had gone first... would he have done the same?"

Laura shook her head. "I don't know." But she did, she realized. She knew all too well.

Adam dropped the pen. He folded his hands on the tabletop. "If we have an opening, we can slot him into one of the VIP bungalows. Would that ease your conscience?"

Laura considered. She opened her mouth to answer.

A knock on the door interrupted.

"Come in," Adam called.

The panel pulled away from the jamb. Laura felt the tension in the room drain instantaneously as Tallulah Deschine peered into the room. The fifty-year-old Navajo woman was head of housekeeping at Mariposa. She'd been with the Coltons since the renovation. In the last decade, she'd become more of a mother to them than a member of staff, and she was one of the few workers at the resort who, like Adam, Laura and Joshua, lived in her own house on property. "I'm sorry to intrude."

Joshua sat up straighter. "No need to apologize, Tallulah. Come sit by me." He pushed out the chair next to his.

Worry lines marred her brow. "There's a situation. Down at the pool."

"What kind of situation?" Adam asked, his smile falling away in a fast frown.

Tallulah's attention seized on Laura. She opened her mouth, then closed it.

Laura saw her chin wobble. Quickly, she pushed her chair back. "What is it, Tallulah?" she asked softly, crossing to the door. She heard Adam and Joshua get up and follow suit. "What's happened?"

Tallulah's eyes flooded with tears. She spoke in a choked voice. "The maid, Bella... She noticed one cabana was never straightened after hours last night. When she went inside to do just that, she found someone there."

Adam touched her shoulder when she faltered again. "Someone who? What were they doing there?"

"Oh, Adam." Tallulah shook her head, trying to gather herself. "Bella thought she'd fallen asleep there, so she tried waking her up. She couldn't. There's something *really* wrong..."

"Who is she?" Laura asked. There was a hard fist in her stomach. It grew tighter and tighter, apprehension knotting there. "Tallulah, who did Bella find in the cabana?"

"It's Allison," Tallulah revealed. "The yoga instructor. Knox knows CPR. He's trying to bring her around—"

"Did you call 9-1-1?" Adam asked, his phone already in hand.

"Alexis made the call."

"EMTs should only be ten minutes out," he assured her.

Joshua pushed through the door. "If she's not breathing, that's not enough time."

Laura tailed him. He'd already broken into a run. She didn't catch up with him until they came to the end of the hall.

If Allison wasn't asleep in the cabana...if she wasn't breathing... What did that mean?

Laura hastened her steps and nearly ran into Alexis Reed, the concierge, and Erica Pike, Adam's executive assistant, in the lobby.

"What's going on?" Alexis asked urgently. "Is Allison okay?"

"I don't know," Laura said. Joshua didn't stop. He hit the glass doors. They swung open. She followed him out into the mountain air. Her heart was in her throat as they raced to the pool area.

The drapes on the farthest cabana were still closed. The pool maintenance person, Manuel, stood outside with his hat in his hands. Their head of security, Roland, stepped out, expression drawn.

"How is she?" Joshua asked. "Did Knox bring her around?"

Roland shook his head.

Laura fumbled for speech. "What?"

Joshua swept the curtain aside.

Laura moved to follow him, but Manuel brought her up short. "I don't think you should go in there, Ms. Colton."

She shook her head. "Why? What's wrong with her?"

Roland took a breath. "I don't know how to say this, but I don't think she'll be coming back around."

Laura couldn't wrap her head around the words. She slipped past Manuel and Roland, ducking through the parting of the drapes. Her footsteps faltered when she saw Joshua and Knox Burnett, the horseback adventure guide, leaning over the still, white face of the woman lying supine on the outdoor rug. Neither of them moved. "Why did you stop?" she asked Knox. "Why aren't you helping her?"

"Laura…" Joshua mumbled. "You need to go."

She crouched next to him. Her hand lifted to her mouth when she saw the tint of Allison's lips.

Knox's face was bowed in an uncharacteristic frown.

Even as she denied what she was seeing, she looked at him. "Why did you stop?" she asked again.

He was panting, his long hair mussed. His face inordinately pale, he said, "She's cold. So cold. I couldn't get a pulse. She never had a pulse…"

Laura looked down at Allison's face. Her dark eyes stared, unseeing. "Oh, God," she said with a shaky exhalation.

Joshua's fingers closed over hers. He spoke in a whisper, as if afraid Allison would hear. "She's gone."

Chapter Two

Laura frowned at the water glass on the table in front of her. She wished for her thermos. Hell, she wished this interview could take place at L Bar. The bartender, Valerie, knew Laura's drink of choice.

Allison, she thought. *Oh, God. Allison...*

Detective Mark Fulton of the Sedona Police Department sat across the table. He hadn't allowed either of her brothers to join her. They had each been questioned separately, as had Bella, Knox, Tallulah, Manuel and Roland.

"I understand you were the one who initially hired the deceased," Fulton commented.

She studied the small corona on top of his shiny, hairless head, a reflection from the wide chandelier above them. Forcing herself to look away, she traced the pattern of his tie with her gaze—circles overlapping circles in various shades of blue, each edged with a thin gold iris. "Allison," she said. She swallowed. She hadn't let herself cry.

Not yet. She'd been surrounded by people—her brothers, the staff, the guests—since the discovery of Allison's body.

Her voice split as if the strain of not crying had injured her vocal cords.

"Sorry?" Fulton said, looking up from his notepad distractedly.

"Her name is Allison," she told him. He needed to stop calling her *the deceased*. It sounded discordant, inhumane.

"Of course," he allowed. He spared her a brief smile. "You hired Allison. Ms. Brewer. Is that correct?"

"I did," Laura answered. "Two years ago last September."

"And when did you see her last?" he asked.

Laura thought about it. "Yesterday. She teaches... I mean, she taught a yoga course in the meditation garden at the rock labyrinth at sunset. I saw her coming back from that around dusk. It was between six and six thirty. I was on my way to check on our chef at Annabeth. He had to have stitches the day before. He cut himself during the lunch rush. I wanted to make sure he was okay to work through dinner. I saw Allison walking from the meditation garden toward C Building, which is where the staff locker rooms, break rooms and café are located. It's also where they park their cars when they arrive for work in the morning."

"Did you speak to her?"

"I did," Laura said with a nod.

"How would you describe her demeanor?"

Laura frowned. "I'm not sure what you mean."

"Did she strike you as happy, tired, angry, upset...?"

It took a moment for Laura to settle on the right description. "She was upbeat. Allison was always upbeat. Even when she was fatigued, which I imagine she was after a full day of classes. She does guided meditation for guests and for anyone on staff who wants to join after hours. One reason I was so excited about hiring her was because she had wonderful ideas for improving the wellness of not just Mariposa's guests but the resort as a whole. She wanted fellow members of staff to have the opportunity to rest and recharge."

"That was generous of her."

Laura nodded. "Allison was always generous with her time and attention. Everyone liked her."

"What did you speak to her about when you saw her yesterday evening?"

She narrowed her eyes, trying to recall the exact words of the conversation. "She wanted to grab dinner and was looking forward to a few moments to herself in the break room before the guided meditation with the staff. Sometimes, she liked to join the stargazing excursion after dinner. She was excited about seeing last night's meteor shower before she went home to Sedona. She had a house there."

"Would you mind telling me what she was wearing at the time?" Fulton asked.

Laura fumbled. She thought again of Allison lying between Knox and Joshua. Her blue-tinged lips. Her blank stare.

Something wormed its way up Laura's throat. The taste of acid filled her mouth. She had to force herself to swallow it back down. "Workout clothes. The same ones we...we found her in this morning."

"Was she wearing shoes last night?"

She narrowed her eyes at him. "That's an odd question, Detective. Do you mind me asking how that's relevant?"

"I'm just trying to get a full picture of the deceased... I mean, Allison...in the hours leading up to her death."

He said it gently. Even so, *her death* sounded so final. Laura reached up for her temples, feeling off balance. "Ah... I believe so. Yes. She wore flexible, lightweight footwear between classes. For the classes themselves, she preferred to go barefoot." Laura remembered the tiny lotus tattoo on Allison's ankle. Her eyes stung. "Do you mind me asking, Detective, if you have any idea *how* she died? It just seems strange for someone so young to just..."

Fulton nodded away the rest. "That's why I'm trying to go through all the details. It will help me understand what happened to her."

"Did she have a heart attack?" Laura asked. Even that seemed nonsensical. Allison was so healthy. She was vegan, preferring to bring her own meals instead of having them prepared by others. "It could have been a stroke, I suppose. Or an aneurysm?"

"Again, Ms. Colton," Fulton said in as kind a voice as he could muster. "I assure you. I will do everything I can to figure out what happened to your employee."

Employee? Allison was her friend. Laura opened her mouth to correct him, but she faltered.

"Was there anyone on staff who Allison didn't get along with?" Fulton asked.

"No. As I said, everyone liked Allison."

"What about guests? Have there been any disgruntled students from her yoga or meditation classes?"

"No," she said, finding the idea ridiculous. "None."

"In two years, she never had a dissatisfied student?"

"Not one," Laura said. She would have known. Allison would have told her.

"Did she have a personal relationship with any of the guests?"

"What do you mean by that?" Laura asked.

"Was she closer to any particular guest?" he elaborated. "Beyond the classes. Maybe one she got to know during the stargazing excursions."

Laura frowned. "Allison would never overstep. She knew where to draw the line. She was the perfect mix of friendliness and professionalism, and she never would have thought of mixing business with pleasure, if that's what you're implying."

"You're sure of this?"

She met his level stare. "Yes."

He made several notes before he asked, "Do you know anything about her personal life? Was she involved with anyone on staff?"

"No, Detective. Relationships among staff members aren't encouraged."

"No one on staff seemed especially interested in Ms. Brewer?"

"I don't think so," Laura said. "There was a flirtation with our adventure guide, Knox Burnett. But Knox flirts with everyone."

"What about outside the resort? What was her personal life like in Sedona?"

"She was in a relationship when she first came to the resort," Laura remembered suddenly. "But it ended a few months after she started."

"Did she seem upset?"

"She enjoyed being single again. Prioritizing herself was important. She enjoyed living alone." She came to attention as something occurred to her. "Oh my God! Have you told her family? She didn't talk about her parents, but there was a brother she was close to. She talked about him regularly. Does he know? Should we have contacted him already? I'm sure she put him down as her emergency contact."

Fulton held up a hand. "We have contacted her next of kin. You don't need to worry about that."

"Still, I'd like to extend the condolences of the family and staff," Laura explained. "There must be something we can do."

"I'd be happy to get you in touch, if you like."

"I would," she said. "Very much."

"I'll have that information sent to you as soon as possible," he stated. "One more question, and I'll let you get back to your day. Can you tell me about your whereabouts between one and two o'clock this morning?"

She felt heavy in her chair, as if gravity were exerting more force than necessary. "Is that when Allison died?"

"Yes, ma'am."

"Why do you need to know my whereabouts?"

"It's simply a matter of routine."

"I was in bed," Laura explained. She'd gone to bed early, her large tabby cat at her side.

"Can anyone corroborate that?"

"No." Was her word not enough? "I took off my smartwatch to charge it. I'm sure there's a time stamp, probably around 11:00 p.m. My alarm goes off at 5:30 a.m."

"Your brother informed me there are no security cameras on the property."

"No. The privacy of our guests is very important at Mariposa."

"He said that, too. I just hope it doesn't make matters more complicated for you."

"Why would it?" she asked.

He closed his notepad and pushed his chair back from the table. "I think that's all I have for now. Thank you for sitting down with me. If I have any more questions, I'll let you know."

If he had any more questions for her? She was the one with all the remaining questions, and none of them had been answered. She sat frozen as he rounded the table. Before he could reach for the door, she snapped to attention, standing suddenly. "Detective?"

He stopped. "Ma'am?"

"You will keep my brothers and me informed of any developments?" she requested. "We all cared about Allison a great deal."

"I will," he agreed. "Have a good day."

She waited until he was out the door before she sank to the seat. Her legs weren't steady enough to stand on.

She should've asked why Allison's lips had been blue. Would Fulton know how long she had been in the cabana?

Had she suffered? Was she scared? How long had she been alone and frightened?

How could this happen? What was she going to do now? How was she supposed to go about their day as if nothing had happened?

Laura's posture caved. She rarely let it, but she folded under the weight of shock and pressed her fingers to her closed eyes.

She hadn't lost anyone close to her since her mother's passing and hadn't forgotten how it felt—the staggering weight of bereavement. It was impossible to forget. But she hadn't expected… She hadn't been prepared to feel it all again.

The shock was wearing away fast. Once it was gone, the grief would sink in. And it wouldn't give way to anything else. She pressed her hand to her mouth, choking it back.

She was afraid of it. Grief. How it gripped and rent. As a child, it had come for her on wraith wings, real but transparent. She hadn't been able to see it, but it had held her. It had hurt her. And it had transformed her into something she hadn't recognized.

Panic beat those wings against her chest now. Her pulse rushed in her ears. She tried to breathe, tried to think through it, but it didn't allow her to.

It was already taking hold.

She'd seen it coming before. Her mother had warned her there wasn't much time. She had told all her children what to expect at the end of her cancer battle. She had prepared them and armed them for the hard days to come.

This wasn't the same. And yet it was.

She thought of her brothers waiting outside the door. Coming to her feet, she walked the length of the conference room. She paced until the panic subsided—until her breathing returned to normal and her heart no longer raced.

Adam might be the oldest, but her brothers had looked to her in the past. For strength. For stability. When their mother died, she had stepped into Annabeth's power—to carry them, to ground them and to keep them together.

They were grown now, but they would look to her, still. They would need her to handle this…and they would need to lean on her. And so would the staff.

She dried her eyes, fixed her makeup and made herself down the entire glass of water in front of her.

A knock clattered against the door. She checked her reflection in the window before she said, "Yes?"

Alexis stepped in. "Hey. How are you holding up?"

Laura made herself meet her friend's gaze. "I'm fine."

Alexis raised a brow. "You want me to pretend that's true?"

"I'm going to need you to," Laura requested.

Alexis nodded. "Okay." She, Allison and Laura had gotten to know each other well. Besides Tallulah and Laura's brothers, redheaded, smiling Allison and dark, no-nonsense Alexis were the members of staff Laura felt closest to. In some ways, they had been her saving grace over the last few years. There were things she couldn't discuss with Adam and Joshua. Just her girls. The three of them had made Taco Tuesdays at Sedona's Tipsy Tacos a weekly escape from the pressures of the hospitality business. Laura lived and worked at the resort. Alexis and Allison had taught her that getting away, even for a few hours, could be crucial for her well-being.

"How about you?" Laura asked. "How are you handling this?"

Alexis's hazel eyes raced across the length of the table, as if searching for the answer there. "I think I'm still processing."

"It's a lot."

"Yeah, and it doesn't make sense, Laura."

"No," Laura agreed.

Alexis glanced over her shoulder before closing the door at her back. She leaned against it. "That detective. Did he say whether she was attacked in any way?"

Laura had to stop and take another steadying breath. "You think someone hurt her?"

"She can't have just died."

Fulton's final battery of questions came back to Laura. She shivered and rubbed her hands over her upper arms. "But who would do such a thing? Who would want to hurt her?"

Alexis's brow furrowed. "I don't know. But it won't take long for the police to find out exactly what killed her. And I have a feeling they're not done questioning everyone."

Laura thought of that, the implications... "Murder doesn't happen at Mariposa. It never has."

"Maybe not," Alexis said, subsiding. "Look, if you need to go home, Erica and I can cover for you."

"No," Laura said quickly. "You're working through this. Adam and Josh are working through this. I'm going to do the same. We have to get through the day."

"Knox is shaken up pretty badly," Alexis told her. "He should go home."

Laura nodded. "Right. I'll handle that." It would give her something to do, someone to take care of for the time being. "I'll check back in with you in a little while."

Sadness leaked across Alexis's features. "Oh, Laura," she said as she grabbed her into a hug.

"I know." Laura fought the knot climbing back into her throat. "What are we going to do without her?"

Chapter Three

Laura knew her presence at Annabeth that evening was reassuring to people. She just wished she was able to reassure herself as she made a point of going from table to table.

For years, she'd watched her mother do this. The real Annabeth had exuded just the right mix of politeness, gratitude and grace to put even the most harried guest at ease. Laura tried to emulate that. She channeled her mother's energy and hoped people bought the illusion.

Under the surface, her duck feet churned. She prayed the diners missed the sweat she felt beading on her hairline and the devastation she knew lurked behind her eyes. Joshua was doing the same at L Bar while Adam did his best to bolster the staff.

Allison's death had hit the heart of the resort.

Laura hadn't found a chance to pull Adam or Joshua aside to ask if Fulton had presented the same questions to them or how they had handled them. Alexis's warning came back to her as she noticed the table with a Reserved card standing empty near the window. The police weren't done asking questions if foul play was involved.

Lifting a hand, Laura flagged the nearest server, a young woman named Catrina. "Isn't this Mr. Knight's table?"

"The actor?" Catrina nodded. "Yes. He normally comes in around six."

Laura checked her watch. "He's running behind. Have some-one place a call to his bungalow, please, and see if he'd still like to dine here tonight. If he's decided against it, there are people waiting who can be seated here."

"Yes, Ms. Colton," Catrina said before hurrying off.

"Laura."

She turned to find Erica Pike. The executive assistant stood eye to eye with Laura at five-nine, and her long brown hair was pulled up in a loose bun. Glancing at the table, she asked, "Is everything okay?"

"I was just wondering why CJ Knight hasn't shown up for his six o'clock table," Laura said.

"Oh." Erica's spine seemed to stiffen. "He checked out."

"Checked out?" Laura repeated. "When?"

"Early this morning," Erica explained. "I thought you knew."

"No," Laura said. "A lot's happened."

Erica nodded, her green eyes rimmed with shadows. "I know. Poor Allison."

Laura tried to think about the situation at hand. "Mr. Knight had spoken to me about extending his stay in Bungalow One for a week or more. Why the change of heart?"

"He didn't say," Erica replied. "Roland asked me to find you. The detective from the Sedona Police Department is back."

"So soon?" Laura said and missed a breath.

"A security person from the gate escorted him to C Build-ing," Erica told her. "He's waiting in the break room."

The police were back with more questions, just as Alexis had predicted. Laura offered a soothing smile to a passing pa-tron before striding toward the exit, doing her best not to rush.

C Building was built in the same style as L Building and the bungalows, but the interior was spartan. Music piped softly from speakers. A fountain in the center of the atrium burbled and splashed pleasantly. Both had been Allison's ideas. Extending the same sense of calm ambience to the employees' building that guests enjoyed everywhere else had brought the Mariposa environment full circle.

Tears stung Laura's eyes again. Allison had left a large foot-print on Mariposa. She'd made it better for everyone.

Laura faced the closed doors of the break room. Halting, she took a minute to breathe and get her emotions under control. She couldn't seem to still the little duck feet paddling under the surface. To make up for it, she encased ice around her exterior. Donning her professional mask felt as natural, as fluid, as freshening up her lipstick.

She pushed the doors open and stepped in. "Detective Fulton…"

The man who stood from a chair at one of the small bistro-style tables was not Detective Fulton.

She blinked in surprise. He was younger, taller, more muscular. His build distinguished him. He carried himself more like a brawler than a police officer. He had brown hair that grew thick on top and short on the sides, a full beard and mustache. A bomber jacket lay across the table. His black button-down shirt was tucked into buff-colored cargo pants, his belt drawn beneath a trim stomach with a bronze buckle. The pants looked almost military. So did his scuffed boots. He'd rolled his sleeves up his forearms while he'd waited, revealing a bounty of tattoos.

No, she decided. This definitely didn't look like a detective. While his attire might have been military-inspired, he didn't carry himself like a military man. More like a boxer. Shoulders square. Hands balled, ready to strike. His hair and ink made him look like a rock star.

He wasn't restful on his feet. He shifted from one to the other, twitchy. His direct stare delivered a pang to her gut, a quick one-two. It was dangerous. Deadly.

Not a rock star, she discerned. A criminal.

She took a step back. "Who are you?" she demanded. The building was empty. The bulk of the staff was in the meeting with Adam at L Building. There was a phone on the desk in the atrium. She placed one hand on the parting of the doors. Should she make a run for it?

That direct stare remained in place. It felt like an eternity before one hand unclenched and sank into a pocket. A badge flashed when he pulled it out. "Detective Noah Steele. Sedona PD."

She wanted to examine the badge. It looked authentic from

a distance, but she hadn't studied Fulton's all too closely when he'd arrived this morning. She wished she could go back and implant the image on her mind so that she at least had something to compare to.

"What do you want?" she asked, forgetting her professional demeanor. Her feet itched to run.

His expression didn't change. Neither did it lose its edge. "Are you Laura Colton?"

"There was another man here earlier," she told him. "Another detective. Mark Fulton. He said he was the lead on the case."

His gaze narrowed. She swore she'd seen a rattlesnake do that once on the hiking trails. Part of her tensed, waiting for the buzzing sound of the rattle.

"So, what are you doing here?" she challenged. "Are you really even a cop?"

"Lady, you'd do well not to insult me at the moment."

She dropped back on one heel and crossed her arms. *Lady?* "Should I call Security and have your identity certified by them?"

"It was Security who dumped me here, away from everybody else," he retorted. "Take it up with the meatball at the gate if you don't like it."

Erica did say that security personnel had escorted the detective to C Building. She frowned, opening her mouth to apologize.

He cut in, "You didn't answer my question. Are you Laura Colton?"

"I am," she said and watched, perplexed, as his eyes darkened and his fists clenched again. "It's been a long day... Detective. I'm sorry for the misunderstanding."

"A long day," he repeated, low in his throat. He let out a whistling breath. Was that his excuse for a laugh? Mirth didn't strike his expression. If anything, it tensed. "*You've* had a long day?"

"Yes," she said. She had the distinct impression that he was mocking her—that he disdained her. The level of malice coming off him was insupportable. She'd just met him. What could he possibly have against her? "I'm sure you're aware one of Mariposa's employees was found this morning...dead." She swallowed because her voice broke on that unbelievable word. "Isn't that why you're here?"

He came forward, stepping quickly between the tables. "You're damn right that's why I'm here."

She dismissed the inclination to put her back up against the door. There was a gun in a holster on his hip, she noticed. Her pulse picked up pace. He had no reason to hurt her. None whatsoever. And yet he looked capable of murder. "*Why* are you so angry?" she demanded.

"Why is your family so determined to keep Allison Brewer's death quiet?" he challenged.

She searched his eyes. They were green. Not leafy green, or algae, or even peridot. They were electrodes. Vibrant, steely, stubborn. She saw downed power lines, snapped electrical cables, writhing and sparking—about to blow her world off the grid.

She had to focus on the music, flutes and pipes, something merry and soothing Allison would have loved, to maintain a sense of calm. "What are you talking about?" she asked.

"Your brother Adam told officers at the scene this morning that Allison's death should be kept quiet," he seethed. "You'll tell me why. Why do you and your brothers want this buried? What happened to her?"

"You're acting like there's some sort of cover-up."

"Is there?"

She would have laughed if he were someone...*anyone* else. "No. This is a resort. People come here for privacy. To get away from the world."

"So close."

"What?"

"Close the resort," he said. "Let the police come in and investigate properly."

"There are over eighty people booked at Mariposa through this week alone," she explained.

"If you really care about Allison—"

She stepped to him, fears squashed as her ire rose. "Allison Brewer was my friend. She was one of my closest friends. And

I will *not* be accused of covering up her death. Who are you to march in here and accuse me of that?"

If she'd expected him to cower, she was sorely disappointed. He closed the marked bit of space between them, lifting his chin. "If you're so close to her, why has she never mentioned you before?"

He spoke in present tense, just as she had even after witnessing the coroner carrying Allison's body away under a sheet. His fury...his near lack of control. It was cover for something else.

Adam had done this, she realized. After their mother's death. He'd been angry, precarious, until he'd learned to put a lid on it. Until he'd developed control and that laser focus that was so vital to him. "You knew her," she realized. "You knew Allison."

He blinked, and the tungsten cooled. Going back on his heels, he moved away.

She watched him rove the space between tables and chairs, his head low.

Allison hadn't had a type, Laura recalled. But Laura couldn't see her with someone this high-strung. Someone this lethal. She had, however, spoken of her brother often—her foster brother. *As thick as thieves*, Allison had said regarding the two of them.

Laura's brow puckered. "Your last name is Steele."

He turned his head to her, scowling. "So?"

"You don't share a last name," Laura pointed out.

He cursed under his breath. Was he mad that she'd made him so quickly?

"Are you really a detective?" she asked, bewildered.

"Of course I'm a detective," he snapped, pacing again from one end of the room to the other. "Why else would I be here?"

"Other than to accost me and my family?" she ventured. "You act like we're culpable."

"Everybody's culpable," he muttered.

Her eyes rounded. "So...there *was* foul play involved in whatever happened last night?"

He stopped roving. His palm scraped across his jaw, the Roman numerals etched across his knuckles flashing. "Nothing else makes sense."

"Murder at Mariposa doesn't make sense," she said. "The people here aren't prone to violence."

He dropped his hand in shock. "You actually believe that?"

She didn't answer. His mockery locked her jaw.

"Here's a news flash," he said. "Most people are inherently violent."

"If you actually believe that," she countered, "then I'd say you have a very narrow view of humanity. And so would Allison."

He flinched. "Someone at your resort killed my sister, Ms. Colton," he said. "I'd advise you to watch your back, because I won't rest until I have proof."

The quiet warning coursed through her. She sensed, if this man had his way, Mariposa would be reduced to rubble before he was done.

Chapter Four

Goddamn it. She had to be beautiful.

Inside C Building, Noah watched Laura Colton and her brothers through the glass doors of the atrium. Legs spread, arms crossed, he listened to harp strings and water cascading cheerfully from the fountain to his left, trying to read the exchange. Trying to discern what was on her face.

He didn't have to. He recognized it, and it drove a knife through him. She was grieving. The tension around the frown lines of her mouth were indicators, just like her heartbreakingly blue eyes drawn down at the corners. She eyed him, too, through the glass doors as Adam and Joshua Colton stood on either side of her, debating what to do about the situation.

Although he gathered sadness and confusion from her face, she didn't waver. She was a winking star at the edge of the galaxy—remote, out of reach and somehow constant.

His shoulders itched. He didn't roll them, but the urge bothered him. It raised the hair on the backs of his arms and neck. The supernatural sense strengthened as she continued to stare.

He could be constant, too—like a roadblock. An obstacle. He would stop traffic. He would dent fenders. He would do anything to find out what had happened here.

It didn't matter if it made waves for these people. Nothing mattered except Allison.

He hadn't been there. The hopeless thought burned on the edge of his conscience. It burned and smoked, and he hated himself.

He hadn't been there for Allison. Not in the last few months. Not like he should have been. He'd been distracted by work, his closure rate at the SPD and the rise in homicides around the area.

And now Allison was dead. If it wasn't someone else's fault, it was his.

He was responsible...until he found who was to blame.

He couldn't live with her death on his conscience. That sweet little girl. She'd had no one, and he'd promised her. He'd *sworn* he would be there for her—until the last breath.

That last breath was supposed to be his, not hers. It wasn't supposed to be her. It should be another person lying under a sheet at the coroner's office.

He'd known she was too soft for this world—too pure. Too good. And, like a son of a bitch, he'd neglected her.

Her voice came to him. *I'm an adult. Noah, you don't have to chase my monsters out of the closet anymore.*

Are you sure about that? he'd challenged.

She had laughed, dropping her head back and belting. Allison never did things halfway, especially when they brought her joy. She'd taken his hand as she'd said, *There are no more monsters. We're free of them now.*

He was the monster, he realized. He was a monster who'd abandoned her to the real world, and she was dead because of it.

As if she could read his thoughts, Laura Colton shivered. She broke the staring contest by turning to gaze at her younger brother, folding her arms around herself.

She was cold, he mulled. Of course she was cold. She was standing outside with the barest of snow flurries falling at a slant from the north. Her white dress was long-sleeved, with a leather belt cinched at the waist and a rustic blue handkerchief tied elaborately at her throat in a Western knot. The handkerchief wasn't meant to keep out the cold. It was silk, for Christ's sake. The dress may have been long, but there was a slit on one side.

As she shifted, he saw a flash of creamy skin. Her boots,

the same blue as the handkerchief, with custom floral tooling, rose to just below the knee. Her shoulder-length blond hair swung as the wind flurried and spiraled. She shivered again, visibly.

Noah clenched his jaw. *Morons*, he thought of her brothers. Couldn't they see she was cold? Couldn't *one* of them loan her a jacket?

Adam caught on first. He swung his jacket off in a quick motion and draped it across the line of her shoulders.

Not enough, Noah chided even as Laura acknowledged the gesture by touching Adam's arm just above the elbow. Joshua braced his arm across her shoulders and huddled her against his side. He rubbed a hand up and down her arm for friction.

Good, Noah thought. Maybe he could stop feeling sorry for her long enough to separate the woman from the adversary.

She was beautiful. So what? He'd seen icebergs. He'd seen one calve and flip over, churning the sea like a bubbling witch's cauldron, exposing its breathtaking glass underbelly. Unspoiled, untouched. Secret and forbidden.

Laura Colton was that kind of beautiful. And damned if it was going to distract him.

Icebergs were roadblocks, too. Sure, they contained multitudes, and they were frigging fascinating to boot. But they could be upset. They melted. They flipped. And when they flipped, their spires crumbled.

I won't let you get in my way, he determined as her heartbreaker eyes seized hold of him again. Frost wove delicate swaths around the edges of the door pane, framing her.

Friend? Allison had never mentioned her. He was sure of it. If he wasn't sure, it was because he had forgotten.

He couldn't bear to think that he'd forgotten.

You forgot the last lunch, a voice in his head taunted.

He and Allison normally met for lunch on the first Friday of every month. Tipsy Tacos, the little cantina close to her place that served vegan options alongside the ones with meat he preferred, was her favorite restaurant.

It's perfect, isn't it? she'd practically had to yell over the mariachi music, her dark eyes laughing.

Noah dug his phone out of his pocket. He unlocked the screen, then scrolled through his texts. Her messages popped up on-screen.

There was one from a week ago.

Allison: TGIF! Music fest this weekend?

Noah: TGIF. Gotta work overtime. Don't go home with a stranger. Call me if you need a ride.

Allison: Will do!

Then a week before that…

Allison: Did you read the meditation book I gave you?

Noah: Covered up in work. I'll get to it.

Allison: Promise?

Noah: Promise.

Emojis had followed. Then the exchange before that dated two weeks past.

Allison: Thinking of you.

Noah: Thinking of you, too. You ok?

Allison: Worried about you. Let me book you a massage. You need you time.

Noah: I'm fine. Don't go out with that guy again. He's bad news.

Allison: LOL. He said the same about you.

Noah: Never trust a guy in an El Camino.

Allison: I miss you!

Noah: Miss you, too. Sorry about lunch.

Allison: It's NBD. I know work's crazy. Hugs!

Noah: Hugs to you.

Noah winced as he scrolled through the next exchange.

Allison: I'm at the cantina.

Noah: Damn. I'm across town. Had to make an arrest. I'm sorry, Al.

Allison: It's ok.

Noah: I'll pick you up.

Allison: It's nice out. I can walk.

Noah: Let me know if you change your mind.

Allison: Will do.

A smiley face capped the message.

He looked for subtext. He searched for anger on her part. Blame. Disappointment. Anything to beat himself up with. As ever, he found nothing. Just happy, look-on-the-bright-side Allison.

The only other person who'd loved him like this...who'd worried about him like this and looked out for him...was his mother. Before she was killed and he had gotten dumped into the system.

He'd let her down. Even if Allison didn't know it, he'd let her down.

He had to live with that. He had to live with the fact that there would be no more text messages at 10:00 p.m. telling him to *relax...unwind...life's short...live well...*

Forcing himself to swallow, he took stock of his emotions. He felt raw, unspooled. He'd gone at Laura Colton too hard. If she really was Allison's friend, did she have a litany of cheerful, forgotten text messages that broke her heart in hindsight, too?

There was movement, he noticed. He stuffed the phone back in his pocket as a security guard moved into the Coltons' circle. He placed a hand on Joshua's shoulder. They all turned to listen. Joshua nodded and walked away.

Laura and Adam spoke quietly, nodding back and forth before moving toward the door.

Maybe he should apologize to her, Noah thought. He could have waited to question the Coltons, done some digging into them and Mariposa first... But he hadn't been thinking with his head when he'd left Allison at the coroner's office.

He'd done this before with his mother. There had been grief, and he'd been alone then, too. Nobody had cared about him, much less commiserated with him. He didn't know how to expose the hurt and had no idea how to talk about it. The shock of Allison's death had put his fists up and his head down like a brawler.

He'd swung at Laura Colton, Noah reflected as Adam escorted her into C Building to face off with him again. Noah did his best to relax his stance. *Breathe*, Allison said in his ear as Laura's gaze climbed back to his.

"It was a mistake," he said without taking a beat to think about the wording. He backtracked. "Yelling at you in the break room. It shouldn't have happened. I apologize."

Her hands balled together over the parting of Adam's jacket. After a moment, she nodded shortly. "I accept your apology."

"That doesn't resolve everything that happened here this evening," Adam said evenly. "I intend to call the Sedona Police Department for some clarity on the situation. They wouldn't let you lead this investigation if Allison was a relation of yours, which is why Fulton was the detective on scene this morning. Not you. Does your commanding officer know you're here now?"

Noah studied Laura and her cold, white-knuckled hands.

Then he asked the man, "If it was your sister, what would you do? Would you sit around, bury your head in the sand, hoping somebody else figures out what happened to her? Or would you use every skill, every resource at your disposal, to make sure what happened to her is brought to light?"

Adam tilted his head. "I understand why you're here, Detective. As a brother, I sympathize, and I'm deeply sorry for your loss. If I didn't have Laura…" His shoulders lifted, then settled as he deflated. "I wouldn't be standing here."

"Adam." Laura spoke her brother's name in a whisper. She raised her hand to his arm as she had outside. This time, she held it.

"But the fact remains that we don't know what happened to Allison, precisely," Adam went on. "We don't know that anyone at Mariposa is responsible or if she died of natural causes. That's for the coroner to decide, yes?"

Noah jerked his chin. "Yes."

"So you'll agree that your demand we close the resort is premature at this point?" Adam ventured.

"What happens when the coroner's word comes down?" Noah asked. "What happens when we're certain it was homicide? What then?"

"If that's the case," Adam said carefully, "we'll reevaluate. But I see no reason to close Mariposa."

"You're worried about your bottom line," Noah growled.

"No, Detective," Adam said coolly. "I'm worried about the same thing Allison was, too, every day. The privacy and comfort of our guests."

"You sure it's not the Colton reputation?" Noah countered.

Laura unfolded her hands. "It's late, and the snow's coming in. I'm sure you'd like to get home, Detective Steele, in case the roads become impassable. Why don't we all reconvene after the coroner decides on the manner of Allison's passing, then proceed from there?"

She said it in such a way, Noah felt every argument die.

He didn't want to go home. At home, it would be quiet. He'd have nothing to distract him from the voices inside his head that said Allison's death was on his hands. "Fine."

She offered something of a smile. It wasn't the real thing. Her eyes weren't involved in it. "I'll walk you to L Building."

"That's unnecessary," Adam cut in. "I'll walk the detective back to his vehicle. You go home, Laura. It's cold."

"I'll be fine," she assured him. "I'd like a moment with Detective Steele." When Adam only frowned at her, she added, "Alone."

Adam exchanged a look with Noah, one that warned he'd better tread carefully.

Laura started to remove his jacket. Adam stopped her quickly. "Keep it. And promise to go home as soon as you see him out. You need to get off your feet."

"I will," she vowed.

"A promise is a promise, LouBear," he reminded her. He dropped a kiss to her brow.

The sentiment rang through Noah's head. *A promise is a promise.* He hated himself all the more. Before she could open the door, he reached for the handle.

"Thank you," she said before ducking back out into the cold.

"We'll see each other again, Detective Steele," Adam said in closing.

"You can count on it." Noah left the statement hanging in the air like an anvil. He zipped his jacket as he and Laura followed the well-manicured path back to L Building.

She walked in long strides. "Normally, I love the snow. Tonight, it just makes me sad."

"Allison loved snow." He closed his mouth quickly. He hadn't meant to say it.

"She did," Laura said. "I remember the first winter she worked for us. There was so much that year, she had to move classes inside. She liked watching the snowfall from the windows at Annabeth. She said it was like being trapped in a snow globe."

That sounded like Allison. The black hole in Noah's chest opened further. He felt gravity reeling him in toward it. He hoped it would wait until he was alone to absorb him.

"I need to apologize, too," she revealed.

"For?" he asked.

"I misjudged you," she explained. The cold stained her cheeks. "Back in the break room. I didn't think you were with the police."

"What did you think I was?"

"A criminal." She winced. "I don't like labeling people. But I labeled you right off the bat. And I'm sorry for it."

He didn't know what to feel, exactly. He glanced down at his hands where Roman numerals riddled his knuckles and a spider crawled up the back of one hand. The etchings on the other made it look like a skeleton hand with exposed joints and bones that went all the way up his fingers. On some level, he could understand. He'd spent a fair amount of time undercover because he was good at inserting himself into a certain crowd.

He remembered how in the break room she'd all but backed herself up to the exit door when he'd approached her. Had she thought he was going to hurt her...take her jewelry...worse? A growl fought its way up his throat. He choked it back, along with everything else, and punched his hands into the pockets of his jacket. "I don't expect you to lose sleep over it, Ms. Colton."

"It's Laura," she said as they came to the doors to L Building. She turned to him, the golden light over their heads crowning her. "We're probably going to be seeing a lot of each other. And we both knew Allison. So Laura will suffice." She stuck out a hand for him to shake.

He stared at it. Then her. There were snowflakes in her hair. If someone gave her a scepter and horse-drawn sleigh, she would be a glorified ice princess.

Unwilling to let her shiver a moment longer, he closed his hand around hers. It felt like ice, and it was as smooth as the surface of a mink's coat. He took his away quickly, unwilling to watch his tattoos and calluses mingle with her fancy digits. He pulled the door open for her.

She cleared her throat. "I'm going to miss her, too."

Whatever he could have said was trapped beneath his tongue.

Her lashes lowered, touching her cheeks, before she lifted them again. "As soon as you make the arrangements, I'd like to know. I'd like to say goodbye."

Arrangements. The portents of that barreled down on him.

He was Allison's next of kin, her only relative. It was up to him to plan her funeral.

He couldn't bury her. He couldn't even contemplate it. She didn't belong in the ground any more than she belonged in a morgue.

An unsteady breath washed out of him.

Her hand came to rest over his. "I can help you. I've helped plan a funeral in the past. I was young, but I think my brothers and I managed to pull it off well enough. If you need help—"

"It's fine." He barked it, desperate to be away from her so he could unleash the panic and anguish building up inside him. He held the door open wider. "Good night, Ms. Colton."

Her lips firmed. She strode inside. He watched her long after the door closed. He watched through the glass until she disappeared down the hall, the tail of her white skirt the last thing to disappear. The lights went off seconds later and he was left staring at his own reflection.

A funeral.

Another breath wavered out, vaporizing in front of him. He pinched the bridge of his nose, hard. That black hole had him by the balls.

He'd go home, he decided. And when he got there, he'd drink himself into a stupor.

Chapter Five

Laura opened the door to her bungalow the next morning to find Joshua on her front stoop. His messy hair hid underneath a burnt-umber ski cap with Mariposa's pale yellow butterfly logo. Ice crunched under his boots as he moved his toes rapidly to keep them warm. "I brought pastries," he announced.

She eyed the long white box in his hands. "You mean you brought the bakery?"

"Had it delivered," he boasted. He handed her a large cup. "With coffee."

The way to a man's heart might be through his stomach, but Laura was convinced the way to a woman's was by crossing cell membranes with caffeine. She wrapped her hands around the to-go cup, absorbing the heat through the gloves she'd donned. "It's no wonder every man I meet is a disappointment." Tipping the cup to him in a toast, she added, "You are the standard."

He offered his arm. "Watch your step. It's slippery."

She trod carefully until they reached the golf cart he'd parked in front of her house. "Have you spoken to Knox?"

Joshua got behind the wheel. He waited until she was seated, tucking her long skirt around her legs before he released the brake and shot off. "I checked on him last night. He's okay. Still shaken up. Hell, I am, too."

"Did you tell him he doesn't have to come in today? Carter's already agreed to cover for him. The horseback excursions will be canceled because of ice and snowmelt."

Joshua nodded. "He agreed to take the morning off, but he wants to come in after lunchtime. He said working with the horses will help him through things."

Laura could understand that. As the golf cart careened around the corner, she stopped the doughnut box from slipping across the seat. She opened it, then indulged, choosing a chocolate éclair. Nibbling, she balanced the pastry in one hand and her cup in the other. "I don't know if I should tell you this."

"Well, now you've got to." He nudged his elbow into her ribs playfully. "Spill it, ace."

She watched the gardens whoosh by. White coated everything. Mariposa looked enchanting under a crystal frost.

Underneath, was some part of it—or someone inside of it—deadly?

She shuddered, blamed the cold, then polished off the éclair. "She had a crush on you."

"Who?" When he glanced over, she canted her head tellingly. He gawped. "Allison?"

Laura sighed. "She wasn't the type to hold back. But she worked with you. She valued her job. So she sat with her feelings." Reaching over, she cupped his chin in her hand, helping him to close his mouth. "I promised her I wouldn't tell. But I think you two could have made each other happy, at least for a time, and… I don't know. All this reminds me not to waste time if you know what's right for you."

Joshua looked shocked, bereft and everything in between.

He jerked the wheel onto the scenic path, along the wall that fell away from the ridge where Mariposa dwelled. She looked out over the countryside. Snow, red rocks and the Sonoran Desert clashed to make the view that much more spectacular. "We're going to be okay. Right?"

"We've done this before."

She nodded. The three of them had weathered quite a few storms together. "Should I have kept my promise? Should I not have told you?"

He shook his head. "I liked Allison. I liked her a lot. But I have rules, same as she did."

Joshua liked to have fun, but he didn't date anyone in-house. Mariposa was as sacred to him as it was to Laura and Adam, and that included every single person under its umbrella. "I didn't mean to make this harder for you. I just didn't get much sleep last night, wondering whether you two missed out on something special. She was special, Josh."

"I know." His Adam's apple bobbed. He reached for her hand and clutched it. "It's going to be okay."

She had told him that after their mother's death, every night he'd cried himself to sleep. Eyes welling, she turned them away, feeling his fingers squeeze hers. "It's coming up on that time of year."

He kept driving, pushing the golf cart as fast as it would go. If Adam saw him driving like this on the guest pathways, he would chastise him for it. Laura said nothing, however. When Joshua didn't reply, she added, "The anniversary."

"I know."

Every year on the anniversary of Annabeth's death, the three of them took the day off. They'd disappear for a day, first bringing mariposas to her grave, then embarking on a hike. The date coincided with the bridge between winter and spring. Snow gathered in places along the trail. Snowmelt tumbled down passes, rushing for valleys. And early spring growth punched through the bedrock, clawing for purchase like hope incarnate.

They never spoke much on the hike. They never took photos to capture the day. And while Joshua was a more proficient hiker than both Laura and Adam, he never left them behind. They didn't turn back for the resort until they reached the high point—Wrigley's Rough, a jagged fall of rocks with a view of the architectural site of the ancient ruins of the Sinagua people. From the top, they could see every piece of land Annabeth had left them.

Laura couldn't help but think that this year, the anniversary would be especially hard to navigate.

They pulled up to L Building. "Adam doesn't like when you park here," she reminded him.

"It's freezing," Joshua said, engaging the brake. "I'm not making you walk from C Building. Hey," he said before she could step out of the vehicle. "We really are going to be okay."

She adored him for saying it. "When I figure out when the service will be, would you like to go with me?"

"Of course," he agreed. "Are you ready for what comes next?"

"What comes next?" she asked curiously.

"Drink," he advised as they walked to the door that led to their offices at the back of the building. "I got you the big gulp for the meeting with Dad."

She raised her face to the clouds. "Oh," she said.

"You forgot."

"I forgot," she admitted. Pressing her hand to her brow, she shook her head. "It completely slipped my mind."

"That wasn't something else keeping you awake?"

"I didn't think about it at all." She groaned. "Oh, Josh. He's going to waltz in, being all Clive, and I've had no sleep, no prep..."

He nudged the coffee toward her mouth. "Drink, ace."

"Right," she said, tipping the to-go cup up for a steaming swig. She quickly covered her mouth with her hand. "Lava."

Erica waited for them near the closed door of Adam's office. "Good morning," she greeted them. "Your father's flight gets in soon. The helicopter will pick him up around eight thirty. He asked for a meeting in the conference room at ten."

"How does Adam feel about him running the schedule?" Joshua asked.

Erica arched a brow in answer.

"Oh, boy," Joshua muttered. He offered the box of dough-nuts to Erica. "Lady's choice."

Erica eyed the contents when he opened it. "I want the one with the sprinkles."

"Excellent," he said, using a parchment square to pinch the corner of the pastry and hand it to her.

"Thank you," she said, cradling it.

"Did you get in touch with CJ Knight's people?" Laura

asked. She didn't miss the way Erica tensed, just as she had the night before.

She shook her head, lowering the doughnut. "No. Do you still want me to reach out?"

"Yes," Laura said. "I'd like to know why he vacated Bungalow One so suddenly. He's a valued guest. If his departure had anything to do with the resort, we could offer incentives to bring him back. I have his manager's number. His name's Doug, I think."

"Doug DeGraw," Erica confirmed. "He rarely leaves CJ's side."

Laura frowned at Erica over the lid of her to-go cup.

"What is it?" Erica asked, alarmed.

"Nothing," Laura said. "That'll be all. Thank you, Erica." As Erica moved down the hall, Laura grabbed Joshua by the collar and pulled him into her office.

"Hey, what—"

She shut the door, closing them in. "She called him CJ."

"So?"

She frowned. "Josh, when was the last time you called a guest by his or her first name?"

He thought about it. "Over the summer, maybe. There was that competitive rock climber. The blonde one with the killer— Oh!" He took a step back, holding up a hand. "Wait a minute. You think Erica and CJ Knight…"

"I don't know," Laura replied. "But Erica is a professional. And calling one of our VIPs by his first name was a sight less than professional. You should look into this."

"Me?" he asked, aghast. "Why me?"

"Because the majority of people, including Erica, don't just respect you. They love you. You also have a tendency to meddle in other people's affairs," she stated.

"I do not."

She placed her finger over his mouth to quiet him. "Please. For me."

He frowned, then tugged off his hat and ran a rough hand through his hair. "Fine," he said reluctantly. "But I'm not comfortable with this. What are we going to do if something did happen between Erica and Knight?"

"I don't know," she said. "She's the best executive assistant we could ask for. And I doubt CJ Knight left because of Erica, even if they crossed the line. They could just be friends. If she is close to him, she may have more insight into why he left or if he plans to return. Adam's worried about any hint of wrong-doing coming off Allison's death. Celebrity guests get nervous when bad press starts to circulate. And if word leaks to the media that someone like CJ Knight left Mariposa—"

Joshua nodded off the rest. "I get it. Damage control. I'll talk to Erica."

"I appreciate it," she told him. "Truly."

"I've always got your back, ace," he murmured. "You know that. And, for the record, I didn't sleep last night either. If you toss and turn again tonight, call me. If we're going to be awake, we might as well talk each other through it. Or drink about it."

She raised her hand to his lapel, flipping it the right way out. Smoothing it, she offered him a small smile. "I like that idea."

Someone knocked on the door. Before she could answer, Adam stepped in. "You heard?"

"About our ten o'clock?" Laura asked. "Erica told us."

Joshua lifted the pastry box. "Doughnut?"

Adam frowned over it. "Jelly-filled?"

"Lemon or raspberry?"

"Lemon," Adam said and took the parchment around the doughnut when Joshua offered it to him. "Thanks. By the way, I called Greg. He'll be sitting in on the meeting."

Joshua gave a little chuckle.

"I missed the joke," Adam said critically.

"You're the one who wants our attorney to sit in on a family meeting," Joshua pointed out.

"Why is that?" Laura asked.

Adam shifted his jaw. "I have a feeling Greg should be a part of this."

Laura trusted Adam's instincts. Still, there was another matter. "Clive won't like it. It'll put his back up."

"So will the fact that you still call him Clive," he noted.

"Have you heard anything about Allison's case?" Joshua asked.

"No," Adam said. "I couldn't sleep last night, however—"

"Disturbed, party of three," Joshua inserted.

"—and I had a thought," Adam continued, ignoring him. "I'd like to set up a fund for her family to help cover funeral costs."

"Adam," Laura breathed. "That's a wonderful idea."

"I second that," Joshua said. "And she should have a plaque to go in the meditation garden. It was her idea, her design. It should be in her name."

"Just like the restaurant is in Mom's," she mused. "Of course."

Joshua's phone beeped. "That's Carter. I offered to help him with the morning work down at the stable. I'll be back for the meeting."

"Preferably on time," Adam called after him.

Joshua tossed a wave over his shoulder and shut the door behind him. Adam looked at her. "Since Detective Steele is the only relative so far who's contacted us, do you think we should send the offer through him, or would you be more comfortable speaking with her parents directly?"

"He's her foster brother," she explained. "I don't think her parents are in the picture. She never spoke of them. Only him. And, you should know, last night, I got the sense Detective Steele was overwhelmed by the idea of planning a funeral for her. I offered to help. He refused. Judging by his behavior, I'm not sure he'd be willing to take on financial help."

"Was he a jerk to you, Lou?"

"Hey," she said with amusement, measuring the width of his straight-backed shoulders. He was wearing his best suit today and his muscles were knotted, ready, beneath it. "Easy there, knuckles."

"He threatened you in the break room," Adam reminded her.

"He threatened all of us," she amended. "And underneath..." She sighed, remembering. "My God, Adam. He looked broken."

"I don't envy him," Adam muttered.

"I'll speak to him about the fund," she said.

"Are you sure?" he asked. "Erica can see to it."

"I know she can," Laura said. "But this is personal."

Adam conceded. "Are you ready for Clive?"

Laura eyed the to-go cup she'd set on her desk. "Ask me again after coffee."

At sixty-one, Clive Colton looked shrunken. He still had his spine. Admitting weakness was distasteful to him. But now he cut a less imposing figure, more compact and slightly stooped compared to his once-distinctive six-foot frame. More salt than pepper tinted his hair. His suit was conservative, tasteful and impeccably bespoke.

He hugged her upon entering the conference room, just as he embraced Adam and Joshua. The latter pulled away after a brief clutch. The hug wasn't about warmth or familiarity. It was for form's sake, something Joshua didn't give a fig about.

Greg Sumpter, the siblings' private attorney, shook hands with Clive. "It's been a long time, Clive."

"Sure," Clive said, his smile falling away. "How are you, Sumpter?"

"Oh, just fine, thank you," Greg replied jovially. Tall, fit, Greg was dressed casually. No suit or tie for him. He wore his collar open. His relaxed demeanor, paired with his legal savvy, had appealed to Adam, Laura and Joshua right away. He visited the resort often, not just for business, but to check in personally with the three of them and to see Tallulah. He was forty-eight and unmarried, and Laura knew he had a one-sided love for their head of housekeeping.

"I didn't expect to find you here," Clive told him.

Adam spoke up from the head of the table, where he stood behind his usual chair. "I asked Greg to join us."

"Why is that?" Clive asked.

Greg answered quickly. "He thought you and I could play a round of golf later. It snowed last night, but it should melt off quickly. Do you still get out on the course?"

Clive lifted a shoulder. "Now and then. Can't swing it like I used to."

Joshua groaned.

"We'll tee off this afternoon," Greg said. "How's that sound?"

"Fine," Clive said, pulling out a chair for himself.

Greg sent Adam a wink before taking a seat. Laura folded into a chair between her brothers, smoothing her skirt over her legs. "What do we owe the pleasure of a visit?" she asked Clive directly. "You didn't bring Glenna with you?"

"Not this time," he said, running a hand down his tie.

"And your health?" Adam mentioned. "How are you feeling?"

"Spry enough," Clive said, cracking a smile. That smile had caught the imagination of his wife and mistress and the other women he'd taken a shine to through the years. "Thanks for asking."

"Would you like coffee?" Laura offered. "Tea?"

"Mylanta?" Joshua muttered, earning a nudge from Laura.

Clive didn't seem to hear him. "No. Thank you, though, Precious." His grin broadened. "Anybody tell you lately you look just like your mother?"

"No," she answered.

"Pretty as a picture," he said proudly. "Just like Annabeth. She was stunning. Before the cancer did its bit—"

"What did you call this meeting for?" Adam interrupted as Laura tensed and Joshua muttered under his breath.

"Are you in a hurry, son?" Clive asked.

"We've got meetings scheduled for the conference room at eleven thirty and after lunch," Adam told him. "Spring means nuptials, and Mariposa has become the place for destination weddings."

"Congratulations," Clive said. His eyes were drawn to the view from the windows. "You've built something impressive here. You were so young when you took it on. I didn't think you'd last long in Arizona. Now you've got something to be admired."

"Yes," Adam replied.

Laura's tension refused to drain. Adam had been right to invite Greg. There was something Clive wasn't saying.

They waited him out. He swiveled back to the table. "I've come to ask for your help."

"Our help?" Joshua asked.

Adam rolled over his brother's incredulity. "Are you in trouble?"

"No, no," Clive said, waving a dismissive hand. "Nothing that drastic. The company's just seen better days, is all."

"What could we do?" Laura asked.

"I understand the resort's made some significant gains," Clive said. "I also understand that you've got plenty of capital at your disposal."

"How do you know that?" Joshua asked.

Clive chuckled. "If there's one thing I understand, son, it's business."

"A business you stole from Mom's inheritance?" Joshua parried.

Clive stared at him. "Colton Textiles is in my name, son. Not your mother's. And I'm not sure I care for your tone."

"This is me playing nice," Joshua informed him. "And you may come from money, but you never made your own. You play with everybody else's. You married Mom for hers. If not for her, you wouldn't have a leg to stand on."

"Josh," Adam cautioned. "Maybe you should take a walk."

Joshua looked at his brother. "I have a right to be here, and somebody has to speak for her."

A headache was brewing behind Laura's left temple. She wished for coffee. "It's okay," she said to Adam. "Let him speak for her."

Adam relaxed gradually. He addressed Clive again. "What did you have in mind?"

"A loan," Clive revealed.

"How much?"

"Two fifty to start."

Joshua scoffed. "Two hundred and fifty thousand?"

"If that doesn't get the company back on its feet, then another," Clive added. "This is your inheritance, too, don't forget. My legacy to the three of you. You each have a stake in Colton Textiles. Adam, you especially."

Laura thought about it. Colton Textiles was a fine-fabrics importer. When Annabeth had died, she had left shares to each of her children. Adam had eighteen, and Laura and Joshua each had sixteen. Clive had wound up with the lion's share.

"Don't do this, Adam," Joshua implored. His eyes burned.

Adam considered. "That's a lot of money."

"You'll make it up in no time," Clive said smoothly. "And it's a loan. You'll have a return on your investment in due time. With interest."

Laura shook her head. "You can't expect us to decide on the spot. We'll need to discuss it and come to an agreement. Together."

"The three of you?" Clive questioned.

"That's how things are done around here," Adam informed him.

Clive eased back in his chair. "Good for you, kids. Good for you."

Did Laura imagine his condescension, or was it real? Her father wasn't just the face of Colton Textiles. He was a chameleon who could easily mask his true feeling and intentions when it suited him.

When there was something he needed to hide.

Adam rose and the rest of them followed suit, Clive coming to his feet at last. "We should have a decision for you soon."

"Tomorrow," Clive requested as they hovered around the door. "By the end of business hours. If I'm to make gains, too, I'll need that money as soon as possible."

Adam gave a nod. "Fine."

"How 'bout you and Laura join me for lunch?" Clive asked, putting his hand on Adam's shoulder. "Just the three of us. I hear your restaurant's five stars. What's it called again?"

"Annabeth," Joshua retorted.

Clive smiled, nonplussed. "Of course it is."

"I'm due in Flagstaff at lunchtime," Adam explained.

"Laura?" Clive looked to her, expectant.

No plans came to her mind. "All right."

"Splendid," he replied. Reaching out, he gave her chin a light pinch. "Are you still seeing Quentin Randolph?"

The name struck her off guard. "No. How…how did you know about Quentin?"

"I knew him before you did," he said. "I told him about Mariposa. And about you."

She stared, unable to believe a connection between her father and the man who had grossly betrayed her was possible. "He never mentioned you."

"A shame it didn't work out," he said. "You were quite the power couple. What happened this time?"

He'd turned out to be just like Clive—a chameleon. She ignored the question and moved to the door to open it.

Joshua beat her to it. "I need some air," he muttered to her.

"Same," she whispered.

"There's something sketchy going on," Joshua said. He pointed to Laura. "You know it. And I know it."

Adam crossed his arms. "Why do you think I had Greg sit in on the meeting? I knew there was something off when Dad called initially."

Next to him, Greg planted a hand against the wall in a relaxed stance. "I can look into him. See what's really going on with Colton Textiles."

"If he needs that kind of money, it's bleeding," Joshua said. "It's bleeding badly. And if he needed money, why didn't he go to Glenna? She's got plenty. Why did he come all this way?"

Laura chewed over it. "He was right about one thing. We all have a stake in Colton Textiles. It was Mom's company, too. It's as much a part of her legacy as Mariposa. If it is bleeding, could we really just watch it die?" Wouldn't that be like watching a part of Annabeth die all over again?

Adam turned to Greg. "Can you look into it by tomorrow afternoon?"

"I'll make the necessary calls," Greg said. He pulled a face. "I may miss my tee time with the man of the hour…"

Joshua cracked a smile for the first time since Clive's arrival. "Aw, shucks."

"Let us know what you find out," Laura said. She hugged

him. "And thanks for sitting in. If you don't go soon, you'll miss lunch with Tallulah."

Greg grinned. "You know me too well."

"She's taking her lunches with the kitchen staff now," Joshua pointed out, "since her nephew, Mato, got hired on as sous-chef."

"Thanks for the tip." Greg gave the men a salute before strolling off.

Joshua waited until he was out of earshot. "He's loved Tallulah as long as we've known either of them."

"Yes," Laura said with a soft smile.

"I don't know if I could wait that long," Joshua confessed, "for someone to decide whether she wanted me."

"Yeah, you're much more of the now-or-never type," Adam drawled. "Or now *and* never. Never being next week when you decide you've had enough."

Joshua pursed his lips. "Is that any worse than the kind of man who's married to his desk?"

"Enough," Laura said. "Both of you."

"What was all that business about Quentin Randolph?" Joshua asked. "Clive was the one who set you two up?"

"No," she said automatically. She didn't want it to be true. The idea made her feel ill.

Adam's phone rang. He took it from his pocket. "I have to leave for Flagstaff shortly." He glanced up at Laura. "You can cancel lunch. Dad can dine alone."

"I'm not afraid of him," she claimed.

"I never said you were, Lou," he told her.

"You don't owe him anything," Joshua chimed in.

"I'll be fine," she explained. "Maybe I can get some more information about Colton Textiles out of him."

Joshua sighed. He patted her on the back. "Good luck with that, ace."

Chapter Six

The following afternoon, Noah flashed his badge at the man in the Mariposa security booth. The uniformed guard waved him in. He steered his car into the same lot he'd parked in two nights prior. Then he followed the path to L Building and ventured into the open-air lobby.

The clerk at the front desk's name tag read Sasha. She smiled, waving him forward. "How can I help you?"

"Laura Colton." Noah didn't know why her name was the first thing out of his mouth, but there it was.

Sasha picked up the phone on the desk. "Do you have an appointment?"

"She's expecting me," he said, sidestepping the real question.

"Name?"

"Steele."

"Just a moment."

After placing a call, she revealed, "Ms. Colton is at L Bar. Go through the doors here and take a left."

Moving briskly, Noah heeded her instructions. He found himself inside an impressive room. On one side, liquor-stocked shelves sprawled from floor to ceiling. The bartender moved tirelessly from one patron to the next. Music played at just the right volume, not too soft, not too loud. Here, the atmosphere felt easy, not stodgy, like he'd expected.

He saw her at the same time she saw him. Laura's dress flowed around her, long and red with turquoise necklaces stacked above the V-necked bodice. Her boots were black leather to match her wide belt. Large earrings dangled from her ears. She'd swept the strands of hair that framed her face back in a subtle half-do.

She looked perfect. Noah felt his joints lock up in response. What was it about this woman?

She walked to him slowly, offering a nod to a patron who acknowledged her in passing. "Detective Steele," she greeted him. "Back so soon?"

He could see the apprehension lurking behind her icy blues. "Is there a place we can talk?"

"Detective Fulton didn't mention an update in the case," she said. "Is that why you're here?"

The envelope from Steinbeck weighed heavily in Noah's pocket. "Is there somewhere we can talk?" he asked again.

She looked around and seemed to decide that the bar was not the place to have this conversation. "Follow me."

She led him to a back hallway with windows where paintings would have been in any other setting. The Coltons' resort decor leaned heavily on their natural surroundings.

She swept keys out of the small jeweled bag she carried and unlocked one of the closed doors. "Have a seat," she said as she pushed the door open and switched on the light.

Her office, he decided. With its buttery-leather ergonomic desk chair and the wide crystal vase overflowing with fresh desert blooms, how could it be anything but?

"Coffee?" she asked as she rounded the desk.

"No." He didn't sit, although the plush chair looked inviting. Was that a real cowhide or just for show?

She remained standing, too. "Well?"

He pulled the envelope from his pocket and handed it across the desk. "Coroner's report."

She held it for a moment, then turned it over. The flap wasn't sealed. She pulled it back, then pried the report from its pocket. Unfolding it, she gathered a steadying breath in through the nose.

He watched her eyes dart across the page, reading Steinbeck's findings, and knew the exact moment she learned the truth. She raised her eyes to his in a flash of disbelief before staring at the paper again. "She died of an overdose?"

"Of fentanyl," he said grimly.

She shook her head. "That can't be right. That would mean..."

"Somebody drugged her," he finished, advancing another step toward the desk. "The coroner showed me the entry site. The needle went in above her left hip."

The page and envelope fluttered to the surface of her desk. Her hands lowered, limp, to her sides. "You were right," she breathed. "How is that possible?"

"She was killed," he reiterated. "At your resort. And you're going to let me find who did it. That was the deal."

Fumbling for the arm of her chair, she sank into it.

He gripped the edge of the desk, fighting impatience. Fighting the inclination to circle the thing and put his hands on her. Whether it would be to help her snap out of it or just to see if she would let him, he didn't know. "Look, my CO doesn't want me on this. He asked me to back off. Stay home. Wait for Fulton to tie up the case."

"Something tells me you're not going to do that," she said wearily.

"If I had your cooperation," he replied, very close to begging, "if I had your permission, I could dig through back channels. I could find what's under the surface. The underbelly."

Her throat moved in a swallow. "This morning, I would've argued that Mariposa doesn't have an underbelly. But this..." She touched the edge of the autopsy report. "Who could have done this? Who here could be capable...?"

He went around the desk. Instead of touching her, he gripped the arms of the chair. He pushed himself into her space and watched her eyes go as round as pieces of eight. "I'll help you. I won't rest until the person responsible is behind bars. But you have to help me."

She bit her bottom lip carefully. It disappeared inside her mouth as she searched his eyes. Her guarded expression closed him off and he was certain the answer would be no.

Her lip rounded again, pink. Perfect, like the rest of her. She canted her head to the side. "You need a reason for being here," she said. "In case Fulton or your CO catches you on-site."

She was...saying yes? He missed a breath. "If I could pass under the radar...if everyone could see me as something other than a cop...a guest, maybe, or a new member of staff, they could be inclined to talk. That would make my job easier."

"Not staff," she said contemplatively. "That wouldn't be right."

He frowned at the tattoos on his hands. They were right there for her to see. "What, you don't hire criminals?"

"That's not what I meant," she said defensively.

"Then what did you mean?"

"A guest, maybe," she decided. "That would get you in the restaurant, the bar, the spa, the golf course and stables...everywhere but C Building." Her eyes cleared. "Oh."

"What?" he asked, feeling his stomach muscles tighten as he watched her pupils dilate.

Her gaze trickled down his throat, over his shoulders and down his chest. "It's that simple...and that complicated."

"Throw me a bone here, Colton."

"You need to immerse yourself among staff and guests. You need a cover. Being my boyfriend would guarantee access to pretty much anything."

"Your boyfriend." He heard his tone flatline. It was the worst idea he'd ever heard.

And it was the best idea he'd ever heard.

She was right. Being Laura Colton's paramour wouldn't just open doors. It would make people openly curious about him. Those people would lower their guard enough...maybe be clumsy or trusting enough to let something slip. To let him in.

The possibilities came tumbling down as reality set in again.

Who the hell was going to believe that she would date *him*? She ruled this high-class joint. She was Mariposa's princess. He lived on a city salary, drove a decade-old city-issue sedan that ran rough in the winter, and he had no family left to speak of.

Who would buy that Laura Colton would choose to slum it with Noah Steele?

He backed off. "Yeah, that's not gonna work."

"Why not?" she asked his retreating back. She gained her feet again. "If someone here killed Allison, they have to be found. They have to be brought to justice. What if they strike again? What if someone else is killed? I have to protect the rest of the staff, the guests, my family... You're the man to help me do that. Not Detective Fulton."

Fulton had cop written all over him while Noah...didn't. "I don't exactly fit into the woodwork around here either. I'm not the country-club type."

"I told you I don't like labels, and we get many people here of different backgrounds, Detective."

"I bet I don't know a single person who could afford a night in one of your bungalows. What's the going rate these days?"

"For a night?"

"Yes."

She paused. "Five thousand."

A strangled laugh hit his throat. "Holy sh—"

"That includes food and all resort amenities except alcohol, spa packages and special excursions," she explained. "Our guests are happy to pay the price because they know it means we take care of their privacy and security while they're here. They can immerse themselves in the resort and landscape."

"And there are no cameras anywhere," he recalled.

"No."

He cursed. "That's going to make my job difficult."

"All staff members also sign nondisclosure documents when they join the Mariposa team," she warned.

"Then you're wrong," he said, crossing his arms. He eased back against the wall, tipping his head against the plaster. "It's the perfect place for a murder. And I bet Allison's killer knew it."

"That doesn't make me feel any better."

"I'm not here to make you feel better," he reminded her. "I'm here to catch a killer."

She drifted into thoughtful silence. Finally, she came around the desk. "What if you weren't Noah Steele from Sedona? What if you were Noah Steele, the politician's son?"

"Do I look like a politician's son to you?"

"You could be the son of a shipping magnate. Or you could be an entrepreneur."

"I knew I should've packed my sweater-vest."

Defeated, she sat on the corner of her desk. "You're not making this easy."

He swallowed the inclination to apologize to her. Again.

Her chin snapped up. Her stare roamed his boots, his hair. As she perused him, it made him come to attention. "What're you doing?" he asked, bracing himself for whatever thought bubble she'd conjured.

Prospects flashed across her face. They practically glittered. "When I first saw you, I thought you could be a rock star."

"I can't carry a tune."

"You don't have to," she said. She crossed to him. "You're not here to entertain. You're here to get away from shows. Touring. The loud party atmosphere. You're here to disconnect. Recharge. It's a commonality many of our guests share, so you'd have a good jumping-off point for conversation."

She was close enough he could see the beauty mark she'd tried to hide under her concealer. It lived, camouflaged, near the corner of her mouth. "And what band am I supposed to be from?"

"I don't know. You could be a cover band, a good one that tours nationally. And you don't have to be the front man. You could be a bass player. A drummer."

"Maybe I just got out of rehab," he muttered, his voice imbued with sarcasm.

"The people who know me will never buy that I'm dating an addict."

"Speaking of people who know you," he said, "Adam knows who I am. He won't buy any of this."

"Adam will have to know," she agreed. "Josh saw you through a window two nights ago. If he remembers you, we'll let him in on the scheme. If not, then I'll tell him. I prefer not to."

"Why?"

"Because he can be terrible at keeping secrets," she admitted. "I love him, but he wears his heart on his sleeve. When would you like to start?"

They were really doing this—this fake dating thing? He took a long breath. "As soon as possible if I'm going to make headway."

"Tomorrow morning, then. Be here at nine. We'll have a champagne breakfast at Annabeth. That way, I can start introducing you as—"

"The boyfriend." He shook his head. "If I saw you and me together, I wouldn't buy it."

"Not everyone's a detective," she said. "Most people take what they see at face value. They don't analyze. If we play it off right...if we're convincing...then you have free rein over Mariposa for the foreseeable future."

"You'll need to tell big brother," he warned. "Tonight. He'll need to play along, too. I have a feeling he won't approve."

"Let me worry about Adam." She hesitated. "You should come earlier than nine. Can you be at my place at eight? To be convincing as a couple, we'll need to establish history. Basic facts like where we met, how long we've been dating and so on."

"Why not now?" he asked. Last time they'd been together like this, one-on-one, he'd been desperate to get away from her. Now the space between them was no longer a minefield of fresh-turned grief. It felt...warm and, yes, precarious. But he wasn't alone. Here, with her, he wasn't a victim to his thoughts and the self-blame that had plagued him since finding out Allison was gone.

Laura drooped like a flower without water. "I have a meeting tonight. It's a family matter. My...father's in town."

Why did she pause before the word *father*? He still knew very little about the Coltons and Mariposa. He could use the time tonight to research. "Eight o'clock."

"I'll tell Roland you're coming. You won't have trouble getting in." An indentation appeared between her brows.

"What?" he asked.

"I'm sorry," she said, shaking her head. "I didn't know how to say goodbye for a second."

Amused, he wondered what path her thoughts had gone down. "No one's looking. I think a handshake will do, Ms. Colton."

"Of course." She offered her hand. "And no need to call me Ms. Colton anymore, remember?"

He gripped her hand softly. Cradled it. What else did someone do with a hand like hers? "Laura," he said, hearing how it left him like a prayer.

The other night, he'd dropped her hand like a hot potato. Now he made himself hold it. He made himself picture it—her and him. Together. If he was going to convince anyone else they were an item, he had to convince himself first. For one dangerous moment, he let himself imagine pulling her closer. He imagined holding her, the smell of her hair, pressing his lips to the curve between her neck and shoulder, running his hands up the length of her spine...

He imagined the shape of her under his hands, how a woman like her would respond to his touch...

"Noah," she replied.

Heat assaulted him. Before he could hit the safe button, a vortex of flame swept him up. It refused to spit him back out.

Noah took a step back. The doorknob bit into his hip.

Shaking her hand had been too much? What was he going to do tomorrow when they had to convince Laura's family, friends, employees and guests that they were a couple? Flame-retardant gear wouldn't keep him safe from this inferno.

Allison's death had ripped his defenses wide, exposing him. He couldn't let Laura Colton take advantage of the fact.

"Good night," he said shortly.

"Good night," she returned, and the slight smile on her face stayed with him long after he left.

"Have you lost your mind?"

Laura stood her ground. "It's a good plan, Adam."

"He's the wrong cop," Adam reminded her. "He's emotional. According to his commanding officer, he's not even supposed to be anywhere near this."

The guy in her office hadn't seemed emotional. Determined? Yes. Standoffish? Absolutely. Underneath, Laura was certain

Detective Steele—*Noah*—had to be hurting. But his clear-cut focus had struck her, inciting her own.

Someone had drugged her friend, cut her life short... She couldn't walk away from that. "I'm doing this," she told Adam. "We're doing this—him and me—whether you think it's advisable."

"Laura—"

"This happened on our watch," she said, and the horror of that made her stomach lurch. "Someone killed her here. This is our home, Adam."

Adam planted a hand on her shoulder. "You are not responsible for Allison's death."

"Then help me catch who is," she insisted. "Don't get in the way. Please."

The last word splintered. He closed his eyes in reaction.

Voices down the hall echoed toward them. Adam's hand lifted from her shoulder. "We'll finish this discussion later," he concluded.

She raised her chin in response. Recognizing the voices as those of Joshua, Greg and Clive, she braced herself for what was to come. The family attorney stood as a buffer between father and son as he escorted them down the hall to the conference room. His Hawaiian-print shirt seemed loud and cheery, his smile in contrast with Joshua's scowl and Clive's expressionless face.

The only nondescript thing about Greg was the beige folder he was holding. He raised his free hand to wave at Adam and Laura. "We're not behind schedule, are we?" he asked them.

"We arrived early," Adam replied. He stepped aside, motioning for Clive to go ahead into the conference room. As his father moved beyond him and Laura, they both raised questioning looks at Greg.

He offered them a slight nod.

Laura's lips parted. She glanced between her brothers, noting Joshua's grim intent. She watched Adam button his suit jacket, the galvanized rods of his business mien snapping into place. He let Greg follow Clive into the room first. "Shall we?" he asked the others.

Laura wished she knew what was in that folder. As she and Joshua entered the conference room, she leaned over and whispered, "Did Greg tell you what he found?"

"Nothing," Joshua answered.

She took her seat. They would each have a vote, she knew. It was how they handled anything that involved their mother's estate, resort capital or unnecessary risk. She folded her hands on the table, watching Clive settle in. He seemed relaxed. Expectant.

His statement about Quentin Randolph from yesterday came back. Had her own father sent a wolf to her door? She could hardly stand to look at him with that knowledge. Throughout lunch the day before, she'd wanted to ask if it was true. Had he known who Quentin was?

Would it influence her vote if she knew he had? She prided herself on separating business Laura from personal Laura. That was part of her success, just as it was Adam's.

That task was hard enough knowing how Clive had treated her mother through the years, and how he had neglected Adam, Joshua, her and their half sister, Dani. Adding the implications surrounding Quentin's place in her life would make being objective that much harder.

Clive adjusted his cuff links. He grinned. "Who calls the meeting to order?"

"It's nothing so formal as that," Adam informed him. "Though this time, I will ask Greg to start."

Greg took a pair of reading glasses from the neckline of his shirt. He put them on and opened the folder. "After yesterday's meeting, I placed a couple of calls to colleagues with a vested interest in Colton Textiles."

"Why?" Clive drawled. "This is a simple family matter. Nothing worth meddling in."

"I asked Greg to look into it," Adam told him.

Clive's serene smile dimmed on his eldest. "You don't trust me?"

Laura spoke up. "If we agree to your terms, we could risk as much as half a million dollars."

"Risk." Clive batted the word away. "Come now, Precious. I said it was a loan, and that I'd pay you back with interest."

"You wanted us going into this blind," Joshua surmised. "Look around you. We built this place because we were smart. You still think we're children you can easily bait and switch, don't you?"

"I'll ask you again to modulate your tone when you speak to me," Clive told him.

"Greg," Adam prompted again, "tell us what you found. Once the cards are on the table, the three of us will put it to a vote, yes or no, and that majority decision will be the one we go forward with."

Greg cleared his throat. "Right. The reality is that Colton Textiles is going under."

Palpable silence cast the room in a long shadow.

"I knew it," Joshua said under his breath.

Laura stared at her father in disbelief. "Going under? How?"

Adam frowned. "How long has it been in the red?"

"Two years," Greg revealed. "There are other investors, none of whom have seen a return on their investment."

"How could you let it get this far?" Laura asked. "If you were going to come to us, you should've done it from the moment there was trouble."

"Well, I'm here now," Clive said, dignified. He spread his hands. "You must want to save your birthright."

"If you cared about our birthright, you would have told us the truth," Joshua retorted.

"You owe me this."

Laura froze, feeling her brothers do the same. "What did you say?"

"You owe me," Clive stated again. "I paid for it all, didn't I? The house in LA. The private schools you attended."

"Let me stop you right there," Adam said. His hands slid onto the table, palms down. He leaned forward. "Because I sense this discussion going sideways. Our mother may have died when we were young, and you weren't exactly there to take her place. But I'm fairly confident when I say a proper parent doesn't talk like that."

"Now wait just a second—"

"No." Adam's voice invited zero rebuttal. "She paid for the house in LA. And she paid every dime of our tuition. And before you claim you put me, Laura or Josh through college, we paid our way through the trusts she left in each of our names, the remains of which we pooled to make Mariposa what it is. You have no fingerprint here. If you're going to come running to us to save the family company, I suggest you avoid leading with lies and grandiosity. That may have worked with your investors, but we know you. We know the real you."

"What good's a vote when you're all prejudiced against me?" Clive demanded.

"In this room, we're not your sons or your daughter," Adam pointed out. "In this room, we're owners and directors of Mariposa Resort & Spa, and we'll vote accordingly. All in favor of loaning Clive Colton half a million dollars to save Colton Textiles, say 'aye.'"

Neither Laura nor Joshua spoke up.

Adam raised a brow. "The nays have it."

Clive leaned back. In a jerky motion, he pulled down the front of his vest. "Very well." Climbing to his feet, he took turns frowning at each of them. "I should have expected as much. You chose your side years ago."

"Right around the time you made it clear you wanted nothing to do with us," Joshua returned. "How does that feel, by the way?"

Laura crossed to her father, keeping her voice low. "If you had come to us as soon as the trouble started, we would have helped you. We could have saved the company together."

"You can't dress betrayal up with excuses, Laura," Clive said. "Didn't your mother teach you that?"

She felt the breath go out of her. "No. But she did teach us common decency."

"Then why not throw the company a lifeline?"

Joshua stepped up behind Laura, supportive. "You can't save a man from drowning when history tells you he won't hesitate to hold you under water to save himself."

"Or bring down the entire ship," Adam chimed in as he stacked papers on his end of the table.

"*And* he insults your mother," Joshua added. He made a face. "I mean, come on. That's just wrong."

Laura couldn't look away from Clive's angry face. "I've been trying to forgive you for over a decade. She taught us to forgive. She forgave you—more times than any other woman would have had the grace to do so. And it didn't stop you. Still, I thought I could—one day—offer my forgiveness. And maybe I will. But not today."

"You know what I learned from your mother?" he asked. "Beauty can be all ice. She must've taught you that, too. Cold suits you."

Heat flooded her face. She felt it in the tips of her ears. "Please, leave."

Clive held her gaze for several seconds before his eyes cut over her shoulder and locked on Joshua. He glanced to the head of the table at Adam. Without saying another word, Clive stepped toward the door.

Laura didn't breathe easily again until he was gone.

Joshua echoed her thoughts. "He'll be back."

"Maybe," Adam granted. "He's wrong, Laura. You're not cold, any more than Mom was."

"Of course not," Greg chimed in.

But the cold had seeped into every part of her, and she couldn't think how to comfort herself with Clive's accusations loud in her ears.

Chapter Seven

Laura woke the next day with her father's words still echoing. Would they bother her so much if they didn't correlate with Quentin Randolph's remarks when she had broken off their engagement a year ago?

She switched on the kitchen light and went straight to the coffeepot to wake it up, too. She left it running before bending down to scoop up the mass at her feet. Her long-haired tabby, Sebastian, cried out as she dropped kisses to the back of his head. She cradled him against her. His purring reverberated into her chest, easing the dregs of another terrible night of sleep.

She closed her eyes for a moment, pressing her cheek to his soft fur. "Good morning, handsome," she whispered.

Feeling generous, Sebastian let her cuddle him, only growing restless when the coffee maker hissed as it percolated. When he wiggled, she set him on his feet and followed him to his food bowl. "Breakfast," she agreed and set about preparing his morning noms.

Her mother had adored big hairballs like Sebastian. When it had come time to leave the house in LA, her brothers had agreed that Laura should take the cats. She had cared for her mother's felines for the rest of their natural lives.

Sebastian was the first cat she'd brought home after burying the last of her mother's. While shopping in Sedona one afternoon on her own, she'd stopped at the animal shelter. It hadn't been the plan, but two hours later, she'd returned home with Sebastian in her arms.

After the relationship with Quentin had blown up in her face, her failures regarding marriage and starting her own family had trapped themselves in an echo chamber in her mind. The humiliation of learning Quentin's true intentions had almost been too much. If not for Sebastian, work and her brothers... she'd still be living in that echo chamber.

Allison and Alexis, too, had helped. Their girls' nights had increased in frequency. As Laura slid aside the long glass door leading onto her patio, she thought of all the evenings she and the girls had spent talking, laughing and commiserating.

She closed the door so Sebastian would stay in. Unknotting her robe, she slid it off. The pool beyond the deck chairs and firepit was heated. She cast off a shiver at the cool kiss of winter's chill, setting the robe on the back of a chair. When she'd moved from her suite at L Building, she'd asked the bungalow's designer to include a starting block next to the pool. She stepped onto the platform and hooked her toes over the edge. Folding, she gripped the edge of the block with her fingers. She counted off, imagined the starting bell and sprang forward, streamlined from fingers to toes.

No sooner had she hit the water than she started swimming. She flutter kicked, rotating to one side as her arm swept over her head, digging into the water, before she repeated the motions on the other side. The freestyle strokes took her to the end of the pool and back before she flipped over and started backstroking. She did a lap down and back this way before she flipped again and crossed the pool by butterflying. Finally, she finished with the breaststroke.

She'd done the relay so many times, she knew how many repetitions of each stroke it took to get from one end of the pool to the other. She knew, down to the inch, how much space she needed between herself and the wall to flip and change direction. When she finished, she gripped the edge of the pool, catching her breath.

Her time was slower today. Hooking her arms over the lip,

she tilted her head to one side to let the water drip from her ear. Maybe it was the sleepless nights. Maybe her thoughts were weighing her down. She wanted nothing more than to cast them off. She no longer wanted to dwell on her father or Quentin Randolph.

Boosting herself over the edge, she sat with her feet dangling in the water, letting the cold prickle across the wet skin around her one-piece bathing suit. She watched her legs circle under the surface and contemplated another relay to drown the voices in her head.

She heard Sebastian scratching at the glass door. Her coffee would be done, and she would need to eat, shower and complete her hair and makeup routine before her morning meeting.

She toweled off, then draped the robe over her shoulders as she went inside. The house felt warm. She sat before the glass door with Sebastian at her side, watching the colors of breaking day stain the sky over silhouettes of peaks, enjoying the ritual of her first cup of coffee.

As she washed and dried her mug, she heard the knock at her front door. She set it on the drying rack and sidestepped Sebastian so she wouldn't tread on his tail and upset him.

Joshua normally didn't show up for another hour. She snatched open the door regardless.

Dressed in a leather jacket and blue jeans that looked like a flawless fit, Noah Steele brooded behind a pair of dark sunglasses.

He stared at the parting of her robe and the black bathing suit with cutouts above each hip. His frown deepened. "You always answer the door like this?"

She drew the robe around her, belting it tight. "You're early."

"Yeah, well," he rumbled, removing the sunglasses. "I figured the sooner you and I figure out how to do...whatever the hell it is we're doing...the better."

"Come in," she said, stepping back to admit him. As he moved inside her bungalow, she dragged a hand through her wet hair. "I'm sorry I'm not dressed. If you give me a moment, I can—"

"No need for formality," he said. He stared at her in the low morning light from the windows. "Seeing the princess of Mariposa at the start of the day without makeup or any of the polish…" His mouth shifted into a side-cocked half smile. "It's a trip."

She looked away quickly. "There's coffee, if you'd like some."

Sebastian jumped onto the counter, eyeing the newcomer. Noah eyed him in return. "Who's this?"

"This is Sebastian," she said, dragging her fingers through the fur over his spine.

"You're a cat person."

"Yes," she said. "What about you?"

"I don't have pets."

"Oh," she said. She tried to contemplate coming home after a long day with no creature there to greet her.

He looked around, cataloging her everyday surroundings. "It's too neat."

She glanced around at her living space. There wasn't much out of place other than the throw blanket she had used the night before on the couch and the hardback she had left face down on the coffee table. "I have someone who cleans for me once a week."

"Must be nice."

She fought the inclination to sigh over his presumptive tone. "If you don't want coffee, we should get started."

"It's why I'm here."

She sat on the sofa. Because her legs were bare and the robe reached midthigh, she twitched the throw blanket into place over them as he sat on the other end. She curled her legs up on the sofa beside her to disguise the move. "I thought about it a lot last night. I think, if people ask, we should put our relationship at six months."

"Why six?" he asked.

Sebastian hopped up between them. When he sought the space next to her, she waited until he folded into a rest position to pet him. "Because that's enough time for us to get to know each other. Since we decided you're a musician and I'm here at Mariposa, we've been courting mostly over a long distance. Calls, texts, the occasional rendezvous."

"'Rendezvous,'" he repeated. "So the relationship's sexual."

She found she could blush. And he hadn't even smiled at the suggestion. "Do you know many rock stars who abstain from sex?"

"I don't know one rock star, period," he replied.

She eyed the leather jacket. It was soft from wear, scarred in places and sheepskin-lined. He hadn't bought it just for the cover story. And he wore it all too well. "Have you considered which place in the band you would like to be?" she asked, changing the subject. "Bass? Keyboards? Drums?"

"Rhythm guitar," he responded readily.

"Can you play the guitar?" she asked, curious.

"No," he admitted. "But, as you say, I'm not here to entertain. I'm here for a little R and R. And to see my girl."

She tried to ignore the sudden rush of feeling…the wave of sheer heat at hearing him refer to her as his girl. Tamping down on it, she turned her attention to Sebastian's belly when he rolled to expose it. "Six months will have given us plenty of time to grow loved up enough. There will be hand-holding involved. Hugging. Maybe kissing, to seal the illusion. Are you okay with that?"

"Are you?" he challenged.

"Yes." She hoped.

"I've done undercover work," he revealed. "It's all part of the act."

She opened her mouth to ask if he'd ever pretended to date another woman for the sake of work. The question washed away quickly. That wasn't what she needed to know about him. "How old are you?"

"Twenty-nine."

"So am I," she said, offering a stilted smile. "My birthday's May sixth. When's yours?"

"November seventeenth."

She nodded, filing the information away in case she needed it. "My middle name is Elizabeth."

"Why do I need to know that?"

"It's the sort of thing lovers would know about each other after a time," she commented.

He looked away. "My full name's Noah Nathaniel Steele. Nathaniel for my dad."

She felt a smile warm her lips. Nathaniel seemed awfully formal. Like a nice tie he kept tucked away in a drawer because he'd decided it didn't suit him. "Your real dad?"

"For this," he said carefully, "maybe I shouldn't be Noah Steele, former foster kid. Maybe the rhythm guitarist, Noah Steele, comes from a traditional home. A normal one. It's less complicated."

"Great artists rarely come from normal homes. But that's your decision. Where do you want the new Noah Steele to come from—California?"

"Washington," he decided. "I spent some time there with my mom before..."

As he trailed off, she willed him to say more. Was he speaking of his biological mother or his foster mom, the one he'd shared with Allison?

"Before...?"

He shook his head. "It doesn't matter. I'm from Washington State."

"I'm originally from LA," she pointed out. "Just for the record."

"I know."

She blinked. "Oh. You looked into me."

"Part of the job," he excused. "You want me to apologize?"

"No," she blurted. "There's nothing available that most people don't know. And it's good you know. For the sake of what we're doing."

"In that case," he said, "why don't you tell me what happened with Quentin Randolph a year ago? Why did you break off your Page Six engagement?"

She should have seen the question coming. It hit her like a wall. "He wasn't who I thought he was."

He lifted both brows when she said nothing more. "That's it?"

She felt her shoulders cave a bit. "Quentin loved the idea of my wealth more than he loved the idea of me. He wanted the connections that come with the Colton name more than he wanted me. And he fooled me into thinking otherwise for a lit-

tle over a year before my brothers caught on to his schemes."
She paused in the telling, then asked, "Is that enough or do you
need more?"

Noah's tungsten eyes flickered. "Did you love the guy?"

"Would you agree to marry someone you weren't in love
with?" At his marked silence, she rethought her answer. "I loved
the version of Quentin he built for me—the one that turned out
to be false. So, in a way, I suppose I didn't. Not really. And that
makes it easier...until the humiliation sets in."

"He's a moron."

She blinked. "I beg your pardon?"

He spoke clearly, drawing each word out. "The guy's a stage-
five moron. If someone like that had come sniffing around Allison, I would've taken care of him."

He would have, she realized. A shiver went through her. She
blamed it on her wet hair and bathing suit, gathering the lapels
of her bathrobe together. "When was your last long-term relationship?"

Rebuke painted his hard features.

She stopped his protest before it began. "These are things
couples know about each other."

A disgruntled, growly noise lifted from his throat. "Six...
seven years ago?"

"And how long did it last?"

"Five months."

"That's long-term?" she asked.

"I don't know." He cast off the admission. "What's your idea
of a long-term relationship?"

"A year," she stated. "Or more."

"Women tend not to stick around that long," he revealed.

"Maybe you're dating the wrong type," she advised.

"What type should I be fishing for?" he demanded. "You
know any trust-fund beauties who wouldn't mind slumming it
with an Arizona cop?"

Laura chose not to answer.

"Before Randolph, did you date anybody else?" he asked.

"Yes," she said. She didn't want to talk about the other men.

But she had probed him about the women in his life. It was only fair.

"Who?"

"Dominic Sinclaire."

"The diamond guy?"

"Why do you sound so derisive?" she asked.

"I don't know. Who ended things there?"

"I did," she said without thinking.

He narrowed his eyes. "I'm sensing a pattern."

"Should I have stayed with someone with a wandering eye?" she asked.

"The son of a bitch cheated?" he said, voice going low.

"Yes."

"He cheated. On Laura Colton."

Exasperated, she repeated, "Yes."

"What an ass."

"Charming," she commented.

"Sounds like he was charmless."

"Dominic has a great deal of charm," she explained. "The problem came when he employed it elsewhere. We're off topic." She tried to think of another question for him. The ink peeking out from underneath the collar of the jacket drew her gaze. "How many tattoos do you have?"

"I stopped counting." When her eyes widened, he asked, "Is that too many for you?"

"No," she said. She'd never known someone with too many tattoos to count. "Which one is your favorite?"

"I don't have a favorite," he claimed.

"I don't believe that for a second," she told him. "Even Francis Bacon had a favorite painting."

"Who?"

She redirected the conversation again. "It's your turn to ask a question."

"Okay," he said. "Morning or night?"

She frowned. "Really? You think that's relevant?"

"It would be," he weighed, "if we were really into each other."

"Ask something else," she demanded.

"Fine," he consented. "What's your drink of choice? No, let me guess. White wine spritzer."

"Martini," she corrected. "Dry. Yours?"

"A boilermaker."

"That's not a real thing," she assumed.

"Yes, it is. It's a glass of beer with a shot of whiskey."

"You can't have one, then the other?"

"I like to multitask."

Trying to plumb the depths of this man was more difficult than she had imagined. Noah didn't have quills. He had a hide like a crocodile.

Wanting to dig deeper, she asked, "What do you do for exercise?"

One corner of his mouth tipped into a grim smile. "I'm a morning guy."

She fought the urge to strangle him with her terry-cloth belt. "You wanted to do this, too. If you won't make something of an effort, what's the point of being here with me?"

The smirk fell away. A breath left him in a tumultuous wash. Shifting on the sofa, he leaned over, planting his elbows on his knees.

"I'm sorry," he said after a while. "I'm not used to this."

"Answering personal questions?" she asked. "That makes sense. You're the investigator. You ask the questions. Don't you?"

"No. I mean I don't really get close...to people," he told her.

"Weren't you close to Allison?" she asked.

"We met when we were kids," he muttered. "She was my sister in all but blood. That may not make sense to you—"

"It does," she explained. "I have a half sister. Dani. She lives in London. We don't see each other much anymore. But it doesn't change the fact that she's my sister."

"Your father had an affair."

So he'd found that corner of the family history. She tried not to bristle. "He had many affairs. He paid off his main mistress. As a result, she gave up custody of Dani. She was mourning the loss of her mother as Adam, Josh and I were, too. The four of us... We were a mess." The house in LA had felt like a cavern of lost hopes. They had been four sad children, desperate for someone who wasn't there.

"I'll try harder," he said. "For Allison."

"Me, too," she promised. She nearly reached for his hand, then stopped, uncertain.

No, if they were going to do this, one of them had to break the intimacy barrier. Her heart flipped as she eyed the denim covering his thigh. She touched it in a gesture of support.

When his eyes swung to hers in surprise, she felt her face warm. A chain wrapped around her navel flashed to life, glowing orange, as if it had been living in hot coals.

He didn't move, didn't look away. His tungsten eyes brought to mind electrical storms. The severe line of his mouth didn't ease as his gaze swept over her. She saw it land on her mouth.

She wasn't just playing with fire. This was a California brush fire with the wind at its back. Out of control. Destructive.

It would devastate her if she let it.

Her hand shied from his thigh. She gripped the edge of the cushion, wishing she knew what to say next. Wishing she knew what she was doing.

Would helping Allison's brother burn her to the ground?

He was still watching her. She felt his stare drilling into her profile. His voice was rough when he spoke again. "Do you want to keep going?"

Could she? Closing her eyes, she gathered herself, wishing the flush in her torso would cool. The robe felt stifling suddenly. She flicked the blanket off her legs, planting her feet on the cool tiles of the floor. "Where do you live?" she asked quietly.

"Sedona. I have a house there. And I row."

"What?"

"It's how I stay in shape," he revealed. "Rowing. There's a park near my house with a small lake. During the winter, I use a rowing machine at home."

Rowing. It made sense, she thought, judging by the muscles packed underneath his jacket. She tried not to think about muscles bunching along his back and stomach as he worked the oars. The flame inside her kicked up regardless. "Do you like to dine out or in?"

"Eating out is expensive."

"So you drink your boilermakers at home," she discerned.

"I'm more of a social drinker, I guess."

"You don't really strike me as a social guy," she admitted.

He made a satisfactory noise. "We *are* getting to know each other better," he murmured.

The rumble of his voice was appealing. She shrugged to release the knots of attraction digging in everywhere. "Is there anything else about you I should know?"

He was quiet for a moment. Then he said, "I was in the navy."

Her eyes went to his boots. They were the same ones he'd worn the first night. She'd thought some part of him was military—or militant. "For how long?"

"I enlisted out of high school. I left when I was twenty-three."

"That's when you became a cop," she realized.

"A rhythm guitarist for an Eagles cover band," he corrected.

She nodded swiftly. "Right." *Stick to the story, Laura.* She checked her smartwatch and stood up. "I really must get ready. Please, have a cup of coffee while you wait."

"So we're still on for breakfast?" he asked, getting to his feet, too.

"Of course." A romantic champagne breakfast for two at Annabeth with the entire resort watching. Nerves flared to life. "Give me forty-five minutes to make myself presentable," she insisted. "Then you can get started on your investigation."

"What should I call you?" he asked suddenly.

"I told you last night. Laura will be fine."

"Yeah, but don't most couples have sentimental names for each other?"

Distracted, she replied, "I believe I can trust you to come up with something."

"Are you sure about that?"

"Yes," she decided. Then she paused. Couldn't she?

"Are you ready?"

Noah cataloged the faces milling beyond the open restaurant doors. Turning to Laura, he thought again of the way his tongue had practically lolled out of his mouth when she had emerged from her bedroom back at her bungalow perfectly coiffed and dressed to the nines in a black maxidress. This one had a transparent lace collar and sleeves, with a line of ruffles below her clavicle. The skirt was a mix of ruffles and lace. A buff-colored belt tied it together with a hat in the same color. The keyhole in the back of the dress had made his palms itch as much as the cutouts in her bathing suit.

He'd wanted to say something then.

You look stunning.

You're too fine for the likes of me.

Instead, he'd just stood there with his mouth hanging open like an idiot.

He took a steadying breath. "Let's get this over with."

"Take my hand."

Cursing inwardly, he snatched her fingers up in his and hoped to God his palms weren't sweaty.

"There's Tallulah," she murmured. "She's our head of housekeeping and has been with the resort as long as my family has. She lives on property like Adam, Josh and me, and she knows everything there is to know about her staff and the guests."

"Good to know," he said, sizing up the woman of average height and weight. When she saw Laura, her face lit up. "Last name?"

"Deschine. And she's not a mark," Laura warned under her breath. His steps had picked up pace and she hurried to catch up. "Everyone adores her. *I* adore her."

"Everyone's a mark," he informed her.

"Tallulah," Laura greeted her, going straight into the woman's arms.

Noah relinquished her hand as she hugged Tallulah. The woman placed both hands on Laura's shoulders and searched her face, speaking quietly. "How are you doing—with everything?"

Laura's smile dimmed slightly. "I'm okay. Are you?"

"I'm still in shock, I think," Tallulah murmured. "Poor Bella. She remains out."

Laura nodded. "Knox has taken some time off, too, but he's returning full-time today. We need him, but I hope it's not too soon."

Tallulah eyed Noah. "Who is this?"

Laura pivoted to him. She took his hand again, fixing that poised grin into place. "Tallulah, this is Noah. My boyfriend."

"Boyfriend?" Tallulah's focus flitted over the tattoos on his neck and hands, the leather jacket and rustic boots. She shook her head. "You didn't tell me you were seeing anyone."

"I've been keeping it quiet," Laura explained. She placed her hand low on Noah's back. "*We've* been keeping it quiet."

"We haven't had enough time together over the last few months," Noah said. "Have we, Pearl?"

Laura's gaze snapped to his. After a beat, she remembered herself. "No. But once Noah heard everything that's happened, he flew in to be with me."

"That's nice," Tallulah said, a smile warming her mouth. "She needs someone. It's good to meet you, Noah."

"It's nice to meet you, too, ma'am," he returned.

When Tallulah swept away, Laura took a moment to gawk at him.

"What?" he asked. "Have I done something wrong already?"

"No," she said with a slight shake of her head. "You called her 'ma'am.'"

"Shouldn't I have?" he asked.

"You absolutely should," she agreed. "It was just odd hearing something that polite come out of your mouth."

He rolled his eyes. "Right. Because I'm uncivilized."

She sighed at him. "Never mind."

As they ventured into the restaurant, heads swiveled in their direction. He tried not to squirm under the attention. Up front, he'd known that being Laura Colton's boyfriend would make people openly curious.

He had been right. The maître d' took his coat. Noah had put more thought into his appearance, for once. The black T-shirt with the Metallica logo exposed the web of tattoos down both arms. He placed his hand on Laura's waist as they were led to their table and could practically hear the buzz of speculation surrounding them.

"Thank you," she murmured when he pulled out her chair, aiming a high-wattage smile over her shoulder.

There was a flirtatious note in those baby blues. When they heated like that, they no longer reminded him of ice floes. They made him think of hot springs, and his body tightened. His hands hardened on the back of the chair. Leaning over her shoulder as she lowered to the seat, he whispered, "Don't lay it on too thick, Colton. Neanderthal like me might get the wrong idea."

He saw the tension weave through her posture again. She said nothing as he moved to the chair facing her and dropped to it. Without opening the menu, she told the server, "Billy, may we have the champagne breakfast?"

Billy looked back and forth between them, owl-eyed. "Just for the two of you?"

Laura smiled Noah's way. "Just us two."

Noah shook out his napkin. Billy skipped off to the kitchen, no doubt to spread the gossip. "We're an organized spectacle."

"You wanted in," she said, not losing the smile. "Too late to turn back now."

"You could make a scene," he pointed out. "Scream at me. Throw something at me. Demand that I sleep with the horses tonight and be on my way in the morning."

She shook her head. "I don't believe in making a scene."

He shot off a half laugh. "You enter a room and it's a scene, regardless of what you say."

She propped her chin on her hands. "I believe you're trying to give me a compliment."

"I'm telling you the truth, Pearl."

Her nose wrinkled. And even that looked pretty on her. "'Pearl'?"

"You said I could call you whatever I want."

"It makes me sound like a member of *Golden Girls*," she complained.

"What's wrong with *Golden Girls*?" he countered.

"Nothing," she said. "But I am still three months shy of thirty."

A woman passed their table. She did a double take and skidded to a halt. "Laura?"

Laura beamed. "Alexis! Noah, this is our amazing concierge, Alexis Reed."

He dipped his head to her. "Nice to meet you, Ms. Reed."

"And who're you?" she asked, skimming her gaze over his torso.

"This is Noah Steele," Laura said. "He's my...boyfriend."

Alexis slowly turned her stare on Laura, her shock plain. "Girl, you've been holding out on me."

"Noah's in a band called Fast Lane," Laura said. "We've been keeping things quiet because he's been touring."

Brows arched high, Alexis turned her stare back to Noah. She offered him her hand. "Is this your first time at Mariposa?"

"It is," he granted, taking her hand in his. He squeezed it lightly.

"How long are you staying for?"

"As long as it takes to make sure Laura's okay. The last week has been tough on her."

"I'll say it has," Alexis seconded. "Well, I'll let you two get back to it." She sent Laura a meaningful look. "You owe me a long talk over white wine."

"I do," Laura agreed. "Are there any problems I need to see to this morning?"

"Nothing I can't handle," Alexis answered smoothly. "Enjoy your champagne. I'll check in later."

Noah waited until Alexis walked away before speaking. "Fast Lane?"

"It's an actual band," she said. "If I'd given her a fake name, nothing would pop up if she googled it."

"Let's hope she doesn't google Fast Lane and Noah Steele together," he said. "That may blow my cover."

Laura shook her head. "I hate lying to the people I care about. This is going to be harder than I thought."

"Relax," Noah advised. "Once I find out who's responsible for Allison's overdose, you can tell everyone the truth."

Laura didn't appear to be consoled. Billy came back, setting a bottle of champagne and glasses on the table. He popped the cork, let the champagne breathe as he set a plate before each of them with a fruit medley and a croissant that smelled incredible. Then he poured the champagne into a pair of crystal flutes. "Can I get you anything else?" he asked.

"This is perfect," she complimented him. "Thank you, Billy."

As he walked away, Laura sipped her champagne. She lowered the flute, tapping her finger to the side. "I like your arms," she noted.

He glanced down at his forearms. The spider went up one wrist. Webbing chased it up his forearm. The primary feathers of the falcon on his upper arm peered out from underneath his sleeve. On the other arm, more bones. "Sure you do."

"I mean it," she said. "You're practically a work of art."

"Well, that was the idea," he drawled.

"You have to get better at this."

"At what?" he asked. Eating the croissant with his hands didn't seem right. Not with a grand piano snoozing nearby and crystal dripping from the ceiling. He picked up his knife and fork and sawed off a corner.

"Letting me be nice to you," she added.

"Hmm." The croissant practically melted on his tongue.

Carefully, Laura set the champagne flute down. "We've got Adam incoming."

Noah set his fork down. He lifted the napkin from his lap and wiped his mouth. "How did he take the news?"

"Not well," she warned. "Please, be good."

"Really? 'Be good'?"

She gave him a squelching look before greeting her brother. "Adam. Will you be joining Noah and me for breakfast?"

When Adam only turned a discerning eye on Noah, Noah lifted his hand. "Howdy."

Adam didn't respond. Noah noticed that both his hands were balled at his sides. Amused, he asked Laura, "Is he going to call a duel or what?"

She frowned at him. "Noah."

"Will he accept pistols, or should I borrow someone's small sword?" Noah continued, undeterred.

"You're both being stupid. And everyone's watching."

Adam glanced around at the interested parties. His fists relaxed. But the sternness refused to leave his face. "Do you know what you're doing?"

"Of course we do," she said.

"I'm not asking you," Adam said.

Laura looked at Noah, pleading.

He stood up from the table and stepped into the aisle to face Adam squarely. "I'm here to see that Laura's okay," he told Adam, planting a hand on the man's shoulder. He had the satisfaction of seeing a nerve in Adam's temple vibrate. "She's lost a good friend, and she needs someone to lean on."

"And you're that person?" Adam asked skeptically.

"You're damn right I'm that person," Noah snapped. "The real question is whether her big brother is going to stand in the way of that."

Adam looked as if he'd rather swallow a handful of broken glass than allow Laura to continue this charade. He measured the hand on his shoulder with its skeletal ink. "All right," he said, his hard jaw thrown into sharp relief when the words came out through clenched teeth.

Laura stood, too. "I think Noah should stay in a bungalow."

Adam's eyes shuttered. "I think that's asking a bit much."

"There are a couple of empty ones," she stated. When he remained unmoved, she tilted her head. "I'll pay for it, if you're worried about that."

"Don't be ridiculous, Lou. This has nothing to do with money."

"Then say yes," she insisted. "The sooner Noah finds the perpetrator, the sooner everything can go back to normal."

Adam groaned. "He can stay in Bungalow Fifteen. It's better than him bunking with you at your place, which is where you'd put him if I refused."

"Thank you," Laura said. "You won't regret this."

Adam waited until she settled back at the table before turning fully to Noah. He leaned in, lowering his voice to a fine edge. "My sister just vouched for you. Don't let her down."

"And let you run me through with your princely sword?" Noah ventured. He shook his head. "I don't think so."

Adam shrugged his hand from his shoulder before he walked away.

Amused, Noah sat again. "I think he's starting to like me."

Laura gave him a discreet roll of her eyes, reaching for her champagne again. He didn't miss the way her lips moved around a whispered prayer before she tipped it back.

Chapter Eight

"You're dating again?"

Laura didn't think she could take another brother's disapproval. She swallowed, watching Joshua's expression as he took in the news.

"Why didn't you tell me?" he asked.

"I was being cautious," Laura tried to tell him. "Can you blame me?"

Joshua squinted off in Noah's direction. The pair had come to the stable so she could familiarize Noah with the grounds and introduce him to other members of staff. She hadn't expected Joshua to be there at this hour. His shock was palpable.

"Laura." Joshua's face broke out in a grin. "This is great!"

She blinked. "It is?"

"Of course it is," he said. "I didn't think after the Quentin situation you'd put yourself out there again. But look at you."

A relieved laugh tumbled out of her as Joshua gathered her in for a hug. "You're not upset?"

"Why would I be upset?"

"After everything with Quentin… You were so angry."

"He hurt you," Joshua told her. "He broke trust with all of us. Tell me you trust this guy, and I'm here for you."

"I do trust him," she breathed.

"That's fantastic," he said, pulling away. "Do I know him from somewhere? He looks familiar."

"You must've seen his band," she blurted. "Fast Lane."

"Maybe."

Before he could think more of it, she asked, "Did you speak with Erica?"

His smile tapered off. "Yeah, I did. She said nothing to make me think her and CJ Knight are more than they should be. Apparently, his manager—that Doug guy—isn't answering her calls."

Laura thought about that. "That's not good."

"Is there anything we can do about it?" Joshua asked. "What we should be worried about is Dad causing trouble for us."

"You think he will?" she asked.

Joshua nodded. "He's going to get that money somehow. And we know he plays dirty when he has to. Roland's been informed not to let him on the property without notifying one of us first."

"That's good, I suppose," Laura conceded. She watched Noah pet one filly who had come to the corral fence. The horse nickered as she nudged her muzzle against his chest. Noah's hands roamed into her mane before teasing her forelock and stroking her ears.

"Does he make you happy, ace?" Joshua asked.

Laura watched Noah and the horse, and something somewhere softened. It was difficult to associate the gentle horseman with the bullheaded one she knew. "Yes."

"Then I don't care who he is," Joshua explained. "I don't care where he comes from or what he does for a living. You deserve to be happy."

She looked back at her brother. "Thank you."

She would have hugged him again, but Knox hailed him. Joshua tossed her a wink and roamed back into the stable.

Laura crossed to the fence where Noah stood. "Penny has a taste for rebels."

"She's got spunk," he said, patting the horse's flank when she sidestepped for him to do so. "I like that in a filly."

She tried not to watch his hands. She couldn't miss how

Penny nodded her head, as if agreeing with his every touch. "Do you ride?"

"I used to take Allison horseback riding on her birthday," he said.

"That's sweet," she said, trying to align him with Allison's indulgent brother. The pieces wouldn't have fit together so well if he wasn't giving Penny everything she wanted, including a treat he'd nabbed from the feed room.

Noah's head turned her way. "Do you ride?"

"I did," she replied. "My horse, Bingley, died last fall. I bought him when I moved to Arizona. He colicked overnight and…that was it."

"And you haven't ridden since?"

She shrugged. "I haven't had the heart to."

"You know what they say," he suggested.

"What?" she asked when he left the words hanging.

"To get back on the horse."

Her lips parted in surprise. "Allison said the same thing."

He stilled. "Did she?"

"Yes."

He looked away quickly. "If I'm going to stay on-site, I need to go back to my place to pack some clothes. I also need to go by Allison's."

"Why?"

"To look for anything that may point to her killer," he said. "She might have written something down. She could have received a note or a gift from someone. Since I don't have CCTV footage to fall back on, I thought that would be the best place to start."

"Let me come with you," she blurted.

He lifted his shoulders. "What good would that do?"

"Her killer is linked to the resort, and apart from my brothers, no one knows the resort like I do," she explained. "You could miss something I won't."

He shook his head. "I don't know…"

"I won't get in your way," she pledged. "If you need to take a minute when we get there, I can walk outside." She wrapped her hand around the spider etched on his forearm. "Please, Noah. This is something I need to do as much as you do."

He rocked back on his heels, pulling a breath in through his teeth. "You talked Adam into letting me stay and investigate," he said. "I owe you one."

"Is that a yes?"

"It is," he admitted.

"We can take my car."

"At what time does it turn into a pumpkin?"

"Ha." She gave his shoulder a light pinch. There was no give in the tight-roped muscle underneath his sleeve. He didn't even flinch.

Rowing, she thought in wonder. Turning away from him and Penny, she looked across the corral. "Oh," she said as Knox and Joshua looked away quickly. She dropped her voice. "Maybe you should kiss me."

"Now?"

"We have an audience," she whispered.

He stopped himself from looking around. Just barely, she sensed, as the muscles of his throat and jaw jumped warily. Somewhere far away, she thought she heard her heart pounding. Or was that his? She didn't see his chest rise. Was he even breathing?

The chain around her navel heated again. She still held his arm. Of its own accord, her thumb stroked the spider's spinnerets, soothing the cords of sinew underneath.

He took a half step closer.

Her pulse skittered. Every inch of her was aware of him, tuned to him.

He seemed to hesitate, uncertain. Then his head lowered, angled slowly.

He dropped a kiss onto the corner of her mouth. His hand skimmed the outside of her lace sleeve, and he lingered, head low over hers.

She wished he'd take off his sunglasses. Would the storms reach for her as they had on the sofa this morning? Would his eyes be tender? Were they capable of that?

She wondered what that would look like.

"We should go," he said.

The words skimmed across her cheek. Then he moved away, and she drew in a stuttering breath.

"This isn't a car."

Laura kept her eyes on the road and her hands at ten and two. "What are you talking about? Of course it's a car. It's got an engine and tires—"

Noah held up a hand to stop her. "This is a Mercedes G63 AMG. Calling this bad boy a car is like calling Cinderella's glass slipper a flip-flop."

Her lips curved. "You should see how she handles off-roading."

"You off-road?" When she lifted a coy shoulder, he tipped his head back to the headrest. "Don't take this the wrong way, Colton. But that is *sexy*."

"I've opened her up a couple of times on the interstate." She bit her bottom lip. "She goes really, really fast."

Reaching up, he gripped the distress bar. He shifted in his seat. Was she *trying* to turn him on? "You're killing me."

She snuck a glance at him over the lowered, fur-trimmed hood of her puffer jacket, her smile climbing. She wore large sunglasses that hid her eyes, but the smile may have been the first full, genuine one he'd seen from her. "Maybe we should take this time to keep getting to know each other."

"We're only a few minutes from my condo," he claimed. Their morning session of Twenty Questions had nearly been his undoing. It had exposed more than he'd intended.

His walls were already down, he reminded himself. He may not have completely come to terms with Allison's death. But he was an open wound, one Laura's questions had gone poking at without mercy.

"One quick question, then."

He tried not to squirm. "Fine. One question." Damn it, he could handle *one question*.

She took a minute to consider. Then she asked, "Tell me a secret."

"A secret?"

"Something about you no one else knows," she added.

He shook his head. "I don't have any."

"None?"

"No," he said.

She looked pointedly at his tattoos. "Do you really expect me to believe that?"

"Sure." He glanced at her. "How about you? What're your secrets?"

"I'll tell you mine if you tell me yours," she offered.

"This match is a draw," he concluded. He pointed to the end of the street. "Turn left there. My condo's on the right."

She made the turn, then swung into the inclined drive. She leaned over the wheel to get a look at the white two-story. "This is you?"

He popped the handle and pushed the passenger door open. Dropping to the ground, he dug his keys from his pocket. "You don't have to come in."

Laura was already out of the vehicle. She walked around the hood, zipping the silver puffer to ward off the dropping temperature. "You don't want me to come in?"

He'd been in her place, he thought. What did it matter if she saw the inside of his? "It won't take but a moment."

"I think I can handle that," she said, on his heels as he followed the path to the front door. He'd dumped rocks into the garden beds so that only the heartiest of desert plants jutted up through them.

There were two dead bolts on the door. He unlocked them both and the knob before pushing it open. After scooping up the mail on the welcome mat, he tossed the keys on the entry table. "Make yourself comfortable," he said, eyeing the return addresses. He set aside the bills for later and tossed the junk mail into the kitchen trash on the way to the bedroom.

He took down his old duffel from the top of the closet. Then he opened and closed the dresser drawers, selecting what he would need for a few days at the resort. He tossed his toothbrush, toothpaste, shampoo and beard trimmer into a toiletry bag. It fit inside the duffel.

On his bedside table, he exchanged his everyday watch for

his good one, flipping his wrist to fasten it. In a small ceramic dish, he saw the leather bracelet Allison had given him when he'd left for the navy to match her own.

The evil eye in the center of the braided cord stared at him, wide-eyed. It was blue—like Laura's eyes.

He frowned as he scooped it up. Shoving it in his pocket, he knelt on the floor and opened the door on the front of the nightstand. His gun safe was built in. He spun the lock once to the left, then the right, left again. It released and he turned the handle to open the lead-lined door.

Inside, he palmed his off-duty pistol. It was smaller than his service weapon. Since his work at Mariposa was off the books, he couldn't carry his city-issue.

He tucked the pistol in its holster before strapping it in place underneath his leather jacket. He picked the duffel up by the handle. Through the open closet door, he could see the black bag that held his suit.

Steinbeck hadn't released Allison's body. But that time would come. There would be a funeral.

Noah had to bury her. He drew his shoulders up tight, already hating the moment he would have to unzip that bag, don the godforsaken suit she'd helped him pick out for a fellow cop's funeral years ago and stand over her coffin.

He pushed his fist against the closet door, closing it with a hard rap. Then he switched off the overhead light and walked out of the bedroom.

Laura stood in the center of the living room.

He followed her gaze to the large painting above the couch. Looking back at her, he raised his brow. "You look like you've seen a ghost."

She lifted her hand to the painting. "It's Georgia O'Keeffe."

"Is it?"

She squinted at him. "You didn't know?"

"Allison bought it shortly after I moved in," he said. "She said it was a replica. But she thought it'd look good in the space. She teased me for never putting anything on the walls. I waited a long time to own a home, and I didn't want to put holes in the plaster. I put the damn thing up to make her happy." And it had, he thought, remembering how she'd beamed and clapped her hands when she'd seen it on the wall for the first time. His chest ached at the memory. "What about it?" he asked, wanting to be away from it. There was nothing of his sister here. And yet there was too much.

"The painting's called *Mariposa Lilies and Indian Paintbrush, 1941*," Laura stated. "It...was a favorite of my mother's."

Noah made himself study the painting again. This time he shifted so they stood shoulder to shoulder. "Yeah?"

"Mariposas were her favorite flower," Laura breathed.

"Hence the name of the resort," he guessed.

She nodded silently. Abruptly, she turned away from him. "I need some air."

He veered around her quickly. If she cried...here, of all places...he didn't know how he'd handle that. Opening the door to the back patio, he held it wide.

She didn't thank him. Head low, she stalked out on long legs.

He gritted his teeth, wondering whether to follow or hang back. Watching, he tried to gauge how unsteady her emotions were.

She crossed the terra-cotta tiles to the railing. Clutching it with both hands, she viewed the sheer drop to the crevasse below. In the distance, the sun slanted low over white-tipped mountains. The clouds feathered overhead, wild with color. Her shoulders didn't slope. Her posture didn't cave. She stood tall, another exquisite fixture on the canvas he saw outside his back door.

After a while, she said in a voice that wasn't at all brittle, "I can see why you picked the place."

Noah tried to choose a point on the horizon just as fascinating as she was. His attention veered back to her, magnetized. "It was this," he admitted. "And the quiet. It's far enough outside the city, I don't hear the traffic."

She folded her arms on the railing and didn't speak. It was as if she was measuring the quiet. Absorbing it.

Quiet strength, he thought. It came off her in waves. He opened himself to it, wishing he could make room in his grief for it. How had she learned to do that—move past it? Or was he supposed to move *through* it?

Was that why he felt like he was losing this race? He had to stop trying to go *over* the grief and go through it?

Somehow, that seemed harder.

He jangled the keys he'd picked up from the counter. "We should get to Allison's."

She waited a beat. Then she turned and crossed the tiles to him, placing one boot in front of the other. She gathered her jacket close around her, her breath clouding the air.

As she breezed past, her scent overcame him. He felt his eyes close. Even as he wondered what he was doing, he caught it, pulled it in deep and held it.

It was a classy fragrance, something no doubt with a designer price tag.

He swore it was made to chase his demons.

That was his secret. And he'd take it to his grave.

He shut the door and locked it, promising himself he'd come back to the view when Laura no longer needed him. When she was gone. When he'd found Allison's killer, put him or her in a cell...if he didn't kill the person first.

He'd come back here and learn, somehow, to wade through the fallout.

Allison's one-story house was a little Spanish-style residence across town. Noah had a key to the door on the same ring as his. Silently, he worked it into the lock before pushing the door open.

The lights were out. He switched them on as the door squeaked, echoing across hard floors.

It was the opposite of his place, Laura observed. It smelled faintly of incense. The walls were bright yellow and cluttered with artwork. There were little eight-by-ten paintings, woven dream catchers, and a whole quilt draped on the wall of the dining room. The plush rugs sank under Laura's boots. As Noah flipped on more lights, Laura caught herself clasping her elbows. There was a hammock hanging in the dining room where a table should have been.

A pair of UGGs sat by the back door.

Noah bent over a table where books were stacked. He went through them one by one.

She circled the space once before she saw the little notebook on the edge of the bar. She opened it and was confronted with Allison's pretty, sprawling handwriting. "I might have something," she whispered.

Noah looked up. He saw the notebook splayed across her palms and rose.

As he crossed to her, she turned so he could see what Allison had written. "It's not really a journal. It's mostly Zen proverbs." She flipped a few pages and shook her head fondly. "She dotted her *i*'s with hearts."

He said nothing as he pried the notebook gently from her hands. Lowering to a stool at the bar, he journeyed through the pages, one after the other.

She turned away. His expression might be inscrutable, but she could feel the sadness coming off him.

The photo on the fridge caught her attention. It was a stunning snapshot of Allison in dancer's pose on top of Merry Go Round Rock. Underneath, a flyer was pinned with Allison's yoga class and guided meditation schedule for the New Year. She'd made small notes next to each time to help keep track of repeat students with their initials and Vinyāsa sequences.

Laura took down the flyer and folded it in two, wondering if Noah would find something useful on it.

The photograph behind it slipped to the floor. Laura crouched to pick it up and was shocked to recognize a young Allison next to a fresh-faced Noah.

In the photograph, Noah was clean-shaven. The wide, uninhibited smile underneath squinty green eyes and the brim of a navy dress-blue cap struck Laura dumb. His smile made him ridiculously handsome, not altogether innocent, but happy.

She stood to pin the photo back to the fridge with a Buddha magnet. A glass of water had been left on the counter. There was an empty breakfast bowl in the sink, unwashed. Alstroemerias in a vase next to the sink drooped.

She couldn't stand to think of them being left to die. Laura picked the vase up by the base and lowered it to the bottom of the sink. She turned on the tap and filled it halfway.

Noah stood. He tucked the notebook into the back of his jeans under his jacket before wandering toward what could only be Allison's bedroom.

Laura didn't want to follow. But she couldn't imagine him facing everything in there, in his sister's most private space, on his own. She tailed him.

The bed was half-made. Dirty clothes were still in the hamper. Noah had switched on the bedside lamp and was dragging the tip of a pen through the little ring bowl on her dresser. He opened a drawer, then another.

"What are you looking for?" she asked.

"Bracelet," he said, riffling through a jewelry box.

"I can help," she told him. "What does it look like?"

He shut the box, then thrust his hand deep into his pocket. He opened his fist to reveal an evil-eye pendant on braided leather strings.

"That's Allison's," she realized.

"This one's mine," he argued. "I picked it up at the condo just now. She wore hers, always."

Laura frowned. She couldn't remember Allison without the bracelet either. "Wasn't it on her when she…?"

He shook his head. "I viewed the personal items found on her person. The bracelet wasn't among them."

Laura looked around. "If it's not here…"

"Then it's lost," Noah finished, "or her killer has it."

"I'll look over here," she said, pointing to the bathroom.

They searched for another twenty minutes, combing each drawer, cabinet and closet space. The bracelet was nowhere to be found. Laura gathered the scarf she'd bought Allison for Christmas. She'd seen the warm, cozy wrap with its bright rainbow pattern and fun fringe at a local arts and crafts festival and had instantly thought of her friend.

She ran her hands over it and felt tears burn behind her eyes.

"Did you find it?" Noah asked from the door.

She lifted her gaze to his.

He froze, wary, and turned his stare elsewhere. "You need to come out of there."

Relinquishing the scarf, she stepped to the door. He let her pass under his arm before he closed it. Once more, she hadn't let tears fall, but she rubbed her hands over her cheeks anyway, to be sure. "I didn't find the bracelet," she told him. "I take it you didn't either."

"No dice," he replied.

There was violence in him, she saw in his taut jaw, his electrode eyes. He barely had it restrained. She saw him as she had the first night. Only this time, the readiness and anger weren't gunning for her.

She wasn't sure why she did it or what compelled her. She simply thought of the way he'd kissed her at the paddock. Just that brush of his mouth at the corner of hers and the softening she felt inside herself...

Fitting her hand to the bulge of his shoulder under the jacket, she held him.

His brows came together. "What are you doing, Colton?" he asked, hoarse.

She didn't answer. She didn't have to lift herself all the way to her tiptoes to stand chin to chin with him.

Just enough, she thought, touching the hard line of his jaw. She brushed her thumb over the center of his chin. The hair there was thick and soft. Up close, he didn't smell nearly as dangerous as he looked. He smelled like worn leather and clean sweat.

She leaned in. Even as he tensed, she closed her eyes and touched her mouth to the corner of his.

She felt his hands gather in the material of her jacket over her ribs, but he didn't wrest her away. Nor did his body soften, even as she pulled away, lowering to her heels.

His eyes searched hers, scrambling from one to the other and back in escalating questions. "What was that for?" he asked.

She considered what was inside her—what he was fighting. "You're not alone."

His brows bunched closer. The skin between them wrinkled in confusion.

She licked her lips, tasting him there. "I have something to tell you."

"What?" he asked, the line of his mouth forbidding.

"Adam's setting up a fund in Allison's name," she informed him. "It's to help pay for funeral costs."

He shook his head automatically. "I don't need your money."

"Noah, please. We just want to help. Let us. You must be overwhelmed by all this—"

"I'm fine." He moved away.

"She told me once that for the longest time you were the only person she had in this life," she blurted. "It's the same for you, isn't it? She was the only person you had. And now she's gone and a big part of you is lost. Even if you don't want anyone to see it."

"I think we're done here," he said.

She rolled her eyes heavenward. She might as well bang her head against the wall.

In the living room, he'd switched off all the lights. As he went to the front door to leave, she caught sight of the alstroemerias. The petals were so delicate, she could see the light from the window through them.

She'd take them home. She'd care for them, as Allison would have. Then she'd return the pretty crystal vase to Noah when they wilted.

As he locked up, she cradled the vase against her chest and frowned at the stiff line of his back. "What was Allison's favorite flower?"

"How should I know?" he grumbled, checking the handle to make sure it was locked. Shoving his keys in his pocket, he stalked back to her Mercedes.

"You can't expect me to believe that you never bought your sister flowers," she retorted.

It wasn't until she'd fit the base of the vase in the cup holder between the driver and passenger seats that he spoke again.

"Orchids."

She fastened her seat belt and paused, then started the car. "What?"

"Allison liked orchids," he said again, his expression flat as he stared out the windshield. "Not that I know why. They're fussy. She was the opposite of fussy. I got her these blue and purple ones once. She cried when she had to throw them out."

Laura was happy she'd taken the flowers from Allison's. She couldn't think about them falling to the countertop one petal at a time. Methodically, she shifted the Mercedes into Reverse. "Let me know when you decide the funeral should be."

"Why?" he asked.

She set her jaw, watching the backup camera and turning the wheel as the Mercedes reversed onto the street. She could be stubborn, too. "If you won't accept my family's help with the service, you can expect several dozen orchids to grace the proceedings."

Noah thought about it. Then he bit off a laugh. "Before this is all over," he contemplated as she pointed the vehicle toward Mariposa, "you're going to drive me crazy."

She mashed the accelerator to the floor and watched the needle on the speedometer climb. "The feeling's mutual."

Chapter Nine

Bungalow Fifteen had every amenity Noah didn't need. The decor was tasteful and minimal. He could have eaten off the bamboo floors. Fresh flowers populated surfaces and there were no paintings here either. Just lots and lots of windows framing more showstopping views of Arizona. The bathroom off the bedroom had given him a moment of pause with its plush, all-white linens, marble tub and glass walk-in shower. On the back deck, there was a hot tub.

What Bungalow Fifteen lacked was a murder board.

So the coffee table in the living room had become Noah's work area. There, he'd arranged maps of the resort, lists of names, including staff and guests from the time of Allison's murder, pictures of the discovery scene at the pool cabana, Allison's notebook, and the schedule Laura had pulled from her fridge.

On the couch, folders were open to the Coltons' history. The section on the patriarch, Clive Colton, was doubly thick.

One manila folder lay closed. Inside lurked pictures of Allison's body at the pool cabana and others from the morgue, close-ups of the entry wound from a needle and abrasion marks on the backs of her legs.

She hadn't died in the pool cabana. The killer had drugged

her at an unknown location and then transported her to a public place that would appear less incriminating.

Was Allison aware when the needle had gone in? Was she afraid? Or had she simply floated away like the dandelion tufts she often picked from the cracks in the sidewalk and blew into the wind?

Noah locked down that train of thought as the ache inside him let out a train-whistle scream. He avoided looking at the photos unless absolutely necessary.

He picked up the list of names, culling members of staff, crossing off those he'd been able to pin down alibis for with a few well-placed phone calls. Most people had been at home in Sedona. The exceptions were, of course, those who lived on property—Tallulah Deschine and the Coltons.

The tip of Noah's pen hovered over Laura's name. He wanted to strike her from the list of possibles. He knew on a primal level she had been precisely where she had told Fulton she was during the interview process—alone at home in bed.

But the cop in him wouldn't allow it. Not because he doubted her innocence. Because striking anyone from a list of suspects was impossible without corroboration. The only witness to Laura's activities during the time frame of Allison's murder was the tabby cat, Sebastian.

Noah would have sat the feline down and questioned him if he could have.

Tallulah, Adam and Joshua were still on the list, too. All claimed to have been in bed, sleeping, according to Fulton's notes. Knox Burnett, the horseback adventure guide who had tried to revive Allison the morning her body was discovered in the pool cabana, hadn't been able to confirm his whereabouts in the wee hours of the morning. He had also taken several days off from his work at Mariposa, claiming emotional distress.

Noah had cleared the concierge, Alexis Reed, whose neighbors had seen her arrive home around dinnertime that evening and whose car hadn't left her driveway until sunrise. But he hadn't crossed off Erica Pike, the executive assistant whose whereabouts hadn't been as easy to establish.

Between security, housekeeping, maintenance, transportation, the spa, gym, restaurant, bar, stable and front desk, there were one hundred staff members at Mariposa. There could also be one hundred guests if the bungalows were booked solid.

They hadn't been, he noted, the day the murder took place. February was supposedly the calm before the storm of the long hospitality season that stretched from March to October. Still, the chill and intermittent snow flurries hadn't deterred everyone. Seventy-two guests had been booked at Mariposa for the week the crime had taken place. With some legwork, Noah had obtained some alibis there as well.

This left less than two dozen possibles on his short list.

Noah rubbed his chin, reading the four names he had circled. There were more questions around these names than others—like actor CJ Knight. Knight had checked out ahead of schedule the morning Allison was discovered in the pool cabana. Noah's calls to his manager, Doug DeGraw, had been pointedly ignored.

He eyed his notes where he'd cross-checked possible suspects with those who had attended Allison's meditation or yoga classes. There were fewer names on the list he'd cross-referenced with the late-night stargazing excursions she had tagged along on.

The bracelet she had given him lay among the maps, photos and notes. The evil eye stared at him baldly. He'd searched the pool cabana. It had been swept already by crime scene technicians, and the police tape had come down, clearing it for use. Noah had found nothing in or around the area they had missed.

He lamented the absence of security cameras. The pool area was along a major thoroughfare. CCTV could have easily picked something up if the Coltons weren't so concerned with the discretion of their overclassed clientele.

A knock made him drop the sheet of paper in his hand. He felt the weight of his off-duty gun on his belt. Rising, he grabbed the leather jacket from the back of a chair and swung it on as he approached the door.

Peering through the peephole, he scanned the two people on his doormat. His teeth gritted. Trying to relax his shoulders, he did his best to cast off the pall of tension that shadowed him everywhere. He snatched open the door and fixed what he hoped was a devil-may-care grin on his face—something befitting a rock-and-roll guitarist.

Adam and Joshua Colton may have shared similar heights, builds and coloring. But they couldn't be more different. Adam stood as high and straight as a redwood. No trace of a smile touched his mouth.

On the flip side, Joshua grinned widely, a sly twist teasing one corner of his mouth higher than the other. His hair was longer than his brother's and carelessly wind-tossed. While Adam's eyes injured, Joshua's practically twinkled. "Hey, Fender Bender!" he greeted Noah, earning a groan from Lurch at his side.

Whether it was because Joshua's enthusiasm reminded him of Allison's or because his ready familiarity with Noah made Adam uncomfortable, Noah felt a strong chord of amusement. "Fender Bender?"

Joshua lifted a shoulder. "Adam told me not to lead with 'Motherplucker.'"

A choked laugh hit Noah's throat. He covered it with a cough as Adam cast a disparaging look over at his brother. The elder Colton shifted his weight and attempted to start over. "We're going for a morning run."

"Okay," Noah said uncertainly.

"You should come with us," Joshua suggested.

"Or not," Adam dropped in. "I'm sure you're booked."

Joshua nodding knowingly. "With Laura."

Adam shifted gears fast. "You're coming with us, Steele. No ifs, ands or buts about it."

"Pretty please," Joshua added, posthaste.

Noah lifted a brow. He glanced at his jeans. "You know, I'm not really dressed for—"

"We'll wait," Adam inserted.

When Joshua moved forward, Noah stiffened. He wouldn't have time to hide the mess on the coffee table. "Ah... It won't take long for me to get changed."

Joshua's smile turned stilted. "What're you hiding in there, Keith Richards?" He craned his neck to get a look. "Burned spoons? Coke? Heroin? Women?"

On the last word, the younger Colton's voice dropped to a dangerous bass. Noah would've been offended if he wasn't so impressed by the hard gleam in his eyes. He tried to laugh it off. "None of the above," he said. "I just don't want it to get back to Laura that I'm a slob."

Joshua lifted his chin slightly. "Sure. We'll wait."

"Just a minute." He shut the door and shrugged off the jacket, cursing viciously. Throwing it over the back of the chair, he then unlaced his boots. In the bedroom, he removed the gun holster and tucked it safely under the mattress.

Quickly, he exchanged the jeans he wore for an old pair of sweatpants. He left on the 1969 Johnny Cash San Quentin State Prison T-shirt and grabbed the sneakers he'd stuffed in his duffel as an afterthought. Happy for the foresight, he scrubbed the back of his hand over his bearded jaw, left his jacket on the chair and opened the door to find the Coltons waiting with varied levels of patience.

Stuffing his bungalow key card into the pocket of his sweats, he injected a hint of nerves into his voice as he asked, "You two are going to go easy on me, right? Being on the road doesn't leave a lot of time for exercise."

Joshua and Adam traded a glance as they led the way up the path. "Sure thing," Joshua replied before he broke into a jog, getting a head start.

Noah caught up with Adam and muttered, "Thanks for your help back there."

"You want Josh's trust," Adam retorted, "earn it yourself."

Adam pulled ahead, trailing behind his brother. Noah was forced to kick it into gear. A cloud of warm air plumed from his mouth as the cold slapped his face.

He kept up with them just fine, even as the path turned rough around the edges and the bungalows fell behind. They passed signs for a trailhead. The path declined, forked, inclined, forked, declined and inclined again. Caution signs zipped past, as well as guardrails looking out over long drops.

They reached a high point and Adam and Joshua let up finally. Adam doubled over, holding his hamstring while Joshua paced, panting.

Noah tried not to grope for the trunk of a nearby shrub tree. He liked to think he was in good shape, but he sipped air that felt thin. They'd pushed him, either to test his mettle or as some kind of Colton initiation rite.

They would need to work harder to throw him off the scent, he thought with a lick of triumph as he caught Adam's wince. "Is this the halfway point?" he called out.

Joshua spared him a look over his shoulder. "This is as far as we go, Steele."

No more "Fender Bender." Not even a "motherplucker." Noah circled, swept up in the panorama. "Hell," he whispered, impressed. He could understand why people paid thousands of dollars to stay at Mariposa. The state parks were littered with people. To find a solitary hike these days, a person had to wander off the map.

Here, there didn't seem to be anyone around for miles. The quiet struck him. He raised his face to the sun. No wonder Allison had been in love with this place.

I get it now, he told that part of his mind that still felt connected to her somehow.

Another thought struck him. He'd been lured away from other guests with only Laura's brothers for company. He eyed the long tumble of rocks down to the bottom of the hill. "Is this where you kill me?"

A laugh left Adam. It sounded grim. "I wish."

At least big brother's honest, Noah mused.

Joshua turned on him, hands pressed into his hips. "What do you want with Laura?"

The question shouldn't have caught him off guard. He'd have done this, too, had Allison brought a man around to meet him. He searched his mind.

And found that some part of him could answer the question. Something inside his chest that had cracked like an oyster.

What did he want with Laura?

Everything.

No, he schooled himself. That wasn't the right answer. That couldn't be the answer at all. He didn't want anything from Laura.

Except her mouth. Her smile—the real one he found so elusive. Laughter he'd never heard. Her banter. Hell, even her rebuttals.

He wanted her hands, he thought, unbidden. Soft, clean, manicured fingers tangled up in his, spreading through his hair…

He shifted when that image alone turned him on. Shifting away from the Colton men, he put some distance between them and him. He didn't think they would be amused if they saw what the simple thought of their sister did to him.

Joshua didn't let up. "Answer the question."

Noah thought about it, vying for an appropriate response that would appease them both. What came out was "I want her to know she's safe."

"Of course she's safe," Adam snapped at his back. "Mariposa's safer than anywhere else."

Noah whirled on him. "Is that right?"

The light of challenge died in Adam's eyes.

"Would I be here if she felt safe?" Noah pressed.

Joshua shook his head. "I'm not sure how you could make her feel any safer than Adam and I can."

"Someone was murdered under your noses," Noah pointed out. "Someone she cared about."

"She blames herself," Adam mumbled.

"Allison's death had nothing to do with Laura," Joshua said.

"How do you know?" Noah asked. "How do you know she's not the next target?"

Both men froze. Noah struggled against the need to press further, to question them more about Allison. But Laura had warned him not to give himself away to Joshua if he could help it.

If Joshua did have loose lips, then Noah's cover would be blown before he could avenge Allison. "She needs me," he said and wondered if it was true, because he knew all too well that the next part was. "I can't let her do this alone."

Adam and Joshua remained studiously silent. After a few minutes, Joshua stretched for the return run.

It wasn't until Joshua had started back for the trailhead that Adam spoke up again. "Allison gave private lessons to some guests."

Noah nearly skidded on a patch of ice. "Why didn't you mention it before?"

Adam chose not to answer that. Instead he told him, "She'd go to them."

"Their bungalows," Noah muttered.

"Yes," Adam replied. "When she came to me with the idea, I advised against it. Our goal is to keep the staff presence to an absolute minimum, in and around the bungalows. Maintenance crews and Housekeeping don't go there unless a guest has a spa treatment or excursion scheduled. All requests are seen to personally by the concierge."

"You asked her not to do it?"

"Allison has a way of talking you into things." Adam grimaced. "Sorry—she *had* a way. I told her she could start taking on a handful of private lessons at a time, as a trial run. If everything went well, she could take on more in the spring."

"Do you know which guests signed up?" Noah asked. "Do you know which ones had private lessons scheduled during the week she was murdered?"

"I don't know their names," Adam explained. "I just know she had three signed up during that time, two she taught that same day. She was excited. She enjoyed helping people, whether it was in a group setting or one-to-one." Adam cursed under his breath. "Did she die because I gave in—because I let her go into people's bungalows against my better judgment?"

If the private lessons had led to Allison's undoing, what were the three names on her exclusive list?

Chapter Ten

Laura hurried toward the front desk. A raised voice had brought the lobby to a standstill and one of the front desk clerks seemed to shrink before a painfully thin platinum blonde whose designer handbag swung in a threatening motion. "I don't want Bungalow Eighteen! My husband and I always stay in Bungalow Three! My last name is Colton, too, you know!"

At Laura's side, Roland spoke briskly. "I'm sorry, Ms. Colton. The guard at the gate didn't realize who she was until she was past the checkpoint."

"It's all right, Roland," Laura assured him. Someone needed to rescue poor Clarissa from her stepmother's rant. She picked up the pace to intercept.

"I can escort her out."

"No, that will just make things worse." Laura had never known her stepmother to visit without Clive or to make a scene. But she knew the indicators of escalation. She could feel the open curiosity and horror from people gathered around. "I can handle this."

Alexis breezed in, planting herself behind the desk in front of Clarissa. "Ms. Colton," she greeted Glenna smoothly. "How very nice to see you again."

"Don't patronize me," Glenna snapped. "I've been on a plane for two hours. I want my bungalow!"

"Clarissa has informed you that Bungalow Three is currently occupied," Alexis informed her. "If you had called ahead, we could have told you it wasn't available."

"I don't care that it's not available—"

"Ms. Colton, reservations are required for Mariposa's bungalows," Alexis went on. "We need at least six weeks to see to personal requests. This is a five-star resort. Not a fly-by-night motel. Because you showed up without prior notice, you will enjoy all the amenities Mariposa offers with a complimentary spa package from the comfort of Bungalow Eighteen or I can call Sedona's Hampton Inn. I'm sure they'll be happy to give you their best room."

Glenna bristled. She hissed. But Laura saw the handbag droop as her arm dropped. "I see I've been painted into a corner."

"No, ma'am," Alexis said, her incisive gaze not leaving Glenna as Clarissa handed her the welcome package, complete with key card and spa vouchers. "Our policy is bungalow by reservation only. Anyone who behaves as you have is normally showed the door. And yet *you* are getting a key card and a free massage from Arizona's very best masseur." She thrust the envelope at Glenna. "We hope you enjoy your stay at Mariposa, Ms. Colton. If you need anything further, my name is Alexis Reed. I'll be your concierge. My number's in the packet. Please, *do* call me."

Glenna took the envelope slowly, as if afraid the thing contained anthrax. She tossed her hair over her shoulder and strutted out the entry doors, no doubt to hail one of the golf cart operators to take her to her assigned bungalow.

People roamed the lobby freely again, and Laura approached the front desk. She caught Alexis's eye and mouthed, *You are my hero.*

Alexis lifted both hands in a prayer pose and tipped her chin down.

"Drinks on me at L Bar tonight," Laura told her.

Prayer pose turned into a discreet fist pump. Alexis stopped when the next check-in appointment came forward. Brushing Clarissa out of the way, she said, "Take five. I'll handle this."

"Thank you," Clarissa breathed and practically fled. She looked at Laura. "I'm sorry, Ms. Colton. She just started yelling. I didn't know what to do."

"It's all right," Laura assured her. "Go to the break room. Brew a cup of tea. I believe Tallulah left a dish of brownies for everyone there. Come back in half an hour. I'll help Alexis and Sasha cover the front desk."

Clarissa lit up. "Thank you so much! I was doing the meditation classes with Allison. Since something happened to her, I've been out of sorts…"

"I know exactly what you mean," Laura said. "This has been a difficult time for everyone."

"People keep asking for yoga classes. I just keep handing them spa vouchers."

"That's the best we can do for now," Laura reminded her.

"Any idea when a new yoga teacher is coming?"

Distress trickled down Laura's spine. She hadn't given a thought to hiring anyone else. It would be her responsibility to do so. "Not at this time."

Clarissa nodded solemnly. "I'll be back in thirty minutes, on the dot."

As Clarissa speed-walked out of L Building, Laura pressed her hand to her stomach. The idea of putting out the call for a new yoga instructor, conducting interviews and placing genuine effort into finding a replacement for Allison made her feel sick.

Roland took her elbow. "Are you all right, Ms. Colton?"

She gave him a tight nod. "Sure. Please let me know if Glenna makes any more waves."

"Will do," he agreed. "I'm going into a briefing with Adam. Should I tell him she's arrived?"

"Yes," she said. "The snow's melted off, so Josh is directing Jeep tours. He'll be off property for the better part of the day. I'll text him and warn him before he returns."

Roland walked toward the offices but snapped his fingers and backtracked. "I've got something for you."

"Oh?" Intrigued, she watched him dig a folded piece of paper out of his pocket. "What's this?"

"I ran into your friend Mr. Steele out by the stable earlier," he revealed. "He said he was looking for you."

Laura thought quickly, her fingers tightening reflexively around the note. "I did tell him to meet me there. I suppose I forgot."

"I wouldn't worry about it," Roland returned consolingly. "He was friendly enough."

Laura tried not to laugh at Noah being referred to as "friendly."

"He gave you this?"

"Yeah. He said he knows how busy you are. He knew I'd be seeing you, so he wanted me to pass along a message."

"Thank you, Roland," Laura said. When he nodded and walked away, Laura unfolded the small slip of paper and stared at the tidy, slightly slanted handwriting.

Pearl,
I missed you. There's a new gelding here you need to check out. He's calm and sweet, like you. His name's Hero if you're still interested in getting back on the horse. If you're not busy later, meet me at L Bar at six. I'll have a martini waiting.
Yours,
Noah

Laura lingered on the closing. *Yours.* She felt herself soften again.

The note hadn't been sealed, which meant Roland could have easily read it. Noah would have guessed that. That was why he'd used the nickname he'd picked for her. Was that why he had invited her to drinks this evening? Or why he'd said such sweet things about the new gelding's nature and her own?

She folded the note again, trying to shove the questions into a drawer. What she couldn't ignore was how the written words had made the waves of sickness she'd felt moments before ease.

She made a mental note to drop by both Glenna's bungalow for a chat and L Bar for a date.

* * *

L Bar hummed with activity. Still, the atmosphere felt comfortably intimate. Patrons hovered around high-topped tables or the long bar where the personable bartender, Valerie, built drafts and mixed cocktails.

"You're Laura Colton's man," she guessed when he introduced himself.

"I am," he said.

"How'd you manage that?"

He chuckled because she meant it more as a ribbing than an insult. And she had a point. "Beats the hell out of me."

"Is she joining you tonight?" Valerie asked.

"I hope so," he said, looking at the doors—as if he couldn't wait for Laura's arrival.

Who was he kidding? He'd glanced toward the doors half a dozen times already. "She'll have a martini, dry. I'll have a Corona and lime."

"Coming right up," she said as she built his beer. "You arrived just in time, if you ask me. The boss doesn't burn the candle at both ends. She's too smart for that. But word is, she's broken up about what happened."

"You're right." He tried to think how to broach the subject without drawing eavesdroppers into the conversation. "You never forget the shock when something happens like that. I lost a friend of mine a few years back. It's tough."

Valerie passed the beer to him. She grabbed a cocktail shaker for Laura's martini. "I don't think anyone who knew Allison will get over it."

Noah folded his arms on the bar. He allowed his shoulders to droop over them. "I don't think anyone ever really gets over it. I'll never forget what I was doing when I heard the news about my buddy."

"I won't forget either," Valerie replied. "I closed the bar that night same as always. It was close to the weekend, so it was open later than it is on weekdays. My roommate woke me up the next morning with a phone call from Laura. That's who hired me and everybody else. If there's a staff bulletin, she makes sure everyone knows about it. Even those of us who aren't scheduled to come in until later. That must've made things harder for her—having to call around and deliver the news to all the staff."

Noah nodded. He made a mental note to track down Valerie's roommate and confirm that she had been home around the time of Allison's death.

"I'm glad she has someone," Valerie mentioned as she poured the cocktail into a martini glass. She topped it with an olive. "You're a real sweetheart for being there for her."

He flashed a smile. "Wouldn't have it any other way."

"Is your band coming to Arizona soon?" Valerie asked. "I'd like to check it out."

"I'll have to check our schedule," he said. "We're taking a break right now. We've been touring for a while."

"Enjoy it while you can," she advised. "Nobody knows more about burning the candle at both ends like a genuine rock-and-roll superstar."

"I'm no superstar," he said.

Valerie leaned toward him over the bar, lowering her voice. "Her stepmother showed up this afternoon."

He searched his memory files for a name. "Glenna?"

"That's the one. Made quite a scene at the front desk. I hear there's trouble with her father, too. She and her brothers turned down his request for a loan. Now he may be out for blood."

Lifting the beer to his mouth, he made a noncommittal sound.

"That's how the old man operates, from what I understand," Valerie said, easing back with a shrug. "He never gave a hoot for his kids. But when the chips are down..."

"How else do you expect an eel to operate?" Noah groaned.

Valerie laughed. "Hey, it was nice to meet you."

He dipped his head. "Nice to meet you, too." Backing away with the drinks, he let her move on to the next customer. He saw the empty table in the back corner and made a beeline for it.

Laura arrived moments later in another fur-trimmed jacket—this one camel-colored. It looked as soft as he knew her skin to be. The hem floated around her knees. She stopped to speak to Valerie for a moment, then let a guest snag her attention. She passed around smiles and assurances in a manner any PR representative would have admired.

The smile didn't dim when she found him lurking at the back table. "I'm behind schedule," she said when she reached him. "I apologize."

"No need," he said, standing to take her coat as she slipped it from her shoulders.

Her bare shoulders. *Christ*, he thought, seeing the delicate ledge of her clavicle on display above the off-the-shoulder blouse. Every lover-like thing he could have said seemed too real. Too sincere.

You're a knockout...

I am the envy of every man in this room...

What the hell are you doing with me, Pearl?

He held out her chair for her. When she settled, smoothing the pleat of the sunshine-yellow linen slacks she wore, he draped her jacket on the chair behind her. And, because this was L Bar—because he could feel every Tom, Dick, Harry and Valerie watching—he took her shoulders.

She turned her head slightly, and he felt her spine straighten.

He told himself it was all for show as he dropped his mouth to her ear. "I'd've waited," he murmured for her. "I'd've waited all goddamn night for you, Colton." Even as he chastised himself for being a moonstruck moron, he closed his lips over the perfumed place beneath her lobe.

She tilted her head. Not to shy away. He knew it when she released an infinitesimal sigh, when her pulse fluttered against the brush of his mouth as he lingered, sipping her skin like a hummingbird. He cupped the other side of her face as she presented him with the regal column of her throat.

Her shiver pulled him back. It roped him to the present, to what was real and what wasn't. He wrenched himself away, watching his hands slide from her skin. "You're better at this game than I am," he muttered before slinking off to his chair where he belonged.

She watched him as he set the martini in front of her and tipped the beer up. It took her several minutes to taste her drink, sipping in a ladylike fashion that drove him to distraction.

"What kept you?" he wondered aloud.

She set the glass down without a sound. "My stepmother arrived unexpectedly this afternoon and was disgruntled when she didn't receive the VIP treatment she thought she deserved."

"It fell to you to unruffle her feathers?" he asked. "Don't you have enough to handle?"

"Glenna's family," she said cautiously. "At first, I thought their marriage was more business than anything. Her and Clive's courtship happened swiftly. Before we knew it, they were married. But I know Glenna takes care of him. He's getting older. When they married, I won't lie and say I wasn't relieved."

"Because that meant he was no longer your responsibility."

She winced. "Does that make me callous?"

"Not if the rumors about Clive Colton are true," he said. "Not if he only comes to you and your brothers for money."

Her gaze riveted to his. "How do you know about that?"

"I've spoken to over half your staff over the last few days," he reminded her. "While they respect you, Adam and Joshua, they talk."

She looked away, noting those at the surrounding tables. In a self-conscious move, she ran her fingers through her straight-line bob.

He wanted to tell her how surprised he'd been by the loyalty of her employees—how the ones who knew about Clive's recent visit to Mariposa had sided with the siblings, bar none. Not one disparaging word had been spoken about Adam, Laura or Joshua. Noah knew that had nothing to do with the non-disclosure documents everyone had signed and everything to do with how Mariposa was run, how staff were treated, and how devoted the Coltons were to the resort and the people who worked for them.

She wasn't the princess of Mariposa; she was the queen, and her subjects loved her dearly.

She sighed. "I just want to know why she showed up without warning. Why she came alone. Her behavior is outside the realm of anything I've seen."

"Breaks in patterns of behavior are tells," he advised. "Dig deeper and you'll find a motive."

"Have you made any headway in the investigation?"

"I have a short list of people with no alibis."

"Who?"

He tried dousing the question with a warning look.

She braced one elbow on the table's edge, rested her chin on her hand and leaned in. From the outside, it looked intimate. Especially when her eyes roved the seam of his mouth. "Are we still in this together, Noah?" she murmured.

He, too, leaned in, setting both arms on the table. He hunched his shoulders toward the point of hers. Wanting to rattle her chain as much as she was rattling him tonight, he dipped his gaze first over her smooth throat. Then lower to the straight line of her bodice. For a split second, he wondered what was keeping it in place. The curves of her breasts were visible, and she wore no necklaces to detract from the display. The effect made him lightheaded, slightly giddy. Did L Bar have an antigravity switch?

His gaze roamed back to hers and latched on. He was half-wild with need. The effort to steer his mind back to the investigation and Allison felt arduous.

Frustration flooded him, anger nipping at its heels. *Damn it.* It shouldn't be this easy to make him forget why he was there. "Why didn't you tell me Allison was giving private lessons to guests in their bungalows?"

Her eyes widened. "She...what?"

"I thought you were her friend," he hissed. "You say you knew her. How could you not have known what she was doing?"

Laura's lips parted. "She didn't tell me."

"I'm supposed to believe that?"

Her eyes heated. "Do you really think so little of me?"

"Adam knew."

She gripped the stem of the martini glass. "Why did neither of them think to involve me?"

"You'll have to take that up with your brother. He said she had three clients the week of her death, two the day she died. I need to know who they were."

"I don't have that information," she said coolly, pulling away from him. "You didn't answer my question."

She'd asked about his list of suspects. "You won't like it."

"It's a little late to spare my feelings," she informed him.

Remorse chased off his anger. He fell prey to so many mixed emotions around her, and it floored him. He'd never known anyone who could make him *feel* like this.

"Tallulah," he said.

She laughed shortly, without humor. "If she's at the top of your list, you're reaching."

"Erica Pike," he continued. "Knox Burnett. Adam. Joshua. You."

Laura stiffened. "Me?"

"You don't have an alibi for the time in question," he said. "Not one anyone can corroborate. I can't cross you or the others off my list until you give me one."

"I'm a suspect." On the outside, she was all ice. "This may be the worst date I've ever had."

"It's not personal, Laura."

"No," she agreed. "You've made that very clear. Haven't you? And it's surprising."

"What is?"

"That a guy like you can be so by the book."

He felt a muscle in his jaw flex. "A guy like me?" he repeated.

"You don't really think I hurt her," she said.

"No, I don't thi—" Fumbling, he course-corrected quickly. "That's not the—"

"You don't really think my brothers killed Allison either," she surmised.

He caught his teeth gnashing together and stopped them before he ground his molars down to the roots. "It doesn't matter what I think. I go where the facts are."

"Speculation figures into detective work," she said. "I've read enough true crime to know that. What would be Adam or Josh's reason for drugging our yoga instructor? For that matter, why would Tallulah or Erica do such a thing?"

"I don't have motive," he said. "Just a list of people who claim to be sleeping at the time of her death."

"You've ruled guests out?"

"No," he said. He tossed a look toward a man in an open-collared shirt who was lifting a glass of whiskey in a toast to Valerie. "Roger Ferraday doesn't seem to know where he was or what he was doing during the night in question. As it sits, he's Fulton's chief suspect."

"Ferraday," Laura said numbly. "He's staying here with his teenage son, Dayton."

"Who has a list of hushed-up misdemeanors back home in Hartford," Noah revealed, tipping his beer to his mouth to drain the glass.

"He's fifteen," she said.

"Doesn't make him or Daddy innocent," Noah told her. "I'm also taking a look at CJ Knight."

Her gaze pinged to his, alarmed.

He narrowed his eyes. "Does that name ring a bell?"

"Yes," she said. "He left the morning Allison's body was discovered. We haven't been able to reach his manager to find out why."

"DeGraw won't return my calls either."

"CJ Knight was one of Allison's repeat students," she whispered. "And I understand he has Bungalow One booked again after Valentine's Day."

"Think he'll show up?"

"I can't say at this point."

"If he keeps his booking, I want to know the second he checks in."

She rubbed her hand over her arm, discomfited. "I don't know how you do this—look at everyone…every person without an alibi and peel back the layers to see which one of them has murder written on their heart."

"With some people, it doesn't leave a mark," he said. "For some people, killing is in their nature."

"God," she said with a shiver.

"There are those, too, who don't seek to harm others," he said. "They start small and escalate. Or they claim it was an accident. Throw in the occasional plea of insanity."

"It must do something to you," she said, "to do this every day. To look at the dead."

"You get used to it."

"Do you ever have trouble sleeping?"

All the time, he thought. He didn't grimace, but it was a near thing. "Somebody's got to speak for them. The victims. Some-body's got to fight for them."

Her expression softened at long last. "My brothers took you running this morning."

He rolled his eyes. "If that's how they treat all your suit-ors, I'm starting to understand how so many dickheads slipped through the cracks."

"Meaning?"

"Meaning if they wanted to warn someone off, they wouldn't do it at first light. They'd do it at night. They'd rustle them out of bed, blindfold them and drop them off in the middle of the des-ert. See if they can make it back on their own before daybreak."

"Why does it sound like you've done this before?"

"I plead the Fifth."

"Is this why none of Allison's boyfriends ever lasted all that long?" she asked.

Before he could answer, he spotted Alexis cutting through the crowd. "I think your friend's looking for you."

Laura turned and waved. "I wasn't sure if you'd join us," she said. "I'll fetch a glass of white for you."

"Not just yet," Alexis said. She placed her hand on Laura's. "We have a situation."

Laura's smile dropped like a stone. "What kind of situation?"

"There's been a leak," Alexis answered. "There's a van from the local news station at the gate and the front desk is getting calls. It's about Allison."

Laura rose quickly. "Does Adam know?"

"Yes," Alexis said. "He's waiting in his office."

"Tell Roland to delay the news crew at the gate as long as possible while Adam and I reassess," she said. "We'll need at least ten minutes to shift into damage-control mode."

"I'm on it," Alexis assured her. "Who could have done this? Who would have talked to the press?"

Laura shifted her eyes to Noah.

He understood the question she was asking. "Leave it with me."

She nodded shortly. "I have to go."

"Go," he urged. When she leaned in, he did the unthinkable. She'd meant her pursed lips to skim his bearded cheek. He turned his head automatically and caught the kiss on the mouth.

Her hand gripped his arm. Her fingers dug through his sleeve.

Again, he didn't think. If he had, he wouldn't have opened his mouth. Her eyes watched his. He didn't close his either as he grazed his teeth lightly over her round bottom lip.

A noise escaped her. He pulled back. The heat refused to bank. His heart racked his ribs.

She stared at him, as shocked as he was.

Did she feel the heat, too?

Alexis said her name. Laura blinked. She backed away from him, turned, and followed Alexis to the doors and out.

He caught the curious looks he'd earned from those around him. Turning away, he saw the jacket Laura had left on the back of her chair.

Noah dug the cash out of his pocket, dropped it on the table, gathered the coat and left to fade into the night.

Chapter Eleven

"Why are you here?"

Noah ignored Fulton as he escorted his guest into the station. She'd fought the cuffs like a wet cat. As she bristled against his lead, he warned, "People get tossed into lockup for fighting custody, sweetheart. I'd calm down if I were you."

Glenna Colton twitched in indignation. "You're hurting me!"

"I'm not," he said firmly, guiding her toward the back of the Sedona station, where the interrogation rooms were located.

"I want my lawyer!"

"You're entitled to a representative during questioning," he acknowledged. "You'll need one when this is all over."

"I still don't understand what I'm being charged with," she said.

"Assaulting a police officer, for one," Noah said, knocking on the door of Interview Room 1. When no one answered, he opened it and poked his head in. The room was clear. He maneuvered her inside. "Sit down, be a good girl, and we'll see about getting the cuffs off."

She sneered at him. "I get a phone call. I *want* my phone call."

"In a minute, Veruca," he said.

No sooner had he shut the door behind him than he heard, "Steele!"

Noah stopped, gritted his teeth, then turned to face his superior office. "Sir."

Captain Jim Crabtree, a weathered barrel of a man with twenty-plus years on the force, bore down on him. "Aren't you supposed to be on personal leave?" he asked. "Who is this woman?"

Fulton peered through the blinds of the interview room and cursed a stream. "That's Glenna Bennett Colton. Wife to Clive Colton. His children own Mariposa Resort & Spa."

Crabtree spoke in a steely, quiet manner that wasn't any less threatening than the sound of his yelling. "We went over this. You asked if you could approach Mariposa. You asked me for my permission to investigate your sister's death and I told you it's against departmental procedure."

"Yes, sir," Noah said.

"You are *not* about to tell me you picked this woman up on the streets of Sedona," Crabtree warned.

"No, sir."

A knowing gleam entered Crabtree's dark eyes. "How long have you been poking around the resort?"

Noah pressed his lips together. He respected the hell out of Crabtree and couldn't lie. "Several days."

Fulton let out a disgruntled noise. It was cut off by Crabtree. "You went against orders. That makes you eligible for administrative leave. I could send you before the review board."

Hell. He couldn't lose his badge. Not with Allison's killer on the loose.

Not when being a homicide detective was the only job that had ever made sense to him. It was the only box he'd ever fit in. "Respectfully, sir, I'm asking you not to do that."

"Give me one reason I shouldn't."

Noah caught Fulton's fulminating stare and wasn't cowed in the least. "I've been operating at Mariposa on and off for the last week without the primary investigator any the wiser."

"Jesus, Steele," Fulton tossed out. "You're a son of a bitch. You know that?"

"Also," Noah said, moving on, "with the help and permission of the Colton family, I've been operating undercover. People don't see a cop walking around. They see the man staying in Bungalow Fifteen. Laura Colton's boyfriend."

"How the hell did he pull that off?" another detective, Ratliff, muttered behind him. General assent went up through the ranks of watching cops.

"I have a short list of suspects and inside access to guest quarters and staff buildings," Noah continued. "I've built a rapport with regulars and employees alike, and I'm looking at a handful of people who were close to Allison while Fulton fights for crumbs from the table. If you pull me out now, we lose our best chance of tying up this case."

"You expect me to believe you can think clearly—objectively—when your sister's the victim?" Crabtree challenged.

"I know how to do my job," Noah said. "I've got the best closure rate in my division."

"Yes," Crabtree granted. "But she was your family."

"I'm going to close this case," Noah informed him, "just as I've closed dozens of cases before hers."

"I don't need a loose cannon on my hands," Crabtree warned. "If you find her killer, how do I know you won't take matters into your own hands?"

It was a fair question, one Noah had asked himself a dozen times. When he found the man or woman who'd killed Allison...when he looked them in the eye at last...would he be able to follow procedure? Was his belief in due process strong enough when confronted with the person who'd squashed what was most precious to him?

Noah took a breath. "I won't let you down, Captain."

Crabtree stared him down. "When you're ready to make an arrest, bring Fulton in and let him handle it. Do not approach the suspect. If you so much as touch them, Steele—"

A muscle in Noah's jaw twitched in protest, but he made himself answer. "Yes, sir."

"Now explain to me why the Coltons' stepmother is in interrogation," Crabtree demanded.

"I believe she's responsible for the news leak at Mariposa," Noah said. "When I approached her with evidence, she swung at me. I cuffed her and brought her in for booking."

"Did anyone see you do this?"

"No. My cover's still in place."

Crabtree nodded in Fulton's direction. "Fulton will take care of it. Either go home and clear your head or go back to Mariposa and find me an actual suspect."

"Yes, sir." Noah subsided and let Fulton pass into Interview Room 1 to finish his job.

"It was Glenna?" Laura asked. "She leaked Allison's homicide?"

Noah nodded. "The timing was right. From there, it was just a matter of pressing the right buttons. Once cornered, she didn't hold back."

"She always seemed so even-tempered," Laura said, struggling to understand. "Why would she do this?"

"You can't think of any reason?" Adam asked from behind his desk. "We had Security watching the gates for Clive."

Her lips parted in surprise. "So he snuck Glenna in here under our noses to cause trouble on his behalf?"

"She said something as I was hauling her in," Noah added. "She said her husband would get what he wants, and Mariposa only exists because he allows it to."

"That's inaccurate," Adam said mildly.

Laura's brow furrowed. "Roland asked me if he should escort her out when she made a scene in the lobby. I should've let him. Valentine's Day is this weekend. I should've thought about the wedding party coming in. Once the families hear about the murder…"

"They signed a contract," Adam assured her. "If they cancel, they'll pay the cancellation fee."

"If that wedding falls through, then who's saying the next one won't?"

"How long will Glenna be detained at the SPD?" Adam asked Noah.

"She wasn't just booked on assaulting an officer," Noah said. "You and Fulton had an understanding that the investigation would be kept quiet to aid in the search for the killer. By leaking it to the press, Glenna interfered in a police investigation. Her lawyer's there now, doing his song and dance. She'll likely be released on bail tomorrow morning. But she won't get away scot-free. She's facing charges."

"And she's going to be angry," Laura pointed out.

Adam rolled his pen between his fingers. "We might as well have poked a beehive."

Laura felt tired just thinking about it. "You have to finish this," she told Noah. "You have to find who did this and get them away from the resort."

"I will."

For once, he didn't argue. The little ship in a bottle she carried inside her anchored up to his strength. It was a port in this storm. "We're running out of time."

"So am I," he said. "My CO found out what I'm doing. He's not wild about it."

"You're not leaving."

His eyes didn't stray from her. "I'm not going anywhere."

The assertion made her feel lighter, if only for a moment. She thought things over, picking through the cluttered mess in her mind. She sought something…anything they'd overlooked. "The schedule from Allison's fridge. Do you still have it?"

"It's at my bungalow. Why?"

She faced Adam. "You said Allison had taken on three people for private lessons?"

"As a test run," he said, "yes."

Laura remembered the letters on the piece of paper. "There were three sets of initials written on the schedule. I thought they were repeat students. But what if they're the names of the guests who requested private lessons?"

Noah's eyes cleared. "*CJK.* Those initials were on there."

"CJ Knight," she clarified. "Is that enough evidence to issue a warrant for him?"

Noah shook his head. "I need him to come back to Mariposa. I need him to keep his reservation."

Laura thought about it. Then, injecting as much promise into her voice as he had at L Bar, she said, "Leave it with me."

Chapter Twelve

Laura couldn't cast off the tension. Since she'd learned Noah had taken Glenna into custody, she felt as if she was waiting for the other shoe to drop.

Sebastian was in no mood for a cuddle. Alexis had gone home for the night, so an impromptu girls' night was out of the question. She couldn't call Joshua to confide in him because she was still lying to him about Noah's part in all this.

She winced at that, hating that she and Noah continued to keep him in the dark. What would he think when he discovered her subterfuge?

Laura told herself not to think about that now. She told herself not to think about anything, but her mind was so full, she couldn't relax.

A hard rap on the front door of her bungalow made her jerk. Sebastian hissed. She dropped the book she had been trying to read to the coffee table and rose from the sofa. Tiptoeing to the door, she peered out through the peephole.

At the sight of Noah, she felt a stir. Snatching open the door, she asked, "What are you doing here so late?"

He held up Allison's schedule. "I thought we'd go over this."

"Oh," she said and stepped aside. "Come in." Before Sebastian could dart out between her legs, she scooped him up.

"Naughty," she muttered and waited until Noah shut the door before setting him down again.

"If he wants to be an escape artist," Noah stated, "he should lay off the Fancy Feast."

"He's not fat," Laura said. "He's fluffy."

Noah smiled the knowing, self-satisfied smile that never failed to get her dander up. "Whatever you say, mommy dearest."

"That's my coat," she said, pointing to the camel-colored jacket draped across his arm.

"You left it," he explained, handing it over, "at L Bar the other night."

"You didn't have to bring it to me."

"If you don't leave your things around for others to steal, I wouldn't have to."

Laura tucked her tongue into her cheek. As she led him into the kitchen and den, she indulged herself by asking, "Did my stepmother really hit you today?"

"She grazed one off me," he replied. "What about it?"

"At the moment, I'm having trouble blaming her. You have a very slappable face."

He threw his head back and laughed. A full-bodied laugh, straight from the gut.

It went straight to hers. She sucked in a breath as the corners of his eyes crinkled and his teeth gleamed. For a split second, she saw the man as he had been in the navy uniform in the photograph at Allison's, and her heart stuttered.

He caught her staring at him, aghast, and the laughter melted in a flash. "What? Why are you looking at me like that?"

It took her a moment to speak. "I didn't think you knew how to smile—really smile...much less laugh."

His frown returned, all too at home among his set features. "You sound like Allison. 'You don't smile enough, relax enough. You don't put yourself first enough.'"

The words echoed in her head. Allison had said something similar to her. She shook off the odd feeling it gave her. "What about the piece of paper?"

Paper crinkled as he straightened out the creases and handed it to her. "*CJK* is obviously CJ Knight. But what about these initials? *DG.*"

She studied them. "You couldn't find someone on your short list to match them?"

"No," he admitted. "Is it possible you missed someone when you gave me the names of staff and guests?"

She shook her head. "No. There's another set of initials. *KB.*"

"That's Kim Blankenship, your guest in Bungalow Seven," he proposed, "or your horseback adventure guide."

"Kim Blankenship is in her late sixties. She's here with her husband, Granger. She built a cream cosmetics empire and is here taking a well-deserved break. And Knox?" Laura instantly rejected that idea. "The private lessons were for guests."

"Maybe Allison made an exception," Noah pressed. "Didn't you say he was flirtatious with her?"

"Yes," Laura granted. "But Knox is flirtatious with every woman. Even me."

"Don't like that," he muttered.

"Why not?" she challenged. "It's not like you and I are really…"

As she trailed off, his gaze became snared on her. "Really what? Kissing? We've done that. Touching? We've checked that box. The only thing you and I aren't doing right now, Pearl, is sleeping together."

Her mouth went dry. She forced herself to swallow. "It's not real."

His eyes tracked to her mouth before bouncing back to hers. Her body reacted vividly. Her heart rammed into her throat.

She wanted his mouth on hers. She wanted to know what it would be like, she realized, for Noah to kiss her and mean it. Not for show—for himself and her.

She demurred. They wouldn't be able to uncross that bridge. Once they went to the other side, she wasn't sure she could swim back to safety. She feared what she would find with him. Fire and brimstone, perhaps? Too much, too hard, too fast?

It sounded wonderful. She reached for it even as she turned away. "Knox Burnett didn't kill Allison," she said clearly, walking into the kitchen.

Noah's voice dripped with sarcasm. "The queen of Mariposa has spoken."

She reached for a wineglass. "Quentin called me 'queen.' Or 'queenie.' Sometimes, he just called me Q. Except when he left. Then he just called me a cold hard bitch who would get what was coming to her." She pulled the cork out of the bottle next to the coffeepot and poured a liberal dose. "Dominic thought I was cold, too—in bed and out of it. Do you want some?"

He didn't spare the wine a glance. "You never should've given those assholes the time of day."

"But I did," she said, raising the wine to her lips. She tasted, let it sit on her tongue, then swallowed, swirling the liquid in the glass. "Which makes me either stupid or desperate."

"It's simple," he stated. "Stop dating pretty playboys."

"Who should I date instead?" She gestured with her wine. "You?"

He cracked a smile that wasn't at all friendly. "You'd run screaming in a week."

She lowered her brow. "Why is that, exactly? Do you have pentagrams drawn anywhere on your person?"

"No."

"Are you mangled?"

"No."

"Do you keep tarantulas or dance with cobras?"

The lines in his brow steepled and she sensed he was trying not to give in to amusement. "I told you. I don't have pets."

"Do you have some sort of fetish most women find offensive?"

"No."

She shrugged. "Then why would I run from you, exactly?"

"I'm not Prince Charming."

She clicked her tongue. "I've looked for Prince Charming. No luck there."

"Doesn't mean you and me are meant to be," he asserted.

Some part of her wanted to challenge that. Even the part of her that knew better wanted to know what it would be like…the hot mess they would be together. When heat fired in her again, she drowned the images with more wine.

"And, for the record," he said, "you're not hard or cold. You're calm and together, and you have a strong sense of what's right for you and what isn't. You know how to take out the trash. That's why the playboys have come and gone. And so has your father."

She looked away. "My father has nothing to do with this."

"Your daddy's got everything to do with it," he said. "It was him who taught you what toxic people look like."

She thought it over. "If I'm together or strong, I learned it from my mother. She kept my brothers and me together through the upheaval. Even when she was sick, she had spine. She was incredible. I can't fathom why she never kicked my father to the curb. They lived separate lives by the time she bought this place, but she never divorced him."

"Maybe he made it impossible for her to do so," he intoned.

She felt the color drain from her face. "You're having a glass," she decided, handpicking another piece of stemware. She poured him one and passed it to him over the countertop. "I don't believe in drinking alone."

He lifted the drink, tipped it to her in a silent toast, before testing it.

She watched his throat move around a swallow. Her own tightened. She was growing tired of the tug-of-war between her better judgment and the side of her that wanted to dance in the flames. She was having difficulty quantifying both. "What was your mother like?"

His glass touched down on the counter with a decisive *clink*. "I don't talk about my mother."

She culled a knowing noise from the back of her throat. "That's what's wrong with you."

A laugh shot out of him, unbidden.

Another one, she thought, satisfied.

He shook his head. "God, you're a pest."

Even as he smiled, she recognized the pain webbing underneath the surface. "She died, didn't she?" she asked quietly.

The smile vanished. He masked the hurt skillfully with his hard brand of intensity. "So what if she did?"

She took a moment to consider. "That would mean we have something in common."

He stared at her...through her.

There was a lost boy in there somewhere. The foster kid who'd been dumped into the system while he was still coming to terms with losing the woman who'd raised him. She ached for that child, just as she ached for that part of her that had listened to Joshua cry himself to sleep every night and had been helpless against the tide of grief.

The line of his shoulders eased. He lifted the glass and downed half the wine in one swift gulp. Frowning at the rest, he cursed. "She'd just kicked my stepdad to the curb. He was a user with a tendency for violence. We moved around some to throw him off the scent. I didn't mind. Stability's fine and all, but I had her, and she had me, and that was...everything."

He chewed over the rest for a time before he spoke again. "There was this STEM camp I wanted to go to. I didn't think I'd get to go. It cost money, and she was working two jobs to keep the building's super off our backs. She put me in the car one afternoon, said we were going out for groceries. She drove out of town and pulled up in front of the camp cabins. She'd packed me enough clothes for a week. I was so happy. I don't remember hugging her goodbye. I just remember running off to join roll call."

She waited for him to go on. When he didn't, she asked, "Is that the last time you saw her?"

"Alive?" He jerked a nod. "The son of a bitch found her. Bashed her skull in with a hammer. Next time I saw her, she was lying in a casket."

"I'm sorry." She breathed the words. "I'm so sorry, Noah."

"He got off," he added grimly. "Broke down on the stand and got sent to a psych ward instead of doing his time upstate."

The wine on her tongue lost its taste. She winced as she swallowed. "No closure for you, then."

"Hell, no. All things considered, it's better than what Allison went through before she got shuffled into foster care."

"What happened?"

"The truth's too ugly to speak here," he grumbled.

"Where else could you speak it?" she asked.

Turning up the glass, he swooped down the rest of the wine and reached across the counter to place it in her deep-basined sink. He gripped the edge of the counter, bracing his feet apart. "Her mother was killed, too. Her father did it, right in front of her, before he shot himself."

"Oh," Laura uttered. She closed her eyes. "She never... She never told me."

"And you'd never know." He gave a shake of his head. "Even as a kid, she was all sunshine and rainbows. She had this rag-gedy stuffed bunny she carried around by the ear. There was nothing anyone could say to convince her it wasn't alive or that it should be washed or thrown away. She called it Mr. Binky."

Laura found she could smile after all. "You wound up in the same home she did."

"I'm not sure what would have happened to her if I hadn't."

"Why?"

He hesitated again. "She didn't have anyone else."

"Your foster parents—"

"—didn't give a damn. I was fourteen when I went out and got my first job. I had to. Otherwise, Allison and I wouldn't have eaten. I had to teach myself to cook. There's nothing more motivating than that pit in your stomach—that one that's been there for days because someone drank away the grocery bud-get for the week. I was scared the reason Allison's cheekbones stood out was because she'd gotten used to that feeling. She was so used to it, it wasn't remarkable to her anymore. She'd just come to accept it. So I worked, and I cooked so she'd never have to know what hunger was again."

"I had no idea it was like that for her," Laura said.

"In that home, nobody hit us," he explained. "Nobody snuck into our rooms at night. Nobody screamed at us. But there's a different kind of abuse and that's straight-up neglect."

Laura had felt neglected, too, but not like that. It wasn't the same. Her father's indifference didn't compare to being left to starve or fend for herself.

She had starved, she realized. For his approval. For affec-tion. After her mother died, she'd had to learn to stop. Men had disappointed her, even those before Quentin and Dominic—because she'd half expected their approval and affection to die off, too. She'd taken the safe route out every time.

"Allison told me the same thing she used to tell you," Laura mused. "That I don't live enough. Smile enough. Put myself first enough." Suddenly, what she'd told Joshua the day after Allison's body was found rushed back to her...

I think you two could have made each other happy, at least for a time, and... I don't know. All this reminds me not to waste time if you know what's right for you...

Behind him, she saw the blue glow of the pool through the glass door to the patio. Air filled her lungs, inflating her with possibilities. She set aside her glass and rounded the counter. "Let's go for a swim."

"What?"

"Let's swim, Noah," she said, grabbing his hand. She tugged him toward the door. "Just you, me and the moon."

"Wait a second," he said, trying to put on the brakes. "I didn't exactly bring a bathing suit."

Be brave for once, Laura, she thought desperately. Buoyed by wine and a spirit she'd ignored too long, she told him, "Then I won't wear one either."

Noah's eyes lost their edge. His resistance slipped and he turned quiet.

She slid the door open and stepped out into the cold. "Don't worry," she said when he hissed. "The water's heated."

He stared at the steam coming off the surface, then at her as she took off her socks and untied the drawstring of her lounge-wear pants. "So we're doing this," he said.

She frowned at his jacket and boots. "Are we?"

When she shimmied out of her pants, his brows shot straight up. He shrugged off the jacket one shoulder at a time. "I can't let you swim alone."

"And you say you're not a hero," she said, pulling her shirt up by the hem so that she was standing in the cold in her gray sports bra and matching panties. She shivered, dropped the shirt and crossed her arms over her chest. "Hurry up, Steele, before I lose my nerve."

The jacket hit the ground. He grabbed his T-shirt by the back collar and pried it loose.

Muscle and sinew rippled and bunched under a tapestry of black-and-white pictures. The wings she'd gleaned under the sleeve of his shirt took the shape of a large falcon. It spread across his upper arm and shoulder, finishing with another wing that reached as far as his left pectoral. The designs boasted more bones mixed with clockwork, as if he had tried to convince the world that he was half human, half machine. They were vivid and detailed. Although some lines and shapes had faded more to blue than black with time, none of them bled into others.

The effect was...breathtaking, she found. She was stunned by her own reaction.

Laura tried not to stare at him—at all he was—as he unzipped his fly and pushed the denim down. He fought with his boots before discarding them and the jeans completely, leaving him standing in his boxer briefs.

She reached for him, happy when he let her lace her fingers through his. Drawing him up to the top of the starting block, she grinned. "On three."

"One," he began.

"Two..."

"Three," he said and pushed her.

She flailed for a second before breaking the surface. She opened her mouth to shout at him but shrieked when he cannonballed in after her. The residual splash was impressive. She swept the water from her eyes as he surfaced, grinning. "Prick!" she shouted, tossing water in his face.

"You look good wet, Colton."

She felt more than stirrings of heat. The tendrils of steam off the water's surface could've been from her. Unsure what to do with herself, she floated on her back. The moon was directly overhead. She drifted for a moment, watching it and the stars before flipping onto her stomach for a lazy freestyle lap.

She'd drowned parts of herself in this pool. The pool hadn't been installed for fun or leisure. She'd needed it to stay fit and sane. Water purified. It cleansed. It took away her doubts and reinforced what she needed.

Usually. Still unsure of herself, she did another lap.

"Hey, Flipper," he tossed out when she came up for air.

She swept the water from her face. "What?"

He nodded toward the starting block. "Want to race?"

She laughed at the idea. "Sure. But, fair warning—I won the California state championship two years in a row."

"Do you still have the trophies?"

"Maybe."

"Of course you do," he said knowingly. He gripped the edge of the pool and pulled himself out.

She tried not to groan. He wasn't just ripped and inked. He was wet, his boxer briefs clinging. Peeling her eyes away from him, she climbed the ladder to join him. She slicked her hair back from her face. "Ready to lose?"

He didn't answer. Glancing over, she caught the wicked gleam in his eye as he gave her a thorough once-over. She felt her nipples draw up tight under her sports bra. "Would you like to frisk me, Detective?"

His gaze pinged back to hers. He blinked. His mouth fumbled.

Without warning, she threw her weight into him so that he tumbled into the pool.

Before he could come up for air, she executed a dive. Without looking back, she pumped her arms and legs into motion.

She felt the water churning to her right. As she raised her arm in a freestyle stroke and tilted her face out of the water, she saw him gaining, cutting through the water like a porpoise. She quickened her strokes.

They were coming up to the wall. She reached out blindly, groping for it.

Fingers circled her ankle, bringing her up short. She spluttered, arms flailing, as he held on.

Then she heard laughter—deep, uninhibited. She stopped fighting. As he drew her back against his chest, she abandoned the competition for lightheartedness. Delighted, she dropped her head back to his shoulder and belted a laugh to the sky.

His arms had hers pinned, and he tightened them. She could feel the reverberations of joy from his chest along her back and listened to the colonnades of his laughter. She closed her eyes, absorbing them.

The laughter wound down slowly and his body stilled, an inch at a time. He said nothing, holding her as steam curled around their joined forms.

She felt his breath on her ear. Then the bite of his teeth on the lobe, light and quick. "Laura?"

She shuddered at the sound of her name. "Yes?"

"In our game of Twenty Questions, I never asked you the most important one."

She tilted her cheek against his as he drew her closer still, his lips grazing her jaw. "What's that?"

"How do you like to be touched?"

The breath left her. It bolted. She felt the flush sink into her cheeks. It sank lower, deeper. And it turned darker, more shocking and satisfying.

Take what you want, Laura, she told herself.

She touched the back of his hand. Raising it to her breast, she brought it up to the ache, snug beneath the heavy curve. Spreading her fingers over his so that he mirrored the motion, she let her fingertips dig into his knuckles and encouraged him to grasp, take.

He obeyed. Her mouth opened on a silent cry as he molded her, kneading her through her sports bra.

"Don't be a lady," he told her. "Don't be quiet."

She swallowed, the sounds clawing up her throat. "You... you want to know my secret?"

"All of them," he said, brushing his thumb over the unmistakable outline of her nipple. "I want to know every last one of your secrets, Pearl."

A bowstring drew taut between her legs. Urgency quivered there. "I hate when you call me that," she said. "And I think about you even when I shouldn't."

"When?"

He is so good at this, she thought, arching back as the kneading quickened. "All the time."

"When?" he said again, the note dropping into his chest as his hold tightened.

"I think about you when I work," she rattled off. "I think about you when I'm with others, when I'm alone. In bed. In the shower."

He groaned. Turning, face-to-face, she saw the answering heat and need behind it. "I think about you kissing me...touching me..."

"Is that what you want?" He was close, but he pulled her closer, so his mouth brushed her own. "You want my hands on you? My mouth?"

She heard herself beg, "Please."

His eyes closed but not before she saw his relief. "As you wish," he whispered before taking her mouth in a decisive kiss.

He didn't kiss softly. He took, and she clung. She wrapped her arms around his neck and held on for dear life.

His hands spanned her waist. They cruised, flattening against her ribs, as he licked the seam of her lips, encouraging. She parted for him. One hand rose to the back of her head as he plumbed, touching his tongue to hers.

Her body bowed against his. Every inch of him was hard and fine. She spanned her fingers through the short hair at the nape of his neck, looking for purchase.

There was none. With him, there was nothing but that slippery slope of want and need, and she was going under.

She felt the pool tiles on the wall at her back. Pinned, she felt her excitement focus, sharpen. It arrowed toward her center.

With a harsh noise that sounded almost angry, he snatched his mouth from hers. He cursed, placing his hands safely on either side of her head.

She sucked her lower lip into her mouth. It stung. The tip of her tongue tingled.

His jaw muscle flexed. It was rigid. His eyes were alive, knife-edged, electrifyingly tungsten. The hands planted against the wall clenched in on themselves. She felt him go back on his heels and grabbed him by the arms. "Where do you think you're going?" she demanded.

He shook his head. "I'm no good for you."

"I don't care," she blurted. When he opened his mouth to protest, she reached up to cover it. "You're not Prince Charm-

ing? Fine. But I want this, and you want this." She replaced
her hand with her mouth, skimming softly in a gliding tease.

His hands dropped to her shoulders and latched as she lingered. He drew a quick breath in through the nose.

She broke away and saw the ardor on his face. "I won't run
from you tomorrow or the next day. I'm here." She kissed him
again, deeper. "Take what you want," she invited.

He winced. "There's nothing you could ask me that I wouldn't
give. That scares the hell out of me. I don't care what those
other fools told you. You're not ice. You're a four-alarm fire.
And I'm burning, damn it. I can't afford this. I can't afford you
or what you do to me."

"I'm not going to run," she whispered. She thought of Allison, his mother... "I won't be gone tomorrow."

His hands still clutched her shoulders, firm, but they were
no longer keeping her at arm's length. They pulled her into his
circle of danger and heat. His muscles were still rigid, his grimace unbroken. But she felt him give... With her hands sliding
from his waist to the backs of his hips, she angled her mouth
to accept his.

It wasn't an onslaught this time. His tongue flicked across
hers and he nibbled her lip, but the clash took on a different
hue. She ached with it, the ball of need inside her roughening.
It grew diamond bright.

"Tell me again," he instructed. "Tell me what you want me
to do to you."

Fitting her palms to the backs of his, she used them to sweep
her body from throat to thighs. She slowed the motion down as
they followed up the seam of her legs where her thighs came
together, up her belly, over her breasts, cheeks, hair...

He raked his fingers through the damp strands, then did it
all again on his own. His hands slid firmly down her torso,
teased her inner thighs before putting on the brakes, slowing
the motions, skimming the folds of her sex so that her hips
circled and she sought. She clamped her hand over the back of
his, encouraging.

He didn't whisper so much as breathe the words again. "Show
me. Show me exactly how to make you come alive."

Her touch worked urgently against his, demonstrating.

He caught on. "Like this?"

She nodded, then stopped when he increased the rhythm. She gulped air.

His hand slipped beneath her underwear. She moaned and churned.

This would break her, she decided. That was his endgame. He wanted to watch her come apart one molecule at a time. The flames inside her raced and leaped as she climbed the ladder fast.

She came, biting the inside of her lip.

"Let it go, Pearl," he bade. "For Christ's sake."

She couldn't leash it. A cry wrenched from her, unpolished and visceral. Everything he made her feel.

"Yes," he encouraged, his mouth on her throat.

She shuddered as she came down off the high, messy and resplendent. Something bubbled up her throat. It crested, escaped. A sob, she heard, distressed. "Oh, God," she uttered. She felt rearranged and so sparkly and sated, she thought she could taste stars.

"Hold on," he said, tossing one of her loose arms around his neck, then the other. Grabbing her around the waist, he hoisted her out of the water.

She fumbled over the ledge of the pool, coming to rest on her hands and knees. Every limb felt like a noodle. "Oh, sweet Lord," she said, then snorted a laugh. Quickly, she covered her mouth, wondering where it had come from. When he didn't follow, she asked, "Coming?"

He swiped his face from brow to chin, gave a half laugh and glanced down at his waist.

Understanding gleaned. He may have slaked her need, but not his own. Looking toward the wicker cabinet where she kept towels and a robe, she dragged herself to her feet.

She retrieved two towels, the long ones that wrapped around her twice. She folded herself into one, knotting it beneath her collarbone.

Behind her, she heard a splash and turned to see him emerging from the water. He passed a hand over his head as he turned from her, slicking the hair back away from his face.

She went to him. "Here."

"Thanks," he said and reached for the towel.

She pulled it away, trying to compress the sly impulse to smile.

He saw it form on her lips anyway. "You think this is funny?" he asked.

"I do," she admitted, holding the towel high.

He cursed and rearranged his feet so that he was facing her.

She saw what he'd been trying to hide from her. His erection was at full mast, the soaked boxer briefs straining to contain it. "I think it wants you to let it out."

"You're right." He snatched the towel.

She watched him scrub the terry cloth roughly over his face and hair. He toweled off his chest and arms before wrapping the towel around his waist. "What's stopping you?"

"What if you don't like what happens when I do? What then?"

She considered him. "What wouldn't I like?" When he didn't answer, she gripped the towel on either side of his waist and yanked him toward her. She stole a kiss while she had him on the back foot, hardening her mouth over his to prove a point.

He hummed in unconscious agreement.

She pushed him away abruptly and watched him fumble for a second in protest. "You want to know another secret?" she asked when he opened his eyes.

"I told you," he said after a moment. "I want all your secrets."

"There's nothing I don't like about you, Noah Steele," she revealed.

His chest lifted in a rushing breath.

"Why not show me the rest?" she suggested.

"You don't do this," he ventured. "You don't just take a man to bed. Not without flowers, dinner. Hell, candles. Silk sheets. Some ridiculous dress meant to tie your man's tongue in a knot."

"Maybe."

"We didn't have dinner," he noted. "I didn't bring you flowers."

"No," she admitted.

"I don't see any candles."

The candles were all inside her, she thought desperately. They stood tall under columns of flame. The wax melted away and puddled, refusing to cool. She wanted his hands all over her again, and it was driving her wild.

She wouldn't beg this time. She wanted him to beg.

She would make him.

"I'm not wearing a dress," she pointed out.

"You're not wearing much of anything and damned if that helps."

She smiled. "But I do have a bed with silk sheets."

"And you want me to mess them up?"

"Don't you get it?" she challenged. "You can shred my sheets, for all I care."

A slow grin worked its way across the forbidding line of his mouth. "You are, far and away, the most bewitching woman I know."

She closed her hands over the knot of her towel, untying it. Letting it fall to her feet, she grabbed him by the hand. "You know what's better than flowers?"

"What?"

"That."

Chapter Thirteen

The room was dark. The sheets were blue. Their skin was damp and bare. She clung to him. Afraid she'd see all the dark and treacherous ridges of his desire, he touched her gently, feathering his hands in and out of her curves.

She rained kisses over him as she braced her hands on either side of him. "It's your turn to tell me."

"What?" Indulgent, he blindly traced the raised surface of a mole on her navel.

"How you like to be touched."

He chuckled, then stopped swiftly when she closed her mouth over his nipple. It tautened and grew pebbly. The skin at the small of his back drew up tight and goose bumps took over. She would drive him over the edge.

He rolled over her, pinning her to the sheet. Taking her hand, he moved it between them.

Her gaze didn't stray from his in the dark as he showed her how to stroke him. How to drive him over the edge—a firm-handed hold, a deep-seated stroke, slow to start, then quickening.

She kissed him as he let her take control, curling his hand into the sheet. He breathed hot against her mouth.

"More," she told him.

Something like a growl leaped from his throat as he took her wrist. Taking her hand away, he turned it up against the pillow over her head. "Not yet." He thought about his wallet on the pool deck. Out in the cold. "Damn it."

She pointed to the nightstand. "Top drawer."

Turning her loose for a second, he pulled out the drawer. Relief whistled out of him. "Were you a Boy Scout, Pearl? Because you prepare like one." He tore the corner off the wrapper with his teeth.

She snatched it from him, then shoved his hands away when he tried to fight her for it. "Lay still, hard-ass," she said none-too-gently.

Not only did he obey. He laughed deeply and fully. Then choked when she took her time rolling the condom into place, drawing out his needs. Her eyes glowed at him in the dark, watchful.

"I'm not sorry you're not a hero," she told him. "Or a prince."

"That's good," he said helplessly. He tugged her back to him when she was done. Then he flipped their positions, so she was beneath him. He turned her knee outward with his. "Because I'd hate to disappoint you, like all those other bastards."

He slid home. Her nails dug into the bed of his shoulder blades. They scraped as he took her through the first glide.

It wasn't soft. When she bit her lip, he wondered if he should be.

She has silk sheets, you meatball, he thought. *Of course she wants it soft.*

She sighed, tracing the line of his vertebrae with her fingertips. "Then don't stop."

He lost himself and didn't look back.

She was perfect. The way she held on. The way she met him stroke for stroke. The way she pressed her heels to the bed and said his name. He forgot why they shouldn't be together as she pulsed around him and her fingers found his, clinging.

Raising them above both their heads, he wove them together like a basket. He took her mouth as he tripped toward the edge and flung himself over like a man on fire.

He fell hard, tumbled end over end and face-planted.

Had that coming, he thought. The landing wasn't any softer or safer than their lovemaking. He lay panting, wreathed in sweat, tuning in slowly to the brush of her fingers through his hair.

"Noah?" she said, muted.

"Hmm?" he managed.

"Are you all right?"

He opened his eyes, saw the afterglow shining off her so brightly it made his eyes water.

She was so beautiful it made his eyes hurt.

He swallowed, still unable to catch his breath. "Why wouldn't I be?"

"You're shaking a little."

He took stock and felt the fine tremors in his joints. "I'll be all right. Just give me…"

He trailed off because she was caressing his face in soft, loving strokes that made him still.

Her eyes were all too blue in the dark.

His heart stuttered, banged, fired and drummed. And it hit him.

He'd never loved a woman. Naturally, it took him a minute.

It hit him like a Sherman tank going max speed, artillery firing.

He released her hands, sliding his away. Careful not to hurt her, he pulled out of the nest of her thighs before rolling to his back beside her.

She turned onto her side, skimming a kiss across the ridge of his shoulder. Laying her hand on his chest, she placed her head on the pillow and closed her eyes. "Stay."

It wasn't a question. Still, the answer was there before he could make himself think. "Yeah," he said.

"Your heart's still racing. Are you sure you're all right?"

He gathered her hand from its warm spot on his chest and pulled it away, up to his mouth. He kissed her knuckles to distract the both of them from what was happening inside him. "Pearl?"

"Yes?"

"Go to sleep."

She gave a little sigh. Her fingers played lightly through

his beard until she dozed off and he lay awake—wide the hell awake—trying to fathom how far and fast he'd fallen.

Laura bolted upright in bed, alarmed at the sight of sunlight peeping at her from between the curtains and the sound of knocking from far away. "Oh, no," she said to Sebastian, who peered sleepily at her over his mustache of orange fur.

She slid out of bed, groping for the robe over the back of the purple wingback chair in the corner. She fumbled it on, tied the belt, then combed her fingers through her hair.

Scenting coffee like a bloodhound, she spotted the mug, still steaming, on the nightstand next to the framed portrait of her mother. There was a small scrap of paper next to it with Noah's handwriting.

L.,
Fulton called. I have to run. We'll talk later.
  Made you something. It's in the oven.
N.

The knock clattered again, louder this time, followed by Joshua's voice. Laura stuffed her feet into her slippers and padded quickly from the bedroom to the entry corridor.

When she snatched open the door, Joshua looked immensely relieved. "Ah, jeez, Laura. You had me worried."

"I'm fine," she blurted. "Sorry. I slept through my alarm."

Joshua gave her a puzzled once-over. "You never sleep in."

"I know," she said, frazzled. "I was up late and must have crashed hard."

"Noah spent the night here."

She shook her head automatically. "I don't know what—"

"Come on, ace." Joshua rolled his eyes. "I saw him head out just a few minutes ago."

"Oh." She cleared her throat and reached for it awkwardly. "It's not what it looks like."

His brows came together. "Why not? Haven't you two been together for six months?"

"I…" She caught back up and nodded, clutching the lapels of her robe together over her collarbone. "Yes. Yes, we have."

He lifted his hands. "Hey, I'm not judging. You say he makes you happy. I believe you."

"You took him running," she recalled.

Caught, he lifted both shoulders in a sheepish shrug. "Adam's idea."

"Oh, give me a break, Josh," she snapped. "I heard you were the pace car. I also heard you took him up the advanced hiking trail. Even Adam thought his legs were going to fall off."

Joshua pursed his lips. "It's not my fault I'm in better shape than everybody else."

She gave a half laugh. "If you'd believed me when I told you he makes me happy, would you have put Noah through his paces?"

"He kept up just fine."

He didn't sound pleased about the fact. "You like him."

"Maybe," Joshua said. "And he said something that scared the hell out of me."

"What?" she asked.

Joshua took a breath, rolled his shoulders back as if trying to dislodge tension and said, "He said he was here to keep you safe. He said you could be the next target of whoever killed Allison."

She shook her head. "Nothing's going to happen to me."

"That's what she thought, too," Joshua said. "I may be your brother, but I like that he's staying the night with you. I like that you have someone watching over you when Adam and I can't. Until the police find out who killed Allison, I'm willing to look the other way when Noah's around. Bonus points that he looks like he could scare off a grizzly."

She smiled. It wobbled around the edges. "You don't have to worry about me so much."

"That's the thing," he drawled. "As long as Steele's around, I worry less. Where'd he go, anyway?"

"Sedona," she said. "He had something to do there."

Joshua lifted his chin. "Right. Valentine's Day's tomorrow."

"Valentine's…" She shrieked and ran back into the house, leaving the door open for him. In the bedroom, she dressed quickly, did her hair and applied makeup faster than she ever had before.

How could she sleep in the day before the wedding?

She snatched the coffee off the nightstand and downed half of it as she eyed the cat still curled up at the foot of the bed. Normally, Sebastian woke her if she even thought about sleeping past her alarm. He required a prompt meal at the break of every day.

As she ventured into the kitchen, where she found Joshua pouring coffee from the pot into a mug of his own, she peered into the cat food bowl. The remnants of a feast were scattered across the bottom of the porcelain dish.

Noah had fed her cat? Stunned, she took the bowl to the sink to rinse it. Then she remembered the note. Turning to the oven, she pulled open the door.

One of her china plates sat in the center of the upper rack. She pulled it out and found a still-warm western omelet.

Joshua peered over her shoulder as she set it on the range. "That looks incredible."

"It smells incredible," she said in wonder.

Joshua was quiet for a moment. "You used to make us breakfast—Adam and me. After Mom died."

"Yes." She remembered.

Regret tinged his voice. "Nobody's ever made breakfast for you in return, have they?"

She didn't reply. The note had said Noah had had to run. But he'd made her coffee, fed Sebastian and thrown together a whole omelet?

The walls of her heart gave a mighty shake.

A fork clattered onto the range next to the plate. She turned to see Joshua grin. "Eat your heart out, ace."

The morning meeting wasn't quick, but it was concise. Laura let Adam lead, still reeling from her naughty night with Noah.

Alexis lingered after Adam called the meeting to an end and the other members of staff bustled out to prepare for the next day's event. "I did what you asked," she told Laura. "I called the number you tracked down. It was CJ Knight's cell phone."

"Did he answer?" Laura asked hopefully.

"I left a message." She took her phone from the pocket of her blazer. "He texted me a reply."

Laura tilted her head to read the phone's display.

Ms. Reed, I apologize for leaving Mariposa on short notice. Yes, I will keep my reservation for 2/16.

"He's coming," Laura said to Adam.

"That's good," he said with a nod. "Thank you, Alexis."

"Yes," Laura chimed in. And because she was so sick of withholding information from Alexis, Laura added, "Mr. Knight may have information."

"What kind of information?" Alexis asked, narrowing her eyes.

Adam cleared his throat, warning Laura to tread lightly.

"About Allison," Laura answered.

Alexis assessed them both. "You think he had something to do with what happened to her?"

"No," Laura said quickly. "But he departed Mariposa the next day. Police couldn't question him. It's possible he saw something or heard something that could lead police to the person responsible."

"That makes sense," Alexis allowed after a moment's contemplation.

"If you could avoid mentioning this to him when he arrives, that would be great," Adam added. "We need to let the police handle their investigation."

"Right," Alexis said.

Laura walked with her to the door of the conference room. "You'll see that the other concierges have their assignments as the wedding party filters in today?"

"I will," Alexis replied.

"I appreciate it," Laura told her.

"That was clever of you," Adam noted after Alexis had departed. "You didn't lead her to believe the police are considering Knight as a suspect."

"I want this to be over," she blurted. "I hate hiding things from the people I care about. Alexis. Josh. Tallulah."

"This was your idea, Lou."

"I know," she said with a wince. "I didn't think it through."

"You were thinking about Allison," he discerned.

She nodded, silently knitting her arms over her stomach. It twisted with guilt.

Adam changed the subject quickly. "I just got a call from a friend of mine, Max Powell."

"Yes," she said, remembering. "The celebrity chef. You went to college together."

"Your attention to detail is one of your many strengths," he said fondly. "Max is taking a break from his TV show's filming schedule and wants to spend a few weeks at Mariposa."

"Let me know the date of his arrival," she replied. "I'll make sure he receives the best treatment."

"Thank you." A smile climbed over the planes of his face. It was a relief for her to see it and the light in his eyes. "The bride and groom check in at eleven?"

"Yes," she said. "Alexis and I will escort them to their bungalows. From there, she'll take them to their first spa treatment, and I'll check in with the parents and wedding party at Annabeth. They're surprising the happy couple with a prewedding margarita lunch. I've enlisted Valerie and her bar staff to help the kitchen staff with the drink rotation. I expect the celebration will go on for some time. I also expect every member of the wedding party to be tipsy when the minister arrives for the rehearsal on the golf course at five."

Adam thought about it. "Talk to the transportation staff. See if they can't have shuttles ready to drive them there. We don't want tequila behind the wheel of the golf carts."

"Good idea," she said.

"How's it going with Steele?"

Her smile froze. Joshua knew Noah had spent the night with her. How long would it take for Adam to find out? "It's going."

"When's he coming back from Sedona?"

"I'm unsure," she realized. "He didn't say, exactly."

"He may be keeping his distance."

"Why?"

He paused, planting his hand on the jamb. "Valentine's Day comes with certain expectations."

She lowered her chin. "Are you speaking from experience?"

He evaded the question. "Let me know of any problems between arrival and luncheon. I'm crunching numbers again with the father of the bride."

"Have fun with that," she muttered.

She felt like she was walking on eggshells for the rest of the day. Weddings and talk of murder mixed like oil and water. She felt she and Alexis handled the wedding party's questions about the investigation well, though.

Laura spotted Fulton lurking around the bungalows before the intendeds' surprise luncheon. His badge and gun were in full view. She wrung her hands and wondered what he was up to and if Noah had returned to Mariposa with him.

Thinking about Noah was doing her no favors. Vivid, distracting memories of the night before followed her everywhere. The things he had done to her...the things she had done to him... The heat in her cheeks refused to leave.

Her body carried its own memories, its own markers. She couldn't cross her legs without the tender ache of coupling causing her nerve endings to remember. She'd worn a high-necked blouse to ensure that the marks from Noah's beard on her neck and chest were tucked away from prying eyes.

Wishing he were feeling the aches as he went about his day, she hoped it was distracting him from his work as much as it was distracting her, if not more. And she wondered if she'd left any guilty marks on him to remind him of their exploits.

By the luncheon, her thoughts turned to speculation. Had he really had to return to Sedona—or was he just avoiding her? She had no missed calls from him, no texts. Just the note he'd left with Sebastian and the empty omelet plate at home.

Was Adam right? Was Noah steering clear of Mariposa because he was allergic to Valentine's Day? Would she even see him tomorrow? She'd thought about calling him again to tell him what she'd learned about CJ Knight. To ask if he knew what Fulton was up to, but her doubts had given her other ideas.

"You look ready to tear the heads off those shrimp."

Laura glanced up from where she'd been hovering next to the buffet. Alexis had finished her to-do list in time to witness the end of the luncheon. Laura stepped away from the shrimp bowl. "Sorry."

"Don't apologize," Alexis said, turning to angle herself toward the festivities. "I just thought you'd like to know your face says, 'Approach me and die.'"

Laura smiled a bit. "I'm in a weird headspace today," she admitted.

"Want to talk about it?" Alexis asked.

Did she ever. She wished she could confide everything to Alexis—the whole confusing fake relationship that didn't feel fake but might still be. She felt terrible for making her friend believe that she and Noah were actually... Wait, but weren't they? What did last night mean? Would Allison approve? Or would she hate what Laura was doing with the brother she'd adored?

Laura tried to think about what to say exactly. Something—anything—to make sense of her actions and his. "Noah spent the night last night."

Alexis arched a brow. "Did he?"

"Mmm."

She frowned. "Haven't you two done that before?"

Laura wanted to curse. "Yes." Fighting for an explanation, she continued. "But last night... Last night was..."

"Oh," Alexis said significantly. "What you're trying to say is last night, you and Noah had *the* night."

"Precisely," Laura replied.

"All right." Alexis grinned. "Now that you mention it, I do detect a strong afterglow."

"I'm...*glowing*?"

"Like a menorah."

Laura snorted a laugh and covered her mouth as Alexis folded her lips around a muted chuckle. It took them both a moment to contain themselves.

Laura sighed. "Allison lived for conversations like this."

"She did," Alexis said reminiscently. "She'd say these are the talks that keep us young."

Laura sobered. "Taco Tuesdays won't be the same."

"No," Alexis granted. "She would want us to keep doing it, though."

"Then we will," Laura determined. "After the memorial."

"When is the memorial? Have you spoken with her family?"

"A little." Every time she'd brought it up with Noah, he'd shut her out. She wasn't looking forward to having the same conversation again. "The coroner's office hasn't released her, so I don't think they've put burial plans into motion yet."

"Adam's coming," Alexis said swiftly. "And...good Lord. What is it with you Coltons and your collective wrath today?"

Laura glanced up and found Adam pushing toward her on fast-moving legs. His face wasn't friendly. Her stomach knotted.

"May we speak in private?" he asked.

"Of course," Laura said. She nodded to Alexis, who moved off to give them a moment to themselves.

Adam's eyelid twitched. "Josh tells me Steele was at your place this morning."

"He was," Laura replied.

"Alone. With you."

"Yes, Adam," she said, feeling weary.

"What are you doing?" he demanded.

"It wasn't supposed to happen like this," she began.

"Jesus, Laura." He pressed his fingers into his eyes before remembering himself. He glanced around and lowered his voice. "Are you buying into your own cover story? Is this all some fantasy you had to indulge?"

"No," she said, offended. "Of course not."

"He's not a rock star," he told her. "He's a cop."

"I know that!"

"And he's not actually in love with you!"

Ouch, she thought. Shaking off the strange pulse of hurt, she straightened her posture. "I know."

"Every bit of this with him is pretend," he went on, undeterred. "And you're setting yourself up to get hurt all over again."

"Stop it, Adam."

"I'm not going to let you get hurt again!"

"Please," she begged, eyes brimming with a sudden wave of hot tears. "I said stop."

He saw the tears and his expression darkened. "I'm not a violent man, Laura. You know this. But if he's making you do this, I swear—"

"It was me," she said. "I was the one who told him to stay. He didn't make me do anything. I wanted him."

His jaw loosened.

She shook her head. "Don't act so shocked. I'm a grown woman. I choose who I go to bed with, just like Josh. I'm responsible for my own actions, just like you. If I get hurt, then that's my problem. Not yours."

"I have to watch," he said from the pit of his stomach. "I have to watch you pick up the pieces and move on. And it guts me every time."

She touched his arm. "It's going to be okay. I… I know what I'm doing."

"Are you sure about that?" he asked.

She wasn't, but she nodded. "I do."

He shook his head in disagreement. "You're always so careful. You're not considering the consequences from every angle."

"Maybe not." She could grant him that. "But ask me if I have any regrets."

"I think it's a little early for that," he considered.

"Do not talk to Noah about this," she said, knowing him. "I don't need you chasing him off like a coyote before—"

"Before what?" he challenged. "Before he shows you what kind of man he really is?"

"Don't pretend to know who he really is," she advised.

"Fine," he returned. "Then you shouldn't either." He turned and left her with the shrimp.

She looked around the tables, making sure no one had caught wind of the argument. She caught Alexis's sympathetic gaze from across the room and tried to erect a reassuring smile.

It slipped as she glanced toward the exit and saw Noah standing just outside the doors of the restaurant.

Chapter Fourteen

"Your stepmother made bail."

Laura nodded slowly. "We knew she would."

"You should prepare for whatever else she's planning," Noah cautioned. "I know her type. She's a schemer—a wrench in the system. She'll make trouble for Mariposa and your family again. I guarantee it."

Laura's brow furrowed. "I think you might be right."

"Fulton believes he has enough to close Allison's case by the end of the week."

Laura frowned. "How can he? There's not enough evidence to convict anyone. Is there?"

"No," he said.

"Then why the urgency?" she asked.

Noah shifted uncomfortably as the laughter from the open doors of Annabeth spilled out into the afternoon air. "I told you he was looking hard at Roger Ferraday. While I was at the station, I looked closer at his background and his son's." He showed her the folder in his hand. "Roger Ferraday has one DWI on his record. There were others that've been expunged because he's got money and power and he's got a high-priced lawyer who plays racquetball with judges and prosecutors alike." He opened the folder and angled it toward her. "This is his son's rap sheet."

Her hand touched her mouth as she read the felonies and

misdemeanors. "How is he free to come and go as he pleases with a record like this?"

"Papa Ferraday flew his bouncing baby boy to Arizona on their private jet because whispers of date rape and drug abuse are getting the attention of people who don't care who he or his lawyer are," Noah revealed. "There's talk of locking Dayton Ferraday up for good."

"How does this tie back to Allison?" she asked.

Noah didn't want to spell it out for her. "Dayton has used fentanyl at least once in a case of date rape. The victim was a minor and charges were dropped, thanks to Roger's influence. But the connection's there."

She stared at him, distress painting her. "You think Allison's death had something to do with…rape?"

"Fentanyl is a date rape drug," he confirmed. "Come on, Laura. Think. For what other reason would her killer inject her?"

This time, both hands rose to cover her face. She stood still for a moment. Then her shoulders shuddered.

Noah wanted to take it all away. The likeliest truth was too ugly for him to process. He didn't want her to have to do so as well. "Hey," he said, sliding his palm over her shoulder. When she didn't raise her head, he rubbed circles over her back. "Hey, it's okay."

He didn't know why he said it. Nothing about this was okay. But he needed her to be. If she broke down, he didn't know what he would do. The confluence of rage and violence he felt for whoever had hurt his sister didn't mix well with a lack of self-control.

Laura had to know, he reminded himself. If there was a rapist at Mariposa, no one was safe. Not the maids. Not the concierges, front desk clerks, masseuses… Most especially not its queen bee, who drew playboys like flies and slept alone a heartbeat away from where Allison was killed.

The need to protect her whistled in his ears. He wanted to get her out of there, away from the resort. The danger was too close to her.

Sweeping the soft strands of her hair aside, he lowered his

lips to the nape of her neck. His anger and torment over Allison lived shoulder to shoulder with his panic over what he felt for Laura, his need for her. He felt too small to contain everything inside him. Something was going to have to give soon or he would explode.

"I can't believe..." She took several shallow breaths, trying to get the words out. "...someone would do that to her...take advantage of her like that... Did he mean to kill her or did he just...want to have his way with her?"

"Either way, the son of a bitch is going to spend a long time behind bars. Unless Fulton rushes it, screws it up, and the guy gets off on a technicality. I have to make this right."

Even as her eyes flashed with tears, her voice was firm. "We both do."

He'd denied it for the better part of the day. He'd held himself back from the truth of what he felt. But he felt himself fumbling over that blind, terrifying cliff again. He felt himself go over the edge. Fear chased him, but he couldn't not see her. He couldn't stop feeling what he felt. In what he hoped was a perfunctory motion, he lifted his hand to her face to wipe the tears with his thumb.

Her eyes went soft, and he knew he'd failed. "Thank you for the coffee and omelet this morning."

"It was nothing," he lied.

"You fed my cat."

He had. "I didn't want him to wake you."

"You were trying to sneak out?"

"I told you. I got called into the station."

"Adam knows about us. About last night."

"You told him?" he asked incredulously.

"Josh did. He saw you leaving my bungalow this morning."

He rocked back on his heels. "I'm surprised I made it through the gate."

"Do you still want to talk to CJ Knight?"

He nodded. "Someone needs to."

"He's returning to Mariposa on the sixteenth," she told him. "Looks like you're going to get your shot."

"What's he booked for—spa, golf, excursions?"

"I'll have to check with the front desk," she replied.

"Find me an in," he told her, "and I'll find out if he's Allison's killer."

"I will," she promised. She looked across the grounds, past the pool to the tumble of rocks on the far horizon. The sun was low. It fanned across her lashes, and he saw they were still wet. Something inside him constricted. "Do you want me to keep Bungalow Fifteen available for you?" she asked.

She could smell the distance he was trying to erect between them. "Yes," he said, hating that he was too spineless to spend the night in her bed...too terror-struck to put himself at her mercy again.

He'd be a fool to let her play with his heart again.

"Very well," she said stiffly.

Before she could veer back through the doors to the restaurant, he took her by the elbow. Without thinking, he pulled her in.

As always, he went a step further. He kissed her. Her arms linked underneath his. They fanned across his back, and she made a noise that flipped his restraint like a wrestler's hold.

He opened his mouth to hers, recapturing the heat from last night. He let it coil around him. It was as if he'd never left.

He tipped his head up and away from hers. Her nails scraped across his scalp, making his mind go dangerously blank.

"Last night, you left a path of little reminders across my skin," she told him. "I've spent the whole day hating you for it."

Last night, she'd drawn little maps across his soul in carbon black. He'd spent the better part of the day trying to come up with enough elbow grease to erase them. He'd failed miserably.

"Hate me, Laura," he invited. "It's better for both of us." He touched her shoulders and held her away from him. "I'll see you."

Her expression folded, but her eyes glinted with promise. "Yes, you will."

Between the wedding and resort operations, Laura stayed busy. Too busy to think about the man in Bungalow Fifteen or the path between his bungalow and hers that, as promised, remained scant on foot traffic over the next few days. No one questioned why they didn't spend Valentine's Day together. The wedding was an all-day spectacle that had her limping back to her house well after hours on Saturday. She found Sebastian waiting for her there alone, demanding Fancy Feast and cuddles on his terms. *Just like a man*, she thought as she juggled a martini and Sebastian's large, round form in her favorite corner on the couch.

She ran into Roger Ferraday a handful of times on Sunday and struggled to maintain her demeanor. She skirted Adam, his warnings and assumptions.

Most of which she had to admit were true. She had gotten carried away by the illusion of her and Noah. But not rock star Noah. The real Noah—the one she'd thought she knew. And maybe she *was* setting herself up to get hurt.

Maybe she was her mother's daughter. Maybe she sought the one person she knew would never let her stand beside him without pretense.

When Tallulah tapped on the open door of Laura's office in L Building on Monday morning, Laura couldn't have been more relieved to see her. She closed the proposal Adam had prepared for her about a new line of more efficient bulk washing machines he wanted to splurge on for housekeeping. "Right on time, as always," she greeted her.

Tallulah stepped into the office and closed the door. "Were you expecting me?"

"No," Laura said, propping her chin on her hands as she watched Tallulah settle into one of the faux cowhide chairs across the desk. "But your visits are always welcome."

"You look tired, Laura," Tallulah murmured, studying her.

"Things have been busy," Laura said by way of excuse.

"Yes, they have," Tallulah agreed.

"Do you want to have coffee with me?" Laura asked, already reaching for the Keurig she'd tucked lovingly into the corner with mugs with the Mariposa logo.

"I would," Tallulah admitted, "but I have something I need to speak with you about."

"I'm all ears," Laura said, easing back into her chair.

Tallulah folded her hands carefully in her lap. "It's about Bella."

"The maid?"

"Yes," Tallulah said. "She came to me this morning in tears and handed in her resignation."

Laura blinked in surprise. "I'm sorry to hear that."

"So was I," Tallulah stated. "She's wonderful at her job, and she's a good girl."

"Did she give you a reason for leaving?" Laura asked.

"Not at first," Tallulah said. Her dark eyes flickered. "But when pressed, the story came out."

"'Story'?" That didn't sound good.

"She says she was assaulted," Tallulah said quickly, as if in a hurry to get the words out. "By a guest."

Laura stiffened. "Assaulted?"

"Yes," Tallulah replied. "It happened Friday, and she didn't tell anyone. She didn't tell me."

Laura wrapped her hand over the edge of the desk. "Tallulah, what kind of assault was it? Did she say?"

Tallulah's eyes grew wide. "Oh, Laura. She said she was manhandled, sexually. She was cleaning Bungalow Three because she thought the guests there were out for the day and she was attacked."

"Bungalow Three." Laura bit down on the urge to scream. "That's where—"

"The Ferradays," Tallulah confirmed with a nod.

"Which one?" Laura asked and heard her voice drop low where anger coiled.

"The younger," Tallulah answered. "And after what she told me, I'm in a mind to march down there and pour boiling water over his head."

Laura pushed back from the desk. She stood. "We need to report this."

"She doesn't want to involve police," Tallulah said. "I could hardly get her to talk to me."

"You don't understand," Laura said as she picked up her phone and dialed Noah's number. "This has happened before."

"With the maids?" Tallulah asked, shocked.

"No," Laura said. "Back in Connecticut, where the Ferradays live when they're not here."

"You knew this?" Tallulah stared at her, aghast.

Laura hated herself for it. "He's already under investigation. That's why his father brought him here. Probably in hopes that things would quiet in his absence." She swallowed hard. "Tallulah. I didn't think he'd do something like this. I'm so sorry."

Tallulah nodded in a vague, distracted motion.

Laura wrestled with her guilt. The call went to voicemail and she redialed. "Come on, Noah. Pick up."

"Why are you calling him?" Tallulah queried.

Laura knew she couldn't explain. She waited through a second procession of rings, then all but growled when it went to voicemail. "Noah. It's Laura. I need you to call me back as soon as you get this. It's urgent." She dropped the phone back to the cradle. "Where is Bella now?"

"I had Mato drive her home," Tallulah admitted. "She was too upset to drive herself."

"We'll need her to make a statement," Laura said. "She's already told her story to you. Do you think she'll do so again if you're there with her?"

"Maybe," Tallulah offered after a moment's thought. "But she was adamant, Laura. No police."

"She may not have a choice." Laura headed toward the door. "Can you call Roland and have him meet me at Bungalow Three? I'm going to have a word with Roger Ferraday."

"Ms. Colton." Roger Ferraday grinned winningly when he found Laura on his doorstep. "This is a surprise."

"Mr. Ferraday," she greeted him. Roland hadn't arrived yet, but she'd knocked on the door of Bungalow Three regardless. "Is your son here?"

"Dayton?" Roger gave her a puzzled look. "Why?"

"There's been a security breach. We're just checking to make sure all guests are present and accounted for."

"Security breach?" Roger's smile tapered. "Should I be concerned?"

"We don't believe so," she blurted. "If you could assure me your son is in residence, please…"

"He is," Roger assured her. "I think he's still in bed."

"When was the last time you saw him?" Laura asked.

"You're scaring me, Ms. Colton," Roger said, visibly paling.

"Have you checked on him this morning?" she asked. "Are you sure he's in his bedroom?"

"I'll go check," Roger said, and he left the door open as he fumbled away. He called his son's name, rushing.

Laura took the open door as an invitation and stepped inside the bungalow. She smelled men's cologne and takeout. The table was crowded with to-go containers, and she spied a pile of wet towels through the door to the pool deck. Housekeeping hadn't come through yet.

Thank goodness, she thought.

"Here he is," Roger announced with obvious relief as he returned to the living area with his son. "He was sleeping in, just as I told you."

Laura eyed the slouch-framed boy with a messy lid of black curls. He peered at her, unhappy to have been roused from sleep.

"What's the big deal?" he asked in a baritone. He was of medium height, skinny, but she saw deceptive strength in the long arms that hung from the sleeves of his oversized Ed Hardy T-shirt.

If she searched his room, would she find fentanyl?

Had he killed Allison?

She unscrewed her jaw so that she could speak. Fury tried to bite down on the words. "I'm going to have to ask you to stay here."

"Me? What did I do?"

She glared at him. "You know exactly what you did."

His eyes narrowed, and he took a step forward. "Are you accusing me of something?"

Betrayal and disbelief worked across Roger's features. "You...tricked me?"

"Our security team will be here any moment," she stated. "They'll take your son into their custody and await police."

"Dayton didn't do anything," Roger said with an expansive gesture. "Listen, Ms. Colton. I'm sure there's something I can do, some arrangement we can come to—"

"I'm afraid not, Mr. Ferraday," she said with a shake of her head. Where was Roland?

"In that case, I'd like to speak with your brother," Roger requested. She could see sweat forming on his upper lip. She noted how he'd planted himself between her and Dayton. "Adam, isn't it?"

"You're lucky I'm the one handling this matter," she informed him. "Neither of my brothers would wait for Security to haul your son out."

"You know." Dayton spoke up, inspecting Laura. His pupils were as black as water beetle wings. "You're a smart-mouthed bitch."

"Shut up, Dayton!" Roger snapped. "I'm handling this!"

"No," Laura said, staring back at Dayton. "Go ahead."

"Okay," Dayton said, and his shoulders squared. "You're a big, loud, smart-mouthed bitch and you're going to eat your words. Just like the rest of them."

She took a step forward, drawing herself up to her full height. "You're right about one thing, Dayton. I'm a really big, really loud, really smart bitch. And I'm going to make sure you never hurt another woman again."

Roger held his hands up. "Ms. Colton, please. I'm sure we can solve this unfortunate matter together. There's no need to involve Security or the police. Dayton and I will leave your resort quietly. Just name your price."

"Bribery won't work here," she told him.

He had the nerve to smile. "Only because I haven't named the right price."

"Maybe I haven't made myself clear," Laura said, raising her voice. "Your son is a rapist and, possibly, a murderer, and he's leaving Mariposa in handcuffs."

"A murderer?" Roger repeated, smile fleeing. His face reddened, and he advanced on her. "That's a lie!"

"Yeah," Dayton spit. "What the hell?"

"Get out!" Roger shouted at her.

She heard the knock on the door. "Ms. Colton?" Roland called as he stepped into the open entryway. "Are you all right?"

Roger Ferraday's arm snaked out, hooking her around the throat. The other pinned her arms to her sides.

"What are you doing?" she cried out.

"Back off!" Roger warned Roland. "Back the hell off or I'll hurt her!"

Roland's Taser was already in hand. He didn't back away. "Mr. Ferraday," he said, focused on the face next to Laura's. "You're making a big mistake here. The police are right behind me. If they see you've taken Ms. Colton hostage, you'll be charged with holding her against her will. And the accommodations at the state penitentiary lack the luxury you're accustomed to."

Laura could smell the fear and sweat pouring off Roger. It dampened his shirt and hers as he pressed his front to her back. It slicked across her ear as his cheek buffered against it. Holding herself still, she kept calm, knowing her fright might encourage him to carry this through.

The tension shattered when the glass sliding door exploded. Glass rained, skidding across the floor, and a dark figure darted through the opening, gun between his hands. "Hands in the air!" he yelled.

Laura barely had time to register the lethal focus on Noah's face before Roger shoved her aside. Her boot heel slid across a loose piece of glass, and she went flying. She reached out to grab the table's edge, but she was going too fast. Her head arced down to meet it and she was helpless to stop her momentum.

Little white lights broke across her vision. Then the world came rushing back to her as she met the floor, little glass shards poking through her blouse. She reached for her head as pain split her temples.

When she pulled her hand away, blood smeared her fingers.

Chapter Fifteen

It was well after dark when Noah returned to Mariposa. He wasn't able to go back to Bungalow Fifteen. Not after going several rounds with Roger and Dayton Ferraday at the police station.

He hadn't accepted Captain Crabtree's orders that Fulton be the one to question them. He'd gone about the task himself with grim determination.

Roger Ferraday would do time. The Coltons' lawyer, Greg Sumpter, had shown up with Adam on Laura's behalf to demand that he be brought up on assault charges while Joshua had escorted Laura to the hospital to get checked out.

The younger Ferraday wouldn't get away from rape accusations this time. Bella, the maid, had changed her mind about not testifying after Adam and Tallulah had spoken to her personally. She was traumatized and scared but had seemed determined to put Dayton away once she found out about the other girls he had assaulted in Connecticut.

Fulton, certain Dayton was Allison's killer, had Bungalow Three searched, confident fentanyl would be recovered from the scene.

Instead, small quantities of Ecstasy were found in Dayton's mattress.

When Noah had leaned harder on Roger, the man cracked

under the pressure and admitted the reason he had no alibi for
the night of Allison's homicide was he had found the bulk of
his son's drug stash and the two of them had snuck out under
the cover of night to dump it on the hiking trails.

By the end of the interview, Noah had wanted to lock Roger
up on more than assault. He'd expressed no regret about holding
Laura against her will or harming her, and he'd blamed Bella
and the other girls for his son's criminal behavior.

Noah had thought of little more than punching the bastard
in the face. But he'd known Crabtree was watching through
the two-way glass, anticipating the moment Noah lost his cool.

He'd kept it—but only just.

Now he trudged up the walk to Laura's place. The door
opened before he could get to it and Joshua, Adam, Tallulah
and Alexis stepped out together. They stopped talking collec-
tively when they spotted him.

Tallulah reached for his hand. "Laura's okay. It's good you're
here. She doesn't need to be alone tonight."

The feeling of her hand in his felt foreign, but it was pleasantly warm. "You had dinner with her?"

"You weren't exactly here to keep her company," Joshua said
in accusation.

Adam surprised Noah when he argued, "Go easy on the man,
Josh. I'm sure he has his reasons."

When the four of them looked at him expectantly, Noah said,
"I had to go up to Flagstaff. I got delayed there and didn't get
Laura's message until she'd left the hospital."

"That was hours ago," Joshua pointed out. "Flagstaff's half
an hour away."

Noah swallowed. "I'm sorry."

Alexis eyed the bag in his hand. "Do you come bearing
gifts?"

He thought of what was in the bag. A blip of panic made him
itch for something more—a better offering. "Yes."

"Good," Alexis noted. "There's no concussion, but doctors
advised her not to imbibe for the next twenty-four hours."

"Noted," he said.

"Good night to you, Noah," Tallulah murmured before

walking away. Alexis followed her. Joshua said nothing as he moved off.

That left Adam. "Anything you have to say to my sister can wait until the morning."

Noah searched for the right words. "I'd like to see her."

Adam studied him. "You were good with Bella. You made giving her statement easier."

"So did you," Noah said, "and Tallulah."

"Roland told me what happened at Bungalow Three," Adam explained. "He told me how Roger had her in a choke hold and how you apprehended him."

"She got hurt," Noah noted dully. The scene was on a loop in his mind. Ferraday shoving Laura away to save his own ass, her skidding into the table, knocking her head against it and falling to the floor, bleeding.

"I've asked Roland not to reveal your real identity," Adam pointed out. "Not until your investigation comes to a close."

"Thank you," Noah said.

"Laura says Dayton Ferraday may have killed Allison."

Noah shook his head. "He and his father confirmed each other's real alibis for the night in question."

"So you're back to square one?"

"Not if you tell me CJ Knight checked in this morning," Noah told him.

"He did," Adam confirmed.

Noah breathed a small sigh of relief. "That's something."

Adam gave him a tight nod. He started to go, then stopped. "Go easy on Laura. She puts up a good front for all of us, but she's raw tonight."

"I will." He waited until Adam had gone before knocking.

He lingered for two minutes. When she didn't answer, he tried the door and muttered something foul when he found she hadn't locked it behind the others.

"Laura?" he called through the house as he stepped inside. The door closed behind him. Everything was quiet, eerily so.

"Laura!" he shouted.

He checked the bedroom. Her sheets hadn't been turned down. The door to the connected bathroom was open, and the light was off. He moved to the kitchen. Five plates and cups were stacked in the dish drain next to the sink. The couch in the living room was empty except for the unimpressed tabby who flicked his bushy tail at him. "Where is she?" he asked.

Sebastian lifted a paw and started to clean it.

"You're no help," Noah groaned. Then a movement on the other side of the glass caught his eye. He peered out. The steam of the heated pool rose to meet the cool night. In the blue glow of the pool lights, he could see arms cutting across the water like sharks.

He slid open the door, similar to the one he'd thrown a brick through earlier. Walking out on the patio, he watched her lap the pool four times without stopping, hardly coming up for air in between.

She cycled through freestyle, then backstroke, butterfly, then breaststroke. By the time she stopped, finally, he was ready to go in after her.

She gripped the edge of the pool, gasping. He saw the shaking in her limbs.

"Are you trying to hurt yourself?" he asked.

She jerked in surprise. "What are you doing here?"

He stared at the goose egg on her forehead. She'd taken off the bandage. There were no stitches, but bruises webbed across her brow.

As he surveyed the damage to her face, the fury came sweeping back in stark detail, and it crushed him.

She looked away. Using her arms, she pulled herself from the water.

He gripped her underneath the shoulder, helping her to her feet.

"I've got it," she said, taking a step back.

He dropped his arm. "Sure you do."

She reached for the towel she'd set on the nearby lounge chair. She patted her hair dry, then her face, hissing when she pressed the towel to the bump on her head.

He reached for her even as she turned away to dry her arms and legs. Then she wrapped the towel around her middle and knotted it as he'd seen her do before. Finished, she bypassed him for the door.

He tailed her, feeling foolhardy. "I should've punched him," he grumbled.

"That would have been counterproductive," she muttered. "Isn't your CO scrutinizing you?"

"Why did you go into that bungalow?" he asked. He'd needed to ask from the moment he'd found out she'd gone. "You thought Dayton Ferraday killed Allison, and you went to confront him and his father? Why?"

"It's my fault," she said. "He could only assault Bella because I didn't warn Housekeeping or others that he was a predator. I should've told them to steer clear of Bungalow Three. I went because I wanted to be the one to tell Dayton Ferraday that he will spend the rest of his life paying for what he's done."

"Ferraday didn't kill Allison," Noah told her.

She stopped. "What?"

"Father and son gave their real alibis," Noah explained weightily. "They check out."

"But the date rape…the fentanyl…his attack on Bella… It all fits."

"Small traces of Ecstasy were recovered from Bungalow Three," Noah went on. "There's no sign of fentanyl."

"What does that mean?"

"It means CJ Knight is now the chief suspect in this investigation. But that's for me to worry about. You can't do this to me again. You can't go charging into a suspect's bungalow and try to take matters into your own hands. Whoever killed Allison will most likely kill you."

"I am not Allison!" she said, raising her voice.

"The man had you in a choke hold."

"I was doing my job."

"So was my sister," he reminded her. Unable to stop himself, he reached out to feather his touch across the first stain of bruising. "It's starting to hurt. Isn't it? And he scared you. That's the reason you were doing laps out there. Because you were alone long enough to feel the fear again." He pressed his cheek to hers, felt the shaking in her limbs and pulled her close, not caring that she was wet and he wasn't.

When he lifted her into his arms, she protested. He quieted her by touching his mouth to the rim of her jaw. "It's a soak in the tub for you. Then bed."

"You sound like Tallulah."

"Do you listen to her?"

"Sometimes." She pillowed her head on his shoulder, giving in as he sidestepped through the door to the bedroom so she wouldn't catch her toes on the jamb. There, he set her on the wingback chair.

"Take off your suit."

"Do you want me to dance for you when I'm done?" she drawled.

He ignored that and went into the bathroom to draw her a bath, throwing in some Epsom salts. When he came back for her, she was naked and shivering still. He bundled her up again, took her into the bathroom and lowered her into the water.

She let out a sharp breath as she sank in.

"Too hot?" he asked.

"No." She tipped her head back against the lip. "No. It's perfect." She flicked a glance at him when he lingered. "I'm not going to drown."

Reaching into his back pocket, he took out the little bag he'd brought to her door. "I bought this while I was in town."

She eyed the box he held with mixed levels of curiosity. "For me?"

When she didn't reach out, he opened it himself. "I found it while I was in Sedona." On a small cushion, a delicate strand of gold held a single pearl teardrop.

Her eyes rushed up to meet his. "You bought this—for me?"

He bit his tongue, trying to come up with the right thing to say. "It's not flowers."

"No," she said.

"Or dinner. But it looked…right."

She only stared.

He groaned at her reticence. "If you don't want it, I can take it back. I've got the receipt right here—"

"Shut up," she said without heat. "Just…shut up and put it on me."

She straightened, her shoulders rising above the water. Lifting her hair, she turned.

He took the necklace out of the box, unclasped it and lowered it over her head. Securing it at the base of her neck, he eased back as she turned to him again. The pearl rested just above her sternum in the dip between her breasts. She touched it. "How does it look?" she asked.

He shook his head. "It looks like I brought feldspar to an empress."

She leaned over the tub wall, meeting his mouth with her own, silencing him and his doubts.

He brought his hand up to her face. *Easy*, he told himself, feeling the quaking in his bones again. Not fury this time. The fear was there and the need, too. Always.

She pulled away. Her eyes flashed blue. "Stay with me?"

It was impossible to argue. "That's a hard yes."

Her smile was a tender curve meant for him alone as she reclined again against the tub wall and gripped his fingers on the ledge.

He watched over her until the water cooled. Then he helped her dry and dress for bed.

Back in her sheets, he held her until he felt her soften into repose. It took a long time to follow, but when he did, he had his nose buried in her hair and his arm tight around her middle, unwilling to let her go in the silent, anonymous hours between night and day.

Chapter Sixteen

Noah was relieved when Laura took Tuesday off after waking with a fierce headache. It took everything he had not to stay and take care of her. He made her coffee and breakfast and fed Sebastian again. As he ate over her sink so he wouldn't get crumbs on her spotless countertops, the cat bumped his cheek against Noah's ankle, then, purring, started weaving figure eights around his boots.

Noah watched, puzzled. When his plate was clean, he scooped the feline up in one hand. "It's your turn to watch her," he informed him as he carried the tabby back to the bedroom where Laura dozed. "Don't screw it up."

His phone rang. Sebastian twisted, unhappy as Noah juggled him to dig the device out of his pocket. Setting Sebastian down, he swiped at the long strands of cat hair clinging to the front of his shirt before answering.

"Steele," Adam greeted him.

"Colton," Noah replied just as flatly.

"I have a proposition."

Noah braced himself. "I'm listening."

"I don't expect Laura to come to work today."

"Damn right," Noah said.

"I'll be stepping in for her," Adam told him, "to help with the investigation."

"Thanks," Noah mused, "but I'm good."

"Meet me near the paddock in an hour," Adam said, ignoring Noah's refusal. "Dress for a riding excursion."

The line clicked. Noah looked at his phone and saw that Adam had ended the call. "Sure, cupcake," he muttered, sliding the phone back into his pocket.

An hour later, Noah said, "You know, I don't think me and you kissing is going to have the same effect on people as Laura and I do."

"Just once," Adam said mildly, "I'd like to see you go an entire day without vexing me."

"Not likely," Noah responded. He adjusted the Stetson he wore low over his brow as they walked to the paddock together. "You're sure Knight signed on for this thing today?"

"Yes." The corner of Adam's mouth curled. "But if he backs out at the last minute, I won't lose sleep knowing you're Josh's problem. Not mine."

"You realize I know how the internet works, right?" Noah said. "If baby brother abandons me like a lost calf on the trail, I'm dropping a one-star review for Mariposa on Tripadvisor."

Adam's smile morphed. "You wouldn't."

"How do you figure?"

"Because what you've done for your sister these last few weeks tells me you're a man of honor," Adam admitted. "If you have as much regard for Laura as she has for you, you'll leave Mariposa alone when this is all over."

Noah scowled, eating up the ground with long strides. He could smell the horses, the saddle leather… He could hear the chink of cinches and stirrups and the nickers and snorts of the animals as the guides and riders readied them for the long drive ahead.

All he'd wanted to do over the last few weeks was find Allison's killer. He hadn't considered what would come after. Once the perpetrator was caught and Noah's actual reasons for being at the resort were revealed, would he be welcome there?

He couldn't think about Laura and what he wanted with her when this was all over. He couldn't think about losing her. Leaving her.

"I know you spent the night with her again last night," Adam revealed.

Noah felt a muscle in his jaw tic. "She was in pain."

"So you didn't sleep with her?"

He chose his next words carefully. "I slept next to her." At the sight of Adam's grimace, Noah nearly gave in to his own frustration. "I know the hospital said she didn't have a concussion. I wanted to make sure." He'd *needed* to make sure. "She didn't need to be left on her own. Ferraday didn't just hurt her. He scared her." And for that, Noah wanted to drive back to Sedona and toss the man across his holding cell.

"She shouldn't have been there to begin with."

Finally, something the two of them could agree on. Noah saw the knot of people in the horse paddock and scanned for his mark. "Where is he?"

"There," Adam said with a jerk of his chin to the left.

Noah had memorized the file on CJ Knight. He knew the man was twenty-seven, approximately five-eleven, one hundred and eighty pounds, with brown hair and blue eyes. Noah also knew he was unmarried and that he resided primarily in Los Angeles as an up-and-coming film actor.

CJ removed his cowboy hat, so the wind tousled his wavy locks. Under his plaid button-down shirt and jeans, he had the trim body of a gym rat.

Like a true actor, he'd dressed the part for the day's trail-riding adventure, led by Knox and Joshua. Noah's goal was to ride next to CJ and get to know him and hope Joshua didn't have other ideas—throwing Noah into a gorge, for example.

Among the others assembled, Noah recognized Kim Blankenship and her husband, Granger. He remembered the initials on Allison's refrigerator schedule: *CJK*, *DG* and *KB*.

Maybe today Noah could knock out two birds with one stone. Was Kim Blankenship *KB* or did Noah need to look harder at Mariposa's cowboy, Knox Burnett?

He needed to find the identity, too, of the mysterious *DG*.

Joshua spotted Noah and Adam on the approach and he nodded in their direction. "The gang's all here. Where's your riding gear, Adam?"

"I'm not staying," Adam stated. Everyone fell quiet as he brought his hands together. "I'd just like everyone to know that Joshua and Knox are the two best guides in Red Rock Country. You're in expert hands today." He patted Noah on the shoulder, either in assurance or warning. "Come on. I'll introduce you."

Noah walked with him to CJ Knight and the mare that had been chosen for him from the stable. "It's good to have you back, Mr. Knight," Adam said.

CJ shook Adam's offered hand. "It's good to be back. I'm sorry I left with so little notice before. I got called back to LA without warning."

"Is everything all right there?"

"It was a callback on an audition," CJ said. "And it wound up getting canceled, anyway. I wish I'd never left."

"Let us know if we can do anything to make your stay with us better this time," Adam replied. He turned to Noah. "I don't believe you've met Noah Steele. His band Fast Lane's making a splash. He'll be riding out today, too."

"Nice to meet you," CJ said, reaching out to grip Noah's extended hand.

Noah pasted on a smile. "Likewise. Have you done this before?"

"A few times," CJ said. "I love Red Rock Country. Are you new to trail riding?"

"It's been a long time," Noah admitted. "I hope I can keep up."

"Knox normally rides behind with the stragglers," CJ informed him. "Josh keeps pace, but most of the time it's leisurely, so we can enjoy the view."

A man flanked CJ. He had light hair and dark eyes and an unrelaxed posture that looked almost unnaturally upright. "Doug DeGraw," he introduced, shaking Noah's hand. "I'm CJ's manager."

"Noah Steele," Noah returned. He glanced down at the man's feet. "I believe you're wearing the wrong shoes for this."

CJ chuckled as Doug looked down at the businesslike brogues he had donned. He patted Doug on the back. "Doug's not used to riding." He lowered his voice and said to his manager, "I told you I'd loan you a pair of boots. And you didn't have to come. You hate horses."

"I'll be fine," Doug said with a slight wince, looking around at the bay he had been assigned. "I'm told fresh country air does the body good."

"I can vouch for that," Adam agreed. "I'd better be getting back to L Building. Enjoy yourselves." He exchanged a significant look with Noah before departing.

Knox brought around a familiar horse that had been saddled. "Mr. Steele. You remember Penny?"

Noah couldn't help but smile as he raised his hand to the filly's mouth for a nuzzle. "I do. Is she mine for the day?"

"She is," Knox said. "She's new to the trails, but she's done well in practice. Want to give her a shot?"

"Absolutely," Noah said as Penny blew her whiskered breath across his palm. He took the reins. "Thanks. Hey, by any chance, do you know when a new yoga instructor will be hired? I've got this pain between my shoulders blades, and I really need a stretch."

Sadness lay heavy on Knox's face. "I don't, no. I'm not sure management's even thought about it. You could ask Laura."

"I will," Noah returned. "Sorry I brought it up."

"It's okay," Knox replied. "Allison hasn't even been buried yet. It's hard thinking about a replacement for her."

"It's a shame she died," CJ added. "I liked Allison. I'd just started private lessons with her."

"Oh?" Noah said, feigning surprise. "I didn't know she offered that sort of thing."

"We got one session in before I had to leave," CJ explained. "I didn't hear of her passing until it hit the news. She was so full of life. I don't understand how anyone could hurt her."

"Are you talking about the yoga instructor?" a voice said from the right. Noah looked over and saw that they'd drawn Kim Blankenship into the conversation. "Allison?"

"Yeah," Knox said, his voice lost in his throat somewhere.

"I knew her!" Kim said with wide gray eyes in a heavily made-up face. Under her hat, her bottle-blond hair was perfectly curled. She mixed a down-home, don't-mess-with-Texas attitude with vintage movie star glamour. "She came to my bungalow the morning before she was killed and led me through a personalized yoga routine. I'd overdone myself hiking a few days before, and she knew exactly what to do to help me work out the kinks. She was so sweet and personable." Kim planted a gloved hand on her hip. "Why, if I knew who did such a thing to her, I'd tie them behind my horse and drag 'em across the desert."

"I'm with you, sweetheart," her husband, Granger, agreed.

This struck up talk among most other members of the excursion. Noah watched CJ nod and concur as others voiced their opinions about Allison and the person who had brought her life to an untimely end. Noah wondered how good an actor the guy really was.

"You ride well, Steele."

Noah looked around as Joshua pulled his big, spirited stallion, Maverick, alongside Penny. "I detect disappointment."

Joshua laughed. "Did Adam tell you I'd leave you for the coyotes?"

"Something like that," Noah drawled.

"You can stop looking over your shoulder, Fender Bender. Accidents on the trail are bad for business."

"That's reassuring," Noah grumbled.

"You've been talking to CJ Knight."

"And you've been keeping tabs on me," Noah acknowledged.

"Part of my job," Joshua explained. "Did he mention Erica Pike?"

"Your brother's secretary?"

"Executive assistant."

"He didn't. Why?"

"No reason," Joshua said quickly.

"Why?" Noah pressed.

Joshua nickered to the stallion when the animal bobbed his head impatiently. "Laura thinks something may have happened between her and Knight. I asked Erica. She said it didn't."

"You don't think she's being truthful?" Noah asked.

Joshua shrugged, obviously uncomfortable with the subject.

"It's no good—relationships between staff and guests. Or management and staff, for that matter."

"No wonder you think so little of Laura and me," Noah noted.

"That's another matter," Joshua told him. "You met her before you came here. And you're hiding something." He spotted Noah's look of surprise and snorted. "I'm the second son of Clive Colton. I know when a man isn't being truthful. I don't expect you to tell me what you're lying about, but I will ask you not to lie to Laura. Come clean with her or coyotes will be the least of your worries."

Noah knew what it was to be a brother. It was a shame Joshua would never know that he and Noah had something so crucial in common. "Laura knows who I am."

"I hope so," Joshua said sincerely.

Noah glanced back at CJ Knight. He was lifting his canteen to his mouth and taking a long drink. His manager, Doug DeGraw, unsettled on his mount, struggled to keep up. "That guy's a nuisance."

"Who?" Joshua turned in the saddle. "CJ's manager? We rarely get inexperienced riders on challenging drives like this one. But he insisted."

"Doesn't look like he's having much fun," Noah said.

"The man's sweating bullets," Joshua observed.

"I'm surprised he hasn't turned back."

"Knox offered to take him. He seems determined to stay by Knight's side."

Noah frowned. "Seems more like a nanny than a manager."

"I'm surprised you and Knight are getting on so swimmingly."

"Why's that?"

"Unlike you," Joshua said, "he's a Boy Scout."

"You think so?"

"Yeah. Like any celebrity, he values his privacy. But he's personable with other guests and staff. He's uncomplaining. He tips well and not because it's expected of him—because he's grateful."

"You like him," Noah stated.

"I do," Joshua said.

This coming from the guy who claimed he could spot a liar at fifty paces. If Joshua had guessed that Noah wasn't being entirely truthful, wouldn't he have been able to do the same with Knight if he was the killer?

Joshua tapped Maverick with his heels and rode ahead. He turned the horse to face the riders. "Congratulations! You've all reached the south point. We'll rest our mounts for a while before the return journey. Dismount. There's a creek down at the bottom of the hill where you can lead your horse to water."

A resounding thump brought Noah's head around.

Doug DeGraw sprawled beneath his horse.

CJ shook his head as his boots hit the ground. Gathering Doug's horse's reins, CJ extended a hand to him. "Something tells me you're going to need a masseuse."

"Forget that," Doug said, brushing himself off. He struggled to his feet with CJ's help. "Get me a stiff drink and an hour with a nimble woman."

Kim Blankenship rolled her eyes. "That one's a winner," she muttered as she led her horse down the hill past Noah and Joshua.

Noah took Penny to the creek. "Good girl," he said as she bent her head to the water that burbled busily over its smooth rock bed. He took a moment to admire where they were. There was no fence to mark the boundary of Mariposa, just an old petrified tree trunk with a butterfly carved into its flank. He could see familiar formations from the state park in the distance.

He'd always been drawn to that perfect marriage between the cornflower blue sky and the red-stained mountains, buttes and cliffs that jutted toward it. The wind teased his hair as he took off his hat and opened his canteen for a long drink.

Someone stumbled over the rocks, making Penny sidestep. Noah patted her on the neck until she settled. Then he watched Doug pry off one dirt-smudged brogue. "I told you those were the wrong shoes."

Doug groaned as he rubbed the bottom of his socked foot. "I miss LA. I can't understand why CJ keeps getting drawn back to this place."

Noah lifted his eyes to the panorama. "Can't you?"

"No." Doug stilled as a woman from their party brought her horse to drink. He lifted his chin to her in greeting. "Ariana, right?"

"Yes," she said. "And you're Doug, CJ's guy."

"Just Doug," he said. "You're the host of that new game show—*Sing It or Lose It*."

"I am," she said, beaming. She was young, a redhead with large green eyes and long legs encased in jodhpurs. "Well, I don't exactly host. I'm the DJ."

"You should host," Doug asserted. He slid a long look over her form. "The network would draw far more viewers if they made you more visible."

She favored Allison. The resemblance jolted Noah, and he fought a sudden overwhelming urge to put himself between her and Doug.

Ariana stepped back a little, as if she didn't care for the way Doug was coming on to her either. Politely, she fixed a smile into place. "Thanks."

Noah cleared his throat, doing his best to draw Doug's attention away from her. "Your shoe's making a break for it."

"Huh?" Doug did a double take when Noah pointed out the brogue racing across the surface of the creek. He swore viciously and ran after it while Ariana giggled.

With Doug out of earshot, Noah moved toward her. "Here," he said, taking her horse's bridle. "They're building a fire. You go get warm. I'll make sure your horse is taken care of."

"Oh, thank you," she said, surprised. "Her name's Autumn. She's a sweetie. But I will join the others. That guy's vibes are way off."

"I'm starting to get that," Noah said.

"Hey." She touched his wrist. "That's an evil eye."

He looked down at the bracelet peeking out from under the cuff of his shirt. "Yeah. My, uh…" Licking his lips, he absorbed the pang above his sternum. "My sister gave it to me," he finished quietly.

"Did you know the evil eye dates back to 5000 BC?" she asked. "It's also used in symbolism across various cultures—

Hindi, Christian, Jewish, Buddhist, Muslim…not to mention Indigenous, pagan and folk societies."

"I didn't know that," he said truthfully.

She rolled her eyes at herself. "I sound like a geek. But I love that sort of thing. You've got a light blue eye. It's supposed to encourage you to open your eyes to self-acceptance and the world around you."

"Interesting," he said.

"Is it?" Doug snarled as he returned with one dripping shoe.

Ariana stiffened. "I'll go get a seat by the fire."

"Sure," Noah said. He blinked when she was gone. For a moment, it had felt like he was talking to his sister again.

"Look at that ass work."

Noah sent Doug a long scowl. "A little young for someone like you, wouldn't you say?"

"I like them young," Doug said as he worked his foot into his shoe. "Things tend to be more high and tight, if you know what I'm saying." He chuckled nastily, cheered by his own imagery.

If the man didn't shut up, Noah was going to shove both brogues down his throat.

Doug stood finally and grabbed the reins of his mare roughly. She rebuked him with a jerk of her head. "I knew someone with one of those."

On the verge of telling him to can it, Noah looked warily to where Doug pointed.

To Noah's wrist. He was pointing at Noah's wrist and the evil-eye bracelet.

Noah felt his jaw clamp and his stomach tighten. "Yeah?" he managed to drawl.

"Yeah." Doug lifted a brow. "That one… Ah, man. She was a real peach."

Was?

Under the watchful gaze of a high-noon sun, Doug led his mount up the hill, limping a little as he went.

"Son of a bitch," Noah muttered, clutching Penny's reins. He fit his hat to his head and led her and Autumn to the cluster of riders, wishing hard for his badge.

* * *

"You're supposed to be resting."

Laura looked up from her desk and spied the dusty man framed in the open door to her office. She noted the Stetson and the wide silver buckle on his belt. Noah looked dirty and dangerous, and her heart caterwauled as he propped the heel of his hand on the jamb above him.

The man was the human equivalent of devil's food cake.

Setting the papers in her hands flat against the desktop, she studied his comfortable scowl and smiled broadly despite the ache in her head that had persisted throughout the day. "You're probably going to take what I say and run with it, but…you look good enough to eat, cowboy."

The scowl wobbled, and warmth chased the moody slant of his eyes. Pushing off the jamb, he closed the door.

As he came around the desk, she turned the swivel chair to face him. Angling her chin up, she tilted her head. "I'm happy to see Josh didn't bring you back to me in splints."

Noah leaned over, pressing his hands to the arms of her chair, caging her in. He scanned the mark on her brow and its ring of dark bruises. Then he searched each of her eyes in a way that made her lose her breath. By the time his gaze touched her mouth, she was shivery with anticipation. She clutched the collar of his shirt to pull him down to meet her.

His arms locked, resisting, when he found the gold chain around her neck. Gingerly, he slid his first finger between it and the skin at the high curve of her breast and lifted it, so the pearl drop rose from the V-cut neckline of her plum-satin blouse.

His eyes crawled back to hers.

"I've been thinking about you," she whispered.

He made a low noise.

Her chest rose and fell swiftly. She wished she could catch her breath. He made it difficult. "And I've missed you," she admitted.

He tensed. Then he lowered to his knees. His arms spanned her waist, and he tugged her to the edge of her chair.

When he buried his face in her throat and pressed his front

to hers in a seamless embrace, she melted. Spreading her fingers through his hair, she latched on.

She couldn't handle him like this—urgent, tender, sweet. It disarmed her.

She swallowed. "Did something happen?"

His lips pursed against her skin. His breath across the damp circle left by his mouth made her skin hum all over. "I have to go back to Sedona."

"Why?" she asked, pulling back far enough to scan his face.

He stiffened. "I think I know who killed Allison."

"CJ Knight?" she asked.

"He was taking private lessons. I confirmed that. But I think I've been looking in the wrong place."

"Talk it through with me," she invited.

He eased back some, his hands lowering to her outer thighs. "*KB* is Kim Blankenship. Allison went to her bungalow for a lesson the day she died. But I don't think it's her either."

"Then who?" Laura asked.

His eyes hardened. *"DG."*

"You know who that is?"

"I think it stands for Doug DeGraw."

She squinted past the thumping behind her temples. "Isn't that CJ Knight's manager?"

"Yes."

"What makes you think he's guilty?"

"Other than that he's a complete and utter douchebag?" Noah drawled.

She sighed, nodded. "Yes."

"He was trying to flex on one woman. Ariana."

"Fitzgibbons," she said, plucking the name out of her memory files. "She's a new television personality. Beautiful, smiley, bubbly—"

"Like my sister."

She stopped. "They look similar," she granted.

Noah swore. "She's a dead ringer for Allison. And she knows things about spiritualism and symbolism. I felt like I wasn't just looking at Allison. I felt like I was talking to her, too."

"Noah," she whispered. "I can understand how that must

have felt. I know how it would have affected me. But is the fact that Doug DeGraw was hitting on Ariana Fitzgibbons the only reason you believe he killed Allison?"

"No," he said vehemently. "He saw the bracelet. He recognized it."

When he lifted his arm, she saw the evil-eye pendant around his wrist. "How do you know he recognized it? Did he say something?"

"Yeah." Noah's jaw locked from the strain. His hands gripped the arms of the chair again. His knuckles whitened. "He said he knew a woman who wore one. He said she was a real peach. I could've killed him on the spot."

"Okay," she said soothingly, laying her hands across his shoulders. "Let's just take a minute." For all his wrath, she could feel the grief emanating off him and she wanted to hold him until those waves came to shore. "I don't think you're in any condition to drive back to Sedona tonight." When he started to refuse, she spoke over him. "There's rain coming in. The roads will be wet, possibly icy. And it's after six—too late for you to make any headway."

"I need to nail this guy," he told her. "I need to look into his history, his record, his behavior—"

"Come home with me." She touched his face. "We'll soak in the pool, order dinner, then turn in before nine. That way, you can be up and out the door first thing in the morning. And you'll have the whole day to do whatever it is you need to do."

His frantic gaze raced over her. "It's him, Laura. He's the one who took Allison's life. He must've lured her to his bungalow, drugged her, then…"

A sob wavered out of her. She shook her head quickly. "Stop. Please, stop."

He released a long, ragged breath, dropping his head. "I still want to kill him. Crabtree was right. If I find something on De-Graw, I'll need to hand the arrest over to Fulton. If it's me… I don't know if I have what it takes not to put a bullet in him."

Her hands gentled on his face. She kissed the broad plane of his cheek. Then the space between his eyes before placing both palms around the back of his head and drawing him against her once more. "It's okay," she said, blinking back tears. "It's going to be okay."

He didn't pull away. They remained that way, still in the upheaval, for a while.

"Noah?" she whispered.

"Hmm?"

"Will you?" she asked. "Come home with me?"

He shoveled out a breath. Then he nodded, reluctantly.

When he stood, he extended a hand. She took it and let him pull her to her feet. Switching off the lamp on her desk, she grabbed her purse. On their way out, she stopped to lock the door.

"You lock your office but not your front door," he grumbled.

She stuffed the keys in her purse and reached for the handle of the glass door that led out of L Building. He beat her to it, shouldering it open and propping it until she'd passed through. He took her hand. "Wait."

She stopped moving. At the sight of his frown returning, she gave in. "I'll start locking my front door if it bothers you that much."

"Yes," he said with a nod. "But there's something else."

She was stunned when he gathered both her hands in his. As his thumbs stroked her knuckles in fast repetitions, she tried to read him. "What is it?"

"Promise me, Pearl," he murmured. "Promise me you won't approach DeGraw while I'm off property. I can't leave you here if I think you'll put yourself in harm's way for even a second."

She nodded. "All right."

"You promise?" he pressed.

"I promise." Unable to watch the conflict clash on the inside of him, she raised her lips to his.

As he inclined his head toward hers and his hand cupped the back of her head, he let it be soft—let himself be, drawing out her sigh with a head-to-toe shudder.

He took her home, where they soaked in the pool. He remained close to her as she reclined on the steps. It was easy with him, she thought, not to cut through the water but to rest and let the moment stretch.

She offered to order in, but he found pesto, grape tomatoes, green beans, tortellini and chicken in her fridge. As she sat with her wine and watched him throw it all together in a pan over the stove, she saw someone channeling his demons. Filling another glass, she took it to him. He stopped long enough to clink it to hers, holding her gaze as he took the first sip. She did the same, then rubbed the bones that had been etched on the left side of his spine, leaving the right side blank.

She half expected to feel the inscribed tears in the flesh that separated the unmarked side of his back from the tattoos as she ran her fingers across his vertebrae. Warm, smooth skin greeted them instead, and she marveled again over the level of artistry he'd placed upon his body.

Noah mixed and flipped the contents of the pan so that the pesto coated everything.

He'd stirred, mixed and flipped her, Laura mused. He'd come at her like a demolition expert, knocking down walls, making a mess, hauling complete sections of those walls out.

He'd rearranged things.

Allison had called Laura a "classic Taurus," no more open to change than she was to heartbreak. *It's why you won't play with risk*, she'd told her.

Laura had shrugged that off. *Risk is overrated.*

Maybe, Allison had replied. Her wise eyes had flickered knowingly. *I'm just afraid that when you find someone who's right for you*—really *right for you*—*you'll shy away from the risk and lose the chance to get everything you've ever wanted.*

The sentiment had made Laura reevaluate everything. What if she'd already done that? What if she'd missed her shot because the risk scared her?

She and Noah were so different. Night and day, as a matter of fact. But as she watched the hair on the back of his head fan through her fingertips, as the tense line of his body eased and he lifted his face to the ceiling briefly to dig into her touch, she caught her lower lip between her teeth.

Could they be this different and this right for each other all at once? All the candles he lit inside her just by being whispered *yes*.

"You keep this up and I'm going to burn the first dinner I prep for you," he noted.

The first? Her heart leaped. She swallowed all the deeper questions and asked, "What's your sign?"

"What sign?"

"Your astrological sign," she clarified. When he gave her a long sideways look, she let a slow grin play across her mouth. "Come on. With a sister like Allison, how could you not know?"

"Please tell me you don't put as much stock in that as she did," he groaned.

"Not really," she said. "But it's a fun question. And I'm curious. You were born in November."

"You remember that?"

"Of course I do," she murmured.

He lifted the wineglass, taking a break to study her.

She smiled. "November either makes you a Scorpio or a Sagittarius. Which is it?"

Ever the man of mystery, he chose not to answer and took a long sip instead. Then he picked up the spatula and continued to stir. "I'm not a wine drinker. But this one's fine."

"It is," she agreed. "It's a rare vintage. One I've been saving."

He raised a brow. "For me?"

Why did he think he was worthy of so little? "Yes," she said, moving closer. "And after we eat, I'm going to find out how it tastes on your tongue."

The spatula clattered to a halt and his eyes fired. The tension hardened his features, but it had nothing to do with anger this time and everything to do with what they had made the last time their bodies had come together in a fit of urgency. He remembered that clash, she saw, and its sensational conclusion every bit as much as she did.

"Is that right?" he ventured.

She saw the smile turn up the corners of his eyes even as his mouth remained in a firm, forbidding line. "How much longer?" she asked.

"Not long," he guessed. He cursed. "Too long."

She wondered if his body had responded as eagerly as hers was. Crossing one foot over the other, she tried to tamp down on it. By pressing her thighs together, she only fanned the flame. She ran her hand over the small of his back, just above the line of the towel he'd wrapped around his hips, and made herself step away. "I'm going to change."

She made it to the corner before he spoke up again. "Scorpio."

She glanced back in surprise. His head was low, intent on the work of his hands. And she grinned because she saw the pop of color in the flesh leading from his collarbone to his ear.

His body *had* responded, and she could think of nothing more than unknotting his towel and letting dinner burn.

Taking a steadying breath, she said, "Of course you are."

In her bedroom, she opened the top drawer and pulled out the black nightie she'd bought online on impulse a few nights before. Lifting it by the straps, she considered. She hadn't thought she'd have the nerve to wear it for him. She'd thrown out all her nighties after the fiasco with Quentin, deciding she wouldn't need sexy finery again.

Carrying the gown into the bathroom, she closed the door after letting Sebastian follow her inside. She discarded her towel and the wet bathing suit underneath and hopped into the shower.

When she came back out, tying the belt of a black silk robe that had lived at the back of her closet for some time, the smell of pesto hit her. She followed the seductive aroma to the dining room table, where he had already plated dinner for them.

She stared at the candle he'd found on her side table in the center of the dining set. "My goodness," she said, at a loss for anything else.

He topped off her wine. "From the moment we met, I knew you were the candlelit-dinner type."

He pulled out a chair for her. Inwardly, she sighed. The hard man in the towel, quietly and devastatingly courteous, had no idea how irresistible he was. "Thank you," she said, turning her mouth up to his for a breathy kiss.

His eyes remained closed when she pulled back. His head followed hers as she lowered her heels to the floor. "You smell good. You always smell good." When his eyes opened, they were unfocused. "I could eat you alive."

"Tortellini first," she insisted.

He dropped his gaze to the silk covering her. "Are you wearing anything under that?"

Later, she cautioned herself when, again, adrenaline and desire surged. "All good things," she whispered before she lowered to the seat, tucking the robe around her legs when it parted over her thighs.

He pulled out the chair next to hers. Lifting her glass, she drank before lowering it back to the table and picking up her knife and fork. "This looks excellent."

"It'll get you by."

"Mmm," she said after the first bite. The different flavors gelled. Together, they were perfectly delectable. "Noah. This is fantastic."

"I just threw things together in the pan."

She jabbed her fork in his direction. "Modesty doesn't suit you. I watched you make this. You'll take credit for it."

"Or?" he asked and popped a long green bean into his mouth, chewing.

She reached for the bottle of wine. "I could pour this fine vintage over your head."

"You'll taste it on the rest of me, then," he said darkly. Wonderfully.

Images hit her brain, inciting more answers from her body.

"What's it going to be, Colton?" he asked, amused, when she didn't let go of the bottle. The delicious light of challenge smoldered behind his eyes.

Jesus. Did he play with fire often? Because he was good at it. She placed the bottle back on the table. "Fortify yourself," she told him, nodding at his plate. "You're going to need it."

Shaking his head, he muttered, "A little over an hour ago, I didn't think there was anything that could make me forget what's going to happen tomorrow. But you could make me forget the world if you put your mind to it."

That had been her goal. Hadn't it? Now she could only think about wanting him in her bed again. He'd been there since that first night they'd made love. He'd slept beside her. But this time, she wanted more. To make him forget, yes. But also because…

Because she *needed* him. "Eat," she said. It was the only safe word she knew.

They cleaned their plates, and he cleared them. She polished off her wine. Before he could think about washing dishes, she took his hand. "Follow me?" she asked, grabbing the soft faux fur blanket draped over the back of the couch.

As she led him to the back door, he said, "Anywhere," before sliding the glass panel open for both of them.

She held that inside her, letting it feed her, as she led him around the chairs and pool to the path that tumbled down one flagstone at a time to the base of the natural hill her bungalow dominated.

The sound of trickling water led her. Little lights on either side of the path would be turned off soon in adherence to Dark Sky Community guidelines. The stargazing party would leave soon in the Jeeps provided by the resort, with the blankets and hot cocoa offered during cooler nights. The chill in the air was sharp.

"Is there a stream here?" he asked as the tumble of water grew louder.

"When I was a kid, it was a river," she told him. "This is all that's left." A small swath of moonlight shimmied over stones as water hurried across them. "My mother would walk here every morning. Sometimes she would bring me and the boys. But mostly this was her spot."

"Is that why you built your place at the top of the hill?"

"Yes," she said. "It was my way of feeling close to her."

His hand didn't leave hers as they stood listening to the water babble. "Do you find that fades…more and more as the years go on?" he asked quietly.

Her eyes sought his silhouette. As they adjusted to the dark, she carved him out of the night. Hooded brow, firm jaw, solid as the mountains that held the sky. "Yes," she admitted.

He nodded slightly. "So do I."

She tightened her hold on him, bringing his attention to her. As his feet shuffled to face her, she let go to reach for the belt of the robe.

He stopped her. "You'll freeze."

"It's why I brought the blanket," she said. "Will you hold it?"

He took the furry coverlet. Anticipation high, she untied the knot.

She wished she could see him better, but the moon was behind him. Knowing it bathed her, she parted the silk and let it slip from her shoulders.

She heard his breath tear out of him. Trailing her fingers over the low-cut neckline and transparent lace, she followed the cascade of silk to her navel. "What do you think?"

"I knew you'd drive me wild."

Intrigued, she planted the heel of her hand against the granite slab of his chest. "You feel okay to me."

"Laura, I—"

She bit her lip when he stopped. "Yes?" she breathed, wanting to hear exactly what he'd censored himself from saying. She waited long enough that she shivered.

"You are cold," he confirmed. He swung the blanket around her shoulders. "Let's go back to the house."

"No." With her hand still on his chest, she backed him up to the large chaise underneath a collapsed red umbrella.

He went down hard, grunting. She knelt on the thick cushion. It was cold, too.

They'd warm it, she knew.

She felt his hands close around the blanket on her shoulders. Using it, he brought her against the heat of his chest and rolled her beneath him.

She did taste the wine on his tongue. She tasted herself there, too, as she lay beneath him, shivering not from the cold anymore but the storm of worshipping open-mouthed kisses. They started somewhere around her instep and spread to the back of her knee, up the inside of her thigh, between them where he lingered, using lips, tongue and beard to push her over the edge. Then his kisses continued over her hips, navel, breasts, to the bridge of her collarbone where he found the pearl. He sipped the delicate ridge of her jaw, and at last took her mouth.

She'd brought him here to seduce him. The thick fur blanket lay heavy over their tangled forms as he joined with her. Long, deep strokes built fresh waves of sensation. The cold didn't penetrate the lovely languid haze of his loving, and she knew she was the one who had been completely, utterly seduced.

"Look at me."

Her eyes had rolled back into her head. She made her lashes lift.

His face was half shadow, half light. His hips rocked against hers in an unbroken rhythm and she found she had swallowed the fire. It burned so good, she wanted to bathe in it.

His mouth parted hers. His eyes remained fixed. "Again," he breathed into her.

She shook her head slightly even as the next climax gathered steam. His hand was between them, coaxing her at the point where their bodies met. She was trembling all over, a string about to break even as his touch made her pliant and soft for him.

His chin bobbed in a listless nod. "Do it," he bade, need bearing the words through his teeth.

She didn't have it in her to shy away. And she realized she'd thrown caution with him to the wind days ago. She burned, feeling like a phoenix as she let the firestorm take her. All of her.

He groaned, long, low, satisfied. "That's right," he whispered and added, "Stay with me," when she pooled beneath him. "Stay with me," he said again, quickening.

The base of his erection pitched against the bed of nerves at her center, and she dropped the crown of her head back, gasping at the assault of unending pleasure. He had to stop. She was going to catch fire.

No one… No one had ever brought her this close to blind rapture. No one had made her bare her soul like this before.

"Noah."

His response hummed across her lips as his brows came together.

Ardor painted his face, and she moaned. "I'm yours."

He swore. The word blew through the night as he buried himself to the hilt. His body locked, arcing like a current, and he slammed his eyes closed, suspended in the rush.

When his muscles released, he made a noise like a man drowning. She raised her hands to him, stroking as his lungs whistled through several respirations and his heart knocked like a ram against hers. Lifting her legs, she crossed her ankles at the small of his back and dragged his mouth back to hers, not ready to give up the link.

"I'm crushing you," he said when he caught his breath at last.

"No."

"Laura, baby. I'm heavy."

Baby. Her smile was as soft as the blanket. "You're perfect, Noah Steele."

He stilled in her embrace. It even seemed like he stopped breathing.

"A little while," she sighed soothingly, running her nails lightly over his upper arms. "Let's stay just like this a little while longer."

He made another noise, this one of assent.

Eventually...eventually, she agreed they had to get out of the cold. And when he wrapped her in the blanket and carried her back up the flagstone steps to her house, she was speechless.

Chapter Seventeen

Mariposa's anniversary always felt bittersweet. Twenty-two years ago, Annabeth Colton had escaped Los Angeles for Red Rock Country, where she'd purchased the hotel.

Today was cause for both celebration and reflection. As Laura went about her duties, she couldn't help but wonder whether Mariposa reflected her mother's vision two decades prior. For Annabeth, it had been both home and a place of hope and renewal.

Laura tried to focus on that and not everything she had learned from Noah the night before.

When CJ Knight and Doug DeGraw crossed her path, however, she thought even Noah would agree the mission verged on impossible.

"Ms. Colton," the actor called out, forcing her to stop on the path to S Building. "I hear there's going to be a show tonight."

"Yes," she replied. "We'll have music and canapés in the rock labyrinth from six to seven this evening, with fireworks to follow. Will you be joining us?"

"Wouldn't miss it," CJ asserted.

Laura looked at Doug. "And you, Mr. DeGraw?"

"If it's better than the excursion yesterday and today's massage." Doug rolled both shoulders back in a discomfited manner. "I wonder why Mariposa is the go-to destination for the rich and famous. I can't find much to recommend it."

As Laura's face fell, CJ cleared his throat. "Come on, Doug. You don't mean that." To Laura, he offered an apologetic smile. "I enjoyed the horseback excursion, and my massage was more than satisfactory. We're booked for lunch at Annabeth. I've told Doug your chef never disappoints."

She returned the smile. "I'm glad you think so." Uncomfortable, she looked at Doug again. "Is there anything I can do to make your stay more enjoyable, Mr. DeGraw?"

He raised a discerning brow. "You wouldn't know what bungalow Ariana Fitzgibbons is staying in, would you?"

"I'm afraid I can't divulge that information," she told him when she regained her voice. "It's against our policy to invade the privacy of our guests."

"Pity," Doug drawled. His mouth turned down at the corners, dissatisfied. "I guess I'll have to find out myself."

"I'd advise you not to do so," she cautioned.

Doug gave a small laugh. "Can't anyone around here take a joke?"

As he walked away, limping slightly on his right leg, CJ's smile deteriorated. He lowered his voice. "I'm sorry. He isn't normally like this. I've noticed he's been out of sorts lately. He practically begged me not to come back here."

She tried to appear as unaffected as possible. "Red Rock Country doesn't agree with everyone."

"I'm not sure how," CJ noted. "I get that Doug's a city guy. He's LA to the bone. But there's nothing I don't love about this part of the country."

"I'm happy to hear it," she said truthfully. "If there's anything you or your manager can think of to make your stay better, please let me know. I'll see to it."

"I appreciate it, Ms. Colton," he returned before hurrying to catch up with Doug.

Laura rubbed her hands across the surface of her arms. The chill had gone deep into her bones despite the desert sun doing its best to ward off the nip of late winter. Thunder rolled in the distance. She looked out across the ridge.

Steel wool storm clouds converged in the east, washing away everything except the foreboding that had been with her since Noah had kissed her goodbye in the wee hours of the morning. He had thought she was still asleep as he'd bent over her still form and skimmed his lips across the point of her bare shoulder before brushing the hair from her neck to repeat the motion there.

She'd wanted to turn onto her back then, ring her arms around him and roll him into the sheets with her. But she'd kept her eyes closed as he'd kissed her cheek and lingered there, his hand moving down her spine to rest warmly in the curve of her hip.

He spooked so easily when he was like that—tender and unguarded. She'd continued to feign sleep, absorbing the sweetness and tranquility.

It wasn't a simple thing, giving her heart to a man who could so easily break it. And yet, in that moment, she'd had no choice. She'd given it as she never had before. Freely.

Laura stared those storm clouds down, daring them to intrude on tonight's festivities. She wanted to follow Doug, track his movements, make sure he stayed far away from Ariana Fitzgibbons and every other woman at Mariposa.

"Come on, Noah," she whispered desperately before continuing to S Building.

The storm split and spread its quilting across the sky. Sunset burned ombré shades across, so the clouds glowed terra-cotta and apricot one moment, then orange and mauve the next. At last, the day died in a somber cast of mulberry, inspiring a round of applause from the multitude of guests who gathered at the rock labyrinth over steak and blue cheese bruschetta bites and spicy blue crab tapas.

"And that wasn't even the part we planned," Joshua said, amused, as he passed Laura a tall glass of champagne.

"No," she said. She sipped. "You cleaned up well."

"Thank you," he replied, running a hand down the front of his blue button-down. He'd popped the first few buttons on the collar, but the shirt was pressed, and he'd combed his hair back from his face, leaving his striking features to be admired by all and sundry. He glanced over at her. "Let's not pretend I'm the one turning heads tonight."

She peered down the front of the glittering, long-sleeved cocktail dress she'd donned. Its color brought to mind champagne bubbles, and its open back from the waist up made her aware of the swift decline in temperature. "A girl needs to shine now and then," she mused.

Joshua's lips curled knowingly as his champagne hovered inches from them. "If Steele were here, he'd swallow his tongue."

The thought brought out a full-fledged grin. "Perhaps that was the idea. It might've worked if he'd made it on time."

Joshua raised his wrist to peek at his watch. "He could still make it."

"I've learned not to hold my breath."

Joshua sipped, swallowed and looked at her contemplatively.

She narrowed her eyes. "What is it, Josh?"

"Is there something you want to tell me?" he asked. "About you and Fender Bender?"

"What makes you think there is?" she asked, tensing.

Joshua lowered the glass. "Because I looked him up. Noah Steele has never played for Fast Lane."

Her smile fled swiftly.

"How could he when he's been working for the Sedona police for seven years?"

Oh, no. "Josh," she began.

He stopped her with "Is he really even your boyfriend?"

She couldn't miss the light of hurt beyond the forced jocularity on his face. "No. Yes." Closing her eyes quickly, she shook her head. "I don't know. I—"

"How could you not know?" he asked, bewildered.

"I don't know how to explain," she tried to tell him, but he was on a roll.

"Is this about Allison?" he asked. "Is that why he's here? Did he manipulate you into being part of his cover?"

"He didn't *make* me do anything," she argued. "It was my idea."

"So he's not the reason you've been lying to me all this time?" he asked. "You decided that on your own?"

"I'm sorry." She grabbed his arm before he could walk away. "I couldn't tell you. He needed intimate knowledge of Mariposa's staff and guests. He needed to know the resort from the ground up, every operation, inside and outside."

"I knew he was hiding something," Joshua muttered. "I just didn't think you were in on it. We've always told each other *everything*, Laura."

"I know," she said, forcing herself to look him in the eye, however much the accusation in his wounded. "I'm so sorry."

"What's going on?" Adam asked.

Joshua pointed. "Our sister's been keeping things from us."

"About?" Adam prompted.

"Steele," Joshua said. "He's a cop."

"I know."

Joshua stared, aghast. "You know?"

"Yes," Adam said.

"So you've both been keeping things from me."

"Mariposa had to continue as usual," Adam stated, not missing a beat, "with no one the wiser except Laura and myself."

"Why not me?" Joshua asked. "You didn't think you could trust me?"

"Of course we trust you," Laura told him.

"But you have a tendency to wear your heart on your sleeve," Adam informed him. "You also party and socialize more extensively than the two of us. I'm sure you would have had every intention of keeping Steele's actual reasons for being here to yourself. But it would have been all too easy to let something slip."

Joshua's jaw worked as he digested the information. His accusing gaze sought Laura again. "He spent the night with you."

Adam shifted uncomfortably beside her. Awkwardness pressed against her. It clung like shrink-wrap. "He did," she said.

"You don't think that's taking your role a little too seriously?" Joshua questioned.

She swallowed when the taste of anger coated her mouth. "I'm not going to take that—from you or anyone else. I don't have to explain what Noah and I have to either of you."

"I'm not asking," Adam pointed out.

"Not now," she granted. "But you have questioned it."

"Because I thought you would get hurt."

"I'm in love with him," she blurted. "If we're being honest, I might as well throw it out there. I've fallen in love with him and we're all going to have to come to terms with that."

Neither of her brothers seemed to know what to say anymore. Laura was relieved by the reprieve, though she sensed this wasn't over. They would need to discuss this more at another time and place. She and Adam would need to address Joshua's hurt. He would need to know the full details of Noah's investigation. There was no going back, no hiding anything from him anymore.

"He's making an arrest soon," she told them both.

"When?" Joshua asked. "Tonight?"

"I don't know precisely," she said. "I haven't heard from him since this morning. But he's gathering evidence to secure a warrant. Soon, he'll go, and this will all be over." There was relief and dread in the finality of that. With luck, Allison's killer would be locked away for good.

But Noah would be leaving Mariposa.

"Who?" Adam asked quietly.

She searched the crowd for the person she couldn't deny she had been keeping tabs on since the party began. She located him over at the buffet table, not far from CJ. "I'm afraid I can't say. Not without Noah's authorization."

Joshua wasn't heartened by the news. "Fantastic. I can't believe I actually liked the guy. I can't believe I trusted him with you."

Laura glanced around quickly to make sure no one would overhear. Then she hissed, "Allison was his sister!"

"What?" Joshua exclaimed.

"She was his sister," she repeated. "He needed help. I gave it—for her."

Joshua stepped back. He pinched the skin at the bridge of his nose, closing his eyes. "This is a lot to process."

"Then take a beat," Adam advised. "We'll speak about this, however much you need to. But come back when you're ready to do so civilly."

Joshua dropped his hand. He glanced in Laura's direction but didn't quite meet her eye. "I've said some things tonight I'm going to regret later."

"Adam's right," Laura said. She tried swallowing the guilt and hurt. Together, they formed a knot that was anything but small. "We'll talk more when you're ready."

He lifted his empty glass. "I need another."

As he moved off, Laura dropped her face into her hand. "Oh, God, Adam. He's so angry at me."

"He's angry at us."

"I made you keep this from him," she reminded him. "You didn't have to take any of the blame."

"I may not understand all the reasons you did this," Adam explained. "But I will never not stand beside you. I thought you knew that."

His ferocity was something to behold. She wanted to tell him she loved him—that she was sorry that he had to weather Joshua's resentment and accusations, too.

Before she could put any of that into words, Erica said, "Excuse me?" In a black cocktail dress and heels, she looked elegant, but her beauty was subdued by the frown playing at her mouth.

"Yes, Erica?" Adam asked kindly.

"They're ready for your speech," she said, gesturing to the stage.

"Right." Adam downed the last of his champagne. He took the note cards Erica had at the ready, then straightened his collar and tie. "Wish me luck?"

"You always bring down the house," Laura murmured. "But good luck."

He gave her a single nod before taking the steps to the bandstand two at a time.

"I was wondering if I could speak to you," Erica said to Laura. Embarrassment and hesitancy battled for purchase on her face.

"Certainly," Laura told her, trying to inject some measure of cheer into her voice. It didn't work as well as she'd hoped.

"I heard a rumor," Erica said. "About the investigation."

"What kind of rumor?" Laura asked.

Erica coaxed the words out, paling as she did so. "They say that CJ Knight is a suspect."

Laura pressed her lips together, wondering what exactly to say. "He may be," she said, hesitant.

Erica shook her head. "That isn't right. I mean, you see, I..." Releasing a breath, she lifted a trembling hand to her head. "He has an alibi."

"He does?" Laura asked, surprised.

"Yes," she decided. "I lied to you and to Joshua. I'm not entirely sure what came over me that night. The night Allison was killed."

"You were with him," Laura intoned.

"I was with him," Erica agreed with a nod. "CJ and I...were intimate. It happened in his bungalow. So he couldn't have done it. He couldn't have killed Allison. And he wouldn't have. He may be the one-night-stand kind of guy. But he's not the type of man who would murder someone."

Laura set her champagne aside. She placed her hand considerately on Erica's arm. "You need to tell the police. You'll have to in order to clear Mr. Knight of all suspicion."

Erica absorbed this news. Her eyes widened, but she nodded slightly. "Of course."

Laura squeezed her arm gently. "It's a good thing you're doing, Erica."

"Do you think Adam will fire me?" she whispered faintly.

"It hasn't interfered with your ability to do your job," Laura noted. "I think we can all vouch for that. I'll speak with Adam, and we'll see about moving forward from this once the investigation's over."

Erica nodded. "Thank you, Laura—for being so understanding."

Laura simply nodded. As Erica slipped away, Laura looked around. She found Joshua near the bar, talking to Valerie. Adam was at center stage, cuing the band for his speech. Alexis and Tallulah stood shoulder to shoulder as they chatted with Greg and Tallulah's nephew, Mato, who held a tray of canapés on an upraised palm.

She spied CJ Knight at last as he spoke with Knox and Kim Blankenship.

If CJ had been occupied with Erica at the time of Allison's death, Noah was right. Guilt now lay squarely at the feet of...

"Ms. Colton."

The chill started at the base of her neck. It trickled down her spine as she pivoted on her heels to confront Doug DeGraw. He wore a suit in charcoal gray with a black shirt underneath. He'd gone without a tie, and the shirt was buttoned to his throat. His Adam's apple jutted over its neat collar and his cool smile turned her blood to ice.

"Mr. DeGraw," she greeted him. "I see you decided to join us. How was your lunch at Annabeth?"

"Superb."

She forced a smile. "Mr. Knight is correct. Our chef rarely disappoints."

"The food was all right," he said with a wave of his hand. "It was the company that was divine."

Her brows came together. "The company?"

"I slipped the maître d' a fifty. He seated CJ and me next to Ms. Fitzgibbons's table."

The smugness of his grin...the light that entered his eyes... They made Laura take a steadying breath. "Is that so?"

"Yes." He took a step toward her while Adam spoke into the mic on stage and those around them quieted. "You needn't worry. Ariana knows she will benefit from the attention of a man like me. And she's more than willing to take it."

Her lips numbed, and she realized she was pressing them hard together. "What did you do to her?"

"Do?" He chuckled. "Nothing she didn't ask for. In her own way." With a wink, he slithered off to stand with CJ and the others.

Laura's heart drummed. She barely resisted the urge to place her hand over her mouth as she searched the crowd desperately for the red hair of Ariana Fitzgibbons.

When she couldn't find her, she walked briskly to Roland. When he leaned down to hear what she wanted to say, she kept her voice low. "Doug DeGraw. Do you know who he is?"

"CJ Knight's manager," he said.

She nodded. "Can you keep an eye on him for me?"

"Yes."

"If you see him leave the party, I'm going to need you to call me on my cell phone," she explained. "Immediately. Can you do that?"

"Of course I can." His wide forehead creased. "Should I be concerned about anyone's safety?"

"Not at this time," she said, again looking around, wishing Ariana's face would pop out of the crowd. "The moment De-Graw exits the rock labyrinth…"

"I'll place the call," he finished. "You have my word."

"Thank you," she murmured, then walked away as Adam's speech wrapped to the roused clatter of applause.

"Ms. Fitzgibbons?" Laura called. She knocked again on the door of Ariana's bungalow, louder this time. "Ms. Fitzgibbons!"

No answer came. The windows remained dark. Laura cupped her hands around her face to peer through the nearest one.

A shaft of moonlight revealed an empty couch and table.

If Ariana had returned to the bungalow before sunset, she would have left a light burning before she'd departed again.

Trying not to panic, Laura sprinted along the path to the VIP bungalows.

When she reached Bungalow Two, where she knew Doug was staying on CJ's dime, she slowed.

Noah had made her promise not to approach a suspect. That promise made her hesitate on the doorstep.

She wasn't approaching a suspect, she reasoned. Doug was back at the rock labyrinth, where she knew Roland would watch him.

Raising her fist, she knocked on the door. When she heard nothing inside, she pressed her ear to the door, willing her pulse to stop knocking so that she may better hear a call for help.

When none came, she peered through the window. The blackout curtains had been drawn.

Frustrated, she tore open her beaded handbag and extracted her master key. If Ariana was in there and she wasn't answering, Laura could only assume she had been drugged, like Allison. That maybe she, too, had been given too much and was...

She swiped the master key. The lock chirped and a green light blinked. Laura pushed the door open and stepped inside.

She switched on the light beside the door.

There was no sign of a struggle. As she shut the door behind her, she peered at the couch. The cushions weren't mussed. A pair of men's shoes sat tidily near the door to the patio. There was a glass of wine, unfinished, on the kitchen counter.

Laura stared at the last sips of dark red wine. She saw the faint impression of lips on the rim. No lipstick.

Through the glass door, the pool sat undisturbed. Folded towels lay in the corner on a raised surface, compliments of Housekeeping. Laura counted one, two, three. None of them had been used.

She twitched the curtain back in place. There was no sign of a woman here. No sign that anything nefarious had taken place.

She eyed the short passage to the bedroom and clutched her handbag tighter.

If she could find proof...if she could help Noah nail Doug DeGraw...this would all be over. Allison's killer would be caught.

Laura stepped toward the bedroom door. It was open. She turned on the overhead light, illuminating the white linens on the bed.

She scanned the space, wondering where to start. Doug's toiletry bag lay on the dresser. His suitcase was open on the rack near the bathroom.

She searched all the outside pockets first, then lay a hand flat between folded shirts. After running her hand around the inside rim to no avail, she checked the toiletry bag. Careful not to disorganize the high-end men's products she found inside, she shifted them one by one. Nothing hid underneath them except a sample sleeve of under-eye cream.

She stepped back, making sure everything looked exactly as it had before she'd begun her search. Frowning, she turned a slow circle.

Where else would a guilty man hide evidence of wrongdoing?

She opened the drawer on the nightstand. Nothing there—not a single dust mote.

The corner of the sheet stuck out kitty-corner underneath the coverlet. It had slipped from its holding under the mattress.

...under the mattress...

Hadn't Fulton found Dayton Ferraday's drug stash under the mattress or inside it?

She went down on her knees. Like she had with the shirts, she reached underneath the mattress and felt around.

Her hand met something cold. It rolled, then tinkled against something else. She grabbed the thin item and pulled it out into the light.

The vial was translucent, but she could see the liquid within. On the side, there was a label.

Fentanyl.

Holding her breath, she reached underneath the mattress and found the other vial and a ten-milliliter syringe, empty and capped. It looked like the kind used for insulin.

She placed them on top of the bed and dug into her bag. Remembering to breathe, she pulled out her cell phone and stood. When she unlocked the screen to place the call to Noah, she paused.

She'd missed a call—from Roland.

She checked the time stamp. He'd tried calling ten minutes ago.

It hasn't rung, she thought.

She checked her notification settings and her heart dropped.

After exiting the party, she'd forgotten to take her phone off Silent.

Don't panic, she coached herself. She'd simply take a picture of the evidence, then replace it and slip safely out of Doug's bungalow.

Quickly, she framed the vials and syringe in her camera view. She tapped the screen when it tried focusing on the fibers of the comforter underneath and ignored the sound of her heartbeat in her ears.

She snapped a couple of pictures, then stuffed her phone back in her bag. Replacing the vials, she left the covers on the bed as they should be. Then she stood and took two steps to the door before an item on the floor made her stop.

It lay innocently enough underneath the hook where Doug had hung his overcoat. A leather string with an evil-eye pendant.

Laura bent down to retrieve it. She raised it to get a better look and her lips trembled.

It must've fallen from the pocket of his coat without his knowing.

A sob rose as she studied the evil eye. Unlike the one she had given Noah, Allison's was light green. She'd once told Laura it granted her success in dreams, good health and contentment.

Laura felt a whisper of air across the bare skin of her back and the hairs on her arms and neck stood on end.

Before she could turn, he took her down at the waist.

She met the wall with a clatter, knocking the lamp over on the bedside table. The impact knocked the wind out of her.

Fingers raked through her hair and drove her face into the wall.

A dull gray film slanted across her vision. Her ears rang. She blinked, trying to bring everything back into focus as he spun her roughly around.

It took several seconds for Doug's face to solidify in front of her.

"Ms. Colton," he said with a sneer.

She saw his fist raised to strike. Before he could swing, she took up the fallen lamp on the bedside table. The lampshade fell. She arced the neck of the lamp toward his face and threw her weight into it.

It hit him. The bulb shattered and he toppled sideways on a shout.

She made a break for it, fumbling for the door.

She slipped in the hall. Her heel came off. She left it, scrambling to her feet as his footsteps chased her.

She ran out of Bungalow Two, screaming.

Chapter Eighteen

Fireworks crackled and thundered. Their lights sparkled across the path to L Building, illuminating her escape route in intermittent bursts.

She melded into the manicured hedges and cacti that lined the path, willing the rocks under her feet not to give her away. She'd lost her other heel. The sharp edges of stones bit into the undersides of her feet. She didn't slow. With her knowledge of Mariposa, she could locate help before he found her.

There was blood in her mouth. She'd bitten her tongue when he'd mashed her face into the wall. She swallowed it and kept going. Something dripped across her lips. She licked them and tasted blood there, too. Reaching up, she swiped the space above them. It came away wet and warm.

Her nose was bleeding. The pulse of pain around the bridge alerted her to the damage there.

Her fist was still knotted around Allison's bracelet. She hadn't lost it in the altercation.

She wouldn't lose it, she determined as she pushed on. The roof of L Building was visible through the foliage. She could see the lights of the pool. Her heart lifted. She was almost there. Someone would be there. Someone had to be.

First, she had to cross the open pathway. She glanced around. Hearing no footsteps, she made a break for it.

A cut on the bottom of her foot slowed her, but she half sprinted for the shape of the first pool cabana—the one where they'd found Allison.

Before she could reach it, fingers dug into her arm. She fought them, reaching for escape.

Doug shoved her off the path into the rocks on the other side. Her hands and knees scraped across them.

He covered her mouth before she could scream. "You couldn't leave it alone, could you? Couldn't live and let live?"

His hand covered her nose. She fought for air, her nails digging into his hand. Desperate, she threw her head back into his face.

He grunted. His hold loosened.

She turned over, scrambling away from him. Her back met the long stalk of a cactus plant. Its fine needles dug into the exposed skin of her back.

Doug was on her in a flash. She did scream now—before he could silence her.

He struck her across the face. The shock of the blow silenced her, as did the fingers he wrapped around her throat. The pressure he exerted made little rockets of flame blossom before her eyes. Her ankles kicked against the rocks. The stones scattered, preventing her from gaining purchase. Again, she clawed at his hand. The bracelet dropped.

He glanced down at it, then back up at her. "I don't like killing," he groaned as he watched her struggle. He shook his head to emphasize the point. "I never meant to kill anyone. If she'd been willing…if she'd just spread her legs for me… I wouldn't have had to subdue her. I wouldn't have given her too much."

Her lungs burned. Her eyes went blind.

"It was such a waste," he muttered. "Wasn't it? I hate thinking about it. Just as I'm going to hate thinking about you, Ms. Colton. Such a beautiful waste."

She fought to stay conscious. She fought to see something other than the whiteout she found when her eyes rolled back. Still, her kicking slowed and she hooked her hands over his arm because they'd fallen away from his fingers. The ocean roared in her ears. It was so loud, it drowned his words.

His grip fumbled away from her. His weight lifted. She gasped, choked, wheezed and coughed. As she fell sideways across the rocks, she reached for her neck, where the phantom hold of Doug's fingers stayed even as she took a breath that raked across her airways.

In the light from the path and the stunning bright lights screaming into the sky—the fireworks' grand finale—she saw two figures, one on top of the other, struggling on the ground.

Her hearing sharpened with the whistle and boom of rockets overhead and shouting. The haze around her vision broke and she realized what she was seeing.

Noah, his face a mask of fury, arced his fist down to meet Doug's face again and again.

Someone else—Detective Fulton—raced forward to pull Noah off. Noah fought him. Fulton didn't let go.

Doug stayed on the ground, curling in on himself. His face was a mess of blood. He didn't get up.

Noah shrugged Fulton off him. Rocks slid underneath his feet as he scrambled over them. He crouched, his hand going to the back of her head. "Laura."

She was afraid to speak. Her throat felt bruised. Sucking air in and out in careful repetitions, she watched his features sharpen.

There was fury there. But more, there was desperate fear. "Hey," he said. "Can you hear me?"

She gave a faint nod.

He blew out a breath, then cradled her to him. She closed her eyes because the cold had gone deep into her bones. She didn't know if it was the temperature or nearly being choked to death, but she lay still, absorbing the heat of him as he held her.

He pulled away. His gaze seized on her throat. "I need to get you to the hospital," he said gruffly.

She opened her mouth, but the words got trapped behind the pain. Looking around over the rocks, she fumbled a hand over them, searching.

She found the little braided cord and lifted it.

When she offered it, he took it from her and raised it to the light. At the sight of the evil eye, he stilled. "Where did you find this?" he asked.

Afraid, she locked her lips together.

He searched her face. Then he shook his head. "You didn't."

She lifted her chin in a half nod. A tear slipped past her guard. She wished she could look away. Then she wouldn't have to watch his disbelief meld into disappointment.

"Laura," he said. "You promised. You *promised* me."

His voice broke and her stomach twisted. *I had to*, she wanted to tell him.

His grimace was complete. It went through her. As he looked away, closing his hand around the evil eye, she felt it as keenly as a knife.

Noah spent an hour at the police station, watching Doug De-Graw be questioned, booked and processed. Even if he couldn't be the one leading him through it, he needed to watch, just as he needed to hear the bars roll into place as the man who admitted to killing Allison was locked in a cell.

An accident, he'd claimed. Allison had shown up at his bungalow after dark for his private yoga lesson. When she didn't respond to his attempts at seduction, he dosed her with fentanyl and waited for the drug to take effect before having his way with her.

"After, she didn't come around like the others do," Doug had claimed. "She just lay there. She didn't breathe. I checked and realized her pulse wasn't right. It was too slow. I tried to make her come around. She just lay there. Lay there and died."

"You handled yourself well," Captain Crabtree told Noah after they both watched Doug sign a confession.

"He's beat to hell," Noah pointed out, surveying the damage he'd done to Doug's face.

"You saved Laura Colton's life."

And nearly killed the man who'd almost taken it. If not for Fulton, Noah knew he would have done worse. Each of the knuckles of his right hand ached like a sore tooth from the impact with Doug's nose, jaw and cheekbone. "I've still got a job on Monday?"

"You closed the case," Crabtree noted.

Noah had spent the entire day on the phone, tracking victims in the wind. He'd finally found one—a twenty-three-year-old colleague of Doug's who had quit her job a year ago and moved to Tallahassee to live with her folks. She'd been reluctant to talk, and Noah had thought he would have to fly to Florida to speak with her face-to-face. But then she'd broken, and the story had come out. Doug had drugged and raped her, too, similarly.

There were others, Noah knew. A half-dozen women Doug had sedated and terrorized. Noah would find them all. He would bury the man for hurting them, for killing Allison and for nearly killing Laura.

"He tried to frame CJ Knight," Noah said. "He assumed calling him away from Mariposa soon after Allison's death would throw suspicion on him. It might have worked, too, had Erica Pike not come forward."

"Knight was here while you were in interrogation. He confirmed he was with Ms. Pike during the time in question, but not much more."

"What did he have to say about his manager being the killer?" Noah asked.

"He was in shock. He didn't seem to know what to say."

"I should've seen it sooner," Noah muttered. "It was Doug's office who refused to return my calls, not Knight directly."

"You were pretty deep in the reeds on this one," Crabtree said knowingly. "But Fulton didn't see it any faster than you did. I'd like to give you both credit for the arrest."

"All that matters is that this scumbag is going away forever."

"Now you can focus on laying your sister to rest. And you'll take some time off."

Noah closed his eyes. He needed to let Allison go. He knew that. And Crabtree was right. It was time. "Yes, sir."

The hospital was five minutes from the SPD. Despite the cold and the sleet that fell sideways, he walked there.

"Laura Colton," he said to the woman at the information desk.

"It's after visiting hours."

He dug into his pocket before placing his badge on the desk for her to see.

She frowned. "One moment," she said before tapping the screen in front of her. "Ms. Colton is in recovery. Room twenty-four."

"Thanks," he said before exiting the atrium and following the corridors to the Recovery ward. She wasn't in surgery, he consoled himself. Or the ER. Which meant she was going to be okay.

He'd heard her scream. As he'd followed Fulton across the pool area on the way to Bungalow Two, he'd heard her call for help. At first, he'd thought it had been coming from the pool cabana.

Like Allison, he'd thought, frantic. Then he'd discovered the couple grappling in the dark off the path behind it. He'd seen Doug on top of Laura, his hands around her throat, and he'd nearly screamed himself hoarse.

Noah passed the door to number twenty-four. He halted and backtracked, the soles of his boots squeaking on the clean linoleum.

Through the window, he could see her brothers, one on either side of her. Joshua was hunkered down beside her in bed. Her head nestled on his shoulder while Adam sat on the bed's edge, his arm across the top of her pillows, head low over hers.

Noah thought about walking away, leaving them alone. They were family. A proper one. And a proper family took care of their own.

He watched as his hand rose to knock.

Adam lifted his head as the others stirred. He motioned for them to stay where they were as he stood and crossed to the door. When it opened, he looked at Noah. More, he looked through him before blinking and seeming to come to his senses. "Oh," he said. "It's you."

"Can I come in?" Noah asked.

Adam ran a hand through his hair. It wasn't as neat as it usually was. "Are you here on police business?"

He should have said yes. What came out was "No."

Adam nodded and stepped aside.

Joshua sat up as Noah entered. Noah looked past him to Laura. She had raised herself up on her elbows. He could see the cut on her mouth, the red mark around the bridge of her nose, the fading bruise on her temple, and the shadows of hands on her throat that would soon fly their colors, too. She looked weary around the eyes, but clarity rang true in them.

Joshua rose and moved into Noah's path to the bed. When Noah only sized him up, Joshua offered him a hand.

"What's this?" Noah asked cautiously.

"I'd like to shake hands with Allison's brother," Joshua said.

The others must have told baby brother everything, Noah realized. He reached out and took Joshua's hand.

The man squeezed his. "If you hadn't gotten to her in time..."

Noah had thought along the same lines. If he and Fulton had been a minute behind... If he'd spent any longer on the phone tracking Doug's victims...

"You lost your sister," Joshua said, "and saved mine. I won't forget that."

"Nor will I," Adam added. "We owe you an immense debt of gratitude."

He didn't want their gratitude. He didn't want Joshua's idea of a truce. He'd spent the better part of the evening chiding himself for working after hours. If he'd been with Laura at the party, she wouldn't have felt compelled to run off into the night and...

He saw Doug's hands around her throat again. He heard her choking. His hands balled into fists and he felt the quaver go straight through as fear lanced him.

"May I speak with her?" he asked. "Alone."

"She's tired," Joshua began.

"It's all right, Josh," came the small, hoarse sound of her voice.

Joshua reached up to scrub his temples. Then he turned and went back to the bed. "A few minutes," he allowed, leaning down for a hug. "Then we all need to get some sleep."

"You don't have to sleep here," she told him. "Either of you."

"You don't have to talk," Adam replied as he, too, came forward. Joshua stepped back and Adam lowered a kiss to the top of her head. "Rest your throat. We'll be right outside the door."

"Definitely not listening," Joshua said with a half-hearted, ironic twist of his mouth.

Noah waited until they'd both left. When the latch clicked shut behind them, he approached the bed. Then he halted, conflicted. "I have a couple of questions."

She sat up a bit more. Wincing, she lay back on the pillows. It nearly broke him to see her struggle.

She spoke haltingly, fighting the rawness of her throat. "You *are* here on police business."

"Your brother's right," he said. "Don't try to talk."

She tilted her head. "Questions require answers."

"Just nod," he told her. "Or shake your head. That's all the answer I need."

She sighed and, slowly, subsided into a nod.

"Ariana Fitzgibbons has been located. It seems Doug was just yanking your chain when he claimed he'd done something to her. She left Mariposa for Sedona after lunch with a friend she made during yesterday's trail ride. They spent the afternoon shopping and caught dinner after."

Laura's lips folded as she spun the hospital band on her wrist. She tried clearing her throat and closed her eyes. When she opened them again, there was a pained, wet sheen over them. "I'm glad she's all right."

It was a miracle Laura was, he thought. Digging in his pocket, he pulled out Allison's bracelet and held it up. She watched it swing from his hand.

"Did you find this in Doug DeGraw's bungalow?"

She hesitated. Then she inclined her head.

"You went to his bungalow?" When she nodded, he wanted to stop. He didn't want to know—didn't want to have to replay it in his head repeatedly. "Did you go there alone?"

Laura's eyes were heavy-lidded with fatigue and swimming in regret as she nodded again.

"Did you find anything else in Doug's bungalow?" At her nod, he said, "Drugs?" She nodded once more. He wanted to raise his voice as the storm inside him built. Desperate, scared, angry storm clouds he couldn't lasso. He had to work to keep his next question cool and flat. "Do you remember last night?"

Tears came into her eyes again. For the first time, she turned them away from him.

He gripped the bottom rail of the bed. "I need your answer."

She nodded.

"You remember promising me you wouldn't put yourself at risk?" he asked. "You remember looking me in the eye and giving me your word before you took me home with you and made love with me for the rest of the night?"

Lips taut together, she nodded. A tear slipped down her cheek.

His heart twisted. And it hurt. It hurt so much, he couldn't breathe. "I trusted you," he said in a whisper.

"I'm sorry," she whispered back. "I thought... I thought he hurt her. Like Allison."

He wanted to go to her. He wanted to slip inside the bed with her and hold her all night—until the storm quieted. Until he could breathe right again.

The early bruising on her throat glared at him. She'd made a promise. He'd needed her to keep it. He'd relied on her word. She'd broken it and nearly died before he could get to her.

He turned away.

"Where are you going?" she asked as he made a break for the door.

He wrapped his hand around the handle. Christ, he couldn't breathe. It was exactly as it had been in the autopsy room when he'd viewed Allison's lifeless body for the first time. He felt a part of his mind detach, float away. He wanted to follow it. But his body anchored him. His lungs strained, his chest felt tight and his head spun. Panic sank in. "I need some time."

"I'm okay."

He looked back and felt the quaver go to his knees. He heard the pounding of his heart in his ears. "You're not," he argued. "I can still see him choking you and hear you fighting for air. And I can't do this. Not until that gets quieter. I need time."

"How much time?" she asked.

"I don't know," he replied. He looked away from the tears falling freely down her face now. He had to get out of there before he split in two. "I don't know," he said again, at a loss. He snatched the door open.

"Noah," she called.

"Get some rest," he replied. Then he was out the door. He bypassed Adam and Joshua and their questions, needing to walk until he could no longer feel fear locking up the muscles around his lungs.

Chapter Nineteen

Laura had never seen so many orchids in her life. Most were rooted in pretty pots. The colors ranged from warm to cool. Some clashed, like the one with blue petals and pink centers.

Allison would have loved the symbolism. Laura tried to remember what each color meant. Red for strength. Purple for dignity. Orange for boldness. Yellow for friendship and new beginnings. Being surrounded by them would have made her friend happy.

Laura held that certainty in her chest as the memorial service came to a close. The setting of nature's cathedral—cloudless, open blue sky above, the carpet of earth beneath—brought to mind Allison's teachings of mindfulness and inner strength. *Sky above us. Earth below us. Fire within us.*

Allison's fire had been extinguished. And those who loved her, who came to pay their respects, had to learn to live without her—to move on. It was as simple and as hard as that.

Laura waited in line with her brothers to lay a rose on Allison's coffin. Over a hundred people had come to pay their respects from Sedona, Mariposa and across the country—yoga and meditation students, her friends and, of course, her brother, who had sat alone in the first row.

Alexis met Laura on the green. "It was nice, wasn't it?"

"Yes," Laura said. "Funerals are never easy, but this one made the last few weeks better somehow."

"It reminds me she's at peace," Alexis explained.

"She is," Laura murmured.

Alexis searched the crowd. "If you're looking for a tall, dark and handsome detective, he's doing well to avoid people over there."

She saw Noah's lone figure and her heart gave a squeeze.

"You know you could have let me in on your secret," Alexis told her.

Alexis wasn't accusing or unhappy with her. Still, the guilt came for Laura. "I know. I never thought for a second you would give me or Noah away. And I wasn't thinking clearly enough to realize how the lies would hurt others." She found Joshua mingling, grave-faced, with some former Mariposa guests. "I regret that now."

"Tell me one thing," Alexis said. "That conversation we had at Annabeth—next to those poor shrimp?"

Laura thought about it, then closed her eyes. "Oh. The shrimp."

"You talked about you and Noah spending the night together. Was that part of the act?"

Laura shook her head silently.

"So the two of you really…" Alexis trailed off when Laura nodded. "But he's over there. And you're over here."

"Precisely," Laura said with a weary sigh.

"What happened?" Alexis asked.

Laura felt relieved she was free to tell Alexis everything. Still, she found it hard to explain what had gone wrong the night Doug was arrested. "I broke a promise to him."

"What kind of promise?"

Laura shifted her feet. Her heels poked through the bed of grass, making her reposition them for balance. "He lost Allison in the worst way possible. And before that, he lost his mother similarly. He doesn't get close to people because he's afraid of losing them."

Alexis's eyes strayed to the marks on Laura's neck that were visible above her knotted black scarf. "He almost lost you, like he lost them."

"I promised him the night before I wouldn't confront Doug like I did Roger and Dayton Ferraday," Laura admitted.

"Why did you?" Alexis asked.

"I thought he was going to hurt someone else or already had. It was the same way when Tallulah told me that Bella had been hurt. I didn't think."

"You went into mama-bear mode." Alexis nodded. "I get it."

"Those men brought terror, rape and murder into my home," Laura said. "They brought it into a place where those things were never meant to exist."

"Have you told the man this?" Alexis asked.

"We haven't spoken since the hospital. He said he needed time."

"Allison would take this moment to remind us that time is fleeting," Alexis said, "and there's no time like the present."

"She would," Laura admitted.

"Is that Bella?" Alexis pointed her out in the crowd.

Laura shaded her eyes with her hand and waved when she spotted the young woman standing close at Tallulah's side. "Yes."

"Is it true she's coming back to Mariposa?" Alexis asked.

"Not yet," Laura said. "She still needs to heal. But I think she will, eventually. Tallulah won't be happy unless she has her under her wing. And I think Bella's learning how strong she really is."

"We'll all take care of her," Alexis asserted. "Not just Tallulah."

Laura couldn't agree more. "Are we still on for Taco Tuesday?"

"Absolutely," Alexis confirmed. "The Tipsy Tacos' owner called to say they're planting a tree in Allison's name in the courtyard where they're opening up the space for outdoor dining."

"I love that," Laura declared.

Adam and Joshua walked to them. "We're going to pay our respects to Noah," Joshua told Laura. "Want to come?"

She took Adam's arm when he offered it. "Of course." To Alexis, she said, "We'll talk later."

"You know it," Alexis returned.

As the three Coltons ventured closer to the tree line, Laura watched Noah. She knew the moment he spotted them. He didn't so much stiffen as still—like a deer in the headlights. Laura felt her stomach flutter with nerves.

Sensing her agitation, Adam whispered, "Steady on, Lou," and curled his hand around hers.

She fought the inclination to lean on his solid form, especially as the distance to Noah shrank to inches and, suddenly, they were face-to-face.

"It was a beautiful service," Joshua told him.

"You did well," Adam pointed out.

Noah looked past them to where the coffin stood. "Thanks," he replied. Sliding his hands into the pockets of his black suit jacket, he shrugged. "I'm not sure what I'm going to do with all the orchids."

"You could take some home and donate the others to the hospital or nursing homes," Joshua suggested. He glanced at Laura and Adam in question. "Didn't we do that when Mom…?"

"That's right." Laura smiled at him softly. "We did."

Noah cleared his throat. "You guys reached out to help, and I refused it. I just want you to know I appreciate the offer."

"We're going to miss her," Joshua said. "Allison was the kind of light the world needs."

Noah lowered his head and nodded. "She was."

Laura could hardly stand to watch his shoulders rise and fall over a series of hard breaths.

"We're dedicating the plaque to her in the meditation garden tomorrow evening at six," Adam said quietly. "You should come. The plan is to light a paper lantern and let it fly. Laura and Alexis will light it. We'd like you to be the one who releases it."

Noah kept his head down. He bobbed it in a solitary nod. "I can do that."

Joshua reached out. He grabbed Noah's shoulder. "You need anything, Detective, call me. Penny's available whenever you need a long country drive. I can accompany you as a guide... or as a friend."

Noah looked at him with the light of surprise. "Thank you."

Adam reached out to shake his hand. "I'm holding on to Allison's fund. I don't care if it's now or thirty years from now. If you think of something you'd like to do in her name, all you need to do is let me know."

"I'll remember," Noah pledged.

Adam looked at Laura. "You need a minute?"

She nodded. "Please."

"We'll wait by the car," Joshua told her before he and Adam strolled off.

Noah ran his eyes over her. He pulled a long breath in through the nose, his chest inflating. "You look stunning," he said on the exhalation.

She lifted a hand to the neck of her dress. "That's sweet of you."

He glanced around at the lingering mourners, unsure what to say or do.

Laura reached out, then stopped. "Are you all right?" she asked.

"No."

He didn't dress it up or deflect. That was something.

"What can I do?" she asked. He hadn't accepted help with the service. He would hardly lean on her now, she knew. Still, she had to ask.

"You're here," he replied simply.

"Of course I am," she murmured.

"Let me look at you a minute," he requested after some thought. "Would that be okay?"

She nodded. "More than okay."

He took a step back. His eyes didn't dapple over her. They reached. The yearning in them, the necessity, made her heart stutter. They started at her feet before winding up the path of her skirt to her waist, her navel, her bodice, before landing on the bruising that hadn't yet faded from her neck. He blinked several times, lingering there, before circling her face.

She saw so many things in him, and they matched what was

inside her—regret, need, longing, hesitation... There was so much she wanted to say to him. *I miss you. I love you.*
Please, lean on me. Just...lean.

Her breath rushed out. "Noah."

He muttered a curse. "Part of me wants to chase these people off so I can have a single moment alone with you."

A match touched the dry tinder inside her. Hope flared as the fire caught.

"What would you do with that moment?"

His tungsten-green eyes spanned her face. They landed on her mouth as he answered quietly. "Beg."

Her breath caught. "No."

"Yes," he argued. "I told you I needed time. But I should've called. I should've checked on you."

She smiled knowingly. "Adam told me you called him to check on me. Every day."

"I should've grown a pair and called you," he grumbled.

"Why didn't you?" she asked. The distance had convinced her he didn't want this—whatever they'd made between them. And it had hurt—more than the bruises on her throat.

"Because I'm a goddamn coward," he said plainly. He paused, considering. Then he closed the distance to her. "You still want to know my secrets, Laura?"

She could smell the light touch of cologne he'd put on his skin. The flame popped, lighting little fires everywhere else inside her to catch and grow, too. "Yes," she breathed.

"I'm hands down, one hundred percent, head over heels in love with you," he said.

She closed her eyes. "You don't have to—"

"I do," he asserted. "I didn't call. Not because I couldn't move past what happened the night of the arrest. I didn't call because I've been grappling with the fact that you are the only woman in this world that I want. You're the only person I want next to me. And I don't deserve you, because what kind of man walks away from Laura Colton? What kind of man runs from the chance to be yours?"

"It's okay—"

"No, it's not."

"But it is," she said, bringing her hands up to his lapels. She traced them with her palms, caressing him as his lungs rose and fell under them. "We're both here now. You're saying these things. And you won't walk out again. Will you?"

He gripped her wrist. He didn't pull her away. Instead, he touched his brow to hers. "No." He ground out the word. "I won't walk out again."

They stood together as a strong breeze swept across the cemetery, lifting flowers and hats into the air. Laura felt the skirt of her maxidress flapping around them like wings, but she didn't move.

As the wind died down in increments, she said, "Tell me another secret."

He made a noise. After a moment, he answered. "I used to braid her hair when she was too little to do it herself."

She smiled at the image. "Softy."

"Yeah," he admitted. "She was the only person who knew that side of me—until you."

"Say more things," she requested.

He thought about it for a second. Then he lifted his wrist, pulling back the cuff of his jacket sleeve. Here, she'd noticed he carried a solitary feather on the inside of his arm. "This was my first tattoo. It's my favorite."

"You *do* have a favorite," she mused, touching it.

He nodded, his head low over hers as she traced the feather's shaft. She heard his slow inhalation and knew he was smelling her hair. "It's for my mother."

"Oh, Noah," she sighed.

"Every Christmas, I drive up to Washington and retrace my steps with her there. I go to the coast and hole up in a cabin we used to rent in the summer. I don't have anything of hers. We didn't have much. And everything that was hers got lost after she was killed. I only have memories. Every year, I'm afraid I lose more. I go to the cabin to remember, because if I don't, did she really even exist?"

"Yes," Laura assured him. "You're proof of that. Not just because you're here. Because you are the man you are—the kind that would take care of a little girl who had no one. The kind who puts bad guys behind bars and who does your sister and your mother proud every day."

He turned his lips to her cheek and kissed her softly. Lingering.

"I want this," she told him, her hands grabbing his lapels. "I want you. And if you try to tell me again that someone like you doesn't deserve me, I've got some ideas how my brothers can alter that line of thinking."

"Coyotes?"

"There's a gorge, too," she added. "What do you say, Detective?"

He scanned her, and his eyes were so tender they made all those little fires inside her hum. "I'm going to keep calling you Pearl," he warned.

"I'm used to it."

He nudged the pearl drop on the end of the gold necklace she hadn't taken off since he'd put it there. "My pearl."

When he said it like that, she shuddered and understood. "Do you want me? Do you want this?"

"Yes," he said, finite. "I want you. *All* of you."

She brought her hands up to his face. "Then you should know," she said, "I'm hands down..." She canted her head at an angle. "One hundred percent..." She skimmed a kiss across his mouth. "Head over heels in love with you, too."

His hands caught in the belt of her dress. "Come home with me," he said, whispering the words across her mouth.

"What about Sebastian?"

"Bring him."

"You don't like pets."

"I said I've never had one."

"You do now. I'm going to need my own drawer."

"Baby, you can take the whole damn closet. I'll have a key made for you. Just stay with me. Please."

She heard the plea and melted. "We both know my answer."

"I need to hear it," he told her. "Say yes."

"Yes," she told him. "I'm coming home with you, Noah. And I'm staying."

When he kissed her, his intensity brought her up to her toes.

Incapable of letting go, she wrapped him in her arms as his banded around her waist.

Laura knew he would be the fire her heart would warm itself by for a long time to come.

* * * * *

Don't miss the stories in this mini series!

THE COLTONS OF ARIZONA

Colton's Last Resort
AMBER LEIGH WILLIAMS
December 2024

Colton's Deadly Trap
PATRICIA SARGEANT
January 2025

Colton At Risk
KACY CROSS
February 2025

MILLS & BOON

Don't miss the stories in this mini series!

THE COLTONS OF ARIZONA

MILLS & BOON

Arctic Pursuit
Anna J. Stewart

MILLS & BOON

Bestselling author **Anna J. Stewart** honestly believes she was born with a book in her hand. After growing up devouring every story she could get her hands on, now she gets to make her living making up stories and fulfilling happily-ever-afters of her own. Her dreams have most definitely come true. Anna lives in Northern California (only a ninety-minute flight from Disneyland, her favorite place on earth) with two monstrous, devious, adorable cats named Sherlock and Rosie.

Books by Anna J. Stewart

Harlequin Romantic Suspense

The McKenna Code

Arctic Pursuit

The Coltons of Owl Creek

Hunting Colton's Witness

The Coltons of Roaring Springs

Colton on the Run

Colton 911: Chicago

Undercover Heat

Visit the Author Profile page
at millsandboon.com.au for more titles.

Dear Reader,

When I wrote the final Honor Bound book, I had no idea a character would appear who would launch The McKenna Code series. Love when that happens. But—that hero (Aiden McKenna) is going to have to wait a bit. His law-enforcement siblings are going to get their stories first, beginning with his sister, FBI special agent Wren McKenna.

For years I've wanted to set a suspense in a locale inspired by Whittier, Alaska. So much about this town fascinated me, so of course I had to create my own version. Hence, Splendor, Alaska, population 443, was born. Sending longtime FBI partners Wren McKenna and Ty Savakis on an off-the books case to protect Ty's former witness was the perfect fit, and personally, I love writing friends to lovers. Or in this case, best friends to lovers.

Wren and Ty are fearless in their jobs, but when it comes to love and taking a chance on each other, that's a different story. These two are definitely made for one another. Even her family thinks so, and as Wren knows, family is always right. I hope you enjoy their roller-coaster journey to happily-ever-after.

Happy reading,

Anna J.

For Mom

I miss you every day.

Chapter One

"No! Wait, Wren, don't go chasing him without…"

The rest of her brother's command fizzled in Wren's ear as she slammed out the back door of The Murky Mermaid and ran face-first into a winter storm. She pivoted, sweeping the rain out of her eyes as she scanned the back alley. There! The shadow shifted just out of sight around the corner.

FBI special agent Wren McKenna's sneakered feet barely hit the pavement as she raced after their drug-trafficking suspect; a suspect she'd been keeping under surveillance for the past four days. Normally she didn't mind surveillance duty, but in this instance it required her to take a bartending job in one of the seediest establishments in all of Seattle. She'd be washing off the grime, stink and misogyny for weeks.

Her earpiece crackled and popped before the static settled in, no doubt taking exception to the rain that had drenched her from head to toe. She ran full bore, lungs burning for an instant before her breathing found a familiar rhythm. Arms pumping, her skin puckered against the chill, Wren rounded the corner just as her suspect stopped and turned, unfortunately for him directly under one of the few working streetlamps in the area. Even from here Wren could see the panic in his darting eyes, see his hands shaking in a telltale sign he'd been doing far too much sampling of his own product.

He spun, lost his footing, did a bit of a flail before he caught himself and beat it around the corner and out of sight. At two in the morning, the nonexistent traffic allowed Wren to make easy work of the remaining distance. She ran across the street in a diagonal path, cutting through a pair of parked dilapidated sedans, stopped at the corner, panting a bit as she peeked around the side of the building.

He ducked inside an abandoned warehouse in the center of the block. She looked up. Eight stories. She shook her head, reached into her back pocket for her cell and quickly texted Aiden an update of her location. She was on the move again when his response came in.

We're two minutes out. Wait for backup.

Can't. She texted back even as she heard her big brother's voice echoing in her head.

Might be a back exit. Catch up.

Her confidence wasn't arrogance or even rebellion. It was seven years' experience as an FBI agent specializing in drug trafficking and distribution cases that had her dismissing the order. She'd worked everything from deep undercover to van surveillance. She knew how these guys thought, she knew their tendency to panic, and she knew what they were capable of when they were cornered.

She turned her phone to Silent, slipped it back into her pocket and pulled out the 9 mm Glock she'd been issued upon graduating from the FBI Academy. Before she ducked inside the building, she could hear the rumble of the surveillance van Aiden and his team had been living out of for the past few days. The engine had an odd clinking to it and the sound told her the team would be right on her heels.

She sucked in her stomach, squeezed carefully between the wall and the askew plywood covering the doorway. A button scraped against the wood, echoing up and into the emptiness of the dank, musty building. She froze, waiting. Listening.

Something plinked in the distance, scurried. Weapon raised, finger posed against the side of the barrel, Wren shook her wet hair back and stepped carefully forward. Another step, then another, until she was deep in the building's belly, turning, scanning.

A gentle thud had her spinning, weapon aimed at the door beneath a dead exit sign. She advanced, heard the rustle of footsteps back at the entrance. She pushed down on the metal bar, shoved gently to open the door to the emergency staircase.

"Wren." Her brother's hushed, irritated voice echoed behind her. She held a finger up to her lips as he approached and pointed up.

"I've got three men circling around back," Aiden said. "Blueprints we pulled up don't show a back way out."

"Meaning he could only go up or down." Two choices were better than three.

"Trapped either way," Aiden confirmed. Two Minotaur Security agents from Aiden's private security firm joined them. "You want up or down?" His smile reminded her of when they were kids and dedicated to challenging one another. He knew exactly which she'd prefer. She'd take rats and a sewer over a fire escape and a roof.

"I'll take up."

His brow arched and she rolled her eyes. "The best way to deal with a phobia is to confront it, right?" Anything over three stories and she got the lurches. Even now, the thought of eight stories up had her stomach pitching and her toes tingling. "Besides, I've been stuck behind a bar for four days. I need the workout."

"Your choice." Aiden shrugged. "Talbert, on her six."

"Sir." Rico Talbert, a former navy SEAL with a sometimes unpredictable temper, nodded once, then looked to Wren. "On your go."

Wren shoved the door all the way open and moved through. "Go!"

She and Rico made quick work of the first three floors, circling up and around, aiming their weapons in preparation for a sneak attack. Her suspect wasn't known for being armed, but he hadn't been tagged by a special investigative unit before. Word was a major meth shipment was hitting the West Coast in the next twenty-four hours and this guy was their best shot at gleaning any details.

She hadn't heard any other doors open, but every once in a while she thought she could pick up the distinct shuffling of feet above them. As they rounded the fourth floor, she stopped, inclined her head, looked back at Rico.

The man was the very definition of intense with his dark lock-jawed features. Given that buff physique and curly black hair, not to mention an all-assessing gaze, she might have found herself tempted were it not for the fact that he had an equally buff navy JAG husband waiting for him at home.

More scampering overhead, slower now, and Wren sighed. "He's going all the way up."

Rico nodded. "Sounds like."

"Let's hit it." She picked up her pace, taking the stairs double time now, and had to admit that when they reached the roof level, she was feeling the burn. "You take right." She stood on the left side of the closed metal door. "I'll go left."

Rico nodded, placed his hand on the bar and shoved the door open.

The rain was still pounding when she spun out. Weapon raised, she moved forward, squinting against the weather. The temperature had dropped in the last few minutes, but she was too charged up to shiver. She stopped at the outcropping of a brick wall, back pressed up against it as she crouched, leaned out and peered around.

The suspect was standing on the top rung of an old fire escape, looking down but not moving. She could hear the pounding of footsteps on the metal rungs far below.

She swore, leaned her head back and drew in a steadying breath. "You're locked in, Jackson!" Wren called as she slowly rose to her feet, held her weapon out to her side as he spun around. Moonlight caught him in its grip, cast him in light as he stood far too close to the edge for her liking. "Just come in with me." She held out her free hand. "Let's talk. You help us, we'll help you."

Jackson swooped strands of damp hair out of his eyes. "How can you help me?" he called into the wind. "You're just a bartender. And a crappy one at that."

He wasn't wrong.

"My name is Wren McKenna, Jackson. FBI special agent Wren McKenna. I work with Ty Savakis. You know Ty, don't you?"

"Yeah." Jackson trembled, looked back down as the arc of flashlights from street level cut through the midnight darkness. "I know Ty."

"I can take you to him," Wren lied. "He's down in the van overseeing the entire operation. You want to talk to Ty? All you have to do is come with me."

"No, man." Jackson shoved his hands in his pockets, took a step backward and nearly toppled off the edge. Wren lurched forward, ready to reach for him, but he grabbed hold of the rounded railing and caught himself. Only then did he cast a longing gaze to the roof across the alley.

Wren holstered her weapon, felt Rico come up behind her. He laid a hand on her shoulder, letting her know he had her back.

"You won't make it," Wren called as the rain finally began to ease. "You can't make that jump, Jackson." She inched forward, mentally willing Jackson to come down off the edge of the roof. She really, *really* didn't want to have to look down. "It's wet, it's slippery, and no matter how much you want to, you can't fly." Another step. She was just inches from him now. She could smell the booze and street wafting off him.

Rico circled around her, looked down the fire escape. "We've got him!"

Wren winced. She wasn't so sure. Her gaze locked on Jackson's. She saw the desperation on his face, the panic in his eyes. He was weighing his increasingly limited options.

"Come with me, Jackson. Please." She was almost close enough to touch him, almost close enough to— "Jackson, don't! There's a way out of this. I promise. Let us help—"

"Ain't no way out," Jackson laughed, and in that moment, she saw the manic acceptance. "Vex doesn't let anyone talk."

"You can be the first," Wren said quietly, desperately. She

needed this guy alive. Ty had been trying to get him to turn for months, but Jackson had disappeared three weeks ago, right before Ty's mandatory vacation had started. She'd promised Ty she'd keep an eye out for Jackson, do what she could to finish the job he'd started. One thing she would never do was let her partner down. "Give us a chance to help you, Jackson." One more step.

She locked her hand around his wrist, felt rather than heard his gasp of surprise. "I've got you, Jackson." *Don't look down. Don't look down.* She resisted the impulse to squeeze her eyes shut.

The tension in Jackson's body lessened and he let out something that sounded like a sob. "You can really help me? You can keep me safe from Vex?"

"I really can." It always disturbed her how easily the lies came. "Give me a chance, Jackson. I won't let you down."

"You got him?" Rico asked as Jackson grabbed hold of her with his other hand.

"Yeah," Wren said quietly. "I've got—"

A shot rang out, loud even against the rain. She jolted, tightened her hold on Jackson, but as she met his gaze again, she saw the dazed, dead look coming across his face.

He looked down as a large red pool seeped across his shirt.

Jackson fell back, his grip still tight on Wren. She cried out as he pulled her forward, nearly off her feet. She slammed hard into the edge of the roof, the cement cutting into her stomach as Rico reached around and pried Jackson's hand free. He dragged Wren back and down behind the cover of the roofline just in case the shooter took another shot.

"No!" Wren pounded frustrated fists against her knees as she sat beside Rico, purposely blocking out the abject fear of nearly pitching off an eight-story roof. "Almost had him."

"Yeah, I don't think we did." Rico poked his head over as three armed Minotaur security specialists reached the top of the fire escape. Their guns were poised and pivoting back and forth, looking for any sign of the gunman. "You see anything?" he yelled at them.

"Nothing," a female specialist shouted back.

Rico clicked on his shoulder radio. "Sweep a three-block radius, rooftops included." But Wren heard it in his voice. Whoever had taken Jackson out had been a professional. He was gone seconds after he fired the shot. Rico swore, let out a slow whistle. "Long way down."

Wren gulped. Very long way. She shoved herself up, promised herself one very big glass of Jack Daniel's when she got home. "Well, that's three months of Ty's life he won't get back." Her partner had made the conviction of Dante Vex his life's mission for more than three years. The case had eaten away at his soul, not to mention eviscerated Ty's marriage, and had their superiors at the agency wondering if, once again, Ty had gotten too personally involved. All she'd had to do was get this one witness to turn—

"You okay?" Aiden approached, flanked by two of his men. He touched her arm, flexed his fingers once, an action the McKenna siblings had developed decades before to silently check in.

"I'm fine." Her temper snapped through the words. "How'd they know he was up here?"

"Not sure. Something more to look into where Vex is concerned." The drug supplier had been making steady progress up the criminal racketeering ladder ever since Ty had locked up his boss, Ambrose Treyhern, almost ten years ago.

Wren shook her head. "Jackson was the only potential source Ty could come close to locking in. No one else would talk to him." She knew what was going to happen when Ty found out what had happened. "He's going to blame himself."

"Then he'd be wrong," her brother said, moving closer and resting a hand on her shoulder. "If what you told me about Ty's investigation is true, chances are they'd have taken him out, too. Might just be lucky they missed you."

"Or they figured I wasn't worth the effort," Wren said. "Treyhern got charged with almost killing Ty. Vex would have learned from his boss's mistake."

"Doesn't mean he won't next time," Aiden commented. "You get in his way enough, you won't leave him a choice."

"Right." Wren sighed. "Next time." She shivered, the cold

of the night finally seeping into her bones. "I'd better call this in. Thanks for lending a hand. Sorry it was a waste of time."

"Hey, when my baby sister calls—"

"Regan is the baby." Wren cut her brother off with a gentle slug to the shoulder. "Although don't let her hear you say that."

"All the same, we McKennas stick together. You ask for help, you've got it. No questions asked."

"There might be some questions," Wren said. "I didn't exactly clear your involvement with my bosses."

"Typical Wren." He slung an arm around her shoulders and led her back to the stairs. "Rather ask forgiveness than permission. You want my help explaining?"

"No." She'd gotten herself into this mess. She'd get herself out of it. Besides, dealing with her superiors at the agency was going to be far less painful than telling Ty she'd lost his best lead. "When are you headed back to Boston?"

"Tomorrow afternoon. You want to hitch a ride on my plane?"

"Well, duh." She rolled her eyes. "You really think I'm going to risk missing another family dinner?"

"I think Mom would understand," Aiden said.

"That's because you never miss," Wren countered. "But then I guess that goes with being your own boss." One of the perks to being one of the premier private security experts in the country meant her big brother could come and go at his leisure. An added bonus? Setting his own hours pretty much ensured he'd never miss the mandatory monthly McKenna dinners that kept the tight-knit family on an even keel.

They ducked inside, made quick work of the eight flights down, but once they got to the bottom, the adrenaline coursing through Wren's system was evaporating. She was ready to crash.

"You going to call Ty tonight?" Aiden asked as they walked outside and into the carnival of flashing police lights surrounding the building.

"I—" She was cut off by her cell phone buzzing against her butt. She pulled it free, stared at the screen for a good long moment and muttered, "I swear my partner is psychic." Ty always knew when something was seriously messed up.

"Or," Aiden said in too innocent a tone, "he's just that into you that he can read your mind."

"Stop it." The warning wasn't the first one she'd given. For years, Aiden—okay, all three of her siblings—had teased her about her relationship with Tyrone Savakis. Thankfully they knew to keep their comments under control this past holiday season when Ty had come for Christmas dinner at the McKenna house. It had been difficult enough to convince him to spend the day with her family without him knowing what all of them somewhat believed about their relationship.

It wasn't as if there had ever been anything romantic between them. She'd been married when they first became partners and he'd gotten married a year after. Didn't matter neither marriage survived; they were each other's best friend.

And, okay, she'd be lying if she didn't admit to having had a major crush on him at one point. And she'd have to be foolish not to genuinely appreciate a tall, incredibly fit blue-eyed man who gave his godlike Greek ancestors something to be proud of.

Getting involved with one another was only going to make their professional lives messy and complicated. Neither of them wanted that. Still…there were times when she let herself think maybe—

"You going to answer or just speak to him telepathically?" Aiden asked.

"Shut up." She glared at her brother as she answered her phone. "Ty, hey. We were, um…" She shoved her sopping hair out of her face once more. "Aiden and I were just talking about you." She frowned when he didn't immediately respond. "Ty?"

"Yeah, I'm here."

Wren straightened. Ty sounded distracted. He rarely sounded distracted. He was arrow straight on concentration 24/7. Heck, he could probably set a world record for not blinking. It was one of the qualities that made him such a good agent. "What's wrong?"

The teasing light in Aiden's eyes faded.

"What isn't wrong?" Ty said in a frustrated tone. "There's way too much…" He trailed off. "Sorry. I haven't slept in a couple of days. You still in Seattle?"

"Yeah." She stepped back as the rest of Aiden's men filed out of the abandoned building. "Um, I've got some cleaning up to do here before I head home to Boston."

"Okay, when you're done, and before you head back, I need you to meet me." He rattled off the name of some private airport outside of Seattle she'd never heard of. "Sunrise. A friend is going to fly me back in time. I'll grab some sleep when we land."

"Fly you back from where?" As far as she knew, Ty had been holed up in his Boston apartment serving out his forced vacation time as if it were a prison sentence. "Where are you?"

"Right now? Anchorage. I'll explain when I see you, okay?"

"Ty? What's going on?"

"I don't want to get into it on the phone. Just meet me, yeah? I really need your help, Wren. As always, you're the only person I can trust."

"Okay." He had a tendency to get a bit overdramatic when a case wasn't going his way. Was it possible he'd already heard about Jackson? Not likely since it was still in local law enforcement jurisdiction. "Just tell me one thing. Are you all right?"

"Yeah, I'm okay. For now. I'll see you in a few hours. Thanks, Wren. Oh, one more thing?"

"What?" She didn't like the uneasy, queasy sensation in her belly.

"Don't tell anyone official we spoke, okay? No one. Especially anyone at the FBI." He hung up.

Wren stared at her cell, then looked up at Aiden.

"Trouble?" Aiden asked.

"Looks like. For you, too," she added as she headed toward the alley to speak with the officers on scene. "You'll have to tell Mom I'm missing this month's dinner."

Chapter Two

The knots in Ty Savakis's stomach didn't loosen until he saw headlights turn in his direction. His breath erupted in thick puffs of white, disappearing into the cold February air that had frozen his face to the point of numbness. Hands shoved deep into the pockets of his fleece-lined jacket, he remained stone-still, standing in front of the private airplane hangar that housed a friend's impressive aircraft collection.

He had no doubt Wren was behind the wheel of the approaching car. He'd always been able to tell when she was near and, given the way he was finally starting to relax, the car couldn't be carrying anyone else. As she pulled the dark sedan to a stop, his gaze shifted to the passenger seat. He'd set the odds at fifty-fifty she'd bring her brother Aiden along for the ride.

But she'd come alone. He hadn't asked her to, but the request had been implicit. There truly was no one else in the world he could trust more than his partner.

His hands clenched as she shoved open the door and climbed out. Her fit five-foot-five frame, primarily constructed of muscle and sass, was bundled up cozily in snug jeans, black tactical work boots and a puffy dark jacket. The knit cap tugged onto her head covered some but not all of her sandy blond hair she normally wore in a messy ponytail to keep it out of her face. She slammed the door and headed in his direction. "You okay?"

Wren wasn't a worrier, so the fact that she asked told him he'd sounded more frazzled on the phone than he'd hoped. "Not remotely. Coffee?"

"Bathroom," she corrected as she followed him into the dimly lit hangar. Half a dozen aircrafts ranging from restored historic models to a modern-day two-seater sat on display. "I drank a tankard of coffee on the drive up."

"Over there." He pointed to the restroom in the back corner of the metal industrial-style building. He didn't ask a second time if she wanted more coffee; Wren McKenna had it running through her veins. Her drug of choice, if one didn't count the occasional Jack Daniel's she downed after nastier resolutions to cases.

He rotated his neck, then his shoulders, trying to work out the exhaustion that had been creeping over him the past few days. That sleep he'd hoped to catch hadn't materialized as his mind wouldn't shut down long enough to reboot. Rubbing his palm across his whisker-covered face, he shoved at the guilt trying its best to grab hold of his throat and choke him.

These days he seemed to spiral from one disaster to another, with bad luck nipping at his heels every step of the way. Given how the last couple of days had gone, that wasn't going to change anytime soon. But now, with Wren by his side, the odds were more in his favor.

"Okay, whew." Wren reappeared, her cuddly jacket unzipped to reveal the thin rock band–inspired T-shirt she wore. "That feels better. That for me?" She pointed to the steaming paper cup near his hand.

"Yeah." He stood back, offered her the cup. He should have realized.

She eyed him over the rising steam. "You heard about Jackson?" She sipped and, true to form, let out a sigh that rivaled that of a woman in ecstasy. An electric jolt shot through his body; an increasingly familiar sensation he found himself experiencing when the two of them were together.

"I heard."

"I'm so sorry. The last thing I expected was for someone to take him out. Not like that."

"Not your fault. I mean it," he added at her scoff. "If anyone's to blame, it's me. I let my focus get foggy. The agency was right to bench me. I should have done a better job. Brought Jackson in on my own, through procedure instead of getting creative and letting him convince me he was fine on his own."

"You only got creative because you couldn't get Jackson the guarantees he wanted," Wren reminded him. "You were looking out for your informant."

"Guess I'm off the hook now." The bitterness in his voice was only countered by the warming air around them.

"Jackson didn't have to run," Wren told him. "He made his choice, and it cost him his life. Still trying to figure out how someone knew to take that shot, though. We had the surveillance locked down tight," she muttered. "Only a handful of people at the FBI knew what I was doing."

"What're Aiden's thoughts?"

"Many and varied." She winced. "You ticked I brought him in?"

"Not remotely." He only wished he'd thought of bringing Wren's brother in sooner. Maybe then Ty would have managed things better. Wren's older brother had the habit of getting through Ty's stubbornness more effectively than most. "Glad he was there. Sorry you got saddled with it."

Wren glared at him. "That sounds disturbingly like self-pity, which you don't do. What's going on? What's with the cloak-and-dagger conclave?"

Every emotion Ty had been struggling to keep under control began to cyclone inside him. "You remember me telling you about Alice Hawkins?" Stupid question. Wren never forgot anything.

"Sure." Wren's blue eyes sharpened as she accessed her memory banks. "She was the main witness who testified against Ambrose Treyhern, one of the biggest drug traffickers on the East Coast. She helped put him behind bars for the murder of one of his dealers." She inclined her head. "Which allowed for Dante Vex and his ilk to slither up Treyhern's organization to take it over, and thus here we are."

Right on the nose. Now came the tricky part. "Treyhern was

granted a new trial three weeks ago. His new lawyers are claiming prosecutorial misconduct." Not entirely surprising given the federal prosecutor in charge of the case had recently been indicted on bribery charges.

"Three—" Wren set her coffee down, eyes wide with surprise and more than a little anger. "Three weeks ago and you're just telling me this now? That was the biggest case of your career. You got your promotion because of it. You got partnered with me because of it. What the what, Ty?"

Ty nodded. All true. "I can't—"

Wren swore, held up a hand, began pacing in a circle the way she always did when she was trying to work something out in her head. "Three weeks ago. That's when you started going loopy-loo on me. Why didn't you tell me?"

"Because I was under the misguided perception that I was handling the information okay." It never occurred to him to lie. He and Wren had a long-standing agreement. No lies. No matter what. Omissions, on the other hand… "I messed up."

"Ya think?" She stopped, looked him dead in the eye and arched one brow.

Ty sighed. He didn't think. He knew. That mistake in judgment had resulted in a forced two-week "vacation" that, if he weren't careful, would be changed in his record to a forced leave of absence. A notation like that could turn any promise of advancement into a long shot. "I fully deserve whatever lambasting you're about to give me, Wren, but it's five in the morning. I haven't slept in three days and right now I'm standing upright out of sheer will."

The irritation faded from her eyes, but her suspicion remained. "What is going on with you?"

"Someone ran Alice Hawkins down in the street last week." Considering he wasn't entirely sure what day this was, he couldn't be more precise than that. "Shortly after she agreed to testify against Treyhern in the second trial."

Wren's posture shifted. Her spine went steel straight and her eyes sharpened to the point of slicing through metal. "Is she dead?"

"No. But it's close. She's in a coma. So far the local sheriff's been able to keep her condition quiet, but it won't be long before whoever went after her realizes he didn't finish the job."

"And you think Ambrose Treyhern's behind the accident? Hasn't he been in solitary for the past two years?"

"So we've been told." But as anyone in law enforcement knew, solitary didn't mean powerful prisoners didn't have their way of communicating with the outside world.

"How did you find out? About Alice?"

Ty could all but hear the wheels turning in her brain.

That now-familiar slick, sick sensation slid through him. "I was on the phone with her when it happened." Even now, the haunting screech of tires, Alice's scream, that decidedly heavy thump replayed in his mind. Those horrifying seconds had been on a nonstop loop in his head. "She called me, needing some reassurance about her testifying again. She was concerned for her family."

"Considering what happened, she was right to be."

Ty swallowed hard. "We were talking when it happened. When she was hit. I heard her…land." The sickening sound was going to haunt him if not forever, certainly for the near future.

Wren shook her head, eyes filled with disbelief, irritation and pity. "Ty."

"I know." He ducked his head in shame. There wasn't anything she could say that he hadn't already said to himself. "I spent the entire time getting up to Splendor, trying to come up with a story about how Alice and I met. Shouldn't have worried over it. She'd already come up with one. Her husband knew who I was immediately."

Wren's brows shot up.

"She'd told him I was a friend from her old neighborhood. The only one she kept in touch with. She also told him if anything ever happened to her that I should be his first call."

"He didn't question how you knew she'd been hurt? Or the, what? Six-year age difference between you?"

"They've got three kids," Ty said. "He wasn't thinking about anything other than them and Alice."

"Lucky for you."

She wasn't wrong. They needed to get their stories straight and do it fast.

Wren eyed him in the same way she did a suspect. "I seem to recall you telling me Alice had a bit of a sketchy past. Is it possible something or someone else caught up with her?"

"No. No doubt in my mind Treyhern's behind this. I get that my opinion might not carry much weight at the moment." He hated having to rehash this again, but he didn't have any choice. "Alice was a messed-up eighteen-year-old when I was working the Treyhern case. And, okay, I was new to the job and desperate to prove myself." He'd spent his entire life trying to do just that one way or another. The only person he'd never had to do that with was the woman standing in front of him. "Sure, she had a record, but for petty stuff. Vandalism, pickpocketing. Petty theft. Doing whatever she needed to survive. She'd been living on the street for over a year when Treyhern found her, gave her a job at his nightclub. He paid her enough that she didn't have to live in alleys and share a cardboard box with the rats. But she had, or she has, a code, Wren. Watering down drinks was one thing. Seeing Treyhern kill someone in cold blood crossed a line for her. She wanted to do the right thing and I was more than happy to take her help."

"I seem to recall you telling me she refused witness protection."

"She did." It had been an argument he'd been devastated to lose. What was happening now had been his nightmare scenario come to life, but Alice had been adamant. "She'd finally gotten her life together and knew what she wanted. She didn't want Treyhern messing with her future. She'd just started dating the man who would become her husband. She was happy, and testifying felt like closing the book on a big chapter of her life. Said she knew how to disappear and still keep her identity intact."

"Brave woman. Wrong, but brave."

"I told her she'd be safe," Ty said. "I promised her Treyhern would never get out, that he couldn't hurt her anymore and I'd make sure she could have that life she wanted so desperately." The layers of guilt that continued to build threatened to pull him under. "I went so far as to visit Treyhern in prison and told him that whatever beef he had, it was with me. That I was the one who made her testify. I made him believe she didn't have a choice."

"Something tells me you didn't quite succeed."

"Alice is still alive, Wren." Right now that fact was the only thing holding him together. "She's clinging to it with her fingertips, but she's alive. She has a good life, a wonderful family. I can't walk away from this. From her. Not again. Whoever's gunning for her works for Treyhern and he probably doesn't take failure well. They're going to finish the job, maybe even hurt her family to get to her again. I need to be there when they try."

"You?" Wren picked her coffee back up. "You mean we, don't you?" She sipped, sipped again. "That's why you called me, right?"

"I'd appreciate the assist." A new layer of uncertainty unfolded inside him. "But I also don't want to put you in the position of having to lie. I called Frisco, asked for permission to head up to Alaska to look into this, to make sure Alice and her family stay safe."

"Let me guess," Wren said slowly. "Our commanding officer denied your request."

Not only denied it, but Frisco told Ty if he did pursue the investigation, he could pretty much kiss his career in the agency goodbye. After his insubordination regarding Dante Vex, it made sense the agency would want him far away from the Treyhern retrial. "I promised her she'd be safe. And you know I never break—"

"Your promises." Wren nodded. "Yes, I am aware."

"I just need you watching my back up there. And maybe covering for me with Frisco when he asks where I am. Just say you don't know."

"Well, that'll be a bald-faced lie since I'm coming with you." The ease with which she said it both erased the tension in his bones and awakened new concerns.

Deep down he'd known Wren wouldn't let him do this alone. She'd never let him down. Not in seven years. "You don't have to."

"Please." She rolled her eyes. "Of course I do. If for no other reason than to make sure you don't mess this up. Plus, I really don't want to have to break in a new partner. So." She finished her coffee. "What's the plan?"

"Plan?" He tried to sound nonchalant. "What—"

"You had a list of options mapped out before you even called me," Wren accused. "One option if I bailed on you and told you to handle your own mess. One if I didn't answer the phone, and another for when I agreed to help. Let's get option C out in the open. Where are we going and what's our plan when we get there?"

"Ah." Now came the tricky part. "We'll be going to Splendor, Alaska. A small town on the West Coast, population a whopping four hundred and forty-three."

"Wow. Okay. Well, I guess that'll limit our suspect pool. What?" She narrowed her gaze, pointed her finger in between his eyes. "What's that look?"

He swallowed harder than he meant to and almost choked. "I, ah, may have already laid the groundwork for our cover story." He reached into his pocket and pulled out two gold rings. He watched the shock register first, then dismayed amusement, followed immediately by her you-have-got-to-be-kidding-me look. "What do you say, partner? Will you marry me?"

Wren had flown in military cargo planes with only a thin metal bench as a seat during category two winds. She'd found herself dangling off the side of a helicopter with only Ty's hand locked around her wrist as security. And she'd flown coast to coast in a massive jetliner that lost one engine during a particularly nasty summer storm.

Right now she'd take any of those scenarios over the single-engine 1946 Piper Super Cruiser—suspiciously similar to a tin can—she currently found herself in.

The only reason she could even identify the plane was because its pilot, one forty-something Gabriel Hawthorne, had given her an extensive rundown on the plane's capabilities. No doubt the abject look of horror she'd been unable to conceal when she first spotted the red-and-white-painted aircraft was the reason for the history lesson.

Hawthorne seemed to believe that the fact his grandfather had flown the plane for more than forty years was an endorsement of safety. She might have felt better if the plane had just rolled off the assembly line.

Her pilot slipped right into the stereotype explanation she'd imagined hearing about how she'd be transported north. Big, a bit on the burly side, fully bearded and flannel-wearing cold-weather enthusiast, Hawthorne projected confidence in both his plane and his abilities, which took a bit of the edge off her fear.

A very little bit.

Hugging her stuffed duffel bag in front of her like an already exploded airbag, Wren bounced around on the thinly padded bench behind the pilot's seat. The narrow belt across her thighs dug into her denim-clad legs. Even now, she could feel the pressure bruises forming, but at least they were a reminder she hadn't traveled into the great beyond. The ride had been bumpy since they first coasted into the air, and more than once her head had just missed connecting with the roof. The engine rumbled loudly all around her and she could feel the vibrations through her work boots.

"You doing okay back there?" Hawthorne yelled over his shoulder as they hit yet another air pocket that set the plane to trembling and Wren to grabbing the top of her head with her hand.

"Fine." She really didn't want to talk. It was taking most of her concentration to hold on to the breakfast she'd forced herself to eat before returning to the airstrip. It had been close to thirty hours since she'd left Ty, promising to try to get some sleep at the hangar. At least twenty since he'd returned ahead of her to Splendor, Alaska, no doubt to avoid having to climb into a plane with her.

She couldn't blame him. She was a nightmare to fly with. She imagined every bump and whine was going to lead to certain death. Fliers like her were partly why the pharmaceutical industry did a gangbuster business. Somehow, miraculously, her brothers would say, she'd managed to hide her anxiety well enough where her job was concerned.

"Ty didn't mention you were a nervous flier." Even though

Hawthorne shouted, she could barely hear him through the headset she wore.

"I'm not nervous." Petrified maybe, but she'd left nervous back on the tarmac. "How do you know Ty?" Distraction, she told herself, could work far better than drugs.

"Met him on a wildlife excursion about ten years back. Flew him and four other CSOs up north during the salmon run."

"CSOs?"

"City slicker outdoorsmen." Hawthorne's laughter crackled in her ears. "They like to think of themselves as urban adventurers. Gotta admit, for a townie, Ty has a pretty good grasp of the natural way of living. He and I got along from the jump. Man respects the wilderness. He enjoys it when he comes up here and never loses sight of the fact it can be dangerous."

"Does he?" Wren frowned. She knew Ty took off on his own a few times a year, mostly to decompress and get away. She had no idea he made his way north into the wilderness Alaska had to offer. The engine seemed to strain, causing the entire cabin to rattle. "Well, I appreciate you getting me to Splendor." *Hopefully in one piece.*

She'd done some destination research in the spare hours she'd had after packing. She knew it was a very, *very* small town, but boasted a surprising amount of art and culture pulling from both those of native Indigenous ancestry and other residents. Fishing was a primary source of income for a lot of people, as was the tourist trade, thanks to cruise ships making Splendor a stop along their routes in the warmer months. From what she'd gleaned off the city's official website, the art studios and galleries outnumbered the restaurants about two to one. Skyway Tower, where Alice Hawkins and her family lived, was a bit of a unicorn when it came to apartment buildings.

Considered a self-contained community, the main and first floor of the six-story complex that housed more than a hundred residents included everything from a school to a post office, from a grocery store to even a movie theater in the basement. The library offered not only books but also cooking equipment, board games, puzzles, and hosted numerous classes in countless subjects. In theory, one never had to step outside to get everything they might need.

That didn't mean the surrounding area didn't have its aesthetic offerings as well. But in the dead winter months, when the snow didn't stop and the sun didn't shine, it provided a safe if not locked-down environment for its residents both in and around Skyway Tower.

"You live in Splendor?"

"About thirty miles north," Hawthorne shouted. "This here's my car." He slapped a hand down on the console. "Gets me anywhere I need to go. I like Splendor, though. It's different. Everyone knows everyone. It's both hard and easy to get lost there."

"That's what I'm counting on." Wren's murmur earned her another over-the-shoulder glance. "I'm looking forward to experiencing it," she called. "Where's the best coffee?"

Hawthorne veered the plane east. "Now, that there's a bone of contention. You ask me, Mountain Morning's got the best brews. But Morning Sun Coffee Company's giving them a run for their money these days. Can't go wrong with either."

"That's all I need to know." Although at the moment she couldn't anticipate a time when her stomach would feel settled enough to imbibe anything.

"You like fresh fish cooked well, put The Hungry Halibut on your list, and the Salmon Run Café has an excellent salmon, bacon and tomato on fresh-baked whole grain."

"So we won't go hungry, huh?"

"Definitely not. Not much to do in Splendor if you ain't on a boat or throwing clay on a potter's wheel. Food's a way of life and they take it serious."

"Noted." Always helpful to know she wouldn't starve. "How much longer?"

"We should be landing in about forty-five minutes. Long as those clouds stay at a distance." He gestured out the windshield to the bank of gray. "We should beat it, though."

Beat it they did, but not by much. By the time Hawthorne brought the plane in for a relatively smooth landing, Wren closed her eyes in silent thanks. Her arms had gone numb with how tightly she'd been holding on to her bag. Even as he steered the plane to the dock at the end of the marina, she was unsnapping her belt and scooting to the edge of the seat to make a break for it.

Whatever unease she still felt evaporated as she caught her first glimpse of Splendor. The marina itself was both typical and a bit ethereal. With the way the midmorning sun hit the boats, it set the gleaming paint and the blue of the surrounding sea to glistening. She could smell diesel mingling with the briny air, an intoxicating combination that made her lungs eagerly expand. As the engine on the plane died back, the silence set in and offered a kind of peace she hadn't been expecting or prepared for.

She spotted Ty heading down a marina gangplank and immediately her stomach jumped. The flight had distracted her from the other point of contention on this particular job. Pretending to be married to Ty Savakis. What a can of worms that could open up. They'd had their share of undercover assignments, but nothing quite so...intimate before.

Wren glanced down at the gold band on her finger. It felt oddly heavy. She'd never worn one when she and Antony were married, which had been one of the many points of contention between them. Her then-husband had always accused her of not wanting the reminder of him when she was working. He hadn't been wrong, but by the time she realized her marriage was on life support, she'd lost any desire to resuscitate it. Which made it even stranger she should look upon this ring so fondly. And her heart really needed to stop skipping every time she glanced at Ty.

"Thanks for the lift," Wren said as Hawthorne pulled the plane to a stop right in front of where Ty stood. "Sorry if I was a bit freaked out."

"I've had worse passengers," Hawthorne assured her as he flipped a switch and killed the engine. "All you want is the landings to equal the takeoffs. Anything that happens in between those two things means nothing."

Wren actually laughed. The door popped open, splitting into two, one panel going up, the other providing a solitary narrow step out.

"You made it in one piece, I see." Ty's grin had Wren chucking her duffel straight into his chest. He caught it with a grunt of surprise as she hauled herself out. "Want to kiss the ground?"

"We aren't on ground yet." She could feel the walkway swaying a bit in the barely-there waves. "But when I get there, you bet. You get any sleep?" It sure didn't look it. She hadn't thought he could look more exhausted than he had in Seattle.

"Some. Worried I'd be late to pick you up."

Fat chance. Her partner was predictably punctual. "How's Alice?" She'd half been hoping by the time she landed Alice would be well on her way to recovery.

"Thought we'd head over now and check," Ty said. "This all you brought?" The disbelief in his voice barely reached her ears as she ducked back inside for the wheeled suitcase she'd also packed. "Ah, that's more like it."

"Half of this is courtesy of Aiden," she told him. Her brother hadn't been overly thrilled at the idea of her heading to Splendor off book, but he knew her well enough not to fight her on it. Instead he'd made sure she had plenty of artillery to supplement her Glock and backup piece.

"Love your brother," Ty said. "Always thinking ahead."

"Yeah, well, keep in mind he's not overly thrilled with you at the moment." She thanked Hawthorne again, and after he and Ty settled up in cash, Wren was following the latter through the marina. "He said to call him if we needed help. He's putting Howell on alert."

"And here I thought Aiden had more faith in me. We don't need a marshal running backup."

"Howell might be a US marshal, but he's got more connections than even Aiden has. We might need help if this thing goes feet up." The FBI had a long-standing thing going with the Marshals Service. Personally Wren had never had a problem with them, but that was because she understood them better than most FBI agents. Her brother Howell was one of the best people she'd ever known and that wasn't just familial affection talking. There was a reason Howell McKenna had the respect of every law enforcement officer he'd ever worked with—in and out of the Marshals Service. But then the same could easily be said for any of the McKennas.

Her family covered the law enforcement agencies like a well-worn blanket, and while they had the reputation for being tenacious and tough, they also erred on the side of cautious consistency. McKennas in law enforcement went all the way back to the very first police department in Boston. Their mother, Elizabeth McKenna, had become the first female police commissioner in the city nearly a decade ago and still served in the office with distinction. To say they took their jobs seriously, and with the utmost responsibility, was a massive understatement. Genetics, if nothing else, demanded it.

"Hopefully we won't need the reinforcements. Speaking of which." Ty suddenly seemed very interested in a fishing boat unloading its morning haul. "You talk to Frisco?"

"Nope." She flashed him a smile. "Sent our boss an email, though, said I'd be out of touch for a while. Family emergency." It hadn't been a lie. Exactly. Ty was family and this was an emergency. "Timed the send to correspond with when I climbed on that monstrosity." She pointed back to the plane. "And funny enough, the Wi-Fi and cell service around here sucks." That said, if Supervisory Special Agent Jack Frisco wanted to track her down, he could. Easily.

Ty slung her duffel over his shoulder as a light rain began to fall. When he slipped his free hand into hers and squeezed, she nearly lost her breath. "Keeping up appearances," he said when she tensed. "Been mentioning how my wife is on her way to meet me so I can convince her we need to move here."

"We still going with you having sold off your IT company for a small fortune and therefore have time to play?"

"It's worked before." Ty's smile was tight. "It's a legend I know forward and backward. It's just using my real name that'll be weird."

"Still doesn't sit well with me." Wren kept turning her head, memorizing where things were and how they were set up. The marina displayed an array of various watercraft from large fishing boats to dinghy-sized vessels. There were sailboats with aquatic and ironic names and an actual thirty-foot yacht named the *Titanic Ego*. *Ugh*. She rolled her eyes. *Seriously?*

She watched as additional craft, likely with their morning

catch, made their way to dock. She'd bet she'd find a stellar fish-and-chips somewhere in the area. "I'd feel better with an alias."

"Yeah, well, Alice locked us into the real thing. Should have come up with a fake name for her to use at the beginning."

"At least that's one lie we won't have to remember." She didn't particularly care; she just wanted to be prepared. Her hand tightened around his and the rumble of the wheels on her suitcase offered a bit of a distraction. "Have you seen her husband since we met down in Seattle?"

"Couple of times. Once at the hospital, then once at Skyway Tower. He's bopping back and forth because of the kids. I told him I'd stay close in case they needed anything." He checked his watch. "If we get to the hospital soon, you can probably meet him. Kids'll be in school, though."

"Right. The kids. There's three of them?" Cases with kids always put her on edge.

Ty nodded. "Esme's seven. Bodhi's five, and River is three." He winced into the cloud-covered sun. "Esme's the only one who seems to have a grasp of what's going on. She's a little withdrawn but is playing mama to the little ones."

"Poor kid."

"Their neighbors are helping, keeping them entertained. And they have their classroom in the same building."

"Noted." Keeping them all in the same place where they felt safe was going to be important. "So what's my story?"

"Lawyer. White-collar. Figure I'd keep it to something you have a shot at." He grinned at her. "Serves you right for always talking about maybe going to law school."

"I only say that when I'm frustrated with my job." It never failed to impress her how he actually listened. The very idea she'd become a lawyer, however, would never sit well with her family. A McKenna lawyer? Perish the thought. "I can lawyer-speak well enough to pull that off. I think."

"There is one thing you should probably know."

"Only one?"

"I met the local sheriff." He paused. "I didn't tell him I'm FBI."

"Okay." She noodled that for a moment. "Considering you're

usually pretty big on not stepping on the locals' toes, I'm guessing you have a good reason."

"Honestly?" For a flash of a second, he looked utterly defeated. "I went with my gut, but we both know that hasn't been acting in my best interests lately."

Understatement of the year.

"Alice's accident has got people spooked," Ty went on. "And you and I have been in enough small towns to know that nothing stays secret forever."

"Hearing the FBI is in town, even unofficially, will only cause more problems."

"And could drive whoever hurt Alice underground."

There it was. The rationale he probably needed.

"You did what you thought was right at the time," she assured him, even as she doubted his decision. Ticking off the local sheriff could, in the long run, turn around and bite them. "You get a feel for the sheriff otherwise?"

"I've kept an eye on him. He's good. He's not wearing the badge because it looks pretty. Near as I can tell, he cares. He knows everyone by name, checks in on people, does morning rounds with the shops and stores. He'd notice an unfamiliar face and he definitely noticed mine."

"Ah." Wren ducked her head to hide her grin. "He made you." No wonder Ty's gut was telling him to stay quiet.

"Pretty much," Ty admitted.

They stopped at a park bench that, according to the brass plaque bolted to the back, was dedicated to a Cyrus Ebscomb, who worked the Splendor waterway for more than fifty years. Seemed fitting his bench overlooked the entirety of the marina not far from the central hub of town.

"Things like what happened to Alice don't happen here," Ty said.

"Until they do." Wren stretched her stiff arms over her head, twisted back and forth as she took in her surroundings. "And they always do."

The cool breeze wafting off the sea behind her shifted her focus to the town in front of her. Three streets that she could see, each branching off from the center of Splendor. Not a lot of cars parked in the area, but she suspected that was because there was only one road into the town and that road came through a nearly three-mile-long tunnel that was shared by the railroad.

The buildings were mostly stone gray in color, and didn't climb much above two stories. She saw homey curtains in some second-story windows, indicating people living there. First levels appeared to be relegated to shops, stores and local businesses, including a real-estate office that boasted photos of rentals in their front window.

"That's Skyway, I assume." She jutted her chin toward the massive building that looked closer than it probably was. She knew it had been built originally as military housing, but after a massive shift in defense funding and priorities, the town had bought it for a fraction of its value and turned it into housing.

Since it was past the usual season of darkness—Alaska had had its annual sixty-day-plus period of no sun—it felt a bit brighter than she'd expected. The gray cloud cover that continued to advance, along with the increasing snow-threatening sprinkles from beyond, eked away some of that sunshine, though.

"I found an apartment in Skyway Tower to sublet through that real-estate office," Ty said. "We're on the fourth floor, same floor as the Hawkins family. Place is furnished. Nothing fancy, but we've dealt with a lot worse. Kitchen seems great."

She should have known he'd find a way for Wren to cook. It was a matter of survival for him since he could barely zap a microwave meal without scorching it. "How long are we in for, do you think?"

"Had to pay for the month." Ty shrugged. "It'll be worth it to keep us close to the family. It's a one bedroom."

"Keeping up appearances." She repeated his earlier comment. "That's fine." No need to stand out with multiple bedrooms for a short stay. "The sheriff probably doesn't have any problems, but do you have an idea as to how we figure out who belongs here and who doesn't?"

"Given the attention Sheriff Egbert showered on me, right now, I'm it."

"Man. Egbert. Now, that's a name." Wren laughed and swiped

at her tired eyes. "Since I've got my land legs back, let's say we head over to the hospital and check on Alice."

"You don't want to drop off your bags first?" Ty asked.

"Sooner we figure out what's going on with her, the sooner we can both get back home." Wren tugged her jacket tighter together beneath her chin and shivered. There was cold, and then there was Alaska cold, but she didn't have much time to think on it. Barely three blocks later Ty was headed inside a single-story building. "I thought—"

"Hospital and medical clinic are all one facility," Ty told her as he pulled open the glass door. "Full service, open twenty-four hours. They've got enough beds for twenty-three people. More if they double up in the rooms. Only three ICU beds. Any more who need it are sent to Anchorage."

He'd definitely done his homework. "Personnel?" She could only imagine a facility like this had to be short-staffed.

"Decent. Three on-call doctors, all GPs, specialists get brought in occasionally, otherwise…"

"Anchorage." Wren was sensing a theme.

"Eleven nurses on staff, rotating shifts and departments. Then you have the usual custodial, office, management. All told, twenty-six employees."

He'd definitely done his due diligence. If he'd been hanging around the hospital enough to gather this kind of information, no wonder the sheriff tagged him.

Despite its outside appearance, once inside the Splendor Medical Facility it looked like a welcoming, highly organized and efficient space. Perhaps more so than most big-city hospitals and clinics she'd been in. One thing that wasn't different was that familiar stale, almost too clean medicinal air and overly bright polished floors. The directional signs gave the option of visiting the outpatient clinic to the left or the inpatient services, including the ICU, to the right.

The demarcation between the two was a small desk labeled Security but with a current be-back-in-a-half-hour sign taped on the wall above.

"Alice's room is just there." Ty pointed to a closed door near the nurses' station. "Room eleven."

"Good morning, ladies." Ty set Wren's bag down and greeted the pair of female nurses sitting behind a scarred half-round desk. One wore scrubs in a rainbow pattern while the other was clad in a simple maroon-colored set.

"Hey there, Ty." The older of the two flashed overly interested dark eyes in his direction until she caught sight of Wren. The way she deflated was almost comical.

"Good morning, Aiyana." He leaned an arm on the counter. "How're things going with Alice?"

"Bradley just got finished speaking with Dr. Johansen. No change in her condition, I'm afraid."

Wren resisted the urge to arch a brow. Did HIPAA regulations not make it this far north? Then she realized Ty had no doubt turned his charm on full blast on his previous visits and managed to wiggle his way around medical privacy issues.

Letting the two of them chat, Wren set her wheelie suitcase against the wall and did a quick assessment of her surroundings. Despite its limited size, the facility appeared to be up-to-date and, for the most part, impressive. The noise level wasn't bad, which made sense considering the patient capacity. What noise there was seemed to come from far down in the other direction where the clinic was located.

The halls were quite narrow and didn't echo the way so many hospitals did. Each hospital room appeared to have a window that allowed the patient to see out into the hallway and, more importantly perhaps, for the patients to be observed.

She spotted a male orderly mopping the floor farther down the hallway, past where a nurse's portable computer station was parked just under the exit sign. An elderly woman made her way out of her room aided by a nurse. Another nurse was at the woman's side, wheeling the patient's squeaky portable oxygen tank behind them. Toward the clinic, a tall, thin man in a white medical coat chatted with a mother and her two children.

Wren pushed her hands into her pockets, feigned slight boredom as she paced a bit, nearly running into a doctor coming out of what she saw was a supply closet. Out of habit, she looked down to the ID badge that wasn't where it should have been.

He knocked into her, murmured a distracted "Sorry" before moving on.

Tall, a bit on the bulky side, he wore a long white lab jacket over navy blue scrubs. His black work boots squeaked as he strode down the hall before pausing at Alice's window, where he knocked quietly before pushing open the door.

Something niggled in Wren's mind. Chills erupted on the back of her neck. Wren's gaze dropped again to the doctor's shoes. She leaned over, looked at the nurses' feet. They both wore soft-soled shoes, comfortable. Colorful. Quiet.

The plastic blinds covering Alice's window closed.

Adrenaline kicking in, Wren bolted for Alice's door. She slammed it open, catching the two men inside off guard.

The younger and slighter of the two jumped out of his chair, still clinging to Alice's limp hand. The machines attached to Alice's vitals beeped at regular intervals.

"Who are you?" Bradley Hawkins was instantly recognizable from the photos Ty had messaged her. The man was a little on the thin side, more than a bit geeky and had the appearance of someone who had been kicked by life a good couple of times in the past few days.

"Hi, Bradley. Wren Savakis." She gave him a quick smile. "Ty's wife."

"Oh, sure, yeah." Bradley offered a weak apologetic smile. "Sorry. Ty mentioned you were headed up. Thanks for coming." He glanced at his wife. "I'm sure she'll thank you herself when she's awake." The hope clinging to his words made her heart ache even as it continued to pound in dread.

Alice Hawkins lay stone-still in the bed, the ventilator next to her keeping her breathing. Her left leg was elevated with metal pins held in place by circular metal frames in three different positions. Her right arm was in a cast and lying across her chest. A thick bandage was wrapped around her head, obscuring most of her light brown hair. She was so pale it was almost impossible to see where the stark white sheets began.

She could only imagine Ty's initial reaction to seeing Alice like this. Wren already understood his commitment to the case, but looking at his witness in this condition, she realized just how hard her job would be to keep Ty focused on not taking matters into his own hands. Any more than he already had, anyway.

"Everything all right, Doctor?" Wren asked the physician currently examining Alice's IV bags.

"Fine. Just adding her new medication." He didn't look once in her direction as he reached into his pocket.

Bradley shifted. "Dr. Johansen didn't mention any new medication. What are you doing?"

"My job." The man turned, choosing now to look at Wren directly.

Her eyes narrowed. She flicked a gaze to the hypodermic needle in his left hand. Her eyebrow twitched up.

The man pivoted and instantly locked an arm around Bradley's throat.

Bradley gasped, kicking out as the man dragged him toward the open bathroom door. The move sent Bradley's chair crashing to the floor. Alice's husband's eyes went wide and bulging, clawing at the arm around his neck as he struggled to breathe.

"Stop!" Wren took a step around the bed, heading for them, both hands up as if in surrender. "Think about this. There's nowhere for you to go."

The man's eyes darted to the door, but he remained silent.

"What's happening?" Bradley gasped as his face lost color.

"Let him go," Wren ordered as she continued to advance. She felt Ty move in behind her. She inclined her head to the right, hoping Ty, even off his game, would get the message. Behind Ty, she heard the kerfuffle of voices rising and footsteps echoing. "Let. Him. Go." She didn't flinch as she met the man's gaze over the top of Bradley's curly head.

The closer she got, moving around the foot of the bed, the more clear she could see the man's plan.

Out of the corner of her eye, Ty shifted away. Wren debated about using the gun she had stuffed into the back of her jeans. She didn't want to out herself completely. Not yet, anyway. And a gun in close quarters with a lot of innocents was rarely the wise play. She reached out, caught one of Bradley's flailing hands and tugged.

The man released him with a giant shove. Bradley catapulted

into her. They fell back and Wren managed to control the landing so that her head didn't crack into the tiled floor.

Wren rolled Bradley off her, pushed to her feet and dived forward into the bathroom just as the man exited through the connecting door.

She heard a crash and a lot of yelling. Ty had tripped the man and sent him falling face-first into a cleaning cart. The push-back had Ty on the floor as well. The racket brought patients to their doors, bed alarms clanging and nurses scrambling to keep their charges safe and calm.

Ty reached out, attempted to grab the man's ankles as he stumbled to his feet, but he darted out of Ty's grip and raced off. His feet barely touched the ground as he ran for the emergency exit at the far end of the hall.

Ty practically bounced up, giving chase, as Wren fell in behind him.

The emergency alarm exploded overhead as they bolted outside, mere feet behind their suspect.

Their suspect picked up speed as he ran along the meandering footpath through the courtyard leading to an anemic parking lot. A white SUV sat parked on the other side of the waist-high exit gate.

From behind Ty, Wren saw the driver lean down. At first she assumed they were ducking out of the way, but then they popped back up, flung the door open, gun in hand, and aimed directly at them.

Chapter Three

"Down!" Wren tackled Ty from behind, sent them both tumbling over one another as a bullet whizzed past their heads.

Another shot, then another kept them pinned down as the suspect leaped over the short exit gate and threw himself into the car. They sped away with the passenger door still flailing. Ty untangled himself from Wren, shoved to his feet and ran out to try to get a look at the car. "No plates. White SUV. In Alaska, that's probably like finding a snowflake on an iceberg."

Adrenaline still coursing through her system, Wren got up onto her knees. "We should get back. Check on Bradley. And Alice." She didn't think the man had injected anything into Alice's IV line, but they couldn't be too careful.

Ty grabbed her arms and hauled her up. "I missed something, didn't I?"

She loathed the guilt and self-pity she heard in his voice. "You were charming the nurses to get information we needed." She shrugged. "One of them mentioned the doctor had just left after seeing Alice. Didn't make sense there'd be another one coming in to see her again so soon."

"Damn." His hands tightened around her upper arms and he hauled her onto her toes, pulled her close and pressed his lips against hers.

Her entire body locked down. There wasn't a muscle she

could move or a thought she could process. The only thing that seemed to be getting through was the idea that Ty Savakis had finally, after more than seven years…kissed her.

"Um." It was all she could say once he set her back on her feet. She blinked, uncertain where that kiss had come from or what it even meant. It had to be cover…didn't it? But one quick glance told her there wasn't anyone to witness the moment. That meant… She struggled not to frown. What, exactly?

"You are amazing," he said before he moved around her and headed back inside through the now-open emergency exit door.

"Right. Amazing." She couldn't stop blinking, as if her body was trying to reboot her brain. What on earth was she supposed to do with *that*?

Embrace it, silly girl. Embrace it?! When had her subconscious jumped on board whatever crazy train she'd landed on? She stopped short before reaching the emergency door, lifted a finger to examine one of the wooden pillars and the bullets lodged in it.

She wedged the door open and ducked into an empty patient room. She snapped a pair of purple latex gloves out of the dispenser hanging on the wall. She grabbed a few extra, along with a pen resting on top of an admissions form.

Letting Ty deal with the initial fallout—they knew him better, after all—she returned to the pillar and, as flashbacks from her forensics training assaulted her, carefully pried the first bullet free. She wrapped it in one of the extra gloves, trying not to handle it very much. The heat of the bullet seeped into her fingers, helping to warm them against the chill.

It took longer to get the other two, but they soon joined the first one. She peeled off the gloves and stuffed everything into her jacket pocket. One of the orderlies turned up to pull the door closed and reset the alarm.

"Hang on!" Wren hurried inside. "Thanks."

The incident had brought everyone out of their offices and cubicles. Nurses focused on keeping the patients calm and getting them back into their rooms. The clinic patients had emptied into the hall. Voices remained raised and a bit panicked.

"I heard gunshots!" someone cried. "Did anyone else hear them? Is someone hurt?"

Wren avoided the pointed looks she received as she returned to Alice's room. The first thing she noticed, other than Ty's visible concern over Bradley, was that Alice herself remained completely and blissfully unaware of what had transpired. Good news, Wren supposed. Best she not know someone had tried to finish the job they'd started last week.

Alice's husband, on the other hand...

Ty crouched beside Bradley, who was still on the floor, only now he held an oxygen mask over his face and was breathing deeply.

"Prone to panic attacks," Ty told Wren as she stepped farther into the room. The nurse Ty had been chatting with previously was on the other side, resting a comforting hand on Bradley's shoulder.

"Did you check Alice's IV?" Wren asked the nurse, who nodded.

"First thing." She gestured to the disconnected line. "I pulled it to be safe. Our supervisor is getting a new setup."

Wren nodded.

Bradley tugged the mask off long enough to gasp at Ty. "Why would someone try to kill Alice?" he demanded. "Especially after..." He turned to his wife, his eyes wide with fear. "What on earth is going on?"

"An excellent question."

Wren spun at the deep, gravelly male voice that belonged to an older man standing in the doorway of Alice's hospital room. His hair was thick, more salt than pepper, and he wore a khaki uniform from his pressed trousers to the top of his wide-rimmed Smokey Bear hat. The sharp eagle-eyed expression on his narrow face assessed Wren in the blink of an eye, shifted to Ty before he settled on Bradley.

"Bradley? You and Alice all right?"

Bradley looked a bit confused at the question at first, then nodded. "Uh-huh." He rubbed a hand across his forehead. "Wren broke my fall. Thanks for that."

"No problem." Wren walked around the bed, stepping carefully past the trio of people huddled on the floor, and approached Alice's IV bag. The nurse was right. She didn't find any holes in the IV line or any indication the infusion tube had been tampered with.

Something caught her attention on the floor and she bent down. Peering under the bed, she found the hypodermic needle and the safety cap lying nearby. "Sheriff Egbert?" Wren asked and straightened to face the town's number one law enforcement officer.

"And you'd be Wren… Savakis." The pause in his voice and even narrower gaze suggested he was reevaluating Ty's previous story.

"That's me." She pulled a fresh pair of gloves out of her pocket and shoved her fingers into them.

"You got something?" he asked when she ducked out of sight again, picked up the needle and cap and topped the sharp end. The plunger was high, yet the tube itself was empty.

"Where did that come from?" the nurse asked as Bradley sat up and pushed the mask off his face again.

"Our assailant. It's evidence. Hopefully." She looked to the sheriff. "You'll be wanting this for prints, I presume?"

Sheriff Egbert eyed her for a moment. "Best we discuss that on my turf."

Wren removed the gloves, covering the needle with them to protect it.

"Shall we?" the sheriff asked as Bradley and Ty both pushed to their feet.

"Hang on." Bradley grabbed hold of the foot of Alice's bed as if to steady himself. "I don't know what is going on, but before I forget. Thank you." He looked to Wren. "It didn't occur to me he was anything other than a doctor. This is all so confusing. It's…incredible!"

"I'm just glad you're okay." Wren didn't want to generate more questions than the man already had.

"Yeah." He ran a hand across the back of his neck. "Might need a chiropractor after that, but yeah, I think I am." He looked at his wife. Tears filled his eyes. "Why would anyone want to hurt her?"

Wren's chest tightened with sympathy and more than a little guilt. It was obvious Bradley had no clue about big chunks of his wife's past, which added a layer to the deception that she and Ty were spinning.

"I'm hoping we can figure that out," Ty said. "Remember what I told you, Bradley. Alice is my friend. I'm not going to leave until I know she and the rest of your family are safe."

"The kids." Bradley balked and lost what color was left in his face. "I didn't even... I need to check on the kids. They're supposed to go on a field trip today."

"Deputy Adjuk's gone over to Skyway Tower to check on them," Sheriff Egbert said. "But we can give Mrs. Caldwell a call if it would make you feel better. Ask her to keep them at the tower."

"Okay." Bradley raised a trembling hand to his throat. "It would, thanks."

"I'll do that right now," the nurse offered. "You just stay here with Alice. I'm going to have one of the doctors give you a once-over. Just to be safe."

"Good idea," Sheriff Egbert said. "Mr. and Mrs. Savakis?" He stepped back as if giving them room to exit.

"I feel like we've been called in to the principal's office," she muttered under her breath as she and Ty fell into step.

"Like you ever were," Ty teased. Wren scrunched her mouth to stop from smiling. He wasn't wrong. The principal's office had been more her brother Aiden's territory. He never had done well with being told what to do.

"What's the plan?" she asked as they made their way slowly out to join the sheriff in the hall.

"Tell him the truth," Ty said. "Most of it, anyway. Follow my lead, yeah?"

Her hand tingled from where he'd grasped it. "I always do."

It felt oddly like a perp walk, Ty thought as he and Wren walked out of the hospital behind the sheriff. Strange, being on the other side of one.

"Sheriff!" Behind them a voice had called.

Ty glanced over his shoulder as the sheriff turned, and found a young man, barely out of his teens with shaggy blond hair and slightly panicked eyes. He wore a uniform of sorts, with an oversize dark puffy jacket with a security emblem on the left sleeve.

"Hang on a second." Sheriff Egbert motioned to the marked vehicle parked haphazardly across two spaces at the front entrance.

"Think he's going to run us out of town?" Wren said in her half-teasing tone.

"I bet he's trying to figure out where we fit in." Ty couldn't blame the man. Things had definitely gone a bit off the rails since Alice's accident. He dropped Wren's duffel onto the ground and leaned against the hood of the vehicle. "You get a good look at the guy's face?"

"Enough that I can play around with an ID program."

"On a scale of one to ten, how confident are you you'll find something if we can talk the sheriff into using his computer system?"

"About a three." She dug into her pocket, pulled out a wadded-up purple glove. "No scars, no distinguishing features that I could see. He blends. Dug these out of the pillar, though." Unwrapping the latex, she showed the bullet fragments to him. "Full metal jackets. Good ones," she added. "Military grade, if I had to guess."

And they would have to guess without a lab backing them up. "Military opens up a whole new can of worms."

"'Military grade' doesn't mean military." She chewed on the inside of her cheek, the way she always did when she was puzzling something out. "Private contractors can get a hold of stuff like this. Given that Treyhern's likely behind this, it would make sense he'd hire someone to take care of his witness problem. The hypo was empty, by the way. Probably planned to inject an air bubble into her IV line."

Ty's stomach clenched. "With her injuries, an embolism would be seen as natural causes."

"Risky, though, doing it with so many people around," Wren mused.

"Maybe they didn't have a choice." Disappointment crashed

through him at her previous comment. "I thought you agreed with me about Treyhern being responsible."

"You say Alice wasn't involved in anything else that could be triggering this," she said. "I'm willing to trust you on that, but I'm keeping my options open. Going in blind isn't going to help us protect her. We need to be ready for anything."

Grudgingly, he had to admit she was right. Getting tunnel vision where a suspect was concerned was a surefire way to blow the case. And this was one case he couldn't afford to mess up.

"Sorry about that." Sheriff Egbert left the young man behind looking somewhat less...dejected. "Obie Farland. Been working security for the clinic for about three months. Feels responsible for what happened."

"He wasn't where he should have been," Ty observed. "Saw the 'away from the desk' note when we came in."

"Considering that up until now we thought Alice's accident was just that, Obie was exactly where he was supposed to be." The sheriff's eyes sharpened like a dagger's edge. "Doing his rounds through the clinic. He asked if it would be okay if he worked an extra shift." Sheriff Egbert glanced back at the clinic as he pulled open his car door. "He'll keep an eye on Alice's door specifically."

"Nice one, Ty," Wren muttered as she climbed into the back seat. "Shame the kid for doing his job."

Ty didn't respond. Guilt wasn't an easy emotion to deal with and he'd lived with his share of it. Funny, he'd have thought he'd gotten better at riding that particular wave by now.

"Gotta admit." Sheriff Egbert pulled out of the lot and turned left. "I've been sheriff of this town for going on seventeen years. Seen my share of fistfights and brawls, especially at The Icebreaker during hockey season—"

"Icebreaker?" Wren asked.

"Local bar. Pub," Ty corrected quickly at the glare he got in the rearview mirror.

"That back there isn't something I ever want repeated in my town," Sheriff Egbert told them. "Everyone should feel safe in a hospital."

"We aren't going to argue with you, Sheriff," Ty said.

"I'm a two-person operation here in Splendor. I don't have the staff to go running around looking for assault suspects with needles, or anything else, for that matter."

"But you were already looking for one, right, Sheriff?" Wren said. "The person who ran Alice down in their car?"

"Mrs. Savakis—"

"Wren is fine."

Ty bit the inside of his cheek. He'd been wondering how long it would take for her to get irritated by that.

"Wren." Sheriff Egbert glanced at her in the mirror now. "Yes, I've been doing my best, but something tells me I've been working under some misconceptions. Either of you want to tell me what Alice Hawkins got herself into?"

"She didn't *get* herself into anything." Ty's defense of the younger woman struck like second nature. It took precisely three minutes to drive from the hospital to the dedicated parking space in front of the blink-and-you'll-miss-it sheriff's office around the corner from the main drag of Splendor. This really was a blink-and-you-might-miss-it kind of town.

"I don't like the idea of leaving Alice alone at the hospital," Wren said as Sheriff Egbert parked. He flung open his door, then paused before climbing out.

"Neither do I, but I don't have any spare deputies." He slipped out, retrieved their bags from the back and waited for them to join him on the sidewalk. "Obie and his nighttime counterpart are going to alternate shifts. It's the best I can do." He hefted the duffel bag and pushed it into Ty's chest. It took all of Ty's effort not to *ugh* out loud. "Come on in." Sheriff Egbert pulled open the solitary glass door and waved them inside. "Let's chat."

To call the sheriff's office a hole-in-the-wall could be considered an exaggeration. The space couldn't have been more than twenty feet across, but it was considerably deeper than wide. Two desks sat across from one another, each topped with a computer and various trinkets and mementos. The wooden filing cabinet seemed both outdated yet completely in style with the rustic decor. As with most small-town station houses, this one boasted a pair of jail cells lining the back wall over which two narrow windows sat, the only real light other than the lamps currently glowing.

Cozy to the point of claustrophobic, but with enough personal touches that it worked.

"Have a seat." Sheriff Egbert pulled a couple of folding chairs out from between the filing cabinet and wall. Ty suspected Wren was surprised they hadn't been put in the cells.

"Let's start by reviewing the information you gave me a couple of days ago when we chatted, Mr. Savakis. If that's your real name."

"There's usually *FBI special agent* in front of it," Wren said.

"FBI." Whatever Sheriff Egbert had been expecting, it appeared it wasn't that. "Huh." He sat back, rested a thumping finger against his lips. "Well, that's something. And your relationship with Alice?"

"Professional," Ty replied. "Ten years ago Alice Hawkins was a witness in a murder case I worked. The suspect was a man named Ambrose Treyhern. Thanks to her, he's currently twenty-five to life in a maximum-security prison." He tried to get a bead on the sheriff's thoughts, but couldn't. "Treyhern was recently granted a new trial. My guess is he isn't thrilled with the prospect of her testifying again and he's hired someone to make sure she doesn't. I'm not here to cause problems, Sheriff. I'm here to find out who's trying to kill my witness."

Sheriff Egbert's eyes shifted between them. "Have to admit." He tapped a restless finger against the edge of his desk. "As disturbing as this is, it sits better with me than having to suspect someone in this town is responsible for the hit-and-run."

Ty kept his expression passive. He hadn't thought of that.

"I've spent the last week looking at people I've known for more than twenty years, wondering if they were guilty." Regret and a hint of anger tinged the sheriff's voice. "Would have been nice not to have to do that."

Ty winced. "In hindsight, I see where I should have handled things differently."

"Suppose you didn't know who you could trust, either." Sheriff Egbert's gaze flicked to Wren. "Except you."

"We've been partners for a long time," Wren said. "We have each other's back."

"Even when it means following him up here to the middle of nowhere?"

She shrugged and earned even more respect from Ty. "He needs me, I'm there."

"No questions asked?" the sheriff challenged.

"Oh, plenty to ask," she admitted with a wry smile. "But the answers wouldn't change anything."

She had no idea how much that sentiment meant to him. "I was on the phone with Alice when she was run down." Ty wanted the attention shifted back to him. Wren was going to have enough to deal with once their involvement in the case got out. And it would get out. The more he could get the local authorities to focus on him, the clearer Wren would be. "She needed reassurances about testifying again." His head buzzed with the memory.

"Guess I have me an ear witness instead of an eye one, then," Sheriff Egbert said. "What did you hear?"

"Enough to believe this wasn't anything other than deliberate. No screeching brakes or tires." He refrained from sharing how the sound of Alice's scream and the heavy thud of her body hitting the ground haunted him.

The sheriff looked him straight in the eye. "As you know from our previous conversation, no skid marks at the scene, so I'd agree with your observation. The glass we found is one of the most common used for headlights, according to the crime lab in Anchorage, so no joy there. While it's not tourist season at the moment, we've had our share of visitors over the past few weeks. No one who's raised any alarm bells, other than you. But my deputy and I will ask around. Especially after what happened this morning at the clinic. Question."

"Okay," Wren said.

"That needle you found under Alice's bed." He shifted his attention back to Wren. "Your fancy FBI field office in Anchorage gonna be able to process that for you?"

"Ah." Wren glanced uneasily at Ty.

The office door opened, letting a cold blast of air in. Ty and

Wren both turned in their chairs as a young woman shoved her hood off her dark head and stomped her boots. "All clear at Skyway, Sheriff. Kids are good. I went through the security camera recordings back to yesterday morning. Nothing strange that I noticed."

"Good to hear," Sheriff Egbert said. "Deputy Shelly Adjuk, FBI special agents Ty Savakis and Wren..." He frowned, inclined his head. "It's not Savakis, is it?"

"It's McKenna, actually. Wren McKenna." She stood, held out her hand as Shelly approached. "Nice to meet you, Deputy Adjuk."

"Shelly, please. Wow. FBI, really?" Her eyes lit up with wonder and held more than a hint of excitement. "I would love to talk to you... Right. Sorry. Not now." She held up both hands and backed away. "I can bend your ear later."

"Fair warning." Sheriff Egbert eyed Wren. "She can do that better than anyone you've ever met. Now, about that needle." He reached for the phone. "I'm assuming you're planning on running that up to your FBI lab in Anchorage. Shall I let them know you're coming?"

Ty glanced at Wren, who shrugged. He may as well be sitting in church, given the amount of confessions he was making today. "Actually, we'd rather avoid any official interactions with the agency. My being here isn't exactly...sanctioned."

"Have you two gone rogue?" Shelly asked in a tone that sounded more enthusiastic than disapproving.

"Don't you have to file a report on Mrs. Tachino's prowler, Deputy?" Sheriff Egbert asked.

"Prowler, my left foot," Shelly muttered loud enough for them to hear. "A merry band of raccoons is more like it."

"Look, Sheriff." Ty sat up straighter and drew his legs under him. "I know my turning up is a bit of a complication—"

"*Our* turning up," Wren corrected.

"Right. We aren't here in any official capacity." He stopped short of admitting that should his presence become known to his superior, those complications were going to increase. "Ten years ago I gave Alice my word she'd be safe. I'm not going to go away. Not until I know she is. That said, if our bosses find out we're here before we find the person or persons responsible for hurting Alice, chances are they'll get away with it." Considering Alice's condition, odds were pretty good they already had.

Sheriff Egbert met his gaze with chilling intensity. "My main concern is the safety of my town and the people who live here. I'm beginning to think Alice might be better off being transferred to a facility with more security. There's a hospital in Anchorage—"

"A bigger hospital could give them more cover," Wren said before Ty could. "I understand your concern, Sheriff, but you've taken new measures to keep her safe. People will be on the lookout for unfamiliar faces. I know it isn't your first choice, but these guys have worked themselves into a bit of a pinch point. Odds are better we'll find them here. We just need the leeway to look."

Wren's argument didn't require any backup from Ty. She'd hit it on the head.

"All right," Sheriff Egbert agreed but looked as if he wasn't entirely convinced. "Like I said, we're a two-person operation. It'd be pretty reckless of me not to accept help when it's being offered. Even unofficial federal help. I'd keep that information to yourself around here, though. Not everyone in Splendor has the best opinions when it comes to Feds. You fly low, I'll give you enough lead. But I'll snap it back the second I think you're overstepping with my people."

"Understood." Relieved, he looked to Wren for her reaction.

"What about a lab to process the needle?" she asked.

"I'll see what I can do with our contacts in Juneau," Sheriff Egbert said. "It'll take time."

Of course, time was the one thing Ty couldn't be certain they had a lot of.

"Appreciate your understanding, Sheriff." Ty stood, motioned to Wren's bags sitting by the front door. "I think it's past due we got out of your hair. We'll be in touch."

"Yes," Sheriff Egbert said as they headed out. "You will be."

Chapter Four

"Home sweet home." Ty unlocked the door to their fourth-floor apartment and pushed it open ahead of Wren. "For the next little while, anyway."

The walk from the sheriff's station to Skyway Tower had helped clear his head, but not completely. The closer they got to their temporary residence, the more anxious he became. The idea that his uncertainty had everything to do with Wren only added to the pressure building inside of him.

He hadn't quite been able to reconcile the odd anticipation he'd felt since Wren agreed to play house with him. They'd worked so closely together for the past seven years, it seemed strange to feel anxious or uncertain. They'd done this plenty of times before: gone undercover as a couple. But their obligation to the FBI had always been a kind of protective barrier between them. Here? On their own, without the agency backing them up, that barrier was nowhere to be seen or felt.

One more thing to throw him off his game. His pinballing emotions—anger, frustration, guilt—about Alice and Treyhern left him feeling as if his emotions were scattered all over the place and he lacked the energy to pull himself back together.

The hall of the fourth floor of Skyway Tower hadn't quite shaken that military housing feel. The reconfiguration and rede-sign had added more homey details, of course. The dark-colored patterned carpeting along the hallway. The soft beige walls. The wood color trim outlining the dozen or so apartment entrances. To Ty, it kind of felt like the building was trying a little too hard to be something it wasn't. But what it was, he reminded himself and as he'd just said to Wren, was home. For now.

A door behind them snapped open. Wren stepped back and the two of them looked to the elderly woman poking her gray-haired head out of an apartment a few doors down.

"Newcomers?" she called.

"Yes, ma'am." Ty rested a hand on Wren's shoulder. "Staying here a few weeks. We're friends of Alice Hawkins."

"Oh, Alice. Poor Alice." She emerged from the doorway, her bright pink tracksuit a startling blip of color. "Such a shame. How's she doing?"

"Last we heard, okay," Ty said and hoped that statement didn't come back to bite him. It was only a matter of time before word of what had happened at the hospital today got around town.

"Agatha!" Another voice echoed into the corridor. "I just got a double word and triple letter score. It's your... Oh. New people. Just moving in?"

Agatha rolled her eyes. "This is my twin sister, Florence. People just call us the Thistle sisters."

Ty's brows went up. He might have guessed sisters, but not twins. Agatha was short and squat where Florence was lean and towered over her sister by at least six inches. Where Agatha wore her gray hair neatly up and away from her face, Florence's dark frizzy curls framed her thin face.

"Welcome to Skyway." Florence waved and set the bangles on her wrist to jangling. "Do you like board games? We have a large collection if you're in need of any. Or join us for one! We promise not to win too quickly."

"Appreciate that, ma'am," Ty said with a chuckle. "We'll keep that in mind after we settle in."

"Come on by for tea anytime," Agatha called. "We love visitors. We've lived here going on fifteen years. Can never have too many visitors."

"Leave them be, Ag." Florence tugged on her sister's sleeve.

"Can't you see they're wanting some alone time?" They were still bickering when the door closed.

"They're cute," Wren said. "And maybe a little lonely?"

"Probably why they're happy to see new people."

"Which apartment is Alice's?"

"Two doors down that way, left side." He pointed behind him. "Four G."

"Quiet floor. Soundproofing must be pretty good." She grinned. "Should work in our favor, yeah?"

Her statement sent a surprising array of rather erotic images shooting through his overstressed mind. Images starring him and Wren. Ty shook his head. Why on earth was he going down this road? They were adults. They knew how to keep their hands to themselves. Besides, they'd agreed a long time ago that their friendship and partnership were far more important than any physical attraction. Still. Ty's gaze dropped to her curves on display even beneath her puffy jacket. They'd probably been more intimate with one another than most lovers were.

Sleep, he told himself. He needed sleep. As much as he could get. That should reset the short circuit that had obviously taken place in his brain. And libido.

"Oh, this is cute."

Wren's surprise brought him fully into the apartment. Most of the space was painted a bright white—the walls, the massive floor-to-ceiling bookcase, the trim. No doubt that had been an effort to make the seven-hundred-square-foot space appear larger than it was.

He closed the door, bolted it out of habit. The splashes of color came courtesy of the furnishings and decor, which ranged from blankets and wall hangings of Indigenous patterns to the rustic bric-a-brac scattered about the living room.

"Shipping furniture out here costs a small fortune," Ty told her. "Doesn't make sense to take it with you when you leave, especially if you plan to come back. As you can see, reading's big in Splendor." The enormous multi-shelf bookcase was jam-packed with mostly genre fiction ranging from some of his favorite suspense titles to Wren's preferred epic fantasy novels. There was also a large selection of puzzles, which seemed a not-so-subtle warning of uneventful evenings. "Got plenty of movies to choose from." He indicated the selection of DVDs on a section of shelving. "The place isn't anything fancy, but it looked comfortable to me. We've got internet and cable, but again, they can be spotty."

"Being on the coast probably means a lot of outages," Wren said.

"Got your sofa—a sleeper, in case you were wondering."

"I wasn't." She wandered the room, no doubt making a mental note of the television, comfy overstuffed chair and the narrow doorway leading into a well-organized and arranged kitchen. "It's small but I like that. We won't be falling over one another. Much." She flashed him a smile as she pulled off her knit cap, fluffed up her hair. The blond caught the sunlight streaming in through the window over the back of the sofa. Unzipping her jacket, she disappeared into the kitchen. "Kitchen's serviceable. Better than yours, anyway," she called. "Fridge is bare, though."

So far he'd only eaten at a few of the restaurants in town or gotten takeout. "Didn't get around to shopping."

"Or you were waiting for me to get here because we both know you love my cooking."

He couldn't help but smile. "I'll plead the Fifth on that." He'd missed her these last few weeks. Being around Wren always centered him. Kept him on an even keel. She understood him, even tolerated him without adding drama. Not that she was responsible for his mental well-being. But her presence definitely helped. His vacation punishment hadn't put him in a good place. Hearing about Alice had only dropped him deeper into that spiral.

"Small-town grocery stores are a wealth of information," she said as she came back out. After removing her jacket and hanging it on one of the half-dozen hooks behind the door, she checked the half bath beside the aforementioned bookcase, then went into the bedroom. "If we hit that up later, we should get a feel for what people are thinking about what happened to Alice."

"Scared." He hadn't needed to visit any store to pick up on that. He followed her into the space where a king-size bed sat wedged between two anemic-looking nightstands. The apartment was a bit dated. No USB plugs or a lot of storage beyond the assembled MDF armoire that had been painted to match the blinding white of the walls, but the navy bedspread accented with bright red pillows added a kind of nautical feel. The character of the place seemed a bit disjointed, but they didn't need character. They just needed to be close to the Hawkins family. "They're scared. I got coffee this morning and the hit-and-run was definitely a big topic of conversation. Had a few odd looks shot my way, so the sheriff was right. They're more than aware when someone new is in town. I'd bet that's part of what's got them spooked. I dropped my name. Said I was a friend of Alice's. Just to see how they react to newcomers."

"Sheriff Egbert probably isn't the only person who's been wondering if one of their own was responsible," Wren mused. "If there's one thing a lot of British television has taught me, it's never commit a crime in a small town. The perpetrator won't ever get away with it, if only because everyone knows everyone's business. You know?" She poked her head into the second bathroom, this one with a full shower and claw-foot tub. He could attest to the water pressure being excellent. "It could be someone local. Small doesn't mean it doesn't have crime. And most everyone has a price."

"Presence of a sheriff proves that," Ty agreed.

"We should ask him about the troublemakers in town."

"Give it a day or two," Ty warned. "I think we've earned all the goodwill we're going to get for now."

"His deputy is interesting," Wren observed. "Young, though."

He'd thought the same thing. "Young enough to hurt our egos. Old enough to be competent. One thing." He crouched, pulled his folding pocketknife from his back pocket. The knife had been a gift from his first partner, the same partner who had helped him close the Treyhern case the first time.

"What are you doing?" Wren poked her head out of the bathroom as he slipped the blade in between two planks of the hardwood floor that he'd pried loose upon his first arriving.

"The really good thing about actual hardwood flooring." He pointed, then held out his hand. "Give me your badge and FBI ID."

"Oh, sure. Yeah." She handed him both. "You thinking we might get mugged on the streets and our secret identities will be revealed?"

"I'm not taking any chances with anything where Alice is concerned." He settled her items into the space under the floorboard, then pushed it back into place. He stood and stepped on it just to make sure it was solid.

Wren ducked back into the bathroom, leaving Ty unable to resist temptation.

He sat on the edge of the bed. Then, before he could talk himself out of it, he lay down. He didn't think he'd ever, in his entire life, found a pillow so perfectly soft.

"Now that we're in with the sheriff, that should make some things easier." Wren opened and closed cabinets in the bathroom. "If Sheriff Egbert's been suspicious, he's probably looked into a few people. Be interesting to know who."

"I got the feeling if he suspected anyone, he'd have let us know. Been here a long time." His eyes drooped.

"Yeah." Wren sighed. "He does seem to like his job. For the most part."

"He likes the town." He smothered a yawn. "He moved here with his wife and two kids. Kids have since moved back into the Lower 48. Wife runs the Books & Brews shop on the main street."

"Well, if we run out of things to read here, we know where to go." Wren popped back into the bedroom. "I'm gonna need something to occupy my brain with other than looking at your mug."

He managed a weak smile. Only when he felt the bed dip did his eyes spring back open. "Sorry." He pinched the bridge of his nose. "I'm about out of steam." It didn't escape his notice that it was only now that Wren was by his side that he felt comfortable enough to sleep.

"I can tell." She touched his leg and sent a wave of heat straight to his groin. He nearly groaned. He was more out of it than he'd realized. "I'm still a bit buzzed with adrenaline. Why don't I hit up the grocery, take a walk around town, get acclimated, and you can get some sleep."

"If you're sure." He rolled onto his side facing her, already feeling his body completely relax. "Second set of keys are on one of the bookcase shelves."

"Don't argue with me or anything," she teased. "I'll be back in a bit."

"Just need an hour or so."

"Uh-huh."

Her derisive snort was the last thing he heard before he dropped off to sleep.

Wren pulled her key out of the dead bolt and immediately slid a hand under her puffy jacket to check on the 9 mm she had tucked into the back of her jeans. She did a quick assessment of the long hallway, then quietly and quickly made her way to apartment 4G, Alice and Bradley Hawkins's home.

No sooner had she leaned her ear against the door than she heard the elevator doors slide open and keys rattling. She quickly shifted and rapped her knuckles against the door.

"You must be Mrs. Savakis."

She straightened, stepped back and faced the slightly stooped, middle-aged bald man making his way down the hall. "Your husband said you'd be arriving this morning."

"He was right." She pointed to the door, then dropped her gaze to the man's white-and-gray dog. "When we heard about Alice, we couldn't stay away. I wasn't sure if Bradley was back from the hospital yet."

"Haven't seen him since he dropped the kids off downstairs on his way out." The man shook his head, stretched out his hand to touch the top of his dog's head. The dog turned adoring eyes on him before shifting his suspicious gaze onto Wren. "Darn shame what's happened to Alice. And the family. They're all just torn up. I'm Albert Jenkins, but everyone just calls me Al. Building super." He extended a hand that Wren instantly accepted. Calluses were evident in his strong greeting. "This here is Koda." The dog seemed to relax a little at his owner's friendly tone. "Anything you need, you just let me know."

"Pleased to meet you, Al." Wren straightened, then held out

her hand for Koda to sniff. "Hello, Koda. You're a pretty girl, aren't you?"

"Don't go feeding her canine ego," Al warned with a chuckle as Koda took a step forward and nudged her cold nose into Wren's palm. "This mutt's already a star."

"I'll bet she is." She adored dogs, had always wanted one, but her sister, Regan, was allergic. Now she traveled too much to have one. Wren crouched, held out her hands, and Koda moved into them, pushing her head under Wren's chin. "What kind of mutt are you? Let me guess. She's got some husky in her, I bet."

"Good eye." Al beamed. "Rest of her's Border collie. Too smart for her own good, I can tell you that. But she's great with the tenants."

"Then she's doing her job." Wren gave the dog a final pat before she stood back up. "Ty's grabbing some sleep, so I thought I'd go check out this town of yours. From what I've seen so far, Splendor certainly has its charms."

"A lot more that's hidden, too." Al's cheeky grin carried a hint of pride. "Must be good friends of the Hawkinses if you got here so quick."

"She and my husband grew up together." Not sticking to Ty's story would only create suspicion. "I've only spoken to her on video chat. Makes this a bit bittersweet."

"Poor girl," Al repeated. "Lived here my entire life, never once heard of something so awful happening in Splendor. You planning on staying long?"

"Until Alice is back on her feet," Wren improvised. "My husband takes his responsibilities of friendship very seriously." Definitely not a lie. "We've been meaning to come up and visit. Terrible reason to do so now, I know. Still." She looked over her shoulder to the large window at the end of the hall. The view put the ocean on full display. "It's a beautiful place."

"That'd be my opinion," Al agreed. "Maybe you two'll put this on your list of places to move to."

"Maybe." Ty must have dropped the hint around town that they were looking to move. "It's definitely shot up my list. As long as it's safe," she added, not wanting to get overly enthusiastic. "We have a lot of places in contention, though. A while back we spent a month in Sedona, Arizona. I absolutely loved it. Ty, not so much." While she always tried to stick as close to the truth as possible, lies were a necessary part of her job. Even when she was off book. "Now that Ty sold his company, we've got the means to consider almost anyplace in the world."

Al's bushy eyebrows arched and he shoved his hands into the pockets of his dark blue overalls. Koda let out a bit of a whine before sighing. "Glad to hear we've made the cut."

"Ty's a fan of unique communities." Wren did her best to stave off doubt. "I'm guessing you don't get many strangers around here."

"Get a few," Al confirmed. "You and Ty are the first new tenants since the holidays."

Interesting. "I don't suppose there's a thrift store in town, is there? I know we won't be here long, but I do love me a thrift store. They're such a representation of the area." They also tended to be a wealth of information. Thrift-store owners knew everyone and everything that happened. If they wanted to get the real pulse of Splendor, that was one place to start.

"Got a few stores, but sounds like you'll be wanting to visit Tundra Antiques and Treasures," Al said. "Callie Haller owns the place." He winked. "She thinks putting *antiques* in the title makes it fancier than it is. Truth is the woman's a pack rat. Never throws much away, but she makes an effort at restoring things. Keeps the place pretty tidy. Might be a treasure or two lurking in there for you."

"Sounds like a fun place to explore." She touched his arm as she passed. "Appreciate the recommendation. Be seeing you around. Bye, Koda."

"You call me if you need anything!" Al called after her, his voice echoing down the corridor as she headed for the stairs.

The chill she got the second she entered the stairwell had her zipping up her jacket. Still, she memorized the number of steps, leaned over the railing to see if the stairs went the entirety of the building or cut off before the roof.

Emerging through the door that led to the lobby level, Wren found herself looking at a large open space filled with bright-colored walls and fun geometric carpeting, much like the lobby of a hotel near an amusement park where she'd once stayed. She hadn't paid too much attention when she'd entered the building; she'd been looking forward to unloading her bags and getting a look at where she'd be staying—and sleeping—the next few nights.

The entirety of the lobby level was dedicated to services and office space. The room for the complex's director near the front door had Wren turning back toward the elevator and walking down the east hall leading to the day care and school. She checked her watch. Just before lunchtime. She was hoping the chaos of mealtime might allow her a chance at observation.

She could hear the telltale sounds of singing and clapping. Structured activities, she assumed. That off-key enthusiastic caterwauling shot her straight back to kindergarten, when she'd been subjected to endless show-and-tells and story times. Sitting still had completely missed her DNA. Even now, she felt a bit jittery and jumpy.

Keeping her gaze steady, she scanned the upper corners of the walls, turned occasionally, getting a feel for what, if any, security measures were in place.

The wide hallways were accentuated by large windows. Nothing felt claustrophobic, despite the numerous amenities made available to residents. The beige walls gave way to colorful murals of children cartwheeling and tumbling their way around giant rainbows of bubbles that served as the entryway of the day care.

The second she approached the door, the back of her neck prickled. Leaning inside, she grabbed the door frame, then held up a hand in apology when the young Black woman sitting in the teeny tiny kid's chair shifted immediately to face her. There was an attempt at friendliness, but there was no mistaking the suspicion in her dark eyes.

"May I help you?" The way she stretched out her arm, as if providing protection for the handful of children in her charge, allayed some of Wren's concerns. She counted eight children in the circle, six boys and two girls of varying ages.

"I'm sorry. I'm new to the building," Wren said. "Just getting the lay of the land. Didn't mean to interrupt."

"It's story time!" a little girl of about five announced, her bright blond ponytail bouncing as she jumped to her feet. "We're listening to *Frog and Toad*. They're friends."

"I love *Frog and Toad*," Wren told them. "Again, I'm sorry to interrupt."

She backed away, and as she turned to leave the same way she'd come, she found herself facing a forty-something woman who definitely had the look of a school official.

"Hello." The woman's voice was a bit clipped. She hugged a stack of notebooks against her chest. Her fiery red hair was pulled away from her face, but springy gray curls erupted along her hairline. The color of her cardigan sweater reminded Wren of ripe blueberries.

"Hi." Wren did her best to appear contrite. "I'm not creeping around, I promise. I'm just new to the building. Wren Savakis." She held out her hand. Why did saying that name send chills up her spine? "My husband and I are friends of Alice Hawkins."

"Oh, you're Ty's wife." The woman visibly relaxed. "Nora Caldwell. I'm one of the teachers here at Skyway. I live in 2F."

"It's nice to meet you."

"Just a moment, please." She stepped around Wren and poked her head in the door. "It's okay, Gemma. She's a new tenant and a friend of Alice's. Oh!" She stepped back when a young girl with chestnut color hair worn long down her back stepped outside. "Esme, I don't think—"

Esme turned huge hazel eyes on Wren. "You know my mom?"

"I, ah…" Wren swallowed hard. She had no problem lying to adults. Kids, on the other hand… "My husband does. His name's Ty."

"Is my mom okay?" Esme attempted to leave the classroom, but Nora blocked her with the gentlest of nudges.

"Last I heard." Wren approached, but kept a distance when she crouched down. "We thought we'd come out and see if you all needed some help while your mom recovers."

Tears exploded in the little girl's eyes. "She's hurt real bad."

"I know." The sadness on Esme's face made Wren's heart twist. "But you and your brothers, you're doing okay, yeah?"

"We're taking good care of them," Nora said as if defending herself.

"I'm sure you are," Wren assured her. Two little boys popped up behind Esme, one taller and slimmer than the other; the smaller one had bright blue eyes that sparked as if they'd been charged by the sun. "You must be River. And Bodhi." She looked to the older boy, who took his time following his brother's lead when it came to smiling. "I'm sure I'll see you all a little while later. After school."

"This is not school," Bodhi stated matter-of-factly.

"The rest of the students are on a field trip today." Nora bent down and set her notebooks on the ground, but Wren noticed the way the woman reached her arm out to keep a barrier between Wren and the children.

"We didn't get to go," Bodhi said with a scowl.

"Because Mom's sick and we need to stay together," Esme whispered loudly. "Dad said so. Go back and listen to the story. You, too, River."

"Okay!" River practically hopped his way back to the circle.

"You can go back, too, Esme," Nora said kindly but with a firmness that impressed Wren.

Esme didn't look convinced and met Wren's gaze with a steadfastness that felt a bit unnerving. There were questions in her eyes, questions Wren herself might have been asking in her place.

"I'll see you later," Wren assured the little girl. "When your dad's home. Okay?"

"Okay." Esme let Nora gently push her back inside and Nora closed the door behind her.

"Again, sorry." Wren didn't need to make enemies of the schoolteacher.

"It's all right." Nora picked up her notebooks and, not so subtly, steered Wren back down the hall. "Since you're aware of Alice's accident, I'm sure you can understand why we're being overly cautious." Her gaze fluttered up and to the right.

It was only then Wren caught sight of the camera in the corner of the wall overhead. It was pretty well hidden, thanks to the artwork, but it was definitely there, its little red light blinking away. "How are they doing? The kids?"

"As well as can be expected," Nora said. "I don't mean to be rude, but—"

"I took you a bit by surprise." Wren wasn't going to apologize again. That would be overkill. But it was clear there was more security in Skyway Tower than she'd expected. "I imagine things have been tense since Alice's accident."

"To say the least," Nora said in a way that led Wren to believe she'd been holding that confession in for a while. Once they were in the main lobby area of the first floor, Nora appeared to relax. "It sounds so contrite, but things like this don't happen here. Let's start over." She took a deep breath, closed her eyes, and when she opened them, whatever hostility had been in her gaze was gone. "Welcome to Skyway."

"Thank you. I only wish it were under different circumstances."

"I'm sure Alice will appreciate seeing friends when she's able," Nora said. "Do you have children?"

"No." Why her face went suddenly hot she couldn't quite figure. "Not yet, anyway." At thirty-three she'd already started hearing that distinctive biological clock start ticking, but so far she'd been able to drown it out. "We're thinking about it now. Just need to figure out where we're going to settle down first." Yep, definitely no trouble lying to adults. "It's a unique situation you have here in Splendor. I like the idea of a self-contained community. School in the same building where you live. Is it open just to Skyway tenants or any of the kids in Splendor?"

"We're funded for up to fifty students."

"I was reading up on the town on my flight in." Talk about lies snowballing. "I think I saw where there are three teachers? You, Gemma and, um…" She pretended to have to think. "Celeste Wheeler."

"Four, actually." Nora straightened with pride. "We just got a new one a few weeks ago. Felix Oliver. He's an inventor by trade but teaches science on the side. You're very well-informed."

"I'm an attorney," Wren said. "Which means I'm a details person. So Felix is new to Splendor, then?" At Nora's immediate frown, Wren hurried on. "It would be nice to talk to another newcomer. See what advice he might have for us as far as settling in."

"I can let him know to be on the lookout for you." Something in Nora's voice had Wren ready to move on.

"I'd appreciate that. Nice to meet you." She headed for the door.

"Hang on!" Nora hurried after her, then pointed to the basket on the table. "Gordy from the second floor leaves us a different kind of fresh-baked treat every day." She grabbed the handle of the basket and held it out for Wren. "Today is white chocolate macadamia nut cookies."

Wren's stomach still wasn't eager to be tested. "They look delicious." She took one and bit in. "Oh, my gosh." Unsettled stomach forgotten, she took another fast bite. "These are amazing!"

"Right?" Nora beamed and shook her head. "He hasn't struck out once. Do you bake?"

"Some," Wren admitted. "I'm a better cook than baker." Cooking was a lot of improvising. Baking, on the other hand, required precision and far more attention than she was willing to spend. Wren was more of a wing-it kind of person. In and out of the kitchen. "I'm just gonna take another…" She grabbed a second cookie and stashed it in her pocket. "For my husband. Maybe," she added with a sly grin. "If it makes it back. See you around, Nora."

"Yes," Nora said slowly. "See you."

Wren had no doubt the older woman could be a font of information, but she was also cautious and suspicious. That was going to take a little extra work to get around.

That said, the conversation had been productive. Wren now knew of a newcomer to Splendor that Ty didn't. She made a mental note to do a check on Felix Oliver.

Four teachers in one school of less than fifty students. An impressive student-to-instructor ratio.

The cold air blasted against her face when she stepped outside. Wincing, she drew up her hood, tightened the strings and turned herself into a half mummy. "How do people live like this?" She'd grown up in Boston. She knew cold. Or thought she did. Clearly she'd been wrong. Winter Alaska cold was like blades of ice stabbing into your bones.

A collection of park benches and picnic tables were arranged over a large area currently covered in snow. Wren could imagine families here in the warmer months, enjoying the sunshine. There was a fun direction sign at the end of the curving walkway, with giant arrows pointing toward various locations: downtown, marina, passenger air trams.

She shoved the last of her cookie into her mouth, considered having the second one, too, but told herself to wait instead. Tilting her head, she looked up into the sky. Sure enough, far off, there were thick wires stretching along one of the tallest mountains. Up, up, up... She gulped as a bright red cable car came into view and headed toward what she guessed was the top of the mountain hidden in the clouds.

"Gives you a view like no other."

Wren spun at the voice, feeling a bit panicked, which was not a good state for an FBI agent. It wasn't easy to sneak up on her. "Excuse me?" she asked the young man standing behind her. He looked like a walking rainbow, from his multicolored riot of curls that appeared to defy gravity to the colorful jacket covering paint-splattered jeans.

"The trams." He pointed back to where she'd been looking. "They offer a great view of Splendor any time of the day or night. And the surrounding mountains. On a clear day, at least."

"Where exactly do the trams take you? The closest glacier?"

He laughed, shifted his oversize bag higher up on his shoulder. "Vacation homes. For rich people. Very rich people."

Wren couldn't help but smile. "Why are you whispering?"

"No idea. I'm Doodle."

"Doodle," Wren repeated in disbelief. "Really?"

"Well, it's Leonardo, actually. Leonardo Doodle, but there's only one Leo." He winked. "If you get my drift."

"Ah, actor or artist?"

His grin widened. "What do you think?"

She shook her head. "I think I'm meeting some very interesting people in Splendor." Given her profession, that was saying something. "Hello, Doodle. I'm Wren."

"Ah, Ty's wife. The lawyer." Doodle nodded and sent his curls into overdrive. "Heard you were coming in. I'm so sorry about Alice." He inclined his head. "Are you close?"

"She and my husband have been friends for years." She could tell she was going to have this conversation a lot for the foreseeable future. Best to keep the details simple and easy to recall. "I'm doing a bit of exploring while my husband catches up on his sleep. Al told me about Callie's place?"

"Can't come to Splendor without visiting Callie's place." Doodle tilted his head. "Happy to show you the way. If you don't mind company."

"Not at all." She fell into step beside him, making mental note of every building they passed, every face she saw. She had a talent for recall, sight, sound, smells. It was one of her gifts, Ty had always teased. As far as she was concerned, it just made writing reports a lot easier. Which was probably why she typically got stuck writing them. As soon as she got back to the apartment, she'd put together a detailed sketch of the town. "So how long have you lived in Splendor, Doodle?"

"Going on five years. Came here with a bunch of friends during the summer after art school and never left." He swooped his arm out across the vista that included the marina, sea and the barest hint of his town. "No way I could walk away from this view."

"I have to admit, it's pretty glorious." There weren't many things, people or places that impressed her to the point of taking her breath away, but the beauty that was Alaska was another thing altogether. Biting cold aside, this state definitely put on a show of otherworldly proportions. "So you like it here, huh?"

"Best place on the planet." He hefted his bag. "Carry my easel and paints with me everywhere I go. Want to be able to capture that moment when it happens."

"So you're like a walking camera." They waited for a car to pass. She looked down the street, then in the other direction. "Don't see a lot of cars around."

"Entire town's barely two miles total," Doodle said. "Only time we ever need a car is when we leave town. Most car owners supplement their income renting out their vehicles to tourists. But don't fall into that trap."

"What trap?"

"Most of them are complete junkers," Doodle said. "You need a car, talk to Sully at the Groovy Grub Grocery. He'll hook you up with someone legit. You can call for a cab to come in from the other side of the tunnel, but it'll cost ya."

Other than the plane she'd come in on or a water vessel, the tunnel was the only other way into Splendor. The traffic direction alternated every half hour, but it was only open from seven in the morning until ten in the evening.

Her mind did a quick calculation. According to what Ty had told her, Alice's hit-and-run had happened at nine o'clock at night, which, if the person who hit her had then tried to leave town, they'd only had a half hour to make it.

Or if the perpetrator had to wait, that still cut their escape time in half. She wondered if there were any security cameras at the tunnel entrance and exits.

Across the street and up a little bit she spotted a hanging sign over a door in the shape of a Victorian-style sofa. "I take it that's Tundra Antiques and Treasures?"

"You are correct," Doodle confirmed as they crossed over. "Be careful you don't get lost inside. Place is jam-packed with stuff."

"You're only making it more enticing." A screech of tires had Doodle jumping. His face lost a bit of color as he lifted a hand to his heart. "You okay?" She touched his arm, recognizing fear when she saw it.

"Yeah." He tried to shake himself out of it. "Sorry. Just jumpy. Alice's accident happened a few blocks that way. Still feels impossible. She's such a sweetheart. Why would anyone do that? Just hit her and drive away like that?"

"People do strange things when they're scared." Wren kept her voice sympathetic. "I don't think we've heard the actual details. Do you know what happened?"

"Only what other people have said. No one's come forward as a witness, apparently."

"Really?" Wren pushed the disbelief into her voice.

"Nine o'clock at night, town's pretty much shut down," Doodle told her. "Only reason Alice was out was because she was finishing inventory at the store."

"Right. That's… Wilderness something?"

"Wilderness Wonders Emporium." Doodle filled in some of the blanks. "Her own work's been really popular, so the owner offered her a management position. She and her husband. She'd sent Bradley home early to put the kids to bed. Then blam! She gets hit walking home. It's just creepy!"

"Definitely," Wren agreed. "And no one knows who did it?"

"Not that I've heard," Doodle said. "And I'd have heard. Course, there's the usual suspects."

"Splendor is big enough to have usual suspects?"

"Oh, sure." Doodle had stopped in front of Caribou Crafts, one of the many stores that featured locally made items. A beautifully woven blanket was displayed in the front window. "Davey Whittaker's usually top of the list. He drinks." Doodle dropped his voice. "I heard the sheriff didn't consider him for this, though. Even though no one's seen him since the accident."

"Really." That set off alarm bells for Wren for sure.

"Davey doesn't have a car, for good reason. He's always been harmless, near as I could tell. Like Alice. I hope she pulls through. I thought I'd stop by, take her some flowers." Doodle cringed. "Do you think that would be okay?"

Given Doodle had lived here awhile, she didn't think Alice's recently acquired personal security guards would take exception. "I think that would be lovely," Wren assured him. She hoped Alice would pull through, too. Not just for Alice herself, but for her family and, yes, Ty. Wren didn't want him spiraling further into a miasma of guilt. "I'm going to head this way." She pointed toward the thrift shop. "It was really great meeting you, Doodle. I'll have to check out your work sometime."

He brightened back up. "I have some pieces on display at the Northern Exposure Gallery. They're open from eleven to three most days."

"Thanks. I'll be sure to stop by."

She walked away, mind processing the information he'd inadvertently given her. If someone had waited for Alice to be off work, when it was typically a dead time of night, that meant they'd been in town long enough to know where she was employed. And to wait for the perfect moment to strike. Her gut told her it wasn't a local. Unless Splendor had its own hit man for hire. She and Ty needed to break down the time frame as far as when someone new in town would have arrived. People stood out here. Even people who lived here, like Leonardo Doodle, stood out. Made them hard to forget.

She pushed open the door to Tundra Antiques and Treasures, not surprised in the least when a bell tinkled overhead. The place had an immediate feel of the past, smelling a little musty, a little floral and more than a little promising. Wren offered a quick smile as she passed an older couple debating over a black iron bed frame.

The sheer amount of items should have made Wren feel claustrophobic, but instead she felt a bit enraptured. From old furniture to knickknacks, to cases filled with jewelry, knives, collectibles, and shelves filled with books. Exploring thrift shops in small towns always gave her a bit of a rush. She spotted a few old toys she'd had as a child, a sit-and-spin chair, a doll whose expression changed when you flipped her head around *Exorcist*-style.

Wren couldn't help but pick up a familiar fashion doll wearing a plaid dress. She lifted the doll's arm, a smile spreading across her face as the doll's chest expanded.

"Can't believe anyone would give that one up." The husky voice of an older woman had Wren glancing up. "Still have mine in a trunk in my attic."

"My brothers broke mine," Wren told her. "Then they stuffed her into GI Joe's helicopter and hung her from the ceiling."

"What are brothers for if not to torture us? Callie Haller."

"Ah, the owner I've heard about. Wren Savakis." Wren set the doll down and faced the woman with waist-length silver curls studded with baubles and beads. "Al suggested I stop by. My husband and I are staying in Skyway Tower for a bit."

"Heard you were on your way." Callie nodded knowingly. She looked out the window. "Seems like the storm coming in at your heels banked off. I'll thank you for that. Anything in particular you're looking for?"

"Do you have any embroidered dish towels? I collect them." It was one of her usual cover stories, but happened to be the truth. She appreciated the kind of needlework she had absolutely no talent for herself.

"Do I?" Callie waved her back, then shouted around Wren, "Vicki, you tell me when you and Theo are done arguing about that bed frame." Callie shook her head and sent her beads to rattling. "Don't know why they bother to argue over anything. Vicki always wins and Theo always grumbles."

"It's probably a tradition for them," Wren said. "My parents argue over who's going to cook the Thanksgiving turkey every year, even though we always know it'll be Mom." Mainly because every time her father forgot to remove the giblets bag.

"You're my kinda people, Wren." Callie steered her through the avalanche of items waiting to happen. "Tradition's why I opened this place. Things that mean something to someone can find their way into someone else's life. Now. Let's see what we've got for you."

Wren found herself surprised by the openness of the separate room. Whereas everything seemed a bit dark in the other area of the store, this space was bright and well lit by lamps with colorful glass shades.

"Anything in particular you like?" Callie asked.

"I know it when I see it," Wren said as she touched a beautiful appliqué quilt hanging on the wall. "You certainly have a lot to choose from."

"Twenty years I've been collecting. No place to keep it all at home, so why not sell it. How about these?" She turned with a stack of yellow gingham towels with bright red milk jugs embroidered on them.

Wren wrinkled her nose. "Ah, anything a little less…frilly? I'm not a lace kinda person."

"Hmm." Callie's eyes narrowed. "Give me another second."

While Callie went on a search, Wren wandered the room, debating how best to approach the subject of Alice Hawkins. Callie Haller, much like Nora Caldwell, struck her as the kind of woman who would know everything that was going on in her town, but Wren had already asked Doodle some leading questions about the accident. She didn't want to raise suspicions by pumping everyone she met in Splendor for information.

Given the small-town effect, chances were everyone she met would be the kind of person who would know something. She needed to reevaluate her plan of action.

"Ah! I forgot about these. What do you think?" Callie popped back up with a stack of towels featuring embroidered cats and kittens. "Unless you're a dog person."

"I'm an all-animal person, actually." Wren took the towels and quickly went through them. "They're adorable." And they'd make great gifts for Christmas. "I'll take them all."

"Definitely my kinda people." Callie beamed and pointed at the other items. "You want to just look around some for a while? I'll keep these at the register, which is at the back of the store."

Chapter Five

By the time Wren left the thrift shop, she'd added a funny googly-eyed ceramic frog for Ty to expand his collection and a vintage camera her father would absolutely love.

Reusable tote bag looped over her arm, she headed for the grocery store next. According to Callie, the place was only a block down, but as Wren made her way back to the main road paralleling the marina, she began to wonder.

"Callie needs to redefine her definition of *block*." Arms burning, she was juggling the box into a less painful position when she finally spotted Groovy Grub Grocery. Given its name, Wren was surprised it wasn't painted in tie-dyed psychedelic swirls. The building was larger than she'd expected and boasted a long red awning noting that it was not only the grocery but also the postal annex, laundry and, oddly enough, offered homemade ice cream.

Sweet tooth activated by that cookie, she thought that might be easy enough on her still-queasy stomach. "Ice cream always smooths things out." She pulled open the door and stepped inside.

Immediately she could smell the sweet hint of Freon, no doubt used in the refrigerators lining the far wall. She'd assumed the store would be limited in its offerings, much like the selection in the lobby grocery at Skyway Tower. But given the number of aisles in front of her, she realized she'd been completely wrong.

The walls were covered by a variety of colors, much like that tie-dyed effect the name alluded to. The style reminded her of the artwork outside the schoolrooms at the apartment complex. There were gaps on the shelves, as if they were awaiting new stock, but most items, like bottled juice and boxes of soda crackers, were plentiful.

The selection surprised her, but it was clear that shelf-stable foods were far more affordable than anything fresh. Or baby-related. Anchorage was only about sixty miles away. Given some of the prices she was seeing on things like diapers and laundry soap, she assumed most people would buy their staples elsewhere, probably when they had doctor appointments or other reasons to travel up north. Cookies, cereal and chips, on the other hand? She grabbed one of each and dropped them into the basket she carried.

"Smart woman," the silver-haired and fully bearded man behind the counter said as she passed by. The two other men standing on Wren's side stepped back to size her up. "Stocking up on carbs, I see."

"They're necessary to my survival." Nothing beat a chocolate sandwich cookie.

"You must be Wren Savakis." The man walked out from behind the counter and extended his hand.

"Must I?" she teased and accepted the greeting.

"Maisey Kirkpatrick described you pretty well."

Wren frowned. "Maisey...?"

"She's a nurse at the clinic. Word is you and your husband stopped someone from hurting Alice again."

"Oh. That was just..." She shot an uneasy glance to the other two men standing nearby. "I get these feelings about people, you know. That guy just didn't look right. Ty's always telling me I need to think more before I act."

"Well, glad you didn't think too much," the counterman said. "Poor woman's been through enough. Can't figure why anyone would try to hurt her while she's in the hospital."

"Maybe someone was worried about her being able to identify them," one of the other men muttered and earned a glare of warning from the shop owner.

"Before I go talking your ear off, I should introduce myself. I'm Sullivan Harper. Sully. I own this place."

"He's also the mayor," the second man said. "Funny enough, he tends to forget that part."

Ah, the mayor. Excellent. "Nice to meet you, Sully." She glanced at the other two guys.

Sully continued, "Met your husband a few days back. Plus, we heard the plane come in this morning. Welcome. Sorry your visit started off with a bit of a bang."

"I guess that is what one might call an entrance." Wren feigned embarrassment. "It's a lovely town you have here, Mr. Mayor."

"Sully," he said, his bright blue eyes teasing a warning.

"Right. Sure. Sully."

"This here is Cal Anderson and Nelson Finn. They work the *Fintastic Voyage*."

"My dad was a Jules Verne fan," the larger, rounder of the two men said with more humor than his bearded face belied. "I'm fourth-generation fisherman."

"Hard life." Wren knew the reality TV shows she watched on the subject sometimes didn't come close to the actual "reality" of the profession. But she didn't think the depiction of long hours and rough seas were fictional. "A worthy tradition." She was seeing a recurring theme playing out in Splendor after only a few hours. "What's your main catch?"

"Halibut mostly," Nelson chimed in. The dark blue knit cap he wore was pulled down low to the point of almost covering his eyes. "But we get some salmon and rockfish in there, too."

"We keep the local restaurants in good supply," Cal said. "Sell the rest here or in Anchorage."

"Never lacking for fresh fish around these parts," Sully confirmed.

"Good to know. What did you bring in today?" Always happy to make inroads, she made the decision about what to cook tonight. "Thought I might fix dinner for me and Ty." She flashed a flirty smile. "Haven't seen him in a while. I'd like to catch up tonight."

"Catch up." Nelson snort-laughed. "Funny."

Wren genuinely beamed. She liked these guys.

"Well, now, you just come back with me and we'll see what we've got for you." Sully touched her shoulder and turned her toward the back of the store. He led her through a bit of a maze of items, including an entire wall filled with boxes containing harsh-weather boots and rain gear. There really wasn't anything she could think that was lacking in the store. "Now, personally, I think halibut is the way to go."

She tried not to balk at the list of prices tacked to the wall. For what a half pound of halibut would cost her, she and Ty could probably eat out for a few meals. Still, you couldn't get much more fresh than the catch currently sitting in a metal tray on a thick bed of ice. "Sounds good to me."

"I'll wrap it up for you, then. Got some fresh produce just down there. You're beating the crowd today. In another couple of hours, all this here will be gone."

She made quick work of choosing her veggies, then browsed the rather meager wine selection, settling on a chardonnay that would be good for drinking and cooking. She carried her basket to the counter, barely resisting the temptation of a fresh-baked pear pie sitting on the side rack next to the fruit. Tomorrow, she told herself. Tomorrow she'd come back for pie.

She eyed the small ice-cream counter on her way up to the register and debated her choices.

"Heard you and Ty are friends of Alice's," Sully said as he rang her up.

"My husband is, yes." She could feel Cal's and Nelson's eyes on her. "As soon as he heard about the accident, he headed up this way."

"Sounds like a good friend," Nelson observed. "He's a tech guy, yeah?"

"He was."

"And you're a lawyer." There was clear disdain in Cal's voice.

"White-collar," she said. "I specialize in insider trading and fraud. Big fish, so to speak," she added with a grin. "Those loopholes the rich try to jump through? I like closing them."

"You don't say?" Nelson's voice rose as if impressed.

"I'm a fan of the little guy," Wren said.

"Everyone's littler than us." Nelson chuckled.

Given both men were well over six foot and carried a good amount of weight, she got the joke.

"Okay, then." Sully rattled off the heart-stopping total. "Anything else you need?"

"I would love to try that maple bacon bourbon ice cream. On a cone."

"I'll get that for you," Cal told her. "As a welcome-to-Splendor treat."

"Well, thank you, Cal." She beamed up at him. "That's really nice of you." She'd bet beneath that beard she'd just made him blush. "It's just all so shocking, what happened to Alice," Wren mused as Sully bagged up her items, then headed off to scoop her ice cream. "I heard there weren't any witnesses to her being run down. No one knows who did it?"

"Nope." Nelson shook his head. "Not a clue."

Cal snorted as if he didn't agree. At Wren's frown, he shrugged. "Some of us have our suspicions."

"Now, Cal," Sully chided in a warning tone. "Don't go spreading rumors that have no foundation."

"Ain't no rumor if it's true."

"If what's true?" Wren asked innocently.

"My money's on Davey Whittaker."

The town troublemaker, Wren recalled from her conversation with Doodle. "I heard he was cleared," she said and earned raised eyebrows in response. "He doesn't have a car, does he?"

"He doesn't," Cal said in a leading way. "But his aunt Bea does, and it hasn't been parked in her driveway for going on almost a week now." He glanced at his friends. "Same time Davey's been missing."

"He's not missing," Nelson argued. "You know Davey. He disappears all the time. He'll turn up."

"Or maybe he already did this morning, so now he's beat it out of town for good," Cal countered.

"You're imagining things." Sully handed over the cone with two scoops. "Extra scoop on the house. Welcome to Splendor, Wren."

"Thanks." One mouthful of the creamy concoction and she nearly swooned. The salty bacon against the sweet maple flavor, then the smoky notes of bourbon. Pure heaven. "This is delicious. Do you make it?"

"My wife does," Sully said proudly. "She switches up the flavors every couple of weeks. Got her an industrial ice-cream maker for Christmas a few years back. Thing cost me a fortune, but it's paid off in spades. She loves creating new flavors."

"I'll definitely be back to try the rest of the menu." She shifted her attention back to Cal. "What does this Davey Whittaker look like?"

Nelson frowned. "Scrawny, scraggly blond hair. Always reminded me of a scarecrow."

Sully nodded. "Apt description."

"The guy I saw at the hospital definitely wasn't Davey, then." Nor was the guy driving the white SUV. "Why would you think he was responsible?"

"Who knows why that boy does anything he does? Been a mess most of his life," Cal said.

"He's twenty-six years old," Nelson chimed in. "Hardly a boy anymore."

"He had a hard upbringing," Sully said in Davey's defense. "His father was a big drinker, and Davey followed in his footsteps real early on. Does seem strange, Davey disappearing around the same time as the accident."

Not an accident, Wren thought. *Attempted murder.*

"Which is why it's the only thing that makes sense to me," Cal insisted.

"Davey's been picked on his entire life," Nelson said to Cal. "Never had anyone believe in him or even try to help him. Maybe give him a break until we actually know what happened. And like Wren here said, wasn't him who came after Alice at the hospital."

"I'll give him a break when he shows his face back in Splendor," Cal grumbled.

"Well, I hope he turns up," Wren said even as her mind raced. "And I hope whoever did hurt Alice is caught. I'm gonna get all this back to the apartment and see if my husband's awake. Nice meeting you all. And thanks for the ice cream, Cal." She hefted the two bags in her free hand and headed out.

A hand touched Ty's shoulder.

Still asleep, he reached up, locked his hand around the wrist and pulled forward. Hard. He'd barely blinked his eyes open as he followed through, shoved himself back and dragged Wren forward. She tumbled over him and sprawled on her back on the bed.

She glared up at him with that narrow-eyed gaze that had intimidated many a suspect. "Hey!" She twisted her hand, but he tightened his grip. "Ty, what the heck?"

"Sorry." The shock and embarrassment almost overtook him, until panic and desire struck and he gave in to what he'd been thinking about doing for...years.

He stared into her eyes, unblinking. Barely breathing. Waiting for something...understanding, maybe. Permission. Agreement. He leaned forward, ever so slowly, and watched as the color in her eyes darkened.

"Ty."

He kissed her, catching the last of his name with his lips. It was a mistake. He knew that from the instant his mouth touched hers. A mistake because he realized he'd only want more. He'd never look at her the same way again without knowing what it had been like to sink into her, to devour her in a way that set his entire body to singing.

He'd expected to be pushed away. He'd hoped to be. To be shouted down or looked at in disbelief or shock. If only to finally put an end to the desire he'd been feeling for what felt like his entire life.

But Wren McKenna had always been a woman who defied expectations. It was perhaps the most consistent thing about her. This was the one time he needed her to fall in line, follow the unwritten rule about partners becoming involved. And yet she didn't.

Instead her hands twisted free of his hold and slipped between them, grabbing hold of his shirt. She pulled him closer. And kissed him more deeply.

Reason grabbed hold as well and pulled him back to his senses. He broke the kiss, keeping his eyes closed. He couldn't bear to look into her eyes and see the regret he feared more than anything.

"Ty." His name was a whisper on her lips, a whisper that had him pushing through the doubt. "Ty, look at me."

He shook his head, squeezed his eyes tighter until he saw stars. Stars that would explode and hopefully destroy the last few seconds from ever having existed.

"Ty."

"Sorry," he repeated, loosening his hold, but only then did he notice their legs were tangled together and he was looming over her, his chest pressing her into the soft mattress. "I'm... so sorry."

Her breathing was unsteady. Her breasts were pushing up against his chest in a way that had him, for a moment at least, debating about moving. Slowly, excruciatingly, he opened his eyes and looked down into her beautiful, confused, worry-filled face.

"I'm not." Her smile was sympathetic, teasing even.

He shook his head, refusing to believe. "That was—"

"A long time coming." She tightened her legs around his when he tried to shift away. "Did you get it out of your system?"

He let out a laugh that might have sounded like a sob, dropped his head forward to the point his forehead brushed against her chest.

"What is it?" She slid her hands up, clasped his face in her palms and forced him to look at her. "What's going on? Or maybe I should start by asking if you're awake now."

Oh, he was awake, all right. In this moment the yearslong effort of keeping his attraction to her under wraps threatened to break loose completely. He'd finally taken that taste he'd always been tempted to ask for and now...now he understood that kissing her had been a really, really bad idea.

Not because it hadn't been everything he'd ever wanted and

dreamed about. But because he wouldn't ever be able to get enough. He freed his legs from hers and sat up. She followed him. Reached for him.

"Don't." His order was sharp, far sharper than he'd intended, but true to form, Wren ignored him and scooted closer. "Wren, please—don't."

"Don't what?" She took hold of his hand and squeezed his fingers. "Come on, Ty. We're each other's best friends. One kiss isn't going to change any of that. If you can't talk to me, you can't talk to anyone. It's been long enough. What's going on with you?" Her gentle tone crumbled his reluctance.

"I don't know." It was the biggest lie he'd ever told in his life. And he'd told it to the one person he'd never once lied to before. "Please, just forget this happened. That I—"

"I'm not going to forget kissing you, so let's get that straight off the bat." Her voice was so calm, so...accepting, he couldn't help but wonder why he'd stopped himself from initiating anything for the past seven years. "Something's wrong. It has been for a while. For weeks. And it's gotten worse since you called me." She paused, looked into his eyes in that way she had that made him admit hiding from her wasn't an option. "Is it Alice?" Doubt filled her gaze. "Was there something more to your relationship than you've said? Were you—"

"Involved?" He balked. "No, Wren. No, I'd never get involved with a witness in that way. Do you really think—"

"I don't know what to think because you won't talk to me. Not really." She sank back, her hair coming down from the knot she'd tied it in. The knot he'd wanted to untangle himself. She didn't let go of his hand. If anything, she only held on tighter. "Trust me, Ty. Everything I'm coming up with is going to be worse than the truth, so please just tell me what's happening."

His throat tightened, as if trying to prevent the words from coming out. "Alex called me a few weeks ago. A month ago, in fact." He leaned against the makeshift headboard. Only then did he realize he was holding her hand as tightly as she held his.

"Did he?" He understood the suspicion in her voice. The barely restrained contempt. Before this call, he hadn't spoken to his brother in more than five years. "Why?"

He hadn't let himself think about the call. Not consciously, at least. But the conversation had been playing, over and over, in the back of his mind. When he slept. While he worked. "He told me it was time to come home." He pinched the bridge of his nose, willed the pain to stop him from talking. From thinking.

"Get it out, Ty. It's not doing you any good caught in here." She placed her fingers on his heart and the heat of her touch felt like a branding iron against his chest.

"It's my father. He's got liver cancer and the treatment isn't working." He heaved a sigh and opened his eyes, looked at her. "Alex said it won't be long."

"All right." She nodded as if processing the information he was still trying to. "What did Alex say when you told him you wouldn't be coming?"

Ty couldn't help it. He laughed. She knew him so well. Too well, perhaps. "What do you think he said?"

"I think your behavior these last few weeks suddenly makes an awful lot of sense." She moved closer, held on even tighter. "You don't owe your father anything, Ty. Absolutely nothing. You know that deep down. He was your childhood bully. An unloving, uncaring jerk who never should have had children. Although, to be fair..." She inclined her head in that particular way she had. "I'm glad he did, seeing as he had you. So I guess I owe him for that."

He loved her for the unwavering support. And humor. "I swore when I walked out of that house when I was eighteen I'd never go back." And he hadn't. Not for one second. Not even when his mother had died four years later. He'd gone to the funeral, but he'd been in and out within hours, long enough to say goodbye and lay flowers on her newly dug grave. "I left Alex with all of it. Everything. Why shouldn't I go back?"

"Stop right there. I mean it," she added firmly. "Alex was older than you and already out of the house when you got out, and more importantly, *he* left *you* there to take on everything yourself. Alex even chose to stay in the same town. He could have made a new life anywhere, just like you did, and he didn't. His situation is not on you. And your father's behavior, then or now, is not your responsibility."

"Isn't it?" It amazed him, how clearly she saw his family situation when she came from such an idyllic one. The McKennas were the kind of family others measured themselves by. The family was tight-knit, supportive, loving and, most importantly, welcoming to any and all hangers-on. Like him. Before partnering with Wren, he couldn't imagine a family like theirs. In truth, being around them only shone a spotlight on how bad his upbringing had really been.

"Did your dad stop drinking when you left? Did he even try to get help?" Wren asked him. "Or, I should ask, has he finally stopped drinking?"

"Not according to Alex, no." And that, more than anything, was always the bone of contention between him and his brother. Ty could never get beyond the idea that his father hadn't stopped, and Alex couldn't forgive Ty for not accepting their father as he was.

"Then your father didn't do the bare minimum. He hasn't earned your visiting him and you can't save him, Ty." There was no pity now, only determined support and understanding. "Just like you couldn't save your mother when she refused to leave him." Wren made certain he was looking at her. "You saved yourself. That's what matters."

How did she always see the better side of him?

"I've sent money, in the past," he admitted. "For his treatment. To make things easier for him." He winced. "It doesn't seem like enough."

"It's more than he deserves." She traced a finger over the scar on his neck. A scar he'd received at the hands of his father on his tenth birthday, when he'd accidentally knocked over his dad's celebratory beer. "Hopefully Alex will keep some of that money for himself, if there's any left."

"I told him he could. He told me I couldn't buy my way to forgiveness."

Wren swore so violently and vehemently she broke through the confused grief that had settled around Ty's heart. "You've got to be kidding me. What a jerk. He's a—"

"I don't blame him, Wren."

"Of course you don't. You never blame anyone else when you

can blame yourself. I want you to listen to me, Ty. And just to make sure you do." She slid over him, her knees resting on either side of his hips.

"I don't think you sitting on me is going to make my ears work better." He'd gone rock-hard. It would be impossible for her not to know it. To feel it. But when he looked into her eyes, all he saw was defiance and determination.

"You cannot save everyone. You couldn't save your father from his drinking. Or your mother from her devotion to him. You can't save Alex from not being strong enough to walk away or at the very least not to throw the blame on you. But you know what you can do?"

He was definitely thinking about all the things he could do at that moment.

"You can work this case and find out who tried to kill Alice. You can keep your word to her and protect her and her family. We can do this together. And we will do it. Because that's what we do." She leaned forward, pressed her lips against his. She didn't close her eyes but bored hard into his. "All this guilt you're feeling about your father, I understand why it's there, and while it's easy for me to say, you need to set it aside. When we're done here, we can talk about what you want to do. If you want to go back, fine. Just be warned that if you do, I'm darn sure going with you and I've got more than a few harsh words for your brother. But for now, we work, yeah?"

His hands began to move. They'd lifted to rest on her hips, his fingers kneading into her in a way that had her gaze sharpening. And darkening.

"Don't start something you aren't willing to finish," she warned him. "Because you kissing me after all this time feels like a bit of a starting flag. You've got my engine revving. You want to see how many laps we can go?"

More so than anything else on the planet. But talking had helped reason and logic take over once more. "I'm not sure I'm in an emotionally stable place to be able to answer."

"Okay, then I'll ask later. After we eat." She kissed him again, quickly this time, and climbed off him. "Dinner's ready. That's what I came in to tell you, by the way. It's time to eat. So get yourself together and join me in the kitchen. I've got information from town that you're going to want to hear."

The bands of pressure around Wren's chest didn't ease until she was on the other side of the bedroom door. She stepped to the side, hand pressed against her chest, back resting against the bookcase as she willed her pulse to stop jumping like a salmon headed upstream.

The anger toward his selfish brother almost overtook the still-tingling sensations of Ty's kiss.

Her face warmed, but she didn't try to stop it or cover it. Or halt the smile that curved her lips. After all these years, all this time, he'd kissed her.

She supposed she owed his brother for twisting Ty up into so many knots her partner finally gave in to what Wren had only hoped he'd felt for her. He was, plain and simple, other than her father and brothers, the best man she'd ever known.

One look at Ty Savakis and most women would assume he had the kissing thing down. He had those classic Greek looks with the dark hair and bright blue eyes. He was…the epitome of romantic heroes come to life, right down to the invisible sword and shield he carried, white horse included. It was a secret she'd kept for going on seven years. Through her disaster of a marriage. Through his marriage. Until, it appeared, today.

And all bets may very well be off.

But her imagination about his kissing abilities hadn't come close to reality. That moment, those kisses—they'd been seared into her mind forever. Whatever happened now, at least, she'd have that. And maybe, for as long as they were in Splendor, Alaska, they could both get their fill and work out whatever attraction they shared.

Yes. That was how they should handle it. Like an off-the-books fling, no commitment. No strings. They could just go back to how they were before they'd come to Alaska. Easy peasy.

Right?

She blew out a breath, set her hair to ruffling on her forehead. She could hear him moving around in the bedroom, enough that she quickly went into the kitchen to finish the meal she'd come up with.

Her hands shook as she clicked on the gas burner, set the pan containing the seared halibut with a tomato-and-caper sauce to cooking. She tried shifting her focus away from what had happened in the bedroom to the notes she'd been scribbling in the book on the cluttered kitchen island.

"I see you haven't become any tidier when it comes to cooking." The humor was back in his tone when he joined her. The Ty she was used to. The Ty she...

She barely cast an over-the-shoulder glance at the mess that had overtaken the rest of the kitchen. "*Tidy* is barely part of my vocabulary." Personally, at least. Professionally, she considered herself a real organizer with pinpoint efficiency. Her personal routine was an entirely different story. As far as she was concerned, if the kitchen wasn't a disaster, she hadn't made enough of an effort. "Notes are over there." She gestured toward the spiral notebook on the island. The cover had spatters of tomato and oil, which Ty wiped off with a dish towel.

"You had a busy afternoon," he said as he read through her copious thoughts and observations. "Even met the kids. What did you think?"

She set the water for the couscous to boiling on the back burner, dropped a lid on the pan. "That they're too young to get what's going on. Two of them, for sure. Esme struck me as a small adult."

"Birth order theory in play." Ty didn't pull his eyes from the page. "Visiting hours at the hospital end at six." He checked his watch. "Bet Bradley will be home soon after."

"I suggest we give him tonight, try to catch up with him again tomorrow." She hesitated. "We do need to know what, if anything, Alice told him about her past."

"I'm betting not much since he seems to be in the dark and he believes the story about my friendship with Alice."

Ty wasn't wrong. Bradley didn't strike her as the kind of man who could keep up any kind of pretense for long. He wasn't, she suspected, a very good liar.

"If we need an in, I can cook them dinner tomorrow." She

rose up on tiptoe, checked to see where he was on her notes. "Two more pages and you'll get to something more interesting." She waited, stirring and adjusting the temperature and testing the sauce.

"Last I heard, four other tenants are alternating making them meals." He shook his head. "People go out of their way to cook when it comes to illness or death."

"It's a coping mechanism," she reminded him. One she recognized in herself. "And it's the way a lot of people show they care." She heard him flip the page, then again. "Get there yet?"

"About this Davey Whittaker guy? Yeah."

"It wasn't Davey at the hospital. Forget the fact his physical description doesn't match, but from what Nelson and Cal said, the man can barely stand up, he drinks so much. However, that..." She looked at Ty, waited for him to catch her train of thought.

"Makes him a good scapegoat, doesn't it?"

Satisfied he was back on track, she nodded. "Exactly what I was thinking. We've got the white SUV without plates, a missing local with a well-known drinking problem and..." She snapped her fingers. "I almost forgot." She hurried to where she'd hung her jacket up by the front door and pulled out the hypodermic needle. "We still have this. You didn't mention it before, but did you bring your fingerprint case?"

"No," he replied when she set the glove-covered needle on the countertop. "It wasn't in my go bag."

"I left mine back in Boston." Not that dusting for prints would do much good without a database to run them through. "Okay, so we table this for now. Tomorrow, we find ourselves a car—"

"I've got one," Ty said, cutting her off. "Rental. Grabbed it in Anchorage when I got back from meeting you in Seattle. It's parked in the underground lot."

"Oh." She blinked, impressed. "Great. Okay. I think we should start with the tunnel. The one leading into Splendor."

"Why?"

"Because after doing some research, it might be a good place to disappear."

"Into Alaska, you mean."

"Eventually." She tasted another spoonful of sauce, nodded, shrugged, added more pepper. "There are emergency exit doors, the tunnel's so long. Even a comms room and more. In case the train breaks down or there's weather that makes it dangerous to leave the tunnel."

Ty raised his head. She could see the wheels turning.

"Couldn't hurt to check. Maybe talk to Davey's aunt Bea about her car that's gone missing?" The water boiled and she added the couscous, moved the pan off the stove. "I bookmarked the website about the tunnel construction. If you want to skim through it."

"I'm getting the gist of it from your notes." Notes he was still reading, so she started cleaning up. By the time he stood up straight and closed her notebook, the center island was gleaming once more, the black marble countertop displaying its thin gold lines and flecks.

"Sounds like you made more friends in a few hours than I've made in a few days."

She smiled. "I'm more sparkly."

"That you are." More often than not, their job was made easier by certain people's underestimating his very blonde, very pretty partner. "Trying to kill Alice a second time blew any chance these guys had of blaming Davey for the hit-and-run."

Wren nodded. "I figured the same thing. Throws her accident—" she used air quotes for emphasis "—completely into question and puts the entire town on edge, not to mention high alert. That's pretty desperate, if you ask me. Unless Alice has someone else from her past coming after her, which you believe is unlikely, it has to be Treyhern. He's the only one with a motive to make mistakes like this."

The fact she saw relief in his eyes at her statement made her wish she'd come around to his thinking sooner. "There is another option we haven't considered. It's not one I'm leaning toward, but it's one we should talk about."

"That Davey might have been hired to run Alice down?"

She nodded. "We'd need to know more about him to eliminate that idea. Addicts are unpredictable."

"Then we'll start with his aunt Bea," Ty said. "Sooner we can

get a handle on Davey Whittaker, the sooner we can move on
to more viable answers. That leaves me with one last question."

"What's that?" She put a dash of seasoning into the couscous,
as well as some grated peel from a lemon that cost her more
than her monthly streaming service charge. She fixed each of
them a plate as he set the notebook aside.

The timer dinged and she turned to pull the homemade bis-
cuits out of the oven.

"I'm seriously not going to starve with you around," he murmured when she tucked a golden-topped biscuit on the edge of
his plate. "For tonight. You should take the bed. I'll do the sofa."

She wasn't entirely sure how to follow that. Her heart
pounded in excited anticipation while the back of her mind sent
out warning bells. "I'm not selfish. I'm happy to share the bed."

"You sure about that?"

"Yes." Suddenly she wasn't so hungry for food anymore.
"What about you?"

He ate more, and again she could practically hear the gears
grinding in his head. "We need to be careful about what might
happen."

"You mean besides avoiding back strain on the sleeper sofa?"

"I meant our friendship." He winced, shook his head. "The
last thing I want to do is lose you, Wren. And I'm just afraid—"

"Don't be. Afraid." She reached out, covered his hand with
hers. "I've already decided—if you're amenable, that is—that
whatever happens, it will stay here in Splendor."

Doubt shot across his handsome features.

"You don't think we can do that?" she asked.

"I don't know. That's what scares me."

"Then we take it a day at a time." Or in their case, a night at
a time. "And we agree. When we leave, it stays here. But Alice
and her family come first," she reminded him. "Agreed?"

"Agreed." He shrugged almost nonchalantly. She waited for
him to say more, but he lifted a forkful of couscous to his mouth.
If he could shrug off their sharing the same bed, so could she.
But his less-than-enthusiastic reaction to her suggestion that
they take their friendship to another level definitely required a
glass of that very expensive wine.

Chapter Six

Turned out Wren was right. Sharing a bed with her wasn't an issue.

Trying to fall asleep beside her, on the other hand?

Ty could literally feel the heat of her body radiating across the blankets they shared, and the last thing he needed was to feel... warmer. It was like an ongoing pulse, feeding the attraction both had admitted to but neither had yet to completely act on.

None of this was what he wanted circling in his head at two in the morning.

It probably hadn't helped sleeping the afternoon away, either. Now, instead of falling into the blissful unawareness he longed for, he lay there staring up at the ceiling, unblinking, swearing he could hear her heart beating. Silence, it turned out, was loud. His city self was so used to noise, but up here he had the sneaking suspicion he could hear a fly buzz half a mile away.

Wren sighed a little, shifting and snuggling down to the point she pressed her bare feet against his leg. Ty stiffened, as if preparing himself for a nuclear launch rather than Wren settling back into sleep. He took a deep breath, inhaled the intoxicating scent of jasmine drifting off her skin.

Yeah, this wasn't going to work.

He slid out of bed as carefully as he could, tugging on the jeans he'd left tossed over the back of the one chair in the bedroom. Barefoot, he walked to the window, pulled the heavy curtain back. He had to stop his gasp before it escaped as he blinked, disbelieving, into the night sky.

The interplay of ghostly green light cascading down from the stars took his breath away. He'd heard of the aurora borealis, of course. Even remembered studying it in school. But seeing it now made him realize how completely otherworldly the event was.

His arm dropped and he stood there, watching the show as if it were the season finale of a grand epic. Yet another wondrous bonus of life in the north.

Just the sight of the intermingling lights with stars gentled the edgy thoughts cutting through his mind. He'd been unable to push aside the idea of an angry accusation Alice would aim his way if…when, *when* she woke up.

This was also a reminder that Wren was correct; he couldn't control the universe no matter how hard he tried. It was ridiculous to blame himself for what had happened to Alice, especially given how many years it had been. But he should have at least reached out to her as soon as he'd heard Treyhern had been granted a new trial.

He grabbed a T-shirt and went into the living area, where the enormous plate-glass window provided a big-screen view of the show in the sky. It was like the universe was trying to remind him that in the grand scheme of things he was one very tiny part. Trying to put himself in the middle of it was only asking for trouble.

His internal clock was as messed up as his head. Everything felt like it was in flux. It had been that way even before the news of Alice's accident. Some days he felt completely trapped by the life he'd carved out for himself, despite knowing he was doing the job he was meant to do. He'd had doubts about a lot in his life, but from the second he'd held his FBI special agent badge and ID in his hand, for the first time his world had felt…right.

That was why it made no sense to him that he was making decisions that put his career at risk. His volatile behavior on the job meant his fellow agents questioned whether he could be trusted or relied on. His boss queried every case he was given.

Wren was the only person who hadn't faltered in her support. She was there for him. No matter what.

Where would he be without her?

He sat back to contemplate that question and the sky.

A little over an hour later, answers nowhere to be found, he poured his first cup of coffee. He sat at the kitchen island, went over Wren's immaculate notes again. He had to admit, while he'd skimmed them last night, he hadn't exactly retained much of the information. It had been difficult to keep up the pretense of focus when she'd been talking about them sleeping together.

He was a man, and most definitely not a saint.

"Morning." Wren's slogging into the kitchen had him glancing at the clock. Where had the time gone?

Her bare feet shuffled against the wood floor as if she didn't possess the energy to lift them. "Ah. My elixir. Thank you." She didn't even look at him as she headed for the coffee maker and, after rooting around in the cabinet containing various mugs and cups and glasses, chose the absolute biggest tankard possible.

Coffee, two spoonfuls of sugar and a healthy splash of cream—three big glugs later and he watched her eyes visibly clear.

"Better?" He could think of fewer things more entertaining than watching Wren McKenna wake up.

"You know it." She looked outside, frowned into the darkness. "What time is it?" She glanced at her watch.

"Seven. Late sunrise," he reminded her and watched her eyes roll. "Takes some getting used to."

"Ya think?" She rolled her shoulders, bringing attention to the fitted tank top she used as a sleep shirt. "How long have you been up?" She eyed him with envy.

"Few hours." Long enough to shower, dress and map out a plan of action for the day. "We have to wait until after sunrise at least to visit Aunt Bea."

"It's your show. I'm just along for the ride. You get anything more out of my notes?"

"Davey Whittaker's still gnawing at me."

"Why?" She leaned her hip against the counter, held her mug of coffee as if it were indeed the elixir of life.

"I don't know." Because the few details he knew about the young man reminded him of himself? Of the path he could have easily found himself on. "It would make things easier if he was responsible for the hit-and-run." But he wasn't. Yesterday's events at the hospital had all but cleared him.

"You can't will someone into being a suspect."

"I know." Ty smothered a laugh and covered his eyes with his hand for a moment. He was so tired of complicated. A nice, tidy solution would be such a relief. But given Wren's doubtful expression when he looked back at her, it told him she was remembering what they'd both been taught early on at the Academy. Tidy solutions only happened in Hollywood scripts.

Real life was full of a lot more twists and turns than could be solved in an hour of television.

"What?" he asked at her pensive expression.

"I'm considering what the odds are that you have a copy of the Treyhern file."

"You mean because, legally, I should only be able to access that on my dedicated work laptop that is currently on my desk back in Boston?"

"Yes," she replied slowly. "That's what I mean."

He got up, returned to the bedroom to dig the jump drive out of the protective case he kept in his go bag. He sauntered to the kitchen and dropped it into her open palm. "This is my shocked face," she muttered and retrieved her laptop from where she'd left it in the kitchen last night. "I'll dig into this when we get back."

He could have suggested she email a copy of it to her phone, but that would be crossing too many lines for both of them. "I need you to help me stop spinning, Wren."

"About what? What are you thinking specifically?"

"Honestly?" He shook his head. "I don't know. That's why I wanted you here. I figured you could see what it was."

"Awww." That teasing lilt emerged in her voice. "You think I'm smarter than you."

"I don't think it. I know it." This was probably the one thing he was confident about. "Can you be ready to go in an hour?"

"Please," she scoffed. "I'll be ready in fifteen. Breakfast of champions is in the cabinet there." She pointed to the one near the stove. "Pour me a bowl, will you?"

"Wheaties?" he guessed, walking around the island to do as instructed.

"Be serious." She rolled her eyes and topped off her coffee. "Froot Loops."

"Only in Alaska," Wren said as she and Ty sat in the rented SUV watching a family of moose make their way slowly across the two-lane road headed out of Splendor. She cast a side-eyed look at him, impressed by the patience he showed when he put the car into Park and sat back to wait. "The pilot who flew me in says he's been bringing you up to Alaska pretty regularly."

"Yeah. Been doing that for a while now. It's a kind of reset for me."

"Always knew you disappeared somewhere. Never thought it was in Alaska." Wren returned her attention to the animals, who seemed more than happy to take their time. "Any reason you never mentioned it?"

"Not that I can think of." He reached down for his insulated tumbler mug and took a long drink. "The first time was a total fluke. Friend of mine invited me along for a spur-of-the-moment fishing trip. He didn't realize how much we'd be roughing it. Unplugging nearly drove him bonkers, but not me. I never expected to come back. Then I did." He shrugged. "I didn't keep it a secret on purpose. Just kind of worked out that way. You know, something that was just mine."

"Sure." Growing up in a house with three siblings, she could understand the need for solitary activity.

"You're welcome to come with me next time," he offered, still keeping his gaze firmly on the animals. "Honestly, I wouldn't have thought it was your kind of thing."

"No idea if it is or not," she told him. "But you're right. My family's never been exactly outdoorsy." Family vacations growing up had been limited to destinations within easy driving distance from Boston in case either of her law enforcement parents needed to get back for an emergency. The farthest she could ever remember getting was the Jersey Shore the summer she turned fifteen. "Not a fan of the cold, though."

The last moose finally cleared the road and stepped into the thick brush. "I don't come up during this time of year," Ty said. "Fishing's best in summer, especially for salmon. Hiking trails are pretty awesome. Still a few places you can access the glaciers."

"Listen to you, going all wilderness-camper dude on me." Next thing she knew, he'd be planning survival weekends for them.

He tossed her a grin, shifted the car back into Drive and headed off again.

"What?" she asked.

"Nothing, really." He hit the gas. "Just nice to know that even after all these years I can surprise you."

Oh, he was full of surprises, all right. But now wasn't the time to think about that kiss. Or how she hadn't wanted it to stop. Or how before she'd fallen asleep last night, she'd almost rolled over and…

Nope. Not now. Now was not the time. Officially or not, they were working. Finding the person or persons responsible for what had happened to Alice was the important thing. Everything else…could wait.

At least the sun had finally peeked over the horizon, and boy, was it spectacular. The color playing out around them almost stole her breath away. There really was something ethereal about this place, despite it wreaking havoc with her internal sensors. She couldn't quite shake that barely-there fog in her mind. Chances were she'd finally get used to the daylight and it would be time to head home. To the real world.

The real world…

"What if she's not up?" Wren asked as Ty pulled the SUV to the side of the road. Beatrice Mulvaney's home stood in the distance, in a bit of a clearing of a thick forested area. The weathered structure, from this far away, called to mind old fairy tales where magic and mystery awaited. "She might not be an early bird."

"Someone's awake." Ty gestured to the lights in the front

window and the slow moving shadow on the other side of the curtain. He killed the engine and the sudden silence was deafening. The chill set in instantly and the windows fogged over.

"We sticking to our cover story? We're just nosy people looking into what happened to your friend Alice?"

"Seems to be working so far. No need to change it. If the sheriff's right, I don't want our employment status standing between us and who ran Alice down."

"Doesn't look like we'll have any neighbors to quiz about Davey." One couldn't exactly call the area a neighborhood. Wren was a city girl; she was used to homes being so close you could hear the neighbors' toilets flush. Here on the outskirts of Splendor, the closest house they'd passed on their drive had been a few miles back.

"People definitely get their privacy out here."

Ty sounded as uneasy as she felt. The drive through town and to its surrounding area had provided a different view of Splendor. It was cute where they'd been, but the farther they drove, the more wild things seemed to get. Overgrown areas of shrubbery and fauna. The wildlife. She'd had her share of braking for squirrels or the occasional risk-taking feline in Boston. Up here you needed to keep your attention on the road for any number of creatures. Case in point, the aforementioned moose family.

"Would have been nice to get more information about her before we dropped by," Ty said.

"Google searches don't exactly get updated as fast as we'd like." It didn't help they were both on "vacation" and any logging in to their FBI accounts would alert someone to the fact they weren't exactly relaxing and doing nothing. "We could probably get some assistance from Shelly."

"The deputy?"

"Uh-huh." Wren nodded. "Something tells me she'd be more than happy to help." They just needed to be careful what they asked of her. They didn't want to burn bridges or get the young deputy into trouble. "I could give Aiden a call," she offered. "See if he can bring anything up on the aunt." But seeing as they were already parked outside the woman's house...

"Nah. We'll do things the McKenna way and wing it." There was the sense of humor she needed to hear.

"In that case, follow my lead." She pulled her 9 mm out from her waistband and left it under the seat. "I don't anticipate we'll be needing any weapons in there."

Ty nodded, but didn't repeat her action. "One of us should be carrying just in case."

"Paranoid," she muttered.

"Practical." He shoved open the door. "No one knows where Davey Whittaker is, remember? He could be holed up in her basement."

The chill shot through her the second she got out of the car. Her booted feet crunched in the icy gravel-strewn dirt. Her breath came out in huge white puffs, disappearing into the air around her as she fell into step beside Ty. "I bet people lose weight just stepping outside their homes." She hugged her arms around her torso, feeling the bite of cold seeping through the material. "We stay here for very long, I'm gonna need a heavy-duty parka." She'd seen one at Groovy Grub Grocery that would probably do the trick.

The sound of their walking reminded her of a path of dropped snow cones. *Snow cones.* She shivered and huddled deeper into her coat. She didn't think she'd ever eat another one for the rest of her life. Not without getting frosty flashbacks.

Whatever yard existed in front of Beatrice Mulvaney's house had been thoroughly blanketed by winter. The only pop of color against all the white was the Wedgwood blue of the house itself that was accented with a silvery-gray trim.

The gentle hum of the generator along the side of the house cut through the ear-pinching silence. Wren hopped up the trio of stairs onto the front porch and quickly knocked on the door with her gloved hands.

"Who are you?" The wavering voice came a few moments later. Definitely elderly. Definitely female.

"Ms. Mulvaney?" Wren spoke up and hoped that a female voice in response might be helpful in this situation. "My name is Wren Savakis. My husband and I are staying in town for a while. We're friends of Alice Hawkins."

"Alice?" The white lace curtain pulled back a smidge and a solitary brown eye peered out. "You know Alice?"

"Yes, ma'am," Wren said and swore her breath attempted to freeze into ice midair. "We were curious and hoped you could maybe answer some of our questions, if you don't mind?"

"Questions about what?" She popped open the door a crack, glared out, suspicion evident on her face. "And this early?"

"We're still on Lower 48 time," Wren said. "Please, ma'am. We'd like to speak with your nephew as well. Davey? He might have information—"

The door snapped open. The old woman stood just inside, wearing sturdy fur-lined boots along with a flowered house-dress and at least two sweaters. Her short gray hair was neat and laid flat around her face.

"Davey's a good boy," she stated. "Troubled is all. He didn't have nothing to do with what happened to Alice."

"Yes, ma'am," Wren agreed. "You're absolutely right about that. Do you mind if we come in? It's awful cold out here."

"Sunbelters." Beatrice shook her head and waved them inside. "Y'all freeze if it dips below fifty. Come on. Come on." Wren stepped in far enough for Ty to move in behind her. It was only after Beatrice closed the curtained door that they saw the shotgun leaning next to it. "Can't be too careful," she said, as if reading her mind. "Never know what kind of whackadoodle might come knocking on my door at…" She glanced up at an old weathered cuckoo clock ticktocking its way through the morning. "Not even eight a.m."

She stepped in front of Wren, made her way down the wood-planked hall.

"Come on in. Might as well take the chill off ya and you can tell me what you're really doing here."

Wren cast a look at Ty, who merely shrugged. "Winging it."

She rolled her eyes and followed Beatrice into the kitchen. As weathered as the house was on the outside, the decor inside was surprisingly up-to-date and cheery. Bright yellow walls, beautifully stained cabinetry, and countertops that looked as if they'd been carved out of the finest of quarries. "I ain't seen my nephew for going on six days." Beatrice reached into a cabinet for a pair of worn mugs. "And like I said, he didn't hurt Alice."

"Are you sure about that?" Ty's voice was gentle but firm.

"As sure as you're standing in my home about to drink my coffee," Beatrice countered. "Sheriff Egbert already came out here twice last week looking for the boy. I'll tell you what I told him. Davey couldn't hurt a fly."

"With all due respect, ma'am—"

"That kind of respect ain't nothing but sass," Beatrice told Ty as she motioned for them both to sit at the kitchen table. "Davey had an awful time growing up at the hands of my reprobate brother-in-law. If my nephew were gonna hurt someone, it'd have happened long before now. And it certainly wouldn't have been Alice Hawkins he'd have taken his troubles out on."

"It's awful coincidental he disappeared at the same time Alice was hurt," Wren suggested.

"Coincidences ain't evidence." She straightened with pride. "I worked as a paralegal more than twenty years. Retired a while ago, of course, but I know what I know. And what I know is you aren't friends of Alice's." She shot them a dark look before turning back to the coffeepot. "Real friends would be at the hospital with her or looking after her young'uns, giving that husband of hers a break."

Wren arched a brow. The old woman had a point. "We're trying to find out what happened to her."

"Well, you're wastin' your time here." She set two mugs of coffee on the table. "Ask what you want to ask, drink up, then be on your way. *Paw and Order* starts soon and I don't like to miss Judge Payne's rulings."

"Paw and..." Ty turned somewhat confused eyes on Wren.

"Semi-reality TV show," Wren muttered under her breath. "Ma'am, we really would like to speak to your nephew. When was the last time you saw him, exactly?"

"Already said, didn't I?" She yanked the head off a cartoon-sheep cookie jar and pulled out a handful of what looked like chocolate-covered nuts. "He borrowed my car about a week ago. Haven't heard or seen him since. Ain't the first time he's disappeared for days on end," she lamented. "Won't be the last.

Guess his timing coulda been better. Whole town's probably thinking he ran that girl down, then beat it out of Splendor to avoid getting caught."

"It sounds plausible."

"Course it does." Beatrice sat across from them, a shadow of concern flashing across her face. "That boy hasn't had anything but bad luck since he came out of the womb. My sister, she had a good heart, but a weak one. Didn't live much longer after Davey was born, and his father…" She broke off, her jaw tensing. "Too rotten for words."

Wren chanced a glance at Ty, who was looking anywhere but at her.

"One thing Davey's never been is a shirker. If he did wrong, he'd own up to it. Spent his fair share of time in lockup. Local, mind you. Nothing serious. Loitering, public drinking, the like. But he's harmless. The sooner people start listening to me on that front, the sooner they can get themselves looking for the person who did hurt that girl. Some people can't see nothing but the worst that people's done. Darn shame is what it is."

"Did you often loan Davey your car, Ms. Mulvaney?" Wren asked.

"Couple times a month, mainly to do grocery runs. Try to catch him early in the day about that. So he wasn't…preoccupied with other things." She frowned, her brow wrinkling. "You think maybe you can find him?"

"We're going to try," Ty said. "It would help if I could maybe look through his room? See if there are any clues as to where he might have gone? Does he have a computer?"

Beatrice looked Ty straight in the eye. "He's a good boy."

"Yes, ma'am." Ty nodded. "I'll be careful. And respectful. I promise."

She hesitated another moment. "All right, then. Down the hall, second door on the left."

"Thank you." He gave Wren a look that told her he'd be quick. Then he left the kitchen and clomped down the hall.

"Handsome fella." Beatrice leaned over in her chair as if watching him walk. "Lucky girl."

"He's a good man," Wren felt obliged to share. Ty would

understand, better than most, what Davey had been through. "We're really only looking to find out what happened to Alice."

"I don't know her well, but I've chatted with her a few times when I've gone into town. She even tried to give Davey a job at that store she works at a few months back. Stocking shelves mostly." Beatrice's eyes drooped with grief. "He's a good boy, Davey. Please. Find him. And if you can, prove he didn't do this terrible thing."

"We're going to do our best," Wren said as she sipped her bitter coffee.

"Mrs. Mulvaney?" Ty appeared at the kitchen door again, an old photograph in his hand. "I found this on Davey's dresser mirror." He approached Wren, handed her the picture. "Is this where he grew up?"

Wren looked at the faded image of a couple, the wife holding a baby. She was staring down at the infant with such affection, while the man towering behind her had a hand on her shoulder.

"It is," Mrs. Mulvaney said. "May I?" She held out her hand.

"Of course." Wren passed her the photo.

The tightness around the woman's face eased. "My late husband took this picture shortly after Davey was born. That's him, there." She touched a finger to the infant. "Back then we thought, or we hoped, Davey would help their marriage. Didn't really have a chance to, poor thing."

"Do you remember where this house is?"

Mrs. Mulvaney tsked and frowned at Ty. "Course I do. I'm not addled just yet. Place has been abandoned for years. It's Davey's, of course, but he never wanted it. Said it had too many bad memories. Ghosts, he called 'em. Never known him to go there."

"I'm thinking it might be worth a look," Ty said.

"Suit yourself." Mrs. Mulvaney shrugged. "It's down this road out here. Six, maybe seven, miles." She gestured back toward where they'd come in. "If you make a right at the twisted spruce grove, then keep going about two more miles, you'll run right into it."

"The twisted spruce grove," Ty mused with a look to Wren. "Guess that'll be our next stop."

Chapter Seven

"I feel like I'm sitting on icicles." Wren squirmed uncomfortably in the SUV before reaching out to turn on her seat warmer. She checked her cell. They'd already lost the weak signal they'd had at Davey's aunt's place. "Is it me or are you purposely searching out potholes to drive over?"

He let out a sound that confirmed he'd heard her. She looked at him.

"You're awfully quiet. You find anything in Davey's room other than that photo?"

"The road not traveled." There was a bitterness in his tone and more than a little relief. "Other than a closet full of empty bottles, not much. Struck me as sad, really. Not a whole lot to represent almost thirty years of life."

"Depends on the years, I suppose." She appreciated the idea that Ty could see where his life could have gone if he hadn't made certain tough choices.

"Found a receipt for a winter season tunnel pass he purchased the day before Alice's hit-and-run."

"Can those be traced?" Instead of paying a toll each time a driver used the tunnel, people could buy a pass ahead of time to make travel quicker and easier. "Is there a way to find out if he's used the pass or not?"

"Not sure. Something to ask the sheriff once we get back to town."

The sun had finally risen enough to start the morning thaw. The trees they passed dripped sparkling drops of frozen water from their branches. The light streaming through the surrounding trees and mountains was the proof she needed that they were not on another planet, just in a unique part of the world.

"Have any idea what a twisted spruce grove looks like?" It felt as if they'd been driving forever, which reminded Wren about the locals' definitions when it came to directions.

"She said we'd know it when we see it."

"Is it me or are you having fun with this?"

"It's not fun, exactly," Ty said. "It's a change of pace, not handling one of our ordinary kind of cases. I mean, when was the last time you saw something like that?" He pointed to a bald eagle soaring overhead above the treetops. "We just don't see that in Boston. Or pretty much anywhere else."

"No, we do not." She leaned forward, looked out the windshield. Her experiences with forests were of the cement type; skyscrapers and buildings reaching up to the clouds in a claustrophobic cluster. "You think that's it?" She gestured to a twisted clump of trees on the right-hand side of the road accompanied by a snow-covered turnoff.

"Guess we'll find out." He slowed, made the turn and took the speed down considerably as they bounced their way along the snowy rutted gravel path. "Two miles, she said, right?"

"Yes, hopefully it's close to that." The farther they went, the thicker the canopy of trees and overgrown brush. She held the photograph from Davey's dresser. The faded imagery was wreaking havoc on her heart. Baby Davey was far too young to know anything was amiss, but the vacant, somewhat worried expression on his mother's face shifted Wren's empathy into overdrive.

She never failed to notice those little fragments of people's lives that reminded her how lucky she'd been. The McKenna family was as close as you could get. There had never been a moment when she'd doubted she was loved, wanted or accepted. Despite the stresses that came with her mother's job as a police commissioner, time was always carved out to give each of the four kids the time they needed to grow into confident, stable individuals.

Davey Whittaker hadn't had that.

Neither had Ty. But Ty had something Davey didn't.

He had her.

Eventually the break in the path came and the sky and road opened up. She was back to being focused on where they were headed. Fortunately for her backside, it wasn't a full two miles before they came across the house in the photograph, now dilapidated.

Ty parked and sat there a moment, then powered down his window. "You smell that?"

"Hard not to." The eye-burning stench of burnt rubber assaulted her senses.

She retrieved her weapon from under her seat as Ty hopped out of the car. The smell was stronger out here, so much so she used the cuff of her jacket to cover her mouth as she followed him. "Where is it coming from?"

They silently made their way through the snow, toward the two-story home. As they rounded the first corner, they both stopped and stared at the burned-out husk of an SUV, sagging crookedly near the edge of a small ravine. There was no smoke, but the leftover smell was unmistakable.

Ty coughed as he approached the front of the vehicle, swiped his own jacket sleeve across the ash-strewn plate. "It's Mrs. Mulvaney's car, all right. And burnt to a crisp." He grabbed a handful of snow to clean off his jacket. "No way of proving this was the car that hit Alice."

Wren heaved a sigh of frustration, wishing the grille and windshield were still intact. She stepped back to look up at the house. Part of the exterior wall was scorched nearly to the second floor. All the windows had been blown in, no doubt from when the car's fuel had ignited. "He must be inside." Her hand tightened around her weapon.

"Only one way to find out." Ty began to move back to the front door.

Windowpanes had been broken and covered with crooked

plywood. Shingles hung off-kilter. Rain gutters had dislodged and looked like odd miniature water slides filled with icy moss and weeds.

"I have a question," Wren said.

"Only one? Because I'm closing in on about a dozen."

"Sheriff Egbert must have known about this place. So why didn't he come out to look for Davey?"

"A question we can ask him when next we talk to him. Come on." He waved her forward. "Let's check inside."

Wren followed, keeping a bit of a distance between them as they approached the porch. Ty knocked, then again more loudly. "Davey Whittaker? Your aunt sent us to check on you." He pressed his hand flat on the door and pushed it open.

The smell was worse in here, trapped, no doubt, by the cold and frost. The house was as frozen on the inside as it was outside. Wren tried to snuggle deeper into her jacket as she took up the rear, weapon aimed and trained and moving as they cleared the living room. The dining room. The kitchen.

Old furniture sagged and collapsed all around them. Broken china littered the floor. Papers fluttered in the breeze, coasting through the entire structure.

"He's not here," Wren said quietly as Ty approached the staircase. "Check upstairs if you want, but the place would feel different if he were here."

"Still gonna look. You finish checking down here."

"Uh-huh." She kept her gun raised. Dishes sat piled in the sink, covered in dust, cobwebs and mold. Cabinet doors sat open displaying a smattering of plates, cups and rat droppings.

She heard a rustling behind her, in one of the tall cupboards. She stepped back, giving the ajar door a wide berth as she reached out and whipped it open.

A gray-and-black cat stood facing her, its mouth open in a noisy hiss. The growling sound coming from the back of its throat kept Wren at a distance. *Odd*, Wren thought, as she stepped away, crouched and reached into her jacket pocket for her cell phone. In her experience, most animals would have scurried away upon being discovered. Unless...

She tapped on her flashlight app, aimed the phone down and

crouched lower. "Oh." She blinked at the sight of three kittens pawing their way around an empty box lined with debris.

The mama cat hissed, this time with force.

"It's okay, Mama." Wren gentled her voice, emotion clogging her throat. "You're just protecting your babies. I get it." Wren met the cat's gaze, set her phone down and reached out her hand.

The cat's paw shot up, started to bat at her, but seemed to think better of it.

"That's right. I'm not gonna hurt you." She remained as still as she could, her legs aching as she remained crouched. "Come on. Give me a good sniff." The cat took a hesitant step forward and pressed her cold nose against the side of Wren's hand, then shoved her head under Wren's palm, clearly demanding a pet.

"Whatcha got there?"

Wren glanced over her shoulder to find Ty leaning against the door frame. The cat jumped, hissed and dived back into the cupboard. Wren stood and carefully closed the door. "New tenants. A mama and three babies." She'd spotted a vet clinic on their way out of town. "We can take them to the vet when we leave."

"Okay." Ty didn't sound entirely convinced that was a good idea. "You find anything else around here?"

"Not yet." She gestured toward the mudroom, where an ancient washing machine sat crookedly against the wall. Wren's boots stuck to the floor as she made her way over.

The back door stood wide open. But there wasn't a lot of snow on the floor. There was, however, a mishmash of footprints heading to the back door.

"See that?" She pointed at the floor as Ty joined her. "There's more than one set."

"Or he came and went multiple times," Ty reasoned. "But only that one set continues outside." He indicated the ghostly footprints on the back porch.

They skirted the prints, following them as far as they could. The only indication of anyone walking around here was straight ahead, into the line of trees in the distance. "Good place to try to hide, yeah?"

"Also a great place to freeze to death," Ty countered. "Temperature got down to below ten degrees last night. Hypothermia would set in within minutes, and that's an optimistic estimate."

"Always with the gray clouds," she muttered. "Let's go." She tried to keep her speed up, but soon the snow was calf deep. Her jeans were soaked. Her feet turned to ice blocks as they trudged on.

Her lungs burned. She could hear Ty huffing a bit by the time they reached the trees. "They need to add snow walking to the FBI training course." She stopped, leaned against a thick trunk for a moment, trying to get her bearings. "Snow isn't as thick under the trees." She pointed ahead of them. "See? I bet those are footprints. They pick up again." The indentations in the snow led them into darkness.

"Or we're on the trail of another family of moose."

"Moose or meese?" She inclined her head. "I never do get the plural of that correct."

"If this turns out to be a wild-goose chase..."

"No geese around here." Wren plowed ahead, convinced that there was something or hopefully someone at the other end of these prints. But Ty's estimation was right. It would be really difficult to survive out here for very long.

"Still believe someone was chasing him?" Ty called from behind her.

"I didn't say someone was chasing him," Wren countered.

"You were thinking it."

That much was true. "Here, look." She stopped, crouched and indicated a new scramble of footprints. "Whoever was behind him was stepping where he was. This one step here is a bit more uneven than that one."

"Or he started to run and they went wonky."

"Okay." She stood up, faced him. "Get going, then."

"What?" Ty blinked.

"Start running. Let's see how you do after having walked that whole bit back there." She shook her head. "And here you're supposed to be wilderness-camping dude."

"I come up here to fish and commune with nature, not take suspects on nature hikes."

Wren rolled her eyes. "You're the one who brought me

up here. Let's try to run this to the end before we come to any conclusions."

"Fine. Just sayin'—"

"When we're done, we can get in the car and drive through the tunnel. See where that pass you found in Davey's room might get us." She took a step back, then another, ready to turn on her heel and walk away.

Her foot found only air. She spun as the snow beneath her foot collapsed.

She dropped straight down.

"Wren!" Ty's voice echoed from above.

She flailed, tried to grab out for something, anything to catch hold of. She tucked in just in time to avoid hitting feetfirst. The snow cushioned her landing, but it was still hard enough to drive the air from her lungs. She saw stars, felt that sickening feeling sliding through her stomach as she tried to keep her breakfast down.

"Wren!" Ty shouted again.

"I'm okay." Her voice came out a whisper, so she tried again. "I'm okay!" Her voice echoed as if she'd fallen into a hidden ravine. She pushed up on one hand that went elbow deep into snow. She focused on keeping her breathing even as she did a mental check—feet, legs, arms, shoulders. She ached, but nothing felt dislocated or broken.

She moved, shifting snow out of her way as she confirmed a lack of injuries.

"Hang on!" Ty yelled. "I'm going to see if I can get down to you. I think I see a way."

"Yeah, okay," she mumbled. "Be careful!" she yelled as an afterthought, knowing nothing she said would stop him from trying.

She shifted away from the rock face so she could look up into the line of trees overhead. She'd just stepped straight off the edge of a rock. She wasn't going to call it a cliff because that would just be mortifying. "Wait a minute." She stopped, looked up again. Looked back to where she'd landed. Then to where she stood.

She surveyed the edge of the rock face, how high up it went.

She'd fallen a good fifteen, maybe twenty, feet and luckily hadn't hit anything on the way down. Definitely could have been worse landing-wise. She stepped backward a yard or so, only to have her foot collide with something solid yet soft.

The hairs on the back of her neck prickled as she crouched and brushed at the snow. When her frozen hands felt fabric, she jerked away, gasping.

Swallowing hard, she pushed the dread aside, resumed brushing. She kept at it until she'd completely uncovered the heavy knit sweater.

She recognized the brown-and-burgundy yarn as the same type and color that had been in Mrs. Mulvaney's knitting basket beside her chair in the kitchen.

"Ty?" she called as she touched the shoulder, gently rolled the body onto its back. Strands of wet, scraggly dark blond hair were frozen to the face and forehead.

She stared down at the lifeless eyes of Davey Whittaker.

"Yeah, almost there. I think." His voice sounded strained but seemed closer. "Give me a few—"

"Stop. Stop where you are." She would have blinked back tears if she hadn't thought they'd freeze on her face. "I need you to go back."

"Go back? I'm not leaving you—"

"You need to go back and call the sheriff. We need help." She rested her hand on Davey's chest. "I found Davey Whittaker." Something sticky coated her fingers.

"What? He's down there? Is he alive?"

"No. He's dead. But not from the elements." She lifted her hand, looked at the congealed blood coating her skin. "He's been shot."

Ty lost ten years of his life watching Wren drop out of sight and plummet through the snow. Ten years he suspected he would never get back. He held his hands up to the heat pouring from the SUV's vents and tried to replay how they could have avoided the events that might have nearly killed her.

After she'd managed the uneven and unofficial path he'd found running into the ravine, the trek back to the house had taken a lot out of her. Out of them both, really. Neither of them was in any shape to remain with the body. Not when there was a warmer alternative not too far away.

Ty forced himself to relax his jaw. He was giving himself a headache grinding his teeth and gnawing on something that couldn't be fixed. What had happened had happened. There were no do-overs. But the memory of seeing her disappear right in front of him fed the real fear he had of losing her. They'd had close calls before. More than their fair share. But this time…

This time he'd watched it play out in vicious, heart-wrenching slow motion.

He caught sight of snow pluming up as a vehicle approached and stopped behind him. Recognizing Sheriff Egbert's SUV, Ty flicked off the heat, shut down the engine and got out of the car. He looked beyond the SUV, half-surprised not to find any other cars following.

"You the only one coming?" Ty called as Sheriff Egbert and Shelly climbed out.

"Afraid so!" Sheriff Egbert tugged on a pair of gloves, tossed his hat into the car before he closed the door. "I've put in a request for a forensics team to come out when they can, but Juneau's been backlogged awhile. It'll be a few days at the very least. If it takes much longer, the request will go to Anchorage."

"Right." One of those quirks of a small town.

"Where's your partner?" Shelly asked.

"In the middle of a rescue operation." Ty hadn't even tried to talk Wren out of rescuing the cats. When it came to animals, there was no way to win. No sooner had he explained than Wren walked out the front door, a medium-sized cardboard box in her arms.

"Couldn't just leave them behind," Wren said as Ty opened the back of the SUV for her. "Mama's definitely not happy." She cringed at the howling coming from inside the box.

Shelly pried open the lid and peered inside. "Poor little things. You want to keep them?"

"No!" Ty said.

Wren chuckled. "I'd love to, but no. Thought I'd take them to the vet I saw in town."

"Doc Thompson, sure." Shelly nodded.

"Why don't you two head back?" Ty suggested. "I'll help the sheriff with Davey's body."

Wren nodded in agreement, mainly because they'd agreed to this course of action after calling the sheriff.

"Give me a call when you're on your way back," Wren said as she motioned for Shelly to jump into their SUV. "We can meet back up at the Salmon Run Café."

"Sounds good," Ty said.

"Okay with you, Sheriff?" Shelly asked.

"Keep your cell on you," Sheriff Egbert advised. "I'll run Davey to the clinic, get the paperwork started for the autopsy."

Ty climbed into the sheriff's SUV while the women drove off toward the main road. "Glad we're driving closer," he admitted as the sheriff slid in behind the wheel. "Wasn't looking forward to trekking through all that snow again."

"I'd think once a day for that is enough." The engine rumbled to life and they drove parallel to the tracks Ty and Wren had made both on their way in and out of the tree line.

"I've got a question to ask you," Ty said when the silence stretched thin. "You knew about Davey's upbringing. Where he grew up." He gestured back to the house. "Why didn't you check to see if he was hiding out here when he went missing?"

"Meant to." Sheriff Egbert winced into the bright sun streaming through the windshield. "I was headed up here a couple of days ago, then got called out for a domestic disturbance on the other side of town." He shook his head as if he could clear his conscience. "Went clean out of my head after that. To hear Bea tell it, Davey never wanted anything to do with this place even before his dad died a few years ago."

"Still." Ty wasn't buying it. "If Davey was a suspect in a hit-and-run, it would make sense for him to do something unpredictable. Having a whole house to hide in—"

"Hindsight's always clear. The place is uninhabitable. You saw that yourself. Given the temperature this time of year, it would have been suicide to come out this far without power or water."

"Guess maybe it was," Ty said, acknowledging the fact.

The sheriff swung the car around at the line of trees, backed up a bit before he killed the engine again. "Truth is." He heaved a sigh and Ty saw a flash of guilt he was all too familiar with. "I didn't chase Davey down because I assumed he was guilty. Figured he'd turn up in time. The boy always had a conscience and I assumed at some point it would win. I got enough to mind without worrying about a loose cannon whose only talent seemed to be getting into trouble. I know." He shook his head at Ty's assessing look. "Not very admirable. Or honorable."

"I didn't say that," Ty responded.

"You didn't have to. It's written all over your face." There wasn't just guilt shining in his eyes now, but sorrow. And regret. "I failed that kid. From the very first time I arrested him on a drunk and disorderly a dozen or so years ago. I should have done more to help." He opened his door. "I should have cared. Maybe then he wouldn't be dead."

These were not the words of a calculating individual, but of a man who would carry this loss for a good long time.

Recovery sled in hand, they hiked through the trees to where Wren had discovered Davey's body. The area had been more than a little compromised in Ty's rush to get down to her. When they reached the ledge, they both looked over.

"Wren fell straight down." Even now, the very idea made Ty's stomach hurt. "Hit a soft patch of snow when she landed. Davey's just there." He pointed to the barely-there splash of color a short distance away. "My guess, given the amount of frozen blood that's under his body, he was shot up here and then pushed over. It would take actual velocity to go out like that before landing. If he'd just fallen, Wren would have landed on top of him."

"You've seen more dead bodies than I have," Sheriff Egbert said. "I'll take your word on this."

"It would have been quick," Ty tried to reassure the older man. "I know that doesn't bring any comfort, but still, it'd have been quick." A shot straight to the heart like that? Couldn't have been anything but.

"You're right," the sheriff said as he started down the un-even path Ty had traversed earlier. "It doesn't bring me any comfort at all."

Wren was still trying to thaw out as she and Shelly stood beside the exam table at Thompson Veterinary Services back in Splendor. Personally she longed for a space heater to stick her hands and feet on, but that would have to wait. Right now there were more important things to address.

"Are they going to be okay?" Wren tried to keep the worry out of her voice. The three kittens—two gray-striped and one black—seemed to have no problem mewing their emotions. The wiggly little fur balls were gaining more energy by the second.

"I think they'll be fine." The forty-something woman with stark black hair and bright blue eyes nodded as she pulled out the third kitten and rubbed a gentle finger between its eyes. "They're a little malnourished, but not surprising, given their mama hasn't had much milk lately."

All three of their gazes shifted to the side table where the mother cat was eagerly gobbling up the bowl of food provided by Dr. Thompson's assistant.

"Once she's eaten some, her milk will come back in and she can feed them. In the meantime—" she smiled at Wren "—we'll give them some bottle formula and start bulking them up."

"Thank goodness." Wren breathed a sigh of relief. "What about finding them homes?"

"Shouldn't be a problem," Shelly said. "I can put the word out around town once they're cleared for adoption. It won't take long for them to be claimed."

Wren walked over to the other table, gently stroked her hand down the mama cat's sleek back. "Her, too?"

"She might be more difficult," Dr. Thompson admitted. "Older cats always are. People think they lose their cute fac-tor. But we'll do our best. Don't worry. We're a no-kill town. If no one takes her, we'll keep her around the office as a bonus employee and comfort cat."

The mama cat lifted her head long enough to give Wren a

quick lick on the side of her hand before she resumed eating. Wren took that as a thank-you.

"Can we get her spayed?" Wren asked. "If it's a matter of cost—"

"Way ahead of you," the doctor told her. "Thank you for bringing them in."

"Great. Okay, then." Wren sighed. "I guess we'll be going. I am in desperate need of some coffee." She looked to Shelly. "Why don't you join me?"

"Oh, sure." Shelly looked both pleased and surprised. "I've got time until Sheriff Egbert gets back into town."

"Back? Where did he go?" Dr. Thompson examined the ears of the black kitten.

"He took a drive out to the old Whittaker place," Shelly said without missing a beat.

"Looking for Davey, no doubt," Dr. Thompson said. "That reminds me—how is Alice doing this morning?"

"Last report was there's no change," Shelly said. "But the doctors believe that's positive news."

"Good to hear. I've signed up for the meal chain that's got going for Bradley and the kids. Planning to make them my famous chicken enchiladas for tomorrow."

Wren's stomach rumbled in reaction.

"Thanks again, Doc," Shelly called over her shoulder.

"You bet."

"You handled that really well," Wren told Shelly once they were outside. It took her a second to get her bearings and adjust once more to the cold. "You didn't miss a beat answering her questions about the sheriff."

"I've learned to keep to the truth as much as possible. Makes it easier when the details really do come out." Shelly winced and tugged her gloves back on. "You really need to get yourself some gloves."

"I've been thinking that myself." Her fingers practically cracked when she tried to move them. "So, coffee?"

"Right. Salmon Run Café's this way."

For being such a small town, it always felt like a trek getting anywhere. *Probably the cold*, Wren told herself.

The instant they stepped inside the rustic-cabin-style eatery, Wren wanted to shout in relief. "Ah, nice and warm in here." The vet's office hadn't been cold, exactly, but here she could feel the heat blowing. She cupped her hands in front of her mouth and stomped her feet.

The interior reminded her of a classic-looking cabin with thick wood stained a rich, deep walnut color. Fishing was clearly the recurring theme, with numerous poles and tackle on display, along with photographs of people having caught some serious-looking salmon. A few pictures were in stark color, others in black-and-white, leading Wren to assume this particular eatery had been in business for a good long time.

"Hey, Aurora!" Shelly called to the woman behind the ten-seat counter. "Gonna grab a table right over there, yeah?"

"Go ahead. Coffee?"

"Please," Wren laughed. "A tankard, if you have it."

The woman grinned. "Be right over."

It made sense the place only had a few customers, given she and Shelly had arrived right between breakfast and lunch. The pair of men sitting at the counter watched as Wren and Shelly claimed their table.

"Morning, Deputy." A young man with thick glasses smiled at Shelly from where he sat at a smaller table against the wall. He kept one hand on the laptop computer currently plugged into one of the outlets on the wall.

"Hey, Mason." Shelly's cheeks went slightly pink and she gave Mason a quick wave. "Uh, thanks for your help the other day with that computer glitch at the station."

"Not a problem." Mason's gaze shifted briefly to Wren, but it was clear he only had eyes for Shelly. "Happy to help."

"Mmm. I bet he was," Wren teased Shelly as they took a seat at a table for four by the window. "He's cute. What's the story?" She liked the young deputy. So far, she'd appeared unflappable and easily dealt with whatever was thrown at her. In that way, she reminded Wren of her sister, Regan. There wasn't anything she couldn't handle.

Shelly rolled her eyes, but the pink in her cheeks only intensi-fied. "Mason and I went to school together. We're just…friends."

"Uh-huh." Wren knew how that went. "He calls you *Deputy*. That's kinda hot."

"It's kinda not." But Shelly laughed. Sitting across from Wren, she shrugged out of her coat. "Since we've got the time, can I ask you some questions about the FBI?"

"As long as you keep your voice down," Wren warned as their coffee arrived. "Thank you so much." She had her hands wrapped around the steaming mug in record time. One sip and she nearly went to heaven. "Now, that's perfect. Hits the spot for sure, Aurora," she added, remembering the name that Shelly had mentioned.

"Good to hear. You're a new face. Pretty face," Aurora said, planting a hand on her hip and pinning sharp green eyes on Wren. She had a thick smattering of freckles across her nose and cheeks. There were a pair of turquoise glasses perched on the top of her head, either because she always needed them or because she'd forgotten they were there. "You must be Ty Savakis's wife."

"I must be." She was so grateful the mug was almost big enough to hide behind. "But call me Wren. Nice to meet you. I heard you fix a great salmon, bacon and tomato sandwich."

"You heard that, did you?" Aurora looked impressed and tapped her bright pink fingernails against the white apron tied around her waist.

"Gabriel Hawthorne mentioned it when he flew me in," Wren added. "He said I shouldn't miss it."

"Well, that Gabriel's a charmer." Aurora's face lit up. "I'll have to give him a free slice of pie the next time he drops in."

Wren's eyes went wide. "You have pie?"

"Oh, yeah." Shelly reached over and pulled the laminated card out from behind the napkin holder. "Made fresh every day." She leaned across the table. "You get a discount on the day's special if you order it with a meal."

"Yeah?" Wren's mood immediately brightened. "What's to-day's special?"

"Alaskan blueberry."

It was official, Wren thought. She was going to have to walk back to the Lower 48 after a few days in Splendor. "You'd better set aside two slices. My husband's on his way," she said.

"Sounds like a plan. Nice to meet you, Wren." Aurora moved off with an approving expression on her face.

"So, you have questions." Wren lowered her voice.

"Well, I have a lot of them. Not really sure where to start." Shelly scrubbed her palms against her thighs. "I've been thinking about applying to the FBI Academy."

"Oh?" Wren picked up her coffee. "Not enough excitement around here for you?"

"There has been since you and Ty got here. I mean, Special Agent Savakis."

"Make it Ty," Wren advised. "We aren't spreading the info about our actual jobs."

"Right. Sorry. Nervous, I guess." Shelly laughed and choked down a sip of her coffee. "Is it hard? Getting through the Academy?"

"It's not easy," Wren confirmed. "Getting in isn't a cakewalk, either."

"Oh, that I have covered, no problem. I've got my BA in sociology with a minor in accounting. Plus, I've been a deputy almost two years now, so, education, check, work experience, check-check."

Wren nodded. "You're more than halfway there." She looked to the door when it opened to let a trio of customers in. "They're going to ask when you apply, so I'll ask now. Why do you want to be an agent?"

Shelly's face fell a bit. "I'm… I don't know, really. It just feels interesting. You get to travel and do a lot of really important work. On all kinds of cases."

"You do important work here, Shelly." Local law enforcement, especially in a small town, was vital to the success or failure of a community. It was obvious Shelly and Sheriff Egbert were two of the good ones.

Shelly huffed. "But it's not…it's not anything special. FBI agents, they solve cases that really make a difference. Like you and Ty coming out here to help Alice."

"Yeah, well." Wren was nearly half-finished with her coffee

and already longed for a refill. "You know by now we are here unofficially." And there would be a price to pay once she—once they—got back to Boston. But that was for another time. "I've seen you work, Shelly. You're good at your job. You're good with people. You understand them and they respect you. That's not easy to accomplish."

"I guess." She sagged and looked a bit deflated. "I just want something…more, something bigger to do with my life. I don't want to get stuck."

Wren nodded. "I can understand that. Look. When the time comes, and you make your decision, you give me a call. I'll write you a letter of recommendation."

"Really?" Shelly immediately brightened. "You'd do that?"

"I'd do that." Wren held out her hand for Shelly's phone and added her phone number into Shelly's contact list.

"That would be so amazing. And I hope you know, if I can do anything to help you and Ty with this case, I'm more than willing."

As much as she appreciated the offer, Wren shook her head. "I wouldn't want to put you in a difficult position with your boss."

"I'd let you know if it was something I couldn't do," she insisted. "But I wanted you to know that you can rely on me." She broke off from saying more when the door opened again, and Ty and the sheriff walked in.

"Hey, honey." Wren rested her chin in her hand and beamed up at a rather sullen-looking Ty as the two men joined them. He looked a bit haggard, but just seeing his face seemed to erase the last of her sour mood. Maybe falling off the edge of a cliff—okay, she was calling it a cliff—had shifted some…priorities for her. "Hungry? They've got blueberry pie for dessert."

"Yeah?" He brightened. "I could handle pie."

"Deputy Adjuk." Sheriff Egbert looked to his second. "We've got places to be."

"Sure thing." Shelly jumped up and snatched her jacket off the back of the chair. "Where to, Sheriff?"

"Beatrice Mulvaney's place for the notification." The second he spoke, the quiet chatter in the diner went silent. "Might as well tell you all now." Sheriff Egbert stepped back, took off his hat. "Davey Whittaker's been found dead up at his family's old place."

"Oh." Aurora blinked quickly, touched her hand to her heart. "Oh, that's terrible. Was it...was it his drinking?"

"It was not," Sheriff Egbert said and triggered more than a few expressions of surprise. "I'm not in a position right now to say anything more, but we might as well get the word out. Mrs. Mulvaney's going to be needing our support and I'd consider it a personal favor if, when the time comes, you all pay your respects. I know Davey caused problems around here, but he had a rough life. He didn't deserve what's happened to him, so please. Just...keep that in mind moving forward."

"Sounds like he got what was coming to him," one of the men at the counter grumbled behind his coffee. "Good riddance."

Sheriff Egbert took a few steps toward the man.

Wren shivered against the chill she felt in the room.

"Davey Whittaker was a member of this town, Carl," Sheriff Egbert said coolly. "We don't have any proof yet that he was responsible for Alice's accident. You want to feel that way about him, you keep it to yourself. This isn't just a tragedy for his aunt. It's a tragedy for all of us. We've lost one of our own. That's all that matters." The man opened his mouth as if to speak again, but Sheriff Egbert held up his index finger. "For now, that's all that matters. Thank you, Ty. For the assist. Deputy?"

"Right. Thanks for the talk." Shelly tossed Wren a quick smile before she hurried after her boss, her braided black hair glistening against the overhead lamps.

The chatter started up again, no doubt this time focusing on a different topic. Ty took Shelly's empty seat, set her mug aside.

"Everything okay?" Wren reached across the table and grabbed hold of his hand. "Are *you* okay?"

"Shouldn't I be asking you that question?" He slipped his fingers through hers and held on tight. Tighter than normal. "You're the one who fell off a mountain."

"It was a cliff," she countered, feigning offense. "A small one, but I won't have you take that away from me." The air suddenly seemed charged between them. Something she couldn't bring herself to ignore any longer. Being with him here, in the middle of a snowy nowhere, with the way he'd kissed her yesterday…it felt like uncharted territory. "Seriously, Ty. What's going on in your head?" It was a question she needed to not only ask more frequently, but she needed to start demanding an answer. If only to ease her own worry.

"Uh, I just helped pull a missing kid off the side of a mountain with a bullet hole the size of a crater in his chest. So, yeah, today's been a great day."

"I know." She hated how he took on the pain of other people, as if he'd had any control over what happened to Davey Whittaker. "I know it's going to be tough, but we've still got a case to work. We might even have to start over, now that our prime suspect's gone. Especially if he wasn't responsible for what happened to Alice."

"I guess." He sat back as Aurora approached with a fresh mug of coffee for him.

"And you're Ty Savakis." The corners of Aurora's eyes were smudged with mascara, no doubt after shedding some tears for Davey. "Welcome to Splendor."

"Thank you." He accepted his coffee with a smile. "Long morning. This'll hit the spot."

"Word is you helped Sheriff Egbert bring Davey back." She nodded approvingly. "Not everyone will say it, but he had a good heart. A bruised one, but a good one."

"I don't know if that makes me feel better about it or not," Wren mused.

"He tried," Aurora said. "He even went back to those Friends of Bill meetings they have at the church twice a week."

Ty's hand tightened around Wren's. "When did he start that?"

"Oh, about a month ago or thereabouts," Aurora said. "I thought it finally took. Said he met someone there who offered him a job working home construction. Really thought he had his stuff together this time."

Ty gave Wren the look.

"Any idea who gave him the job?" Wren asked. When Aurora frowned, Wren rushed on. "It would be nice for his aunt to know that he was doing better."

"Poor Beatrice." Aurora shook her head. "He did joke once that the guy was from out of town. Said that was probably why he was willing to take a chance on Davey. Didn't know the history." She shrugged. "Anyway, you two ready to order?"

Wren ordered for the both of them. She knew that look on Ty's face. It was his putting-the-pieces-together look. "What?" she asked once Aurora left again.

"Seems odd, doesn't it? Davey's just getting his life together, hits an AA meeting, makes friends with someone who might not even be from around here, and he's dead shortly thereafter?"

"You always say there are no coincidences."

"I do say that, don't I?" He took a large gulp of coffee. "Let's stop at the church on the way back, see when their next meeting is."

Wren looked down to where their hands were still locked together. "You, ah, have any other plans for the evening?" She stroked her thumb across the back of his knuckles.

"Nothing official. You have something in mind?"

"Maybe." She shouldn't even be thinking about kissing Ty at the moment, not with the mystery of Davey Whittaker's death added to the mix. Still, that drop down the mountainside had flipped a switch for sure. "Don't worry. I'll keep you in the loop."

Chapter Eight

"Church is just up this way." Ty zipped up his jacket the instant they were outside the café. Funny, he would have assumed that it would get warmer as the day progressed, but he could not shake the persistent chill.

"We can't infiltrate an AA meeting," Wren said as she fell into step beside him. "Some lines can't be crossed."

"They wouldn't tell us anything, anyway." This little town really was growing on him. The laid-back pace, the small specialized stores, the friendly way everyone smiled or said hello as they passed. "They take the *anonymous* part very seriously."

"You know that for sure?"

"One of my high school English teachers recommended Al-Anon meetings to me when I was fifteen."

"The meetings for family members of alcoholics?"

"When you turn up to class looking like I did, the good teachers take notice." He'd shoved those memories down so far he couldn't believe they had the oxygen to resurface.

"Did you go?"

"Until I graduated. Saved my life. Gave me a support system of people to call when things got really bad." He didn't realize how much the memories stung until Wren wrapped her arms around his and held him close. The instant balm against his heart nearly made him trip over his own feet. "Of course, a massive growth spurt helped a bit more. Along with the box-ing lessons I started taking." His smile was quick and cool. "Phone numbers were great, but seeing the look on his face when he realized I'd learned how to defend myself?" Now, that had been priceless.

"I hate that you grew up that way."

He did, too. But he wouldn't be who he was without it, and, for the most part, he was pretty pleased with who he'd become.

They found the church at the end of the main road of Splen-dor, looking as if it had been cobbled together out of various buildings. The wide arched windows were painted a darker brown than the natural wood that constructed the building. A beautiful shiny white wooden cross sat perched on the angled eaves over the front door. A solitary stained glass window sat below the cross, depicting a colorful scene of Alaskan beauty— the mountains, the water and an eagle soaring into the heavens.

A woman was crouched in front of a line of flower beds, digging through the snow to tend to the barely-there buds at-tempting to burst through the hard soil. She glanced up as they approached, shielding her eyes against the sun.

"Good afternoon!" Her greeting was warm as she got to her feet and pulled off her gloves. "Given the looks of you, I'm guessing you're the Savakises." She held out her hand. "I'm Pastor Lorraine Cunningham. But, please, call me Lori."

"Nice to meet you, Lori. Does everyone know who we are?" Wren asked in what Ty recognized as her half-teasing voice.

"Perils of a small town, I'm afraid." Her brown hair was cut short and on an angle and her thin face carried the barest hint of a sun kiss. She was well clad for a winter's day with her double layers and thick tights and boots. "You look like you've found what you're looking for." She turned to gaze up at the cross. "What can I do for you?"

"We have some questions about Davey Whittaker."

Pastor Lori shook her head. "Davey. I just heard." She touched a finger to the cross at her throat, looked at Ty. "You helped the sheriff bring him back to town."

"I did, yes, ma'am."

"He's having a little trouble processing the whole thing,"

Wren lied. "We've heard so many conflicting stories about him, we thought maybe you might have some insights?"

"Of course. Certainly." She gathered up her gardening bucket and motioned for them to follow. "Come on in. I was just about to fix myself some tea."

"Are we going to get struck by lightning for lying to a pastor?" Ty muttered so only Wren could hear him.

"McKennas have earned a fair amount of goodwill." She glanced to the sky. "Plus, it's for a good reason. And it's not all a lie. You are struggling."

It disturbed him that she saw that. But then whatever was happening between them seemed to have cracked whatever walls remained. Or the filters that kept them from commenting or speaking their minds.

Pastor Lori led them through the small quaint church that on the inside looked as if it had been outfitted by master carpenters. The dozen pews sat neatly arranged facing a modest but elegant dais. The door to the right led to the pastor's living quarters, a practical area neatly displayed with even more hand-carved pieces of furniture and accent pieces.

"My grandfather helped build this church," Pastor Lori said as she urged them to sit at her square kitchen table. "He was a carpenter with a love of architecture."

"It's a beautiful building," Wren said. "Was he also the pastor?"

"No." Pastor Lori set a kettle on the stove and switched on the burner. When she turned, the knowing smile on her face said it all. "My grandmother was." She retrieved a tin of cookies from on top of the refrigerator. "Please. Save me from myself. My assistant makes the best peanut butter cookies. I need them out of the house."

Lunch at the Salmon Run Café had been filling and delicious, especially the pie, but Ty could never resist a cookie. "Thank you." He nudged Wren, who quickly followed suit. "We heard mention that Davey had recently started in a recovery program here at the church."

"Yes." Pastor Lori sat on the edge of her chair.

"Do you know the last meeting he attended?" Wren asked.

"I do." Pastor Lori nodded. "It was the night of Alice's accident. We all thought he was doing really well." She shook her head. "It's not an easy demon to battle."

"No, it's not," Ty agreed before he thought better of it.

Pastor Lori's gray eyes softened. "I'm sorry you understand that."

Ty resisted the urge to squirm. He didn't like being under the microscope. One of the appeals of joining the FBI was to be on the other side of it. He cleared his throat. "What time did the meeting let out?"

"About five. We had bingo that night and I'm a complete stereotype when it comes to bingo." She chuckled as the tea-kettle began to whistle. "I didn't hear about the accident until the next morning."

"Any idea why everyone assumes Davey was the one who hit Alice?"

Pastor Lori glanced away. "I don't suppose it hurts to say. He was seen at the Outlaw that night. It's just a few doors down from Wilderness Wonders."

"Where Alice works," Wren clarified. "We were under the impression Davey didn't drive much."

"Oh, he did when he was sober," Pastor Lori said. "That was usually how anyone knew he'd stopped drinking. And he always drove his aunt's car. Couldn't keep a job long enough to pay for one himself."

"But he did get a new job, though."

"Apparently." Pastor Lori rose to pour the hot water into three mugs. "Is lemon tea all right for you?"

"Sounds great," Ty said. "You were saying, about his job?"

"Now, that I don't have many details about. I heard rumblings that someone he met in the program offered him a job. But it wasn't anyone local." She set their mugs in front of them. "Even if I was in a position to share their identity with you, I'm not sure it would get you anywhere."

"Oh? Why's that?" Wren accepted the sugar bowl and spoon Pastor Lori scooted closer.

"Well, let's just say I tend to know when people aren't telling me the truth. It's a...gift." She raised her eyes to the sky again.

"Just like I'm pretty sure you aren't asking about Davey because of any spiritual crisis you're going through. Or am I wrong?"

Feeling a door open, Ty walked through. "We're trying to find out what happened to Alice. And now to Davey. That's all we want to do."

"I see." Pastor Lori sipped her tea. "Okay, as I said, I'm afraid I can't be of any help as to who Davey might have met at the meetings. We had two guests in the past two months. Don't recall seeing them in town very much, but they were definitely at the meetings. Two, no, three."

"And since Alice's accident?" Wren pressed.

"We had our meeting last night. Not a sign of them."

"Could you describe them, maybe?" Ty asked.

"I cannot." Her expression said she clearly believed in the *anonymous* part of the group's principles. "All I can say is they stood out."

"Male?" Ty tried again.

She inclined her head. "What I noticed was that they definitely didn't look as if they had any interest in being at the meetings," Pastor Lori went on. "We pride ourselves on being welcoming. I got the impression they were both just going through the motions. But I try not to judge. It's kind of in the job description."

Ty chuckled. "Appreciate you spending the time with us."

"I'll do anything to help find out what happened to Davey, and whoever hurt Alice. It's such a tragedy. She and Bradley haven't attended services, but I stopped in after breakfast this morning. From what I hear, the doctors seem to think she's improving."

"That's great news," Wren said.

"I wish there was more I could do. That we all could do for Alice and her family," Pastor Lori said. "If you can think of anything, please don't be shy. Just ask."

"Believe me, neither of us is shy," Wren said.

"So, what do you think?" Ty asked Wren a few minutes later as they walked back through town. "She gave a pretty good description of bachelor number two in the white SUV."

"Yes, she did. Want to test our luck and check out the Outlaw?"

They did, but to no avail. The two employees working the night of Alice's accident—the night Davey supposedly fell off the wagon—wouldn't be on shift until tomorrow. Pushing would only make Ty and Wren stand out more, so instead they headed over to Groovy Grub Grocery.

"Hey, Sully!" Wren called as soon as they walked in the door.

Ty always marveled at how easily she got along with people. One of those McKenna traits, he supposed. They all knew how to interact with others in any situation.

"Oh, hey there, Wren. See you brought your other half today." Sully gave her a wave before returning his attention to the short line of customers at the counter.

Ty wandered while Wren perused the gloves and jackets. Her cold hands could explain her new tendency toward holding his hand whenever she could. Sure, that was it. She was cold. And keeping up the pretense of their "relationship." Still…

He couldn't help but wonder what she'd been talking about at lunch when she asked about his plans for the evening. He knew what he wanted to think about it, but he wasn't going to jump on board that particular train just yet.

"Find something?" he asked when she tracked him down at the back of the store. The selection of hunting knives, especially the carved ones and the more practical military type, captured his attention.

"One pair for me and one for you." She held the gloves up as if for his inspection, along with a new fleece-lined jacket the color of ripe plums. "Couldn't find one that came with a plug-in heater, so this'll have to do."

He trailed behind her to the register, keeping an eye on the customers milling about in the aisles. He got his fair share of looks and smiles and nods of acknowledgment. He received another from Sully, the burly man standing behind the cash register.

"You done good by our Davey," Sully said with a solemn expression on his whisker-covered face. "Heard you gave the sheriff a hand out there."

"Just doing what I could," Ty said as the man rang Wren up for her items. "Wish it didn't have to be done."

"Agreed," Sully said.

"Hey, Sully, I'd like to get ice cream for Bradley's kids," Wren said. "Can you give me a couple of pints of their favorites?"

"Sure can. You want a cone? Got a new flavor today. Mint chocolate chip made with Irish liqueur."

"*Irish*, you say?" Ty teased as Wren groaned. "You might have just said the magic word."

"If you aren't busy tomorrow night, we're having a town potluck to raise money for Alice's medical bills."

"Oh." Wren blinked and then glanced at Ty. "What a great idea. We'll definitely plan on being there."

"Six o'clock, the town meeting hall. You won't have to go far," Sully added with a deep chuckle. "It's in the basement of your building. Just take the elevator all the way down."

"Sounds good," Ty said, thinking that would be a great chance to see if anyone else had run into the two guys Davey had made friends with at his AA meetings. "Thanks for the heads-up."

"I'll have to put my thinking cap on as far as what to bring," Wren said as Sully included three pints of ice cream to her order, then went back to get her cone.

They were stopped again on their way out, more than once, by people thanking Ty for his helping the sheriff with Davey.

"You can see it on their faces," he said once he and Wren were on their way back to Skyway Tower.

"You mean that they maybe feel like they should have paid more attention to Davey while he was still here?" Wren asked. "I noticed that. Even saw it on Pastor Lori's face when we were talking to her. And she did try to help."

A new sliver of anger burrowed beneath Ty's mood. "It ticks me off, thinking Davey might have finally been ready for a change and someone was waiting to pounce on him."

"Wouldn't be the first time we've seen it." She licked the ice cream in a way that had Ty seriously wishing they were already in their apartment. Her gaze went up and her face lost a bit of its color. "Ugh. I've got to stop doing that." She squeezed her eyes shut, shook her head as if trying to erase an image in her mind.

"What?" He looked to where she had. One of the passenger air trams was gliding up the mountainside in the distance. Far above the ground. "You know, at some point you're going to have to get over this height thing of yours."

"Uh-huh, well, I've made it this long," she muttered. "There are some challenges I'm willing to let pass me by. Seriously." She pointed at the cable cars suspended high in the sky, her eyes wide with disbelief. "Why?"

"To reach places you can't get to otherwise?"

"Ha ha."

"It's not that bad, Wren. I took the trip up my second day here. They're automated, accessible 24/7, just someone overseeing the system in case anything goes…" He broke off at her glare. "You sit in the right place, you only see sky. You can almost trick yourself into thinking you're still on the ground."

"Please."

Okay, maybe that was a stretch. "Don't make me issue a dare," he teased. "You know you can't resist that."

"There are few certainties in life, Ty Savakis," she said firmly as she drew her tongue around the top edge of the cone to stop the ice cream from dripping. Every cell in his body tightened to attention. "But I can one hundred percent guarantee I am never stepping foot in one of those…things. What?" She frowned at him, examined her cone, then looked back at him. "What's wrong?"

"Not a thing." For once, everything felt very, very right.

"Want some?" She held it out.

"Of the cone?" he asked. "No."

He couldn't help it. He bent his head and caught her lips with his, tasting the cold of the ice cream along with the tempting combination of flavors that included Irish liqueur, chocolate and Wren. Her mouth opened beneath his, her free hand snaking up to the collar of his jacket to grab hold. She ignited something inside him he'd never allowed himself to stoke before. A fire, a desire that he'd had to bank for going on seven years.

He heard the telltale sound of giggles and whispers moving past him and he lifted his head, looking into her eyes as if she were the only life preserver in an ocean of emotions. After all this time…this, whatever it was between them, might finally happen.

"Is it just me," she murmured and patted a not-so-calming hand against his chest, "or am I the only one who's grateful that potluck is *tomorrow* night?"

"Not just you. Wanna go back to the apartment and compare…notes?" he asked with a grin he had no doubt came across as sly.

"Sure." Her smile matched his and set off all kinds of fiery images in his brain. "If you're sure."

How could he be, given everything making love to her would risk? He should say no. He should be the rational one, the responsible one, and remind her about their professional partnership. Their jobs. The undeniable fact that their attention would be…divided. But he'd spent years longing to touch her in ways he never could. Would he honestly walk away from it now? For so long all he'd had in life was his job, and now, even for a little while, he could have her, too. It was a longing he had to fulfill.

He took the bag containing the ice cream and her old jacket, slipped his free hand into hers. "I'm sure."

There wasn't a power in the universe that could have made him remember that walk back to the tower, or if they took the stairs or elevator to the fourth floor. All he did know was that closing in on that apartment door and the ability to lock the rest of the world completely out—even for a little while—felt like the culmination of a life's goal.

"Keys, keys," Wren muttered as she dug into her pockets. "Where on earth did I put the stupid— Gah!" She ripped the bag out of his hand, yanked out her old jacket and fumbled to find the correct pocket. It did something to him, deep inside where he tucked it safely away, to know she was as anxious and maybe as nervous as he was.

"Want some help?"

"No, I don't want— Oh." She blinked up at the key he held in his hand. "Give me that." She snatched it from him, laughing, and unlocked the door. She spun around, grabbed him by the front of his jacket and dragged him inside. The door had barely closed behind them before she pressed him to the wall and kissed him.

There wasn't a part of himself he didn't want her to touch. Every cell in his being cried out for her. His hands moved as if he were possessed by a restless fever, skimming up and down her back, frustrated by the thick fabric of the coat that separated them.

She pressed his mouth open with hers, dived in, took control of the kiss and swirled her tongue around his in a way that reignited that dormant core inside him. Breathing ragged, they worked at each other's jackets, letting them drop where they were as they went to work on buttons and...

"Wait!" She planted a hand on his chest. He almost couldn't hear her—let alone think—with the blood pounding in his ears. It shouldn't be possible that kissing her, having her in his arms, felt even better than he'd imagined.

"What?" He banged the back of his head against the bookshelves, flexing his hands since he wanted nothing more than to grab hold of her again.

"Boots. Off." She trailed her hand down his chest, scraped her nails under to where he could feel her fingers all but scorching him through his shirt.

"No fair," he teased as she bent down to untie her boots. He squeezed his eyes shut for a moment, getting his bearings before moving far enough away so that he could do the same. "Didn't realize what a hindrance these might be when I got dressed this morning." He fumbled with the laces, finally unknotting them. He hopped around on one foot, then the other, making her giggle while she watched him.

"So gallant," she teased as one boot, then his other, got tossed away. Her socks came next. He followed suit, only to find himself frozen at the sight of her shimmying out of her jeans.

The way she slipped her hands under her waistband and moved her hips so she could slide her legs free made him rockhard in an instant. She reached up, pulled the band from her hair, letting it cascade around her shoulders.

Wren stood before him now in nothing but panties and a thigh-skimming yellow T-shirt that clearly showed the outline of her bra. "Thought I'd save something for you to do," she said, a teasing smile playing across her lips. "Your turn."

He grinned, unbuttoned his shirt, but left it on. "Returning the favor." He reached out, clasped her wrist in his hand and tugged her forward. "The rest is for you."

Ty bent his head, caught her mouth again in a kiss that emblazoned itself so intensely, he couldn't imagine thinking of anything else ever again. The way she moved against him, the way she kissed him back, meeting him stroke for stroke. Feeling her still-cold hands flat against his chest, sliding restlessly over his bare skin.

"We should have done this ages ago," she whispered against his mouth as she pushed him toward the bedroom. Wren shoved his shirt off his shoulders and tossed it aside. She couldn't seem to get enough of touching him, something he could appreciate as he drew the hem of her shirt up until he exposed the tight muscles of her stomach that clenched when he touched her.

She moaned, directing his mouth back to hers as she hooked a leg around his. "Fast," she ordered, her hands fisting in his hair, her teeth blazing a trail down the side of his neck. "I want this fast, Ty."

"I can manage that." Reason sliced through his foggy mind. "Wait. I forgot." Trying to slow his breathing, he pressed his forehead against hers and squeezed his eyes shut. "I can't believe I'm going to say this, but I forgot condoms."

"Clearly not prepared. Tsk-tsk." She kissed him deeply, then looked him in the eye before stepping back and out of his reach.

He watched, dazed, as she kind of twirled her way to the nightstand on her side of the bed, pulled open the drawer.

"You know me." She ripped open the box and pulled out a foil package. "Ever hopeful."

If he'd needed any more confirmation that his desire for her was shared, he finally had it. She walked back to him, hands gripping the edge of her T-shirt, which she then pulled over her head. The resulting image of her there, wearing cute white panties and a bra, nearly had him exploding. She wouldn't even have to touch him again. The very sight of her was enough to push him over the edge.

"I thought that was mine to do." His legs felt weak as he stepped up to her, bit back a groan as her hands got busy on the button and zipper of his jeans.

"Changed my mind." She reached into his pants, slipped her hand around him and set off every synapse in his brain. The feel of her firm touch had him sighing with pleasure. When his eyes finally focused, he looked down at her, only to find her watching him just as intently. "Amazing," she whispered and kissed his mouth, releasing him so she could maneuver him to the bed. With one gentle nudge, she had him flat on his back.

She made quick work of his jeans, throwing them to the floor before she slipped her fingers beneath the waistband of her panties and pushed them down her thighs.

He cursed, hands fisting in the bedspread. He wanted nothing more than to touch her, but that look in her eye, that determined, demanding, powerful gleam, was something he never wanted to be rid of. When she reached back to unclasp her bra, every part of him stiffened.

She drew the straps down her arms, excruciatingly slowly, in his opinion. He'd always been impressed with how she could control a room, an interview. A suspect.

Now she was controlling him. Simply by standing there.

Until she wasn't.

She pressed her knee to the edge of the mattress, between his legs, and leaned over him, her hair skimming parts of his body in ways he'd never allowed himself to think of. Wren dipped, pressed her lips against his throat, opened her mouth and licked the side of his neck before returning to his mouth. He heard the crinkling of the foil packet in her hand, saw the slow, seductive smile curve her lips before she kissed him.

"I thought you wanted this fast." He lifted his hands to her hips, kneaded her soft flesh and felt her breath hitch.

She brought the condom packet to her mouth, clasped it with her teeth and tore it open. "Thanks for the reminder." It was clear by the slow shimmy she did down his body that she had every intention of drawing out his torturous pleasure. She pushed one of his hands away, placed his fingers into the bedspread for him to grip and then shifted back enough to roll the condom onto him.

There was no one else capable of giving him the pleasure he felt in that moment. The touch of her fingers as she protected them both had him shifting on the bed to the point of being unable to control his movements.

When she was done and she rose over him once more, she reclaimed his hands, wove their fingers together.

"Watch me," she said in a tone that would forever be locked around his heart.

She took him then, only enough at first to set her throat to humming. She closed her eyes, arched her back and deepened the connection, clenching her fingers around his as she began to move her hips. Her knees pressed into his and tightened with every thrust he gave. He couldn't look away from her. Mesmerized, he flexed his fingers and raised their clasped hands.

The soft, wet heat of her felt like the fulfilled promise of his life, but it wasn't enough.

It wasn't nearly enough.

He released her hands, grabbed her hips and, in one pulse-pounding movement, shifted their positions so she was under him, surrounding him. Fulfilling him.

She gasped, eyes open and shining into his as he drove himself deeper into her. The sensation of her legs locking around his back, holding him in her, was the only encouragement he needed as the rush overcame him. He thrust with every bit of himself, enraptured by the expression of pleasure crossing her face as she writhed beneath him. There wasn't an ounce of her he couldn't feel. Her heartbeat. Her breathing. Her...

Too much, he told himself as he held back that last bit of hope. It was too much to go there, so he kept it to himself as he began to thrust faster.

"Come with me," he whispered and pressed his hot mouth against her neck as she rose to meet him. "We go together."

She groaned, smiled and turned her mouth to his. "Together," she murmured. "Always. Ah!" She crested first, that look of utter bliss on her beautiful face carrying him over the edge as they rode the wave as one.

As if it was always meant to be.

Chapter Nine

"**Y**ou're thinking so loud I can't sleep," Ty murmured against the top of Wren's head.

"Sorry." Instead of moving away, she snuggled closer, reveling in the sensation of being in his embrace. "Got a lot going on in my head, I guess."

"Yeah? Me, too." His hand stroked down her arm, sending now-familiar and all-too-welcome chills racing through her body. "Anything you want to talk about?"

She lifted her head, found him looking at her with obvious affection, and it unsettled her. As dangerous as their…liaison was, she couldn't help but feel as if a part of her, a part she never wanted to acknowledge, was finally set free. "Why do you think it took us this long?"

He sighed, shrugged, shook his head. "Well, if we're looking at the facts."

"Oh, yes, please, Special Agent Tyrone Savakis." She shifted over him, rested her chin on her hands as his own moved down to her hips and curve of her butt. The latter a part of her anatomy he seemed particularly fond of. "Let's look at the facts."

"To start with, when we first became partners, you'd just gotten married."

"Oh, right." She frowned. "Antony." She'd almost forgotten about him. "Boy, there was a mistake. Poor guy didn't know what he was getting into." And neither, if she were being honest with herself, had she. At the time she hadn't quite figured out who she was. The last thing she should have done was get married, but it seemed like the right thing to do and she couldn't think of a good reason to say no. She had to give her parents credit. They'd supported her and kept their opinions to themselves, even after her divorce. "Mom calls that my rebellion phase."

"Does she?"

"Um-hmm." She loved feeling his hands on her. They had an oddly intoxicating effect on her still-humming system. "Each of us McKennas had one, I just waited the longest. Aiden's was the most typical. He went through his at fourteen."

"Really?" Ty raised a brow. "Can't really imagine Aiden McKenna going through a rebellious stage."

"It had to do with the wrong group of friends, a trunk full of illegal fireworks, a patrol car and a very bad sense of timing."

Ty's laugh drew a smile out of her. She couldn't remember ever feeling quite so...content before.

"What did your parents do?" he asked.

She suspected he was thinking about what his father would have done to him had he been in the same circumstances, and the prospect of that stabbed at her full-to-overflowing heart. "Mom and Dad employed the tough love with him. He spent three days in juvenile detention. They are firm believers in one's actions and poor decisions having consequences."

"I can't wait to ask him for the details the next time I see him," Ty said. "What about Howell? When did his rebellion hit?"

"Second grade. No kidding," she added at Ty's doubtful expression. "He took exception to this kid named Reno, who liked to bite girls on the arm."

"Sounds like a budding serial killer," Ty commented.

"Mmm. No doubt. The story goes that's when Howell developed *the look*."

"The look?"

"Howell has this...ability to just stare. He doesn't blink. He doesn't move. He just looks at you in a very particular way that stops you doing whatever it was you were doing."

"So he stared at this kid?"

"For about two weeks. Followed him around at recess, before or after school. Anytime a teacher wasn't around. He would just be there. But he didn't touch him. Didn't talk to him. Just... watched."

Ty laughed, covered his eyes with his hand. "Oh, man."

"Needless to say, the biting disappeared while Reno was fending off Howell, which was Howell's goal. Reno's parents tried to call for a meeting with our parents to get Howell to leave him alone, but by Reno's own admission, Howell hadn't touched him. And, considering the school hadn't done anything to stop him biting other students..." She shrugged. "Didn't really go their way. I was only in first grade at the time, so I don't remember it happening. I just remember the day Howell politely explained to the principal what he'd not done and, more importantly, why he'd not done it. We all went out and had ice-cream sundaes for dinner."

"I love your family." Ty continued laughing. "How different my life would have been with parents like that. What happened to Reno?"

"The family moved away before the next school year. Aiden says Howell stood across the street from their house the day they moved and watched, but I think that's just him adding to the legend that is Howell McKenna." She had no qualms with the pride she felt when it came to every member of her family.

"You McKennas do have a unique sense of honor about you."

"We are the watchers and protectors," she said, as if by rote. "Mom and Dad always told us to keep an eye on the people who could be easily preyed upon. Sometimes just standing in someone's corner is enough to make a difference. For some, knowing they aren't alone is enough."

His hand sank into her hair. "Like you've always done with me."

She shrugged. "With you, it was more out of obligation." She wiggled a bit and set his eyes to darkening. "I'm kidding. You do okay on your own, Savakis. You don't need a guardian angel."

"Maybe not need." He leaned down, kissed her gently on the lips. "But I'll take the one I've got. I'm enjoying this trip down memory lane with your family. Tell me about Regan. What was her rebellion?"

"It wasn't so much a rebellion as a disturbing dedication to winning." Something Regan had not outgrown.

"Winning what?"

"Anything and everything. Races, board games, bets. Being right." Under *stubborn* in the dictionary, there was a picture of Regan McKenna.

"I do seem to recall a rather vicious game of Scrabble at Thanksgiving one year that…"

"Vicious?" Wren paused, then nodded. "Yep. She hates to lose. And she goes after those triple-word scores with purpose."

"Probably comes from being the baby of the family."

"Don't let the baby hear you call her that," Wren warned. "She's thirty-one and carries her own badge and gun."

"Yeah, but she's ATF, so she's not really—"

She kissed him quiet. "Seriously, Ty. I cannot protect you from her if she ever hears that come out of your mouth."

"Noted for future reference."

Wanting a distraction from talking about the future, she shifted to the past. "So is now a good time to ask you what happened with Felicia? You never did tell me."

"Didn't I?" The overly innocent tone told her he was well aware he hadn't spoken of the breakup with his ex-wife. "Long story short? Never should have married her. It wasn't fair." He smoothed his hand over her shoulder. "To either of us."

"Would now be a good time to admit I never liked her?" A little levity in this moment couldn't hurt.

"Would have been better if you'd told me that before we eloped to Vegas." His hand was back to doing those touchy-feely things that would result in their not talking for a good long while. "Biggest mistake I ever made, but at the time it was a solution to a problem I couldn't solve another way."

"What problem?" She never had understood the impulsive wedding, especially since he'd never seemed particularly happy about the event.

He looked at her, an expression on his face she'd never seen before. An expression that caused her toes to tingle even as an odd panic settled in her chest.

"What?" she asked.

"I married Felicia because the woman I was in love with wasn't available."

"Oh. Well, that's just…" She didn't get it at first, but the longer he looked at her, the harder his heart pounded against hers, the truth settled. "Me? The woman you were in love with was…me?" How she had air left to breathe, she couldn't fathom. This man, this glorious, amazing, frustrating man, loved her?

"Pretty much from the second we met." His smile was quick and somewhat bittersweet. "Postcoital confessions are the ones that can get you in the most trouble, so I'd be grateful if we could just let that go and pretend I didn't say it."

"Then you shouldn't have told me." She curled her legs under her, straddled his hips and drew the sheet up and around the back of her shoulder. Bending over, she brushed her lips against his, her hair dropping around them like a curtain of protection. "All this time? You kept this to yourself all these years?" Even now, he had courage she lacked. The feelings, the emotions, were there. But she couldn't, no matter how hard she tried, push the words free to tell him she felt the same.

His hands ran from her hips up her rib cage and back down. "I think you might be the only one surprised." He cupped her face in his palm, gazed up at her with such affection, such… love, she lost her breath. "The question is, where do we go from here?"

"We agreed." She swallowed hard, tried to remember what they'd said. "This would stay here in Splendor."

"Yeah?" He gripped her hips, kneaded her flesh with his hands as desire built up inside her once more. "You really think that's going to work?"

"We have to try." Figuring out how they could make this work outside this place, back in the real world, where their partnership could be at risk, wasn't something she wanted to contemplate at the moment. She didn't want another partner. She liked working the way they did. But…

She leaned over, shook another condom package free from the box. "Right now, I have other things on my mind."

"I can see why you went after Treyhern as hard as you did."

Ty didn't take his eyes off the scrambled eggs he stirred in a pan on the stove—the quick food was the only dish he was capable of making to any degree of success.

It had taken them until almost midnight before they realized hunger was the only thing that was going to blast them out of the bedroom. His offer to cook came from a purely selfish place. If he was busy with this, he couldn't dive deeper into a conversation about them that she clearly wasn't ready to have.

"Considering all the crimes he was suspected of committing, it's almost a miracle he killed that dealer of his in front of a witness."

"He made a mistake." Ty grabbed two plates from where they'd been drying beside the sink. "He completely underestimated Alice's loyalty."

"Mmm." Wren continued to scroll through the extensive Treyhern file, from the case's inception all the way through to his appeal. "He neglected to realize even people who are down on their luck have lines they won't cross."

"Alice was stand-up from the start." He could still remember how impressed he was looking at a then-eighteen-year-old Alice sitting in an interview room at a neighborhood police station, explaining that Ambrose Treyhern hadn't only murdered the nightclub dealer right in front of her, but had offered her a hundred thousand dollars to keep her mouth shut. "Don't think I have that kind of fortitude now at thirty-three."

"There you go, underestimating yourself again." It wasn't chiding, exactly, but it came darn close. "But that does explain why you're so determined to help her even now."

He popped two pieces of bread into the toaster, retrieved the butter from the fridge. His bare feet slapped against the wood floor. He wondered, not for the first time, if she had any idea how beautiful she was. Not just on the outside. She had that classic blonde-bombshell beauty Hollywood had made a fortune off of. But inside there wasn't any maliciousness to her, no hard edges to scrape past. She was the epitome of goodwill and justice wrapped up in an all too sometimes overwhelmingly appealing package.

"If...when Alice recovers," he said as he retrieved flatware from the drawer, "I might have to take a harder run at her when it comes to witness protection."

Wren nodded. "Good that you're seeing that. Treyhern's got a powerhouse attorney on his side this time around. His first one was good, but this guy?" She tapped the screen. "This guy could very well get Treyhern out. Of course, if anything else ever happened to her, he'd be the first suspect."

Guilt pitched inside him. "That wouldn't stop him. People like Treyhern, they're steeped in the belief that the rules and laws are for other people, not them. He'd take her out, along with her family, and then worry about whatever possible consequences there are later. Maybe not even then."

"I really hate guys like that." She finally glanced up, gestured to the stove. "Turn the flame off."

"Oh. Right." He clicked it off, flinched as he stirred the now-slightly-overcooked eggs. "Sorry."

"They'll be edible, don't worry." The smell of burnt toast coasted through the air. "Those might not be."

He dived for the toaster, but tossed the scorched pieces of bread into the sink.

"Seriously, I'll have to give you some cooking lessons." She pulled the jump drive out of the laptop and tucked it into the front pocket of his shirt that she was wearing. "Otherwise at some point you're going to starve."

"Will not," he argued as he reset the toaster settings and tried again. "Not as long as I've got my cell phone."

"Doubt they've got FlashFeast up this way." She closed her computer, rested her chin in her palm. "What about calling Howell and asking him to come up and talk to Alice? Once she's better." She narrowed her eyes just as he turned his back on her. "You've already considered that, haven't you?"

"It crossed my mind." He dished out the eggs, stood watch over the toaster. "I didn't push her toward WITSEC the first time because with every other aspect of her life she was happy.

I didn't want her to lose what she'd worked so hard to attain. But now…"

"Now there's more than just Alice to think about."

"Let's keep Howell in our back pocket." He buttered the golden toast and slid her plate in front of her. "I'd like to give it a better shot. Besides, we've got time before—"

The screech of the building's fire alarm had both of them jumping. Wren's toast clattered onto her plate as Ty raced out of the kitchen. He yanked open the apartment door, stuck his head out.

Strobe lights flashed in the hall, the high-pitched alarm blaring.

"You think there's a real fire?" Wren appeared behind him, stuffing her legs into her jeans.

"I don't smell anything." Doors up and down the hall opened. Some, like Ty, simply looked out, while others, like the Thistle sisters, emerged in their robes and curlers with their purses looped over their arms. "This happen often?" Ty yelled.

"Not in a long while," Florence called back.

"Take the stairs. Head on down," Ty suggested, then popped back into the apartment to grab a shirt, his shoes and their guns. "Here." He handed hers off and they each hid their weapons underneath their clothes.

Voices were muted, the alarm blared on, slicing through Ty's head like a knife. The lights had started flashing in apartments now, no doubt the next level of warning.

"This could be a false alarm," Wren said as they left with their phones and keys. "A coincidence, but still—"

"Not taking a chance. Did you see Bradley and the kids?" He scanned the flood of residents heading toward the staircase at the other end of the hall.

"No." They looked at each other for a brief moment, then ran to the Hawkinses' apartment. Wren banged both fists on the door. "Bradley!"

When the door opened, Bradley stood there, a sobbing and crying three-year-old River in his arms, seven-year-old Esme clinging to him. His hair was mussed, his eyes wide in panic, and there was little to no color in his face. "I can't find Bodhi."

"I'll get him," Ty said. "Wren, take Esme. Go on down."

"Sure, yeah, okay, honey. Come on. You remember me?" Wren crouched and held out her arms to the nightgown-clad little girl. "We met at your classroom."

Esme nodded, her big eyes filling with tears. "You're a friend of Mom's."

"That's right. Come on." She scooped Esme into her arms and pulled Bradley out of the apartment. "Ty'll get Bodhi. Don't worry. You've got your slippers on, right, Esme?" She glanced down at Esme's feet. "Good girl. And you've got your stuffie."

"But—" Bradley looked beyond terrified, and honestly, Ty began to wonder how much more the husband and father could take. "Bodhi has sensory issues. The noise and the flashing lights, he'll be so scared. I checked under his bed, but he wasn't there." The panic only made Ty more calm.

"I'll find him, I promise," Ty said. "I don't make promises I can't keep."

"He really doesn't." Wren sniffed the air. "That's smoke. And not from your toast fail." She pointed to one of the air vents. Smoke spewed out in puffs. "Ty?"

"Right. Go." The hall was almost empty now. "I'll meet you downstairs."

In the far distance Ty could hear the faint sound of sirens. Either that or he was imagining it. He knew about the police situation, but didn't have a clue about the fire department. Or if Splendor even had one.

He raced into the apartment, barely passing a glance at the mess and chaos a family with three kids could create. When he stepped on a LEGO, he thanked himself for putting on his shoes. Backpacks and schoolbooks littered the area around the coffee table in the living room.

The internal emergency lights continued to flash like some weird disco hall gone rogue. Shouting for Bodhi wasn't going to do any good and could, in his experience with people on the spectrum, be even more frightening.

The three-bedroom apartment was a completely different configuration than his and Wren's. He found himself in Alice and Bradley's room first. He dropped to the floor, looked under the bed, checked the closet. Then went to the bedroom across the hall.

Esme's room. Had to be, with an oversize unicorn that matched the one she was currently carrying painted on the wall. Again, he checked under the bed, the closet. Only one more to go.

"Bodhi?" Ty called loud enough to be heard over the alarm. "My name's Ty. I'm a friend of your dad's. He's really worried about you!" He dropped down; nobody under the bed. He checked the closet, bent to dig through the piles of stuffed animals and clothes. Nothing.

Frustrated, he turned, winced at the still-screaming alarm. "Where would he be?" Ty scanned the room. The pair of bunk beds for the boys, two different desks. A beanbag chair in the corner beside a large toy box wedged under the…

Toy box.

Ty shot forward, pulled up the lid.

The five-year old had buried himself among the toys, curled up almost into a ball with his hands over his ears. He wore pajamas with tiny trains on them. "Bodhi." Ty sat back on his heels, letting out the breath he'd been holding. "Hey there, little man. Did you hear me calling you? My name's Ty."

Bodhi nodded, pointed to the ceiling.

"I know. It's super loud, isn't it? But that's to make sure everyone knows we have to…" He heard a door slam, loud voices. Angry voices.

Torn between desperation to get the boy out of the building, and his instincts screaming at him, he made a split-second decision. "Stay here." He closed the lid again and returned to the door.

There was movement in the living room. "I've got this one!" a deep voice bellowed. "You check the other one!"

Ty flattened himself against the wall and carefully, slowly, leaned over to get a look.

A man in black, masked and covered from head to toe, moved through the living room, a SIG Sauer in his hand with a silencer attached. It was clear from the way the man moved without disturbing anything he was looking for people, not objects.

Ty returned to Bodhi and opened the toy box again. "Hey, Bodhi. Let's say you and me play hide-and-seek. We'll team up, yeah?" He held out his arms, wanting nothing more than to pick Bodhi up, but he didn't want to give the child a reason to cry out. "We need to be really, really quiet, though. Otherwise we won't win."

At the idea of winning, Bodhi's eyes cleared a bit. He sat up and held out his arms.

"Good boy." Ty grabbed hold, and hearing footsteps outside of the bedroom, he quickly ducked into the closet, kicking his way through the clutter, and pulled the louvered doors closed.

"It's loud," Bodhi cried in his ear. "I don't like noise."

"I know." He rubbed the boy's back. He could feel the child's heart pounding against his chest. "Just be really quiet for me for a little while, okay?" Ty tried to shrink back, but he was too tall for the closet and knocked his head on the top shelf. "Just hold on to me, okay? As tight as you can."

Bodhi's arms squeezed his neck with far more strength than Ty expected.

The lights still flashed. Ty could see just enough through the slats in the door. His mind raced. Reaching for his gun meant losing his firm grip on Bodhi, and right now, he had the feeling he was the only thing keeping the boy quiet.

Still...

Wincing, he readjusted his hold on Bodhi, shifting him over to one hip to hold him with one arm. "Shhhh," he whispered not only to Bodhi but to himself. He reached back, under the hem of his shirt, pulled his gun free and, releasing the safety, held it down at his side.

The man in black arrived, swept the room like a professional. Ty watched, memorizing every step the man made. The dim glow from the bedside lamp caught him in just the right light.

A shock of bright blond hair stuck out of the edge of the mask just above the man's eyes.

Ty's grip on the gun tightened. His head pounded against the continuing screeching of the alarm. The lights made it seem as if the man were moving in slow motion.

"I want Mama," Bodhi cried and began to sob.

"Shhhh."

The alarm cut off.

The lights stopped strobing.

Bodhi gasped. Ty shifted his feet, prepared to...

"We gotta go!" The second man slammed into the room, his gloved hand gripping the doorjamb. He was in all black as well, but there was nothing Ty could see to distinguish him. The other man, however... "Now. The police are here."

"They'll go after the smoke first and that's floors away," the first man said.

"Did you get it?"

Ty stiffened.

"Yeah. What about you? Anything in the other apartment?" He did a circle of the room, knocked a robot toy off a shelf.

"Laptop. Clothes. No IDs."

"What about the virus?"

"Installed. We'll be able to see everything they do on it when they turn it back on."

"Good. Okay." He moved to the window, looked out.

Bodhi squirmed and began to make noises.

"Shhhh. Hide-and-seek, remember?" Ty whispered almost silently into the boy's ear. "We're going to win."

Bodhi turned his head and rested it on Ty's shoulder, heaved out a sigh.

"Let's go." The first man shoved the second one out of his way and they left. Ty waited until he heard the front door close before he breathed easy.

He reengaged the safety on his gun, shoved it back into his waistband and carefully set Bodhi on his feet. "You did really great, Bodhi. You were very brave."

"I don't like noise," Bodhi repeated with a bit more vehemence this time.

"Right there with you." Ty pushed open the doors, nudged Bodhi ahead of him.

His cell phone vibrated in his back pocket. He barely glanced at the screen when he answered. "Hey, Wren. I've got Bodhi. He's okay."

"Thank goodness. Bradley's been going nuts. Where are

you?" Ty went to the window to look out. Dozens of people stood huddled around the entrance to the building. He saw the sheriff's SUV, along with a single fire engine. "Why didn't you—"

"Bodhi and I had visitors," Ty said. "Tell Sheriff Egbert and the firefighters to look for smoke bombs either on the first, lobby or basement level. That's what caused the smoke in the vents."

"How do you—"

"We're on our way down now." He hung up and found Bodhi picking up the toy the man had knocked over.

"Goes here." He put the robot back on the shelf, frowning and glaring up at Ty. "Did I win?"

"Absolutely." Ty touched a hand to the boy's head. "And you know what the prize is?"

"What?"

"Ice cream."

Chapter Ten

River Hawkins turned a face-splitting grin up at his father and pulled the spoon out of his mouth. "Yum!"

Wren turned sympathetic eyes on Bradley as he reached out to touch his son's head. The expression on the man's drawn face could only be described as shock and dismay. "What do you say to Ms. Wren and Mr. Ty, River?"

"'Sank you!" He waved his spoon in the air before going in for another taste of the double chocolate chip that Sully had chosen for them.

"Come on, River." Carrying her own bowl of strawberry, Esme grabbed her little brother's hand and tugged him away from the table. "We'll go into the living room."

The little adult, Wren thought as the girl sent Wren a watery smile. Scared, but still determined to play protector for her brothers.

"Bodhi?" Esme called from the doorway.

"He's okay where he is." Ty smiled at Wren and set her heart to melting. The adoration Bodhi cast upon Ty was clearly reciprocated. She wondered if he had any idea what a good father he'd make. She coughed, almost choked and turned away before having to admit where her thoughts had taken her.

"Bodhi, why don't you go with Esme?" Bradley told his son. "I bet she can find an episode of *Proton Patrol* for you to watch."

"Okay." Bodhi slipped off Ty's knee, cradling his bowl against his chest. "Bye, Ty."

"Bye, Bodhi."

"Thank you again, for looking out for him," Bradley said to Ty once they were alone. "That's a level of terror I never want to feel again."

"I'm sorry you were put in this position."

"I can't believe I forgot to have them put on their coats." He rested his elbows on the table, lowered his head into his hands. "I just feel completely scattered and useless."

"You're far from useless." Wren touched his arm. "It's been a rough week for you. And them. But you're doing okay."

"I feel like I'm being held together by will alone." He sighed, and when he looked at Ty, there was an odd light in his eye. "You aren't a school friend of Alice's, are you? There's something else going on. That's why you're here, isn't it? That's why you're both here."

Ty glanced at Wren and she knew what he was thinking. That it wasn't his place to share Alice's story or past; that he didn't want to risk Alice losing the life she had because she'd lied to her husband about things she'd gone through. Things she'd done.

"We're here because Alice is in trouble and we want to help," Wren found herself answering. "I need you to believe that, Bradley. Alice loves you so much. We don't want you doubting that for even a moment."

"I don't doubt it." Bradley seemed confused she'd even say it. "I love my wife, and I know she dealt with a lot before we got serious. She told me most of it, about the trial, anyway. About testifying against her former boss because of the embezzlement. It was my idea to move. I wanted her to have a fresh start."

Any hope Wren had had that Bradley was up-to-date on Alice's past shriveled up and died. "She told you the case was about embezzling?"

"Yes. She worked in the office, knew about a second set of accounting books. She said…" Bradley's eyes went from bright to suspicious. "She said she turned the books over to the Feds and that…" He sat up straighter. "Oh, my God. You're Feds, aren't you? That's how you know Alice. But why…?" His frown returned. "But why are you here now?"

"Bradley, I need you to—"

"Wren." Ty's voice was sharp, sharper than she expected or appreciated. "Can I talk to you for a minute? Alone, please."

Bradley sighed, looked between the two of them. "I'll go check on the kids. Could you…please, could you just get your stories straight and be honest with me? Trust me." He got to his feet. "The truth cannot possibly be worse than what I'm coming up with in my head."

Wren sat stone-still in her chair, watching as Bradley left the kitchen.

"He deserves to know the truth, Ty," she rage-whispered. "He's been in the dark long enough!"

"It's not our place—"

"Those men created a fake fire to empty the building in the middle of the night, Ty."

"I am aware."

"Are you? Are you really?" Wren couldn't quite believe he was taking this tactic. "They evacuated hundreds of people in Alaska in winter so they could get into this apartment. So they could get into ours!"

"Again, I'm awa—"

"Stuff your awareness. That man needs to be able to protect his family, and he can't do that as long as he's in the dark."

Ty shook his head. "Alice would have told him if she'd wanted him to know."

Was he really this naive? This reckless? "Alice is currently in a medically-induced coma, maybe because she didn't tell her husband the truth. It's not just this family that's at risk now, Ty. It's the entire building. Maybe the entire town. They're using cars and smoke bombs as weapons against them. Protecting one person's past isn't worth risking everyone else's lives."

"That's not what I'm doing. I made her a promise."

It didn't escape her notice that Ty was staring down at the tabletop. He didn't look at her. Not once.

"You made a promise to keep her safe. Do you really think she wouldn't want you telling Bradley the truth if it meant putting their children at risk? You and I both know what would have happened if one of those men had found Bodhi in that toy chest."

"But they didn't find him. I did."

"Knowledge is power. Put that power in Bradley's hands, Ty. Alice can't speak for herself anymore. Maybe not ever again. He deserves to be able to decide for himself how he wants this to go."

"How I want what to go?" Bradley's voice was stronger now. He didn't appear as frail and dejected as he had just moments before. "It's funny how a few minutes with my kids clears my head."

"This is my fault," Ty said. "This entire thing—Alice's accident, the break-in tonight, the attack at the hospital. All of this happened because of me."

"Oh, for crying out loud." Wren stood up. "Martyrdom doesn't become you, Ty. This isn't your fault. It's not even Alice's fault. All of this is because the world is a messed-up place and bad things happen. You both got caught up in something that turned out not to be over. You made the choices you could make at the time. As great an agent as you are, time travel is not in your arsenal of weapons."

"You don't understand," Ty said. "I convinced her—"

"You gave her options," Wren corrected. "She chose the path to take. You said you'd back her up and you are. Now let's finish it once and for all. Tell him the truth!"

"I know she kept things from me," Bradley said. "I told her she didn't have to tell me anything she didn't want to. I love her. Nothing's going to change that. I promise. And like you," he told Ty, "I don't make promises I don't intend to keep." He shifted his attention to Wren. "You tell me, then."

Wren purposely didn't look at Ty. "It wasn't an embezzlement case Alice testified in. It was a murder case."

"Wren—"

She reached out, rested her hand on Ty's shoulder and squeezed. "She witnessed her boss, a man named Ambrose Treyhern, kill a man who worked for him. Instead of running or hiding, she gave a statement and testified against him. He was convicted and sentenced to life in prison. Only now—"

"Only now Treyhern's been granted a new trial," Ty finished. "And he doesn't plan on letting Alice testify again."

"Murder?" Bradley wandered back to his chair, sat across from Ty, blinking quickly as if trying to process what he'd heard. "All this time she said that trial was no big deal."

"You didn't see anything in the papers about it?" Wren asked.

"I was barely twenty. I was working full-time and going to college," Bradley said. "I was lucky to see Alice." He shook his head. "I don't think we've even spoken about her testifying for years. Until you mentioned it, it never crossed my... When did word of the new trial come out?"

"About three—"

"Three weeks ago." He dropped his head back. "I knew something was wrong. Something was just off with how she was. She was jumpy, nervous. I assumed she was stressed with work and the kids." He took a deep breath, looked back at Ty. "She called you."

"The night of the accident, yes."

A light flickered to life in Bradley's eyes. "You were who she was talking to. The sheriff, when he found her phone... Okay." He nodded, as if putting the pieces together. "She called and you were here the next day."

"I was one of the agents in charge of the Treyhern case," Ty admitted. "I convinced her to testify. I promised to keep her safe."

"After she refused to go into witness protection," Wren added.

Ty glared at her.

"That's a big piece of this, Ty. Stop acting as if it isn't," she ordered. "Chances are, if she'd gone into WITSEC, none of this would be happening."

"I'm not going to blame her for making that decision," Ty argued.

"Fine," she snapped. "Then stop blaming yourself."

"Stop, please." Bradley held up both hands. "You two bickering isn't helping the situation. She wouldn't have chosen witness protection because of me. We were...getting really close around then. I was head over heels in love already and she...

I'm super close with my family. A family that accepted her immediately. My parents, grandparents, siblings. They love her. Adore her. Probably more than they've ever liked me. She'd never had that before."

"She wouldn't have wanted to be cut off from them," Wren concluded.

"She wouldn't have wanted *me* to be cut off," Bradley corrected. "But I would have gone anywhere she was. In whatever circumstances. I just wanted her." Tears filled his eyes. "I just want her back."

"She's hanging on," Wren reminded him. "You have to hold on to that."

"I don't know how much longer I can do it," Bradley admitted. "Wren's right, Ty. I've been married to Alice for ten years. I know better than anyone that when my wife has her mind set on something, there's nothing that's going to change it. Not me. Not even the FBI." He took a deep breath. "I need to know our options. Moving forward, I want everything on the table. What could, what might, what can happen."

Wren shifted in her seat. "Does that include information on witness protection? Ty—" she blew out a frustrated breath "—if there's a way to get Alice out from under testifying, we'll find it, but right now, we have to go with what we know."

Ty cursed, shoved to his feet and walked out of the kitchen. Wren's heart twisted. She didn't want this to turn into a bigger fight than it already was, but she was in a position to help Bradley in a way Ty couldn't.

Bradley nodded. "I'd like to know what would be involved if we joined the program, yes."

Despite Ty's displeasure with the idea, the fact Bradley was open to it brought her some relief. "My brother is a US marshal. He's worked in the witness protection program for years. I can give him a call, ask him to come up and speak to you personally. One-on-one. No strings attached."

"He'd do that?"

"He can't say no to his little sister." She glanced out the window. Last she'd heard, Howell was working a case out of Idaho.

Since she was going the unofficial route, it would take him some time to get here. "If that's what you want."

"I want my family safe," Bradley said. "All of them. I would like to speak with him."

"Okay." She nodded and sighed in relief. "I'll make that happen. So that's step one done. Now. What else do you want to ask me?"

Ty stopped at the apartment only long enough to grab his jacket before he headed out. He needed some fresh air, even if it was blistery cold air and it was still pitch-black outside.

He needed to get his mind clear and his anger under control before he said—or did—something he was going to regret.

As much as he loved her, Wren McKenna was the equivalent of a human steamroller when it came to doing things her way. It was his own fault, he supposed, for asking for her help. He should have realized once the tides shifted in a certain direction she was going to slip in ahead of him and take charge.

He took the stairs. It had been a couple of hours since everyone had been let back into their apartments. Skyway Tower was still relatively quiet, although he could hear the telltale sounds of chanting coming from the apartment of Zoe Marbury, who had apparently cornered the market on yoga and meditation.

All Ty wanted right now was to walk things off and come to terms with the fact that Wren had hit multiple nails on the head with her accusations and observations. He did feel responsible for Alice's situation. He'd spent an inordinate number of sleepless nights worrying that his inability to convince her to go into witness protection would result in something happening to her. Something like what had happened to her.

He needed to take some comfort in Bradley's declaration, that Alice was her own person with her own mind and she'd made a clearheaded decision.

Upon exiting the building, he found the sheriff's SUV parked where it had been for the past few hours. He turned back to the door just as the sheriff emerged from one of the hallways. He nodded at Ty and came out to join him.

"Figured you'd be out prowling around," Sheriff Egbert said. "Been a bit of a rough night for you."

"I've had worse."

"Bet you have."

"Where's Shelly?"

"I sent her home to get some sleep. She looked ready to pitch over into the snow." Sheriff Egbert eyed him. "Come on. Looks like we could both use a walk." He nodded toward the marina. "You have a chance to watch the sunrise since you've been here?"

"Not intentionally."

"A visit to Splendor's not complete without seeing one. Where's your other half?" the sheriff asked as they fell into step.

"Talking with Bradley." Probably being the proxy for her US marshal brother when it came to signing the Hawkins family up for WITSEC. "What's going in your report about the fire alarm?"

The air was so cold it didn't move. Not a ruffle against his skin. Not even coming off the water in the distance. He was getting used to not feeling his face and had the odd notion that once he left he was going to miss this place.

"That's a good question. Near as Shelly and I can piece together, someone hacked into the building's Wi-Fi, rode it into the security system and deactivated it remotely. They got in, set the smoke bombs off in the basement at the air-filtration unit, then another on the first floor under the smoke detectors. The rest took care of itself. Fortunately, the system acted the way it was supposed to and everyone followed procedure. Scared the life out of some people, but it seems to have also brought everyone closer together."

"Those two guys in black came in looking for something."

"So you said." Sheriff Egbert gave a quick nod. "Haven't gotten reports of anyone else's apartments getting hit. Just Bradley's and yours."

Ty wasn't certain he'd have known they'd gone into his and Wren's apartment if he hadn't heard the discussion.

"Any idea what they took from the Hawkinses' place?" Sheriff Egbert asked.

"None." And that bothered him. Whatever it had been must have been small since Ty hadn't seen the man carrying anything. "Bradley couldn't figure what might be missing, but he was pretty shaken up."

"At least we know they didn't come in specifically for him or the kids."

"That would make even less sense than what did happen." It was what he couldn't wrap his mind around. "Alice is in a coma. She can't talk, let alone testify against anyone right now. If they were smart, they'd lie low and wait to see if she dies." To Ty's thinking, that was the best-case scenario for Treyhern and whomever he'd sent after Alice. "Why expose themselves again by taking such a big risk?"

"If they needed something that bad, maybe it wasn't that big a risk," Sheriff Egbert said. "Evacuate the building when they wouldn't be seen or recorded. They couldn't pull that off during the day. Too many people around. Everyone focused on everyone else. And this way they get the bonus of checking your apartment out as well."

"Did anyone report seeing anyone hanging around the building in the last few days?"

"Shelly checked the security footage going back more than a week. And I asked Al about that," Sheriff Egbert said. "He doesn't recall seeing anyone, but then most of the time he's inside the building. Aside from what happened tonight, we've never had any security issues with Skyway Tower. I checked with a lot of people tonight. The only thing people mentioned that was odd was Alice's accident and you and Wren moving in. Now's gonna be a different story. Everyone's on high alert and jumpy, especially where unfamiliar faces are concerned."

"Unless those faces aren't so unfamiliar." Ty racked his brain. "It's hard to be invisible in a small town, but they have to be staying somewhere close." He turned, looking behind them as they walked. The clear night cast the entire town in a glow he'd never seen before. Overhead the ghostly remnants of the northern lights played against the dark backdrop. "Someone mentioned to Wren about the vacation homes up the mountain."

He pointed in that direction. "Any way to get a list of property owners or renters?"

"Property owners of record, no problem," Sheriff Egbert confirmed. "Renters would take some work-arounds. People who stay up here like their privacy."

Which would make it a perfect hiding place for someone who worked for Ambrose Treyhern. "Is the tram the only way up?"

"There's a narrow road that goes up that way." He pointed toward where the edge of town lay. "Most people prefer the tram, as it is not a fun drive. This time of year, the snow closes the road more than it's open. The entire tram system was overhauled last year. It's almost completely automated now and the cable cars are top-of-the-line. Takes about fifteen minutes."

"How high does it go?"

"About eight thousand feet. There's a gift and coffee shop up at the station, along with a bar that stays open until midnight." Sheriff Egbert pointed to where one of the two trams was parked at the station in town. "Makes for a beautiful observation area, especially on a clear day."

"If you could get me that list of owners, I'd appreciate it." They were at a distinct disadvantage in terms of accessing information since someone had gotten their hands on his laptop.

"I'll get to working on it as soon as I get some sleep."

"Is there anyone around here with some serious computer skills?" Ty asked.

"Sure—Mason Green. Shelly can hook you up with him. He's kind of a one-man tech guru. Makes a solid living hooking up entertainment and computer systems for people. I'll have her give you a call once she's back in the office."

The walk had done its job and taken some of the edge off Ty's ragged thoughts. The sound of the gently lapping water offered a surprising sense of peace as they approached the shoreline.

"Every so often this is where I find myself in the early morning," Sheriff Egbert said as they stood on the other side of the marina fence. "With the town behind me, and all that in front, reminds us what we have here. How special it is." He gestured to the water shimmering beneath the slowly disappearing moon. "I can see everything that's coming at us. Like that bank of clouds out there." He pointed off beyond the horizon. "You see that?"

"Not really." Everything looked like one big, massive blur to him.

"Take my word for it. Storm's coming in. Probably hit late afternoon, early evening."

"Okay."

"You get a feel for a place after a while. That said, I don't think I could've anticipated the last few days even with a crystal ball. I've had more crazy hours since you and Wren got here than I've had since my time on the police force in Chicago. Part of me is tempted to ask when you're leaving."

"As soon as we know Alice is out of danger and there's no more threat to anyone here in Splendor." He already felt a pang of regret.

"I appreciate that. Have to admit, last few days has me thinking about retirement."

"That would be a real loss to Splendor," Ty said. "We'll be out of your hair soon enough. Things'll get back to being uneventful once we are gone." But they weren't out of the woods yet. "Has there been any word from the medical examiner on Davey?"

"Time of death's going to be hard to pinpoint. His body's still thawing out." He shook his head. "But it's not out of the realm of possibility he was killed sometime around Alice's accident. Seeing as he couldn't have shot himself in the chest, I'm leaning toward someone using him as a convenient scapegoat."

Ty agreed. "Troubled local with a history of offenses, a drinking problem and access to an easily-disposed-of car."

"Made him a perfect target. By someone who snuck right by me. That's what's got me spinning."

"At least one of the men in Alice and Bradley's apartment was part of the duo Wren and I chased down at the hospital," Ty told him. "Maybe take some comfort in that all those loose threads seem to be connected to one big knot. Near as we can tell, there's only two of them." He could only hope it stayed that way.

Sheriff Egbert smirked, shoved his hands deeper into his

pockets. "Don't anticipate finding much comfort in anything for a while. Davey's death is going to haunt me."

"Davey was his own man, Sheriff." Ty was all too familiar with ghosts, and now seeing the sheriff wrestle with his own showed Ty what Wren must see when she looked at him. "He made his own decisions."

"Hard to make the right ones without a solid support system behind you."

There was no talking the sheriff out of his feelings of guilt and regret. But they certainly shone a certain light on his own internal demons. The ones Wren seemed focused on helping him exorcise. "Tell you what, Sheriff. You stop blaming yourself for what happened to Davey and maybe I can let go of my own guilt where Alice is concerned." Maybe if they tag-teamed each other, they could both get somewhere new. "I should probably give you a heads-up. There's a good chance Wren's brother's going to be coming up here in the next few days. He's a US marshal."

"Another Fed." Sheriff Egbert sighed. "Sounds about right."

"It's not going to be long before the truth about Alice's situation comes out," Ty advised. "Or about how Wren and I are involved. If the two men responsible for the evacuation know who we are—"

"I'm guessing since they tagged your laptop, we can assume that's true."

"Chances are they've been here long enough to realize the chaos blowing our cover could cause. Like you said, a lot of people around here don't have any love for the FBI."

"The FBI, maybe," Sheriff Egbert said. "But you and Wren are a different story. You came up this way to help one of our own. Folks will see that. Eventually. You get whatever was eating at you put back away?"

"I'm almost there." Admitting Wren was right really was half the battle. Telling her she was would be the other half. "Just working through some issues with my partner."

Another smirk from the sheriff.

"What?"

He ducked his head, rocked back on his heels. "I ever tell

you about my first partner back when I was working for the Chicago PD?"

"Ah, you didn't really mention your previous job, Sheriff." Ty had just assumed the older man didn't want to talk about it.

"The most stubborn person you've ever met. Never knew anyone who could argue with me better but never once did I not think they were watching my back. We worked together for four, maybe five, years before we finally got around to admitting the truth. We've been married more than twenty-five years now." He lifted his head into the fading moonlight. "Partnerships like ours, like yours and Wren's, they're something special. Just so you know, one thing doesn't have to end in order to start another. The work-around is worth it. You've got the friendship necessary to make a go of things, Ty. Don't let fear or worry about what could happen get in the way of what's possible."

"Yes, sir. That's right." Curled up in the corner of the sofa facing the front door of their apartment, Wren looked up as Ty returned. Most of the knots in her stomach eased at the sight of him. The anger was gone. Mostly. The irritation as well. She pressed a finger against her lips.

He pushed the door closed.

"I understand this case is personal to Agent Savakis." Supervisory Special Agent Jack Frisco's rough voice crackled over her cell. "But we don't need anyone involved in the original investigation sticking their nose into Treyhern's reopened case. We can't risk tainting it any further."

"Ty's involvement has never been called into question before."

"His involvement, no," Frisco agreed. "But you and I both know he's not at his best when his personal feelings enter the picture. Keep him away from this case, Agent McKenna. That's an order."

"Yes, sir." She hung up and tossed her phone onto the coffee table. "Our boss sends you his best."

"I'll bet he does." Ty shrugged out of his jacket and hung it up. "Thanks for not ratting me out."

She frowned. Did he think she'd actually do that?

"Did you walk off your mad?" She had no trouble comparing him to a child who had thrown a tantrum. She'd done the same herself at times and therefore knew it rarely produced the desired result.

"I walked off my mad." He collapsed onto the sofa beside her and immediately reached out to take hold of her hand. "You were right. I'm too close to this to evaluate certain aspects properly."

It took all her self-control not to bask in the happiness that hearing the words *you were right* gave her.

"Bradley only wants information, Ty." Maintaining her hold, she turned to face him. "He hasn't decided on WITSEC."

"Yeah, well." He dropped his head against the back of the sofa. "Howell will probably talk him into it in about ten seconds flat."

"His record is seventeen minutes."

"So you called him?" Ty asked.

"I left a voice message, followed up with a text." At his raised brows, she shrugged. "When he's working a difficult case, he turns everything to vibrate. He'll call me back when he can."

"Good." He nodded and managed to only wince a little.

Ty was the kind of man who was quick to react, but often countered a flash of temper with putting some distance between himself and the subject at hand. He also often returned having come around to her point of view. It went both ways, but as their stats currently stood, Ty was the one often taking the walk.

She tried to smile, touched her other hand to his face. "You okay?" Feeling his skin beneath her fingers eased the last of her tension. For a moment, a long few moments, she'd worried they wouldn't find their way back to one another. At least not in the sense their reinvented relationship offered.

"Yeah." He squeezed her hand. "Just tired. We've gone through everything as far as Splendor's concerned. Sheriff's going to get us a list of owner names for the houses on the hill."

"The vacation homes. Huh." That was an interesting turn. "You think there's something there?"

"I think those two guys are hiding somewhere nearby, yet we can't find them. They aren't roaming around town, only showing up to make very specific strikes. They could be coming in and out of the tunnel—"

"Not with the current operating schedule," Wren confirmed without hesitation. "The tunnel was closed when they hit here. They had to go somewhere afterward and that fire alarm and evacuation pretty much woke up the whole town. They're here in Splendor. They have to be. They couldn't have done what they have without staying close by, and hitting the tower took planning. Up the mountain makes sense."

"We're going to need evidence before we go knocking on doors." He smothered a yawn. Outside, the safety buoys clanged in the harbor. "Sheriff Egbert didn't come out and say it, but he treads carefully with the people up there. Too many toes to step on."

"Mmm." Wren shifted and looked out the window. The morning was dawning bright, with only a thin layer of cloud cover overhead. In the distance she saw the teeny figures of early-morning fishermen heading out on their catch boats. She shivered in sympathy even as she gnawed on her lower lip. "What about a boat?"

"You want to buy a boat?" He tugged her down against him, curled his arm around her shoulders.

"As a place to hide." She lifted her head as his eyes drifted closed. It was another avenue to explore.

"I can't think anymore right now," he said on another yawn. "Give me a half hour, okay?"

"Okay." She started to scoot away but his arm tightened.

"Stay with me." He turned his face into her hair, took a deep breath. "I like holding you."

She smiled and rested her cheek against his shoulder. "I like you holding me."

"Half hour," he murmured again.

"Half hour." She closed her eyes and followed him into sleep.

Chapter Eleven

"Let me see if I understand." Mason Green sat behind Deputy Shelly Adjuk's desk at the sheriff's office and blinked disbelievingly. "You want me to see if I can isolate, examine and extract a virus on this laptop that was installed specifically to track what you do on this laptop?"

"That's pretty much it," Wren said. "Can you do that?"

"Well, yeah, sure." It didn't sound like bravado. Exactly. "It's just an odd request is all."

"If you're worried about being paid—" Shelly planted her hands on her hips and glared at him. It was, to Wren's mind at least, a blatant throwing down of the gauntlet.

"No, no, it's not that." Mason waved both hands in the air. "I love the idea of a challenge. I'm just—" He leaned forward a bit, lowered his voice. "Is this legal?"

"It's my laptop," Ty said. "It's perfectly legal. What was installed on it, however, is not."

Wren tried to mitigate Ty's obvious frustration. "It's a weird ask, we know. But we don't have the resources we're used to currently available to us, and Shelly here said you're the best computer guy in this part of Alaska."

"She did?" Mason brightened.

"I did?" Shelly balked.

"Yep." Wren nudged Shelly with her elbow. "Why else would we have asked you to come in?"

"Exactly," Shelly said in an attempt to salvage the meeting. "Best in this part of Alaska. For sure. No one better."

"Don't oversell it," Wren muttered under her breath.

"I appreciate that." He touched the laptop, then stopped. "What resources do you usually have at your disposal?"

"Federal ones," Ty said. "We're trying to keep this on the QT. Wren and I are with the FBI. We're here to find out what happened to Alice and keep her family safe. We need your help to do that." He indicated the laptop. "Can we count on you?"

"FBI? Wow, really? You know, rumor was you two were some kind of private investigators." Mason rested his elbow on the desk. "What with all the questions you've been asking around town and—"

"Mason, we're really short on time right now," Wren said, cutting him off. "I promise, once all this is over, we'll be happy to sit down and chat and answer any questions you might have."

"Right. Sure, yeah, okay." He blinked his doe-brown eyes and gave Shelly a very personal grin. "Can I take you out as payment?"

"I'm not currency," Shelly said in a way that earned her another nudge from Wren. "But okay, I guess. When all this is over, but only if you're helpful." By her tone, it was clear Shelly was not convinced.

"Epic." Mason linked his fingers and stretched them out to crack the joints.

"Apparently they'd be able to track when I turned the machine on," Ty said.

"That's pretty sophisticated programming." He pulled his oversize tech bag onto his lap and dug into it. "I'm going to set up a proxy computer, open it in safe mode and then open yours as a kind of… Never mind." He shook his head. "I recognize those blank looks. Give me a few minutes. Can you help me make some room, Shelly?"

Shelly heaved a sigh, shot Wren an I'm-going-to-get-you-for-this look before helping Mason set up. Wren pulled Ty aside.

"Your grumpy side is showing," she accused gently. "You need another walk?"

"No. I'm just frustrated." He scrubbed his hands down his face and through his hair. "Doesn't help that you let me sleep a lot longer than a half hour."

"Only because I fell asleep myself." She had to admit, the fact they hadn't woken up until almost noon did feel like a hitch in their day. "You're worried about Bradley and the kids, aren't you?"

"I shouldn't be, I know," he admitted. "But Bradley wasn't happy when I told him to stay in the apartment."

"His home was invaded," Wren said. "Obviously, he'd want to get out. But you did a great job convincing him the tower was the best and safest place for him and the kids." But she didn't seem to be getting through. "You had the right idea asking Pastor Lori to check in on them. Hopefully she'll be able to help with Bradley's state of mind and she said she'll stay as long as she feels she's not in the way."

"Right. Yeah, you're right." Maybe their boss was right. Maybe Ty shouldn't be involved with this case.

The front door opened and the sheriff walked halfway in. The stony expression on his face had Wren doing a double take. "What's wrong?"

"Someone called me about an abandoned burned-out car out by the sawmill."

"What sawmill?" Wren asked.

"The one that was shut down before I was born," Shelly said. "Who called it in, Sheriff?"

"No clue. Came in as unknown. That's what had me stopping here." He looked at Ty. "You up for a ride-along, Agent Savakis?"

Shelly frowned. "But I—"

"I need you close to Mason while he works on that computer," Sheriff Egbert said, as if he'd rehearsed his response. "Man the phones. Storm's moving through the area soon, so send out our usual alert. The system may very well wreak havoc with cell service and you know how squirrelly some people get when their phones don't work. Ty?"

"Coming." He squeezed Wren's arm. "I'll be in touch. Hopefully."

"Be careful." Odd. Saying that to him now felt...different. As if she wasn't talking to her partner, but to the man she loved.

Her entire body froze at the thought. It felt right, somehow, to consider the idea. Loving Ty just made sense, and while it didn't freak her out on every level, there were enough questions and uncertainties to have her scrambling for a significant distraction.

"Guess I'll be staying here, then," Shelly grumbled.

"He's leaving the entire office and town in your hands," Wren said. "That's a pretty big statement of confidence. Hey..." She turned to the deputy. "I've been here a few days, never heard this sawmill mentioned."

Shelly shrugged. "Like I said, place has been abandoned for years. Only thing it gets used for really is a landing spot for teenagers and their parties. Keggers."

"So many keggers," Mason chimed in. "Just so you know, this computer thing is going to take a while."

"Why?" Wren asked.

"Because at first glance, what I'm seeing on the back end of this latest installation?" He tapped his finger against a line of code displayed on the second laptop screen. "That's military-grade spyware. Some of the best I've seen."

"Where have you seen it, exactly?" Wren peered closer and tried to make sense of the writing.

"Ah." Mason winced. "In my online training courses?" The high-pitched question gave away he was lying. "I have to be really careful getting into its guts to see where it's coming from."

"Then be careful," Wren said. "What else can I do?"

"Stop asking me questions," Mason said firmly, which had Shelly clearly impressed. "Just let me work."

Shelly waved her over toward the sheriff's desk. "Sheriff Egbert left this for you guys. It's a list of property owners Ty asked for." She handed Wren a stack of pages.

"Oh, right. For the vacation homes."

"I downloaded all the property information on record. That

way if anyone noticed we were pulling anything, they couldn't tell which house we were focused on."

"Look at you, thinking like an agent," Wren murmured as she accepted the list. "Looks like there are—" she quickly flipped and counted "—eleven homes, valued anywhere from..." She let out a low whistle. "No wonder the sheriff doesn't want to go stepping on toes up there. Takes some serious funds to buy one of these. I can only imagine how much it cost to build them." When Shelly didn't respond, she looked to the deputy. "Something wrong?"

"Shelly's parents protested the sale of the land to build those homes," Mason called out. "Even got themselves arrested for trespassing about a half dozen times."

"Shouldn't you be working?" Shelly yelled back before she offered Wren a tight smile. "Those homes are a sore subject with native Alaskans. For a lot of reasons."

"Of course," Wren said. "Sorry to bring up a sore subject."

Shelly shrugged. "You asked me why I want to join the FBI? This is one of the reasons. To get away from things like those homes. They just sit up there, looking down on the rest of us like overlords. Makes it really hard to keep an objective attitude when it comes to offering them our services."

"I hear you. Just keep in mind..." Wren continued to scan the information. "You don't get to pick and choose who you protect and defend at the Bureau any more than you do here."

"Shelly, you're not thinking about leaving Splendor, are you?" Mason asked.

"Mason." Shelly's sigh said it all. "Nothing's written in stone, okay? I'm just exploring my options." The desk phones both rang. "Sheriff's office. Deputy Adjuk—" She was cut off, listened, touched her hand to Wren's shoulder. "Okay. Thanks for letting me know. You're good staying with... Uh-huh. Great. Appreciate that. We'll get him back home as soon as we find him."

"Find who?" Wren asked with a ball of dread spinning in her stomach. "Who was that?"

"Pastor Lori." Shelly yanked her jacket off the hook over her desk, nearly smacked Mason in the head with the zipper. "She said Bradley went to Groovy Grub Grocery about two hours ago and hasn't come back yet. He isn't answering his cell."

"I'll come with." Wren grabbed her own coat and shrugged into it.

"Mason? You okay here on your own?" Shelly asked as she zipped up. "Can you answer the phone if it rings?"

"Like an assistant deputy or something?" His cheeky grin didn't come across as particularly reassuring.

"Or something. Please?" Shelly asked. "I really need to be able to trust you."

"You know you can." He seemed to get the message and turned serious. "Got your back, Shelly. Always. Go. Be safe."

Wren found herself grinning as she followed Shelly to the station's second SUV.

"What's the smile for?" Shelly demanded as she yanked open the driver's door.

"Nothing, really. That's just what Ty and I always say to each other."

Shelly rolled her eyes and climbed in.

"This is truly desolate." Ty leaned forward to look out the windshield as Sheriff Egbert took the winding road into the valley. It wasn't a part of Splendor that had been on Ty's radar before. Despite the snow frosting the area with its usual sparkle and ice, the jagged rocks and terrain on either side of the road felt far more eerie than beautiful.

"This land's first use was as a quarry going back about fifty years ago. After that, they turned it into a lumber mill, but transporting the trees got to be too expensive. Not to mention the drive down into this canyon's a pain. Mill shut down shortly before I got here," Sheriff Egbert told him. The strong winds had begun to howl and buffeted the vehicle, but so far the clouds had banked off and the snow had yet to fall. "My kids were teens at the time. You know the story. Tell a kid to stay away from a place, that's the only place they want to go."

"Looks like a definite temptation." The giant structure ahead was a reminder of just how horrible Davey Whittaker's old home had been. "An ideal location for parties."

"And ghost stories," Sheriff Egbert said. "'Bout five years ago a group of high school seniors from Anchorage got inspired by some TV show, thought it would be fun to make their own videos exploring the spot. Had themselves a pretty big following for a while. Until one of them took a wrong turn, stepped on a bad board and dropped about forty feet. Kid was in traction for three months. Broke both his legs."

"Kids will be kids." Ty was more than familiar with the level of foolishness of some teenagers.

"Don't I know it."

The sheriff eased up on the gas as they reached the base of the valley. The mill loomed large in front of them and blocked out anything behind it. "Place like this, you'd have to know it was here to ditch a vehicle."

"You'd have to know about this place to call it in." Sheriff Egbert slowed down even more. "Appreciate the backup. Call just got my nerves up, you know? No telling what might be waiting for us. Keep an eye out for the car, yeah?"

"Yeah. Those nerves of yours. They why you didn't want Shelly along?"

"Let's just say I'm glad I had someone else to choose from. There." He pointed off to the right as they slowly circled the four-story structure. "They weren't lying, whoever it was that called." He stopped the car a good ten feet away from their target vehicle. "Shelly's got potential but a lot of the job left to learn. Given what these guys did to Alice, tried to do to her in the hospital, I'd like my deputy kept as far away from them as possible."

Ty got out his sidearm while the sheriff checked his own pistol and chambered a bullet. "Does Shelly know you're expecting her to take over when you retire?"

"Not yet."

"Word of advice?" Ty grabbed the door handle. "She's looking beyond Splendor for her future. Asked Wren about applying to the FBI Academy. Says she wants to make more of a difference."

"Shouldn't surprise me, I suppose." There was no mistaking the disappointment on his face. "She'd make a good agent."

"She'd make a great agent," Ty agreed. "But that might not be where she belongs."

"That's up to Shelly to decide. I won't stand in her way if that's what she really wants to do. What about you?"

"What about me?" Ty asked.

"You looking to make a change? If I can't pass this job on to Shelly, you'd be a good fit. I've been watching you. You don't seem particularly...settled with your life choices."

He didn't like the idea of someone reading him so easily. Especially someone he'd only just met. "I'm working through some things. There's an appeal to what you suggest...but..." He liked the town, the people he'd met. The laid-back life he'd found here. He couldn't imagine Wren here. Not permanently. She was made for the FBI. She was a stellar agent with a tremendous future. A future he wanted very much to be a part of. "I belong with Wren." As what, exactly, had yet to be decided. Partners? A couple? A family? He wanted it all, but he'd take what he could get. Life without her simply wasn't an option. No matter how picturesque and beautiful a place was.

"Spoken like a man in love." Sheriff Egbert left his keys in the ignition as he climbed out.

"Hopefully, maybe." Ty laughed as he opened the door. "I'm still working on it."

They walked side by side toward the burned-out vehicle. The acrid smell had dissipated but hadn't been left out here as long as the previous car they'd found at the Whittaker place. Thunder rolled around them as gray clouds overhead seemed to pick up speed.

"I didn't get a plate at the hospital." Ty circled around the car, looking for something, anything, that confirmed it was the one that had picked up the shooter from the hospital parking lot. "Suppose it could be it."

Sheriff Egbert remained where he was, weapon at his side. He shook his head, tipped his hat back. "I don't get it. Why out here? They could have taken it through the tunnel, ditched it on the other side."

"Yeah, but they'd have to come back, wouldn't they?" No, this fed into his and Wren's theory that the two responsible for trying to kill Alice were still here in Splendor. And apparently they were using every bit of local lore and information they could get their hands on. He completed his search and stopped a short distance from the sheriff. "My question is, who called you about it? And why? Do you get a lot of calls about abandoned vehicles?"

"I do not." Sheriff Egbert turned slightly. "As far as anyone knows, it's just a car."

A flash of red caught Ty's gaze. Small, almost imperceptible. Familiar.

It strobed once against the sheriff's chest.

"Down!" Ty yelled and dived for the older man. He tackled him around the waist as the sound of the shot echoed through the canyon. Sheriff Egbert grunted as Ty rolled, weapon raised. "You hit?"

"I am." Sheriff Egbert groaned and started to sit up.

Another shot went over their heads, plowed into the hull of the car. "Where?" Ty didn't dare take his eye off the horizon, trying to guesstimate where the shots were coming from.

"Shoulder. High. It's okay. I think."

"Can you move?"

"To save my life?" The sheriff laughed. "You bet."

Another shot. This one struck in front of Ty's knee that was planted on the snowy ground. One more shot, but this one sounded farther away. "I'll go for your car," Ty said. "You get behind what's left of that one, yeah? I'll come get you."

"Sounds good."

Ty could hear the pain in the man's voice, but he blocked it out. "Okay, in three, two..." He lifted his knee but stayed low. "One!"

He didn't allow himself the indulgence of checking to see if the sheriff had moved. He kept his eyes locked on the SUV, moving in various directions as he raced for the vehicle. More shots rang out, but they alternated, some at him, others at the sheriff. He lunged for cover just as a bullet ricocheted off the hood of the SUV. "Too close."

He yanked open the door, climbed in through the passenger side and shoved himself over into the driver's seat, trying to stay low even as a bullet cracked the windshield. Ty turned the key, barely had the car in Drive before he slammed his foot on the gas.

The car whipped forward. He swerved, trying to keep the truck moving unpredictably so the shooter couldn't get a good lock. The tires spun in the icy mud and sludge. When he screeched to a stop beside the sheriff, the car skidded a bit on its own, as if trying to find a place it wanted to stop.

Ty shuffled over to the passenger seat, then dropped to the ground. He knelt beside the sheriff, who had his right hand pressed against the wound low on his left shoulder. Ty swore. There was blood. A lot of blood. "You lied," Ty accused as he tucked himself behind the sheriff and dragged him toward the truck.

"I fibbed," Sheriff Egbert ground out. There was a weakness in his voice that didn't sound right.

He paid no heed to anything other than hefting the sheriff into the truck via the open passenger-side door. The sheriff gasped and coughed, a wheezing sound emanating from his mouth.

The shot that exploded as soon as Ty jumped in from his side and slammed the door took out the front left tire. He swore again even as the SUV began to tilt slightly down.

"Tire's gone," he muttered as he threw the vehicle back into Drive.

"We'll never make it back into town on three wheels," Sheriff Egbert managed.

Ty glanced at him, looked in the rearview mirror as the telltale sign of someone with a gun stepped out from the cover of the mill. The sheriff's face was losing color. That all-too-familiar pallor of gray was taking over.

"You'll never make it," the sheriff said again.

Ty slammed his foot on the gas. "Watch me."

Chapter Twelve

"Bradley never made it here." Shelly walked out of Groovy Grub Grocery with more attitude than Wren had seen in her previously.

Wren, having checked with the stores on either side, hadn't gotten any sightings of Bradley Hawkins. "He left the tower what, more than two hours ago?" She planted her hands on her hips, turning back and forth as if she could spot him on the street. "That's not good."

"What'd they do? Just snatch him off the street?" Shelly accused. "That doesn't happen in—"

"Neither do hit-and-runs and vehicle burnouts." Wren grabbed her phone, hit Ty's number as the clouds rumbled by. The call went straight to voicemail. "Maybe the cell signal's down already."

Shelly's cell phone beeped.

"Or not," Wren murmured. The look on Shelly's face started an entirely new thread of panic. "What?"

"It's a text from my friend Nancy at the hospital. It's Alice."

Wren swallowed hard. "Is she—"

"She's awake."

Hope sprang anew. "Maybe that's where Bradley is."

They jumped into the car and raced to the hospital. Shelly screeched into the law enforcement–dedicated space minutes later. Running inside, they didn't stop until they got to Alice's room. Obie, the security guard, jumped up out of his seat, his young face alert and anxious.

"Everything okay?" he asked.

"Just here to see Alice." Shelly patted his arm as they stepped inside.

The doctor smiled at them from across Alice's bed. The badge on her white coat identified her as Dr. Maya Rodriguez. "Ah, here you go. Your first visitors. Deputy Adjuk. And friend."

"Alice, hey." Shelly seemed to struggle for control, but she maintained a calm voice as she moved into the room. Alice was still as pale as the bandages on her head, but those eyes of hers were struggling to stay open even as she managed a weak smile. "How are you feeling?"

Alice tried to wet her dry lips. "L-like I got run over by a truck." The monitors beeped irregularly, as if trying to catch up with her recovery.

"Unfortunately, you're close. It was an SUV." Shelly's attempt at humor fell flat. "Seriously, though, do you remember—"

"I'm sorry." Wren didn't want to interrupt but time was of the essence. "Alice, hi. I'm FBI special agent Wren McKenna. I'm Ty Savakis's partner."

"FBI?" Dr. Rodriguez went wide-eyed as she stared at Wren. Wren waved off her surprise.

"Ty?" Alice's voice crackled as she drew in a very ragged breath. "Is he here? Did he come? Funny, I thought I heard him. Weird dreams." She began to hum a little. "Really weird dreams."

"He came as soon as he heard what happened," Wren assured her. "Ty'll be here soon. He'll be so happy to see you're awake."

Alice's smile dimmed and her eyes drooped. "Haven't seen him in an age. Is he still dreamy?" The arm unencumbered by IVs and tubes drifted into the air.

"As a matter of fact—" Wren grabbed her hand and held on "—he's even dreamier."

Alice laughed a little. "Awesome. Pretty man. Pretty, pretty man."

"Alice, have you seen Bradley?"

"Not yet. Said." She started to drift off. "Nurse said she'd call him. Need to see him. Need. To see. My…"

The monitors evened out again, the rhythmic beeping settling into place.

"She's just asleep again," Dr. Rodriguez said quickly. "You're really with the FBI?" she asked Wren.

"Yes. And I'm hoping you can tell us where Bradley might be?"

"I haven't seen him since last evening," Dr. Rodriguez said. "Check with the nurses. Maybe one of them—"

A gentle cough from the doorway had them all turning. "Excuse me. Hey, Shelly. You made good time." Wren recognized the young nurse from her previous visit to the hospital. She'd been the one flirting with Ty.

"Hi, Aiyana." Shelly's greeting sounded tense.

"This was just delivered for Alice." Aiyana held up a small cardboard box about the size of a paperback.

"Were you able to reach her husband?" Dr. Rodriguez asked.

"I'm afraid not. I left two voicemails, though."

"May I?" Shelly held her hand out for the box, cast an uneasy look at Wren.

"Go ahead," Wren said, urging her to open it. No postmark. Nothing to indicate it had been mailed. "Did you see who delivered it?" she asked Aiyana.

"No. It was left at the nurses' station while I was on break and everyone else was with patients."

Wren pulled Shelly off to the side while Dr. Rodriguez gave updated orders to Aiyana. Shelly pulled out a pocketknife, flicked it open and sliced the tape. Inside the box sat a framed photograph of Alice and her family. Bradley's face was marked with a red X.

Wren's stomach clenched. "That must have been what they went into the apartment for." She was careful when she lifted the frame up, mindful of leaving her own prints, and grasped the folded piece of paper beneath it. Every nightmare scenario that could play out in this situation came to mind. Wren tried to shake off the feeling. She needed to stay calm.

"What does it say?" Shelly asked when Wren finished reading.

"It says they have Bradley and that the only way to get him back is for Alice to refuse to testify in the retrial of Ambrose Treyhern. If she doesn't, they'll kill him and come back for the kids. One at a time." Wren gnashed her back teeth to the point of pain. She pulled her cell out, dialed Ty again.

"Yeah!"

"Ty?" She recognized that tone. "What's wrong? Where are you?"

"Heading to the hospital. I'll be there in maybe two, three minutes." The sound of tires screeching came through the line.

"I'm here now. Are you hurt?" She stepped out of the room.

"No. Sheriff's been shot. Lower shoulder. He's losing a lot of blood. Why are you—"

"Alice is awake." She cupped the phone with her hand. "Dr. Rodriguez, is there an emergency entrance, room, trauma unit?"

"There's the ambulance bay at the back end of the hospital. Just to the left once you're in the lot. Why?"

"Ty, you hear that?"

"Yes. Be there soon."

"Sheriff Egbert's been shot," Wren told Dr. Rodriguez and the nurse. "It sounds bad. He's going to need blood. A lot of it. ETA maybe three minutes."

Dr. Rodriguez snapped into action, as did Aiyana. They raced out of the room, running down the hall past the outpatient clinic.

"The sheriff's been shot?" Shelly seemed stunned. "But… by who?"

"Not important right now." Wren pulled out the backup piece she'd borrowed from Aiden's stash of weapons. She cocked the hammer, handed the gun off to Obie. "You know how to use one of these?"

"Yes, ma'am," Obie said, straightening and standing taller.

"Good. You sit. In there." She pointed into Alice's room. "Doctors and nurses only. You don't recognize them, they don't get in, unless they give you the password."

"What password?"

"Winchesters."

"As in the gun? Or the TV show?"

Wren simply smiled. The family code word—based off their

shared obsession over the latter—came in handy more often than not. "Anyone who uses that word you can trust them the same as you'd trust me or Shelly or the sheriff, yeah?"

He nodded.

"Alice. She's your priority, understand?"

"Yes."

Down the hall she saw Aiyana and Dr. Rodriguez running with a trauma stretcher between them. Two male orderlies raced after them. Wren followed with Shelly right on her heels.

The blast of cold air when they stepped through the automatic doors chilled her to the bone. She heard the SUV before she saw it, the grinding noise the same sound she had heard when she was speaking to Ty on the phone.

Sparks flew when the SUV barreled up to the hospital and Ty flew out. He raced around the front of the car and ripped the door open. Dr. Rodriguez shouted instructions to her people and within seconds they had Sheriff Egbert out of the car and on the gurney. As the medical team pushed him inside, Dr. Rodriguez flashed a handheld light into the sheriff's eyes. "Olsen? It's Maya. Can you hear me?"

The sheriff's head flopped back and forth. "Going to take that as a yes. I want him checked and headed into surgery in ten minutes max. Go!" She blocked Wren, Shelly and Ty from coming any farther. "I've got him."

"But—" Shelly tried to dart around her, but Wren caught her arm.

"Let her do her job, Shelly." Wren nodded. "We're good."

The doctor vanished behind a pair of swinging doors.

Shelly shrugged out of her grasp. "I have to call his wife." Shelly's dull voice belied her shock. "I don't understand... How did this happen?" She swung on Ty. "What happened?" Anger filled her eyes.

"It was a setup. They lured him there," Ty said. "We didn't realize it until they took the first shot."

Wren touched his arm. "This isn't your fault."

Ty's glare was filled with disagreement, but he didn't respond.

"This isn't his fault," Wren repeated to Shelly, who looked unconvinced. "This happens, Shelly. It's part of the job."

"And I'm just supposed to get used to it? To be ready for it?" Shelly's voice went up an octave.

"Yes," Wren said firmly and released Ty's arm to grasp his hand. "It's part of the job."

"Well, this job sucks!" She spun on her heel, pulling out her cell phone as she stalked away.

"He knew," Ty whispered when they were alone. He stared unblinking at the double doors. "That's why he didn't want Shelly with him. He was afraid it was a setup."

"So did you." She'd seen it in his eyes before he'd walked out of the station. "You suspected that's what it was, so you went with him." Her heart stuttered. "It could have been you."

"It should have been me."

"No." She turned into him, rose up, wrapped her arms around his neck and drew him to her. "No, it shouldn't have been." Wren squeezed her eyes shut and held on when he tried to pull free. "Don't you dare let go of me. Don't you dare." She needed to feel him, every part of him she could, to remind herself he was still alive.

"Wren." Her name sounded like a prayer, a plea on his lips. Finally his hands moved around her, his arms tightened. And he held on.

"I love you." The admission nearly broke her in two. "Maybe it just happened or maybe I always have, but I love you, Ty. And I will not allow you to die on me before we get a chance at whatever this is going to be."

"Okay."

The simple response had her half laughing, half sobbing. She leaned back, looked into his eyes. Her feet were off the ground. He held her, supported her, comforted her all with a look.

"That's it?"

He kissed her. Like a man who had come too close to dying, he kissed both of them back to life. "That's it."

Shelly returned, her cell in her hand. "Mason called," she snapped. "He's got something."

"What about Sheriff Egbert's wife?" Ty asked.

"She's coming." Shelly visibly swallowed. "We should get back to the station."

Wren shook her head. "You should stay—"

"I'm done being left behind." Shelly cut her off with a furious look that had Wren shutting her mouth. "Let's go."

The short drive felt like they made it in light-speed mode. Wren and Ty didn't say another word, just glanced knowingly at one another as if to say, *Tread carefully with her.*

Shelly swore as she jerked the car to a stop. "Who the heck is this guy?" Yanking the keys out, she unlocked their doors. "I don't have time for this. No new people. Not today."

"Make time. He's here to help." Wren squeezed Ty's hand before she got out of the car and beelined for the man standing in front of the sheriff's station, some of her built-up tension melting away.

Howell McKenna had their father's height, their mother's fair Irish skin tone and the McKenna spark lighting his eyes. His passive expression didn't shift but his eyes did as Wren approached. Seeing him was like coming home. "Hey, Howell." She couldn't quite turn on her high-beam smile. "Thanks for coming."

"You called, I came. It's what we do." Howell pulled her into a quick hug.

"You got here fast." And she was so, so grateful.

"Called in a favor. Caught a military flight out of Boise. You doing okay?"

She nodded, her voice trapped somewhere between shock and dread. "Yep, doing okay." She thought she was handling the situation pretty well, but she absorbed the quick offer of comfort to reinforce her mental strength. A McKenna reboot she hadn't realized she needed. She stepped back as Shelly and Ty approached. "Shelly, this is my brother, US marshal Howell McKenna. I asked him to come up and talk with Bradley and Alice."

"Oh." Given the rapid rise of color in Shelly's face, she was rethinking her earlier comment. "Nice to meet you, Marshal McKenna." She held out her hand. "Deputy Shelly Adjuk."

"Deputy. And it's Howell, please."

"Howell." Ty reached out to her brother. "Good to see you again. Thanks for the assist."

"Ty." Howell offered a surprisingly easy smile. "Wren filled me in on the Treyhern case when she called. Want to bring me up-to-date?" He tucked his hands into the pockets of his too-thin jacket. "Preferably inside?"

"You'll get used to the cold," Wren assured him.

"Not entirely sure I want to." He held the door open for the rest of them before following. "Please tell me there's coffee."

"Pod machine's over there." Shelly pointed to the side table near the sheriff's desk.

Mason spun in his chair, his expression worried as he looked up at Shelly. "How's Sheriff Egbert?"

"Waiting to hear." Shelly's voice was uncharacteristically sharp. "Tell us what you found out."

Wren cleared her throat. "I should probably tell Howell—"

"I can play catch-up later." Her brother rested a gentle hand on her shoulder. "Go ahead," he urged Mason.

"Uh, sure." Mason frowned. "Who are you?"

"Reinforcements," Ty said simply and earned an appreciative smile from Wren.

"Okay. Well, buckle up." Mason turned back to his now three computer screens that were open and siphoning multiple lines of code. "I had to reach out to a hacker friend of mine. He's, ah, intermittently employed by some private companies."

"Everything's a free pass today, Mason," Ty assured him. "Speak freely. It'll save time."

"Right." Mason immediately brightened. "So it was this line here that stood out to me. I've seen it before. Hackers have their own way of identifying themselves in the code they write. They're like Easter eggs in an ego-boosting kind of way. According to my source, they were all written by a hacker named Inferno." He glanced up, clearly expecting a reaction.

"Never heard of him," Ty said.

"Me, either," Wren agreed.

"Make that three," Howell chimed in from where he waited for his coffee.

Mason frowned. "Okay, whatever. Three years ago, Inferno bragged about how he'd been contracted to work exclusively for a private security firm. TitanForge Technologies."

"Now, them I've heard of," Howell murmured as he moved in behind them. "They've got their hands in a bunch of pots. Global operation."

"How does this connect to the Treyhern case?" Ty asked.

"TitanForge is one of a number of subsidiary companies under the Titan Holdings name. They've got a law firm, health research-pharma company and a financial business. The financial firm is called Apex and—" He clicked on one of the screens. Images of a mini mansion popped up. "—they are the free-and-clear owners of this home up on the mountain." He grinned from ear to ear, spinning lazily in his chair again. "Am I good or what?"

"You're definitely something. Any chance you could access TitanForge Tech's current roster of employees?" He glanced at Wren. "Wondering if our blond friend is listed."

"Be pretty stupid if—" Wren stopped, watched as a host of pictures exploded onto the smallest of the screens. "That's a lot of employees."

"Stop!" Ty stepped closer. "Go back. Slowly. Back. Back. And there." He stabbed a finger at the screen. "That's him. It's an old picture, but that hair." The shocking blond hair was slicked back and tamed but impossible to deny. "Barrett Lynch. Personal security specialist."

"That's your guy?" Howell asked.

"That's him, all right," Wren agreed, but didn't feel quite the joy Ty clearly did.

"What's wrong?" Ty asked her. "What's the face for?"

She shook her head. "Something's niggling at me. Titan. I've seen that somewhere." She pulled out the jump drive from her pocket. "Which laptop can I use, Mason?"

"Give it here." Mason cleared one screen and popped the drive in. The FBI's list of official files regarding the Treyhern case displayed. "What am I looking for?"

"Not sure." She scanned the file names. "I read through all of them the other night. Here." She pointed to the file titled Research and Associates. "Now scroll down...down." Her eyes moved back and forth, skimming as fast as she could. "There.

Roy Calvin. He's a former associate of Treyhern's." She glanced at Ty. "You know him?"

"Not personally," Ty said. "He was a person of interest early on in the investigation. He and Treyhern grew up together. They remained friends for years. Gino cleared him."

"Gino?" Howell asked.

"Ty's first partner," Wren said. "Gino Bianchi."

"He was killed two years ago in an undercover sting gone wrong," Ty said.

"Good agent?" Howell asked in a way that had Wren wincing. She knew the subtext of that question. He wanted to know if Gino Bianchi was on the take.

"Taught me everything I know." Ty glanced at Wren. "Most of what I know."

Wren smirked. "I seem to recall skimming through a list of assets for Roy Calvin. Mason, is there a search feature—"

"On it." Mason clicked more keys. "This what you're looking for?"

"Oh, yeah." She moved in, leaned over Mason's shoulder and drew her finger down the lengthy list of assets. "He likes spending money. He likes his toys. And he likes to brag. At the time this report was created, he already had multiple properties all over the world. But…" She shot upright. "That boat. Yacht. Whatever you want to call it. The *Titanic Ego*. I've seen that boat." She spun around to Ty. "It's in the marina. Or at least it was the day I flew into Splendor."

"It's a place to start," Shelly said. "We should go."

"We need more evidence," Wren said. "We need proof of a current connection between Treyhern and Roy Calvin beyond the face of a security professional."

"I don't have—" Shelly snapped. "My boss is in the OR, I've got one murder, one attempted murder, an abduction and a town that's going to start panicking unless we get this under control. We should go to the boat. That may very well be where they're holding Bradley."

"Excuse me?" Howell's baritone pierced the room. "Holding Bradley? Explain."

"Sorry. Part of that catch-up." Wren cringed. "Bradley's gone missing sometime in the last few hours. Shortest version is Alice is awake, Bradley's missing. Their kids are safe in the tower with the entire building watching over them. And whoever took Bradley sent Alice a note telling her they'll kill Bradley unless she refuses to testify at Treyhern's new trial."

"When did that happen?" Ty demanded.

"You were busy trying to save the sheriff's life," Wren said. "Someone lured Sheriff Egbert into an ambush. He's alive." She nodded at Shelly. "Last we heard."

"Treyhern's reach has gotten longer," Ty said. "That's a lot for him to organize from behind bars."

"Impossible is more like it," Howell said. "I made some calls before my flight. With the exception of talking to his attorneys, Ambrose Treyhern has served almost every day of his term in solitary. Voluntarily, apparently. He does not play well with others. Especially in close quarters. He'd be closely monitored there. No cell phones. No outside communications. The only visitors he's had have been his lawyers."

"That must be how he's pulling strings." Wren noticed Shelly was getting antsy, pacing in frustration. "Ty, do you know what law firm is representing him?"

"Uh." He squeezed his eyes shut for a moment. "Brooks, Patel and Pendleton. They're based in New York, I think."

"They are." Mason clicked once on the second screen. "Brooks, Patel and Pendleton is the law firm owned by Titan Holdings. And FYI, the Brooks part is actually Roy Calvin's daughter."

"There it is," Howell said with a nod to Shelly. "That's the connection you needed to lock in on." He turned back to Wren. "Where do you need me?"

On her six. Ty had been joking earlier, but Howell being here, backing them up, was tantamount to reinforcements having arrived. That said… "The hospital. We need someone watching Alice. Someone who can protect her if the need arises." She quickly explained Obie—the security guard's presence. "Someone who will know what to do."

Howell nodded. "Understood." He looked to Shelly. "I'll keep you apprised of your sheriff's condition."

"Thanks." She deflated a little. "I'd appreciate that. Can we go now, please?" She was already walking toward the door.

"She going to be okay?" Howell asked Wren as Ty followed Shelly out.

"Yes." Even though she had her doubts. "We'll make sure of it. If we get into a mess, you'll be my first call."

He squeezed her arm. "Stay safe, sis."

She flashed a quick smile. "You, too. Oh! The secret password is Winchesters."

Howell rolled his eyes. "Of course it is. Go. Do good work."

"I'm a McKenna," she said, heading out. "We always do."

Chapter Thirteen

The wind whipped so hard that flags atop boat masts snapped soundly in the air. Shelly had gone to speak to the harbormaster, who also happened to be a distant relative, while Ty could see the *Titanic Ego* from where he and Wren were standing outside the marina. There were at least two dozen vessels tethered close to the yacht. Anyone on board those vessels could get caught in potential cross fire. It was important to know how many were occupied before they swooped down on the yacht. In the meantime, he and Wren waited across the street, not wanting to be seen until they made their actual approach to the *Ego*.

Anticipation and adrenaline built inside of Ty at an equal pace. He could almost hear the clang of Treyhern's cell door closing once and for all, but everything had to go perfectly in order to make that happen.

And perfectly hadn't exactly been in his repertoire as of late.

"Take it one step at a time," Wren said, as if, once again, she was able to read his mind. "Don't leap ahead, Ty. We get Bradley home. That's what we focus on right now."

Wren, always the voice of reason. "You give any thought to what comes after?" he asked.

"A long, hot shower." She shivered. "Feel like I haven't been warm since I got here."

"How about after that?" It was a distraction. One he needed

before he worried himself through the cement under his feet. He'd obsessed over this case for so long; longer than he felt comfortable admitting. Treyhern had gnawed on him from the moment Ty arrested him ten years ago. That smug smirk on the man's face was haunting. It left him questioning himself in ways no agent ever should. Treyhern had known then this day was coming. Ty should have paid closer attention to his gut. "After we close the case against Treyhern."

"Well, I imagine we're going to be dealing with some disciplinary issues." She winced and turned into the wind. The clouds continued to move past at a clipped pace. Gray, full and threatening. Errant flakes of snow drifted down, a promise of what was to come. "Agent Frisco isn't going to approve of us being off book and ignoring orders. He might split us up."

"Did you mean what you said back at the hospital?"

"I don't say things I don't mean."

He could almost hear her heart pounding over the wind. "Wren—"

She faced him. "I'm not going anywhere, Ty. You're stuck with me. If you want a short, concise answer about our future at this moment, how about my place is bigger than yours and it's closer to work? I'm thinking you sublease your apartment for six months, or however long it takes us to accept that we're going to be in each other's lives until the end of days." She gave him a quick smile. "Does that answer your question?"

It was, he realized, the first time in his life he was looking forward to the future. "Given this some thought, have you?"

"A little." She put her back to him again. "One other thing you're going to need to accept. You're obligated to attend the same monthly McKenna dinners I am. We do this, you're one of us. No way out."

"Sounds like I'm joining the mafia."

"Hmm, in a way…" She trailed off as Shelly jogged over, gloved hands shoved deep in her jacket pockets. "What's the word?" she asked the deputy.

Shelly's breath came out in big puffs. "As far as Roscoe knows, all of the boats are currently vacant. Not many went out to fish this morning because of that." She pointed behind her to the storm approaching. "Doesn't mean someone isn't out there, but officially, they're all empty."

"Even the *Ego*?" Ty asked.

She shrugged. "Let's hope not."

"You need to make sure your mind's in the right place before we go in," Wren advised. "Bradley's our focus. We get him out and safely back to his family. Nothing else can factor into your thinking, Shelly. Not even revenge."

"I know."

"Do you?" Wren narrowed her eyes, waited for Shelly to meet her gaze. "We've got your back. Sheriff Egbert wouldn't want you doing anything to risk Bradley's safety. What you do is important, Shelly. Do it as well as you've done up until now and everything'll be fine. We've got you," she repeated.

A bit of the deputy's anger seemed to fade and Shelly nodded.

Understanding what Wren was trying to encourage, Ty said, "You know boats better than we do. How should we go about this?"

Shelly shifted to stare at the black-and-gold-painted yacht. "I'd send Wren to starboard and you and I take port. There's entryways on both sides of the main cabin."

"You know the layout of the ship?"

"Roscoe's nosy, especially when it comes to boats. He has a tendency to give himself tours when he knows no one is on board."

Ty nodded, impressed. She'd built up sources without even realizing it.

"We get Bradley home," Shelly repeated, as if she'd discovered a new mantra. "Our only goal."

"Our only goal, *for now*." Ty nodded in a way that told her they should get started.

They made their way to the marina entrance, stepped through the swinging gate and drew weapons as they neared the yacht. Their footfalls echoed dully against the wood planks, barely loud enough to be heard over the wind. The boat bobbed in the water, which swelled up and over the edges of the dock.

Shelly turned slightly, pointed to Wren, then to the right side of the yacht, where a short platform was attached. Ty fell in behind Shelly, mimicking her moves as they climbed the port-side ladder. They landed quietly on the deck. Across the hull he could see glimpses of Wren's head bobbing as she crept along her side of the yacht. He focused on Shelly as they made their way, similar to Wren, toward the main cabin door.

He and Shelly stood on either side. Ty pointed down before pointing inside.

Shelly nodded, understanding he wanted her taking a crouched position once the door was open. He'd go high.

She reached out, slid the door open, and they ducked in. Ty took the lead now, moving his weapon from side to side as if clearing a room. The cabin space was larger than his entire apartment. The highly polished wood gleamed almost obnoxiously against the brass fixtures. Plush furniture and a well-stocked bar decorated the room. A ghastly garishly patterned carpet covered the floor.

Wren joined them, merging into their pattern easily. Ty held up a hand. They all froze.

He strained, listening. The roar of the wind was duller in here. But he could hear voices. Two, maybe three. He swallowed hard. Maybe more. Bracing himself, he walked forward, focused on keeping his balance as they reached the staircase that led down into the ship's belly.

Shelly tapped his shoulder, indicated she was going to go back out and around, then down. He took that to mean there was a separate entry into the keel of the boat. He glanced at Wren.

She nodded.

Shelly whipped around and went out the same way they had come in.

Ty placed a foot on the first step. He felt Wren at his back. Took another step. And another. The voices grew louder. He and Wren were headed in the right direction. Near as he could tell, however, he still couldn't see any faces.

He looked back at Wren, saw concern in her eyes before she shrugged. They were in too far now. They couldn't stop. Below there were four closed doors, two on each side of the narrow passageway.

He pressed a hand against the first one on the right. It opened easily. Empty. He shook his head. Instinct told him the next door was going to be the one.

Wren tested the doors on the left. Both unlocked and empty.

The familiar tension built inside him. With it came the calm of having spent so long as an agent. He'd walked through the right doors and the wrong doors and come out alive in every instance. This wasn't going to be any different.

He felt Wren at his back once more. Even if he did have something far more important to worry about now, he took one more step and looked up.

Directly into a security camera aimed at his face.

He straightened, lowered his weapon and signaled to Wren. The door in front of them was ripped open and the blond-haired man they had been searching for emerged, pistol in hand. And aimed directly at Ty's head.

"Just returning the visit, Lynch." Ty raised his arms and let the gun spin out of his grip. The weapon dangled from his finger. "You have something that doesn't belong to you."

Lynch smirked, eyed Wren. "Put it down. Or he gets the first bullet."

Ty had dealt with men like this before. When he'd been up against seemingly impossible odds, Lynch would take them both out if it came down to his own survival. "Don't," he told Wren.

Her finger shifted from the side barrel of her gun to the trigger.

"You don't want to do that." Lynch stepped aside, away from the open door.

Inside the room, Bradley Hawkins sat tied to a chair. His face was battered and bruised. Blood trickled out of his nose and the corner of his mouth, but he was breathing. His swollen eyes widened with hope when he saw Ty and Wren.

"Not much space." Lynch gestured over his shoulder. "You miss me, you might hit your guy. And you don't want to do that, do you?"

"Alice got your message," Wren told him. "She's awake. She's agreed not to testify."

Lynch smirked. "You don't expect me to take your word for it, do you?"

Wren shrugged. "That's your choice. You said you'd let the husband go if she didn't testify." She cocked her pistol. "Let him go."

Lynch looked at her for a long moment, then at Ty. When his gaze flicked back to the stairs, an unfamiliar knot of fear tightened in Ty's stomach.

"Fine." Lynch lowered his weapon, did a little bow and motioned them into the room. "Go on and take him."

Wren's brow furrowed.

Ty's throat was dry. "Do as he says, Wren." He kept a solid gaze on Lynch's accomplice at the top of the stairs. He had one arm locked around Shelly's neck. The other held a gun to her temple.

Shelly's eyes were sparked with fear, but her jaw tensed as if anger was trying to take control.

"Guns down, please." Lynch motioned to the floor. "Now."

Ty bent and did as he was told. He nodded for Wren to do the same. Only then did she turn enough to finally see whom Ty had already spotted.

"Consider this a hostage exchange," Lynch said as Ty stepped into the room, holding out his hand for Wren to join him. "When you're ready to negotiate the deputy's release, you know where to find us."

Ty held on to Wren's shoulders, felt the tension in her body as she prepared to leap at Lynch. He squeezed his hands and she got the message to take a step back. Lynch pulled the door closed and locked them in, presumably to keep them from following.

Immediately Wren went to work on the door. The sound of Shelly's muffled cries echoed through the boat. Ty checked on Bradley, found the man's pulse to be strong and steady.

"Bradley?" Ty untied the ropes to free Alice's husband, then bent down to the point they were practically nose to nose. "You okay?"

"I think so." Bradley wheezed a bit. "Don't know why they did this. Never asked me anything." He spit a little blood.

Ty met Wren's raging gaze. "That's twice they've lured us. What's the endgame? What are they playing at?" She threw herself against the door and bounced off it. She swore and kicked the door. "What do they want?"

"Now? Me." It was the only thing that made sense. "They believe they've taken out the sheriff protecting Alice. So they're going after the agent in charge of the case. Alice doesn't testify, I don't testify, the charges go away. There's no reason Treyhern won't win his appeal."

"But leaving you locked up on a boat isn't really getting them what they want, is it?" Wren tended to get snippy when she was angry. And scared.

Ty looked around. There was a king-size bed, a pair of night-stands and a trio of portholes along the top of the wall.

"They left a way out." Ty yanked open drawers, cabinets, even rooted in the closet, searching for something, anything, he could use to... Diving equipment sat among the clutter. He sorted through the tanks and tubing, found what he was look-ing for. "Diving weights." He hefted them, scooted between Wren and Bradley and climbed onto the bed.

"What are you—"

The rest of Wren's question was lost against the banging of the weight against the porthole. He could feel time ticking away, feel Shelly's life possibly ticking away. Regardless of the noise, he had to try whatever he could to get them out of here. He hit the glass again and again. Finally he cracked it. The pane split like a spiderweb and so he hit it one more time and it shattered. Air whipped in. He dropped the weight, got off the bed and leaned against the wall to keep his balance as the boat swayed. "Out you go." Wren looked dubious when he shoved the discarded coat over the jagged window shards, bent over and cupped his hands. "I'll boost you."

She tucked her hair behind her ears. "If I get stuck, I'll never forgive you."

"You won't get stuck." He couldn't look at her when he said it, though. "You should be able to drop down, then come around and open the door."

"Uh-huh." She shook her head, unzipped her jacket. "No way this is going to fit." Wearing only her jeans, T-shirt and a sweater, she planted her foot in his hands and he raised her up.

She cried out when she grabbed the frame of the window.
"What?"

"Glass shards. I'm fine. Brrrr." She shivered as she wiggled forward. "It's freaking freezing."

"Do you need me to push?" He had his hands out, ready at her butt.

"No, I don't need you to..." She grunted, shimmied some more. Let out a frustrated breath. "Okay, fine. Push."

He tried to be gentle, but that window wasn't forgiving.

"Harder!" she rage-whispered.

He did as she ordered, pushing hard enough that she dropped out of sight onto the deck. "Wren!" He climbed back up onto the bed and tried to see out the porthole, but his downward view was cut off. "Are you okay?"

No response. He shouted again but his voice disappeared into the wind.

The door busted open, slamming so hard against the wall that it bounced closed again. Wren shoved through. Her hair was disheveled, her palms bleeding, and, from her attitude, she seemed seriously ticked off.

"Next time, *you* get the porthole," she growled as she snatched up her jacket. She handed him back his gun and shoved her own into the back of her jeans. "Come on." She grabbed one of Bradley's arms and tucked herself under it. Ty followed suit and they hauled Alice's husband out of the chair. They maneuvered down the hall, up the stairs and out. The boat rocked under their feet but slowly they made it onto the marina.

The storm was almost on them. Besides the howling wind, there was rain and sleet making the situation even more challenging. "Everyone's inside because of the storm!" Ty yelled. "We'll have to get him to the hospital ourselves."

He could see the conflict on her face. She agreed. But she was worried about Shelly. Wren paused and wiped the hair from in front of her face. "Wait. I see something! You got him?"

"Yeah." Ty accepted the full weight of Bradley Hawkins. She ran down the dock, heading toward a fishing boat pitching side to side. She waved her arms wildly and got the attention of two men. Ty focused on keeping his balance. "Hang in there, Bradley. We're going to get you help, okay? You'll be at the hospital in no time. The doctors will fix you right up."

"My kids?" Bradley whispered brokenly. "Are they—"

"They're fine," Ty assured him. The icy air had turned his fingers numb. "The whole tower is looking after them. And Alice is awake."

Bradley's head snapped up. "She's awake?"

"Woke up a little while ago. Wren talked to her. You should be able to see her once you're patched up." Wren raced toward them, two bulky men right behind her.

"Cal and Nelson are going to get Bradley to the hospital," she yelled.

"We've got him." The larger of the bearded men took Bradley from Ty as if he were nothing more than a caught fish.

"We need to get your car," Wren yelled. "We have to get up that mountain and find out which house is Lynch's."

"Car won't do you any good!" the other man hollered. "They closed the road about an hour ago. Snowslide." The two men moved off with Bradley between them.

Ty could feel Wren's anxiety coming off her in waves. She looked to Ty, then over to the tram.

All he could do was shrug and nod. They had to get up that mountain—she'd said so herself.

"You have got to be kidding me." She stared at the dark sky.

"I'm not that funny," Ty said, attempting some humor. "I'm sorry. It's the only way we're going to get her back. We made a promise."

"I know." She shoved her hands into her wet hair and pushed it off her face. The fear was there, but so was the familiar determination of the woman he loved. "Come on. Let's go get our deputy."

Chapter Fourteen

The race through Splendor to reach the tram left Wren's legs and lungs burning. Maybe it was the cold or perhaps the desperation she couldn't shake. Her mind spun around the possibility she'd never see Shelly again. But that was nothing compared to the fear that Ty was most probably Barrett Lynch's main target.

The killer had drawn out this entire thing like some sick game. Going after Alice had done its job. It had lured Ty here. They'd been kept here by the mystery of Davey Whittaker's involvement and the abduction of Bradley Hawkins. The only person left on their list had to be Ty.

The three flights of stairs up to the tram entrance was almost too much. The air had thinned with the incoming storm. She could feel her head spinning, as if she weren't getting enough oxygen. Beside her, Ty seemed to be doing just fine if not for the concern etched on his face.

"When this is over, I want a vacation." She heaved a breath, then another. "Tropical. Warm. Scorching. With nothing to do other than lie on the beach or by the pool."

"You got it."

They rounded the final platform. "Are you planning on being this agreeable for the extent of our new relationship?"

"I'm planning on taking things a minute at a time." His smile was quick and cursory. "I've had seven years to get used to you, Wren. I've been trained."

She laughed, then choked and coughed. She nearly tumbled on the last step, but he caught her and pushed her forward. The ticket booth was empty when they reached the main level of the tower. She slammed her hands on the glass.

"They must have shut it down because of the storm!" Ty said.

"Then how did Lynch— Wait!" She stopped, strained to hear. "What's that?" It sounded like whimpering. She darted around the corner of the ticket booth, saw the door and shoved it open.

Inside, a young woman sat curled up in the corner on the floor underneath the counter, arms tight around her knees as she rocked. Tears fell from her dark eyes to her brown cheeks. When she saw Wren she gasped, tried to push farther back into the corner.

"It's okay." Wren dropped down, held up both hands. "I'm with the FBI. My name is Wren McKenna. This is my partner, Ty."

Her eyes shifted with recognition.

"You've heard our names before, haven't you?"

"Y-yes." She swiped at her cheeks. "This morning. Mayor Sully was talking about you when I picked up my breakfast."

"What's your name?" Ty asked.

"Yara." She sniffled. "Yara Kato."

"Yara, two men scared you, didn't they?" Wren asked. "Two men with Deputy Adjuk."

Yara nodded. "I told them the tram was dangerous. We always stop them during storms. I was supposed to be home, but I stayed here to study. It's quieter."

Wren could only imagine what noise there must be at her home. The wind was howling like a banshee and the entire tower felt like it was vibrating.

"They made me send the tram up." Tears pooled again. "I'm going to be in so much trouble. I'm not supposed to send them in the storm but they had a gun. They pointed it at me." The abject terror in Yara's eyes erased a good portion of Wren's fear.

"It's okay." Wren crept closer, touched the young woman's hands. "You did the right thing." She peeked up enough to see the second tram sitting in its bay. "Yara, I'm going to have to ask you to send us up in that one."

Yara shook her head. "It's too dangerous! The wind—"

"I know, you're afraid of getting in trouble."

"Not just that." Yara looked slightly offended. "I don't want you to die. Then no one will be able to save Shelly."

"Hey." Wren needed every ounce of reassurance she could find. "We aren't going to let anyone hurt Shelly. She's our friend. And we promised we'd have her back. But we can't go get her without your help. We'll be okay." Even as she said it, the fear tasted like a lie in her mouth. "The system's mostly automated, right?"

Yara nodded.

"Okay, then just tell me what buttons to push."

Yara's eyes cleared. "You're really going to go up there to get her?"

"We really are," Ty said.

Yara took a trembling breath and let Wren pull her to her feet. "It'll have to go slower than normal. Otherwise the tram—"

"Don't!" Wren ordered sharply. "Just do me a favor and don't tell me what could happen."

Yara nodded.

"Can you hand me your notebook and a pen?" She flexed her hands, praying she could make them work properly. When Yara gave them to her, Wren scribbled down Howell's number. "If anything goes wrong, I want you to make a call. This is my brother. He's here in Splendor. He's going to need to know."

"Okay."

Wren gave her a quick hug. "Thank you for your help. Open the doors for us, yeah? Then send us up."

"You sure about this?" Ty asked when the two of them were back outside.

"Absolutely not." Never in her life had her heart pounded this hard and fast. At this rate it was going to be able to live outside her chest. She didn't stop moving. She didn't dare to. Arms stiff at her sides, her hands clenched into fists so tight she couldn't even feel them, she approached the shiny red thirty-passenger cable car and stepped through the open door.

"Hold on to me," Ty said and reached for her as the door slid shut behind them. She grabbed hold, tried to remember to breathe. Her feet felt like they were stuck in cement, but she moved an inch, maybe two, to the side, grasped the metal pole with her free hand as the tram glided away from the tower.

As it picked up a bit of pace, the car lurched from one side to the other, buffeted by the strong wind. She let go of Ty and locked her other hand around the pole, hugging it as the tram made its way up, into the foggy storm.

"We're in this together." Ty stood next to her, his arms around her as if wanting to remind her he was there. As if she could forget. The rocking got worse. She could hear the cables overhead straining and whining. The padded plastic seats around the perimeter of the car looked comfortable; she wished she had the courage to try to sit.

"I'm not going anywhere, Wren."

She laughed nervously. "Where would you go?" Her voice sounded like a mouse's squeak. "This is pathetic. I have no idea where it even comes from. But it's just—" she struggled for breath "—paralyzing." The tram seemed to be moving in slow motion. "It's never going to end."

"Nothing lasts forever. And look at the bright side."

She stared at him with narrow-eyed suspicion as fog blanketed the tram.

"After this, I'm betting heights won't bother you so much. Maybe you'll even be willing to go zip-lining with me."

"Keep dreaming, Savakis." But the idea made her smile. They rumbled past something. "What was that?"

"One of three towers," Ty said. "Perfectly normal." He shifted his feet farther apart as the tram swayed more violently. "That's one down and two to go."

"I'd say a prayer if only I could remember any of them."

"I thought you all went to church every Sunday. Another McKenna family tradition."

"Did." She choked down the bile rising in her throat. "Didn't really pay that much attention. Oh, hey, here's a silver lining." She cleared her throat. "If we die, you're off the hook with monthly McKenna dinners."

"Then I've got another reason to stay alive." He pressed his mouth to hers. "I think I'm going to like being a McKenna."

She sob-laughed and grabbed hold of him. "I really, really hate this."

"I know. But in fact, it could be—"

"Do *not* say it," she ordered.

"Worse."

No sooner was the word out of his mouth than the overhead mechanism let out a jaw-dropping screech. The tram slammed to a stop. Wren and Ty were thrown to the floor as the doors on either side slid open.

Wren screamed, flailing frantically for the metal pole as she felt herself sliding toward the opening.

"Hang on!" Ty yelled and gripped the nearest post. With his free hand, he grabbed a fistful of her jacket and tried to tug her toward him.

The storm shot through the tram, filling the thinning air with fog and rain and now snow.

"Ty!" She could feel herself slipping out of the jacket. The weight of her body was pulling her free. The tram shuddered and lurched. Her body twisted and suddenly she could feel her feet, then her legs, dangling free of the tram.

"No!" Ty yelled and groaned at the same time.

She dropped another inch. Wren screamed, fingers flexing uselessly. There seemed no way to stop herself from falling the thousands of feet to the ground.

Panic surged. The edge of the cable car pushed hard into her stomach. Almost the whole bottom half of her dangled out of the tram. She had one hand on the edge, the other barely holding on to Ty's. She turned her head.

"Not. Going. To. Happen." Ty spit out each word as if it were an oath. "Don't look down, Wren. Wren!" he yelled. But she was unable to resist temptation. "Wren, don't!"

It was an odd moment. Certainty descended. She felt the absolute acceptance that she was about to die. She didn't want to, of course. She'd miss her family and she knew they'd miss her. And Ty. Her breath froze in her throat and she felt the tears in her eyes turn to ice. What she could have had with Ty.

The thought reignited her spark to live.

"Wren!"

She looked up, saw Ty had shifted position. He now had his other hand free. A hand that reached out for her now.

"Grab hold!" he hollered. "I won't let you go. I promise. Trust me and grab hold."

He promised.

It took every ounce of strength she possessed to release her grip on the tram. But she did and shot her arm up to where he could latch on to her wrist. Holding both her hands now, he nodded when she met his eyes.

A fierce gust of wind hit the tram and she closed her eyes, surrendered and put her trust in Ty.

He tugged hard, quickly jerking her toward him as the tram rocked. She flew up and cried out as she landed, his hold gone. But in the next second he locked his arms around her and rolled her to safety at the back of the car.

She clung to him, insisting; she told herself that she'd never let him go, not in any sense of the word. Her breathing slowed, his, too, and she tried to remember how to think. Her brain was blank.

The overhead mechanism clanged before they started moving once more. She laughed, long and loud, and felt the tears on her cheeks as she held on to the man who'd saved her life. Just as his hold on her tightened.

"Amazing," he whispered into her ear, his breath hot against her skin. "Thank you. Thank you for trusting me. I love you, Wren." He squeezed his arms so tight he stole what was left of her air. "I love you so much and I'm never letting you go."

"Okay." Her muffled response had them both laughing.

They remained where they were, huddled together as the tram made its way slowly to the highest deck. She didn't think she'd ever heard a more beautiful sound than that of the tram locking into place.

The rocking stopped. The doors slid closed before one side slid open again.

"The thing's possessed," Ty muttered. "Can you move?"

"Right now, I think I can fly." She shoved to her feet, held out her hand to help him up.

Every inch of her ached to the point she'd probably be unable to walk tomorrow. But right now? She checked to make sure her gun was still in place. "You good?" she asked Ty as he seemed to need a moment to get his legs under him.

"I will be." He bent over, planted his hands on his knees. "You ready to finish this?"

"More than and we'd best make it fast. Now even their machinery is trying to kill us."

"What do you mean?" Ty asked. He followed her out.

"That thing. The tram system?" She pointed back at the car of death. "It was built by TitanForge Technologies."

"They hacked into it," Ty said dazedly. "That's why it stopped."

"That's what I'm betting." And the very idea really, really ticked her off.

Apparently sixty-mile-an-hour winds and snow coming down was nothing when in the presence of Wren McKenna.

Ty trudged along beside her, keeping an eye out for the side road located about a hundred yards from the tram deck. The house owned by Apex shouldn't be much farther, but if they didn't get there fast, the windchill was going to take him and his partner out.

"There!" Wren shoved her hood back and pointed to the left.

They headed up a slight hill, found themselves in front of the house almost immediately.

They flanked the door and brought out their weapons. Ty continued to pray that his frozen hands would work. "We expect anything," he told her. "They're expecting us."

"Unless they think we fell out of the cable car." She grinned. "I'm really hoping we surprise them."

She was about to touch the handle when the door opened.

Ty went low this time. Wren went high. They left the door open as they moved through the marble foyer.

They made it as far as the main seating room before a slow clap of applause exploded through the house.

"Impressive." Lynch's voice rang against Ty's ears. "If I hadn't been hired to kill you, I'd recommend TitanForge hire you. Both of you."

"It's doubtful you're going to have a job for much longer," Wren said as the man stepped out of the shadows. The house was cold, unlit and monstrous. Ty bet the power had gone out at the beginning of the storm. "Where's the deputy?"

"She's resting. It's been a long day."

Ty's ears perked at the squeak behind him. He spun and fired.

Lynch's second flew back off his feet and landed dead on the floor.

Lynch rolled his eyes. "Told that moron to get better shoes." The shooting was evidently cause enough for Lynch to draw his own weapon and aim it at Wren. "Put your gun down, Savakis."

Tired of being a puppet, Ty ignored him and advanced. "No."

"Put it down or she's dead."

"You put your weapon down, Ty, and I'll shoot you myself," Wren warned.

"Feisty," Lynch said. "I like that."

Ty took another step forward. Then another. And saw a flash of doubt on Lynch's face. "There's nowhere to go. Storm's locked everything down. Once you leave the mountain, there's a US marshal waiting in Splendor to take you into custody."

Lynch's eyes narrowed. "I don't believe you."

"Howell McKenna," Wren said. "My brother. And trust me when I say you can't hole up in here waiting him out. He'll come get you. Especially if I don't turn up."

"Can he fly?" Lynch asked. "Because in about eight hours a helicopter is going to be arriving with my boss and I'll be out of here." He shifted his gun from Wren to Ty, then back to Wren. "Which one to shoot first?"

"How about you?"

Ty and Wren both jumped at the sound of the gunshot.

Lynch's face went completely white, shock barely having time to register in his dark eyes before he pitched forward and landed on the floor.

He didn't move.

Shelly, leaning heavily against the door frame, dropped her

arm to the side and sagged forward. Ty dived for her, caught her before she collapsed. "Hey. Hey, Shelly. You okay?"

Wren was at his side immediately, helping to prop Shelly up, narrowing her gaze as she checked for any indication of injuries.

"Using your X-ray vision?" Shelly mumbled. "You two sure seem like superheroes to me."

Wren smiled.

Ty slipped the gun out of Shelly's hand, set it aside. "Where did they keep you?"

"Basement. Back there." She pointed behind her. "They drugged me. Offered me water and I fell for it. Ick." She lifted a hand to her bruised throat. "I made myself throw up. I hate throwing up."

"You are going to make a brilliant agent, Deputy Adjuk," Wren said.

"Hmm." Shelly grinned. "I'm tired."

"That's okay. You got the bad guy."

"I did, didn't I?" Shelly managed one more smile before she gave in.

Wren straightened and smiled. "I think we did it. I think we closed the case."

"Not quite yet," Ty said, as a new plan began to form. "But soon."

Three hours, almost to the minute, and Wren and Ty were settled on a sofa in the living room of the mini mansion owned by Apex. They'd moved Shelly into one of the bedrooms for her to sleep it off. She and Ty planned to get the deputy to the doctor as soon as they were back in Splendor. But, for now, they were enjoying the calm after the storm.

"No, we're fine, Howell. But we will eventually need a full team from Anchorage to help clean this matter up." Wren looked over at Ty before she snuggled closer. "Lynch and his buddy are dead. We're just waiting on one more to arrive. As soon as the tram's been cleared for operation, Ty, Shelly and I will be on our way down. Yes." She laughed. "Yes, I said *tram*. It's a long story. Talk soon, okay? Love you." She ended the call, rested her head on Ty's shoulder. "Sheriff Egbert's okay. He'll be away from the job for a while. Rehab's going to be tough, but he's out of the woods."

Ty heaved a sigh of relief. "Now, that's good news."

"Would you like more good news?" She was just getting started. "Apparently my brother took it upon himself to call our boss." She couldn't seem to stop smiling.

"Oh?"

"Mmm. He explained that it wasn't just a witness who was in danger of lethal retaliation, but one of Frisco's own agents, namely you. It turns out, thanks to all of us, that several cases across various agencies were closed. Justice has triumphed yet again, and due to my brother's extra-fast talking, you and I are not only *not* in trouble, but in line for a commendation." She actually giggled. "I bet Frisco had a hard time saying no when he heard. He's not going to be able to fire you or suspend me. Yay!"

Ty didn't respond.

Concerned, she turned her head to look at him. "What?"

"I'm just... That he'd do that." He shrugged. "That's pretty awesome of him."

"It's what family does," she said. "Best get used to it because the word is out. Howell also called my mother, so you're officially on the dinner-invite list."

"No place else I'd rather be." He pressed a kiss to the top of her head. "I do have a favor to ask."

"Anything."

"You say that now," he teased. "You mentioned that if I decided to go see my father and brother, you'd come with me. Did you mean it?"

"I did." She didn't like the idea. She knew how much he'd been hurt by his family. She didn't want him stepping into the line of emotional fire again. "Do you want to go see them?"

"I think I have to. Not for them," he added quickly. "For me. I need to close that book before I can start writing another one."

"Then I will come with you. Can I bring my gun?"

"No." He laughed and they both looked up. There was the distinct sound of whapping helicopter blades. "You ready to do this?"

"More than." But neither of them moved. They simply sat there, on the sofa, staring at the front door.

The key in the lock had them shifting away from one another, both sitting forward as Roy Calvin entered the house. He wore a long beige wool coat, his hair slicked back, his cheeks red and ruddy. He carried a large metal suitcase in one hand that he set on the floor almost immediately.

"Barrett? Is it done?" He took off his jacket. "I've got your money."

"He won't be needing it." Ty's voice froze the owner of Titan Holdings just inside the living room. "Nice to finally meet you, Mr. Calvin." Ty gestured to one of the empty chairs. "Please. Take a seat."

Wren watched with a certain growing pleasure as Roy Calvin walked stiffly toward them. "I take it we don't need to introduce ourselves?"

Calvin remained silent.

"You're a smart guy, aren't you, Roy?" Ty said. "You've stopped talking because you don't want to further incriminate yourself. Good play. It won't help, of course." He set the cell phone they'd found on Barrett Lynch's body on the coffee table, beside the gun they suspected had been used to kill Davey Whittaker and the rifle used on the sheriff. "Funny thing about Barrett Lynch. He didn't trust anyone. Not even you. He recorded every conversation the two of you had over the past month and a half. He even called you when he made contact with Davey Whittaker. Said he'd found the perfect patsy for Alice's accident. She's fine, by the way, in case you were wondering."

Calvin's face went stone-cold still. "What do you want?"

"So many things," Ty said.

Wren's pride in his patience and composure soared. Her joy at seeing him be able to close this chapter of his life once and for all, immeasurable.

"But we're going to start with Titan Holdings writing a very generous check to Beatrice Mulvaney, for the death of her nephew."

"I won't—"

"And then you're going to resign from Titan. You'd have to do that anyway," Ty said before Calvin could interrupt. "Because the Justice Department has just opened an investigation into all aspects of your business practices. Trust me, you aren't going to want to deal with that. You'll have other things to worry about."

"What other things?" Calvin began to sweat. Tiny beads of perspiration dotted his upper lip and forehead.

"You're entering the witness protection program," Ty said. "You'll have to after you testify about your dealings with Ambrose Treyhern. You're going to admit that your law firm took on his case with the intent of eliminating the witnesses against him. I don't think new attorneys—his old ones are being notified of their possible disbarment in the near future—will be easy to find. You're both going to be held responsible for the actions taken against Alice Hawkins, her husband, Sheriff Egbert and Deputy Adjuk."

"I really like that last part." Shelly entered the room, slowly, as if every step she took hurt. Her face was bruised, her lip bloodied, but she stayed on her feet and stood behind Wren and Ty.

"You will testify against Treyhern," Ty said firmly. "You will tell the truth about everything, and you'll be the one who will lock him in his cell forever. It'll let Alice off the hook, so in a way, your plan worked. She won't be testifying. And she and her family will stay here in Splendor, safe. For the rest of their lives." Ty took a deep breath and glanced at her. "Is that everything?"

"For now," Wren said. "You can relax for a little while," she told Calvin as he sat awkwardly in his chair. "The Marshals will be waiting for us once the trams start working again." She stood. "Can I get you something to eat or drink?"

Calvin glared at her.

Wren grinned. "All right, then. Ty? Shelly?"

"I, ah, want to thank you both." Shelly hugged her arms around her torso. "For everything. For coming to get me."

"We promised," Ty said. "Simple as that."

"I, um… I don't think I'm going to be applying to the FBI."

Wren met her steely gaze. "Please don't tell us this incident scared you out of law enforcement. You're a natural at this, Shelly."

She nodded. "I know. That's why I'm going to stay here in Splendor. So I can take over when Sheriff Egbert retires. These guys showed me something that I forgot. This is my home. My people. My town. I'm sticking with it and will make sure every citizen is safe."

Wren's heart skipped a beat. "That sounds like a great plan."

"You'll come back, I hope? To visit?" the deputy asked Wren.

"Oh, we'll definitely be back," Ty said, and he got to his feet to stand beside Wren. "I've had some savings stashed away for a long time. And I think I'm finally ready to invest in a property. Say an apartment in Skyway Tower?" He turned expectant eyes on Wren. "Our home away from home?"

Wren pressed her lips together, hope soaring inside of her. "Do I still get a vacation in the tropics?"

"Absolutely."

"Sounds like the deal of a lifetime to me." She threw her arms around his neck and kissed him. "Partner."

* * * * *

Romantic Suspense

Danger. Passion. Drama.

Available Next Month

Colton's Deadly Trap Patricia Sargeant
The Twin's Bodyguard Veronica Forand

....

Hostage Security Lisa Childs
Breaking The Code Maria Lokken

....

 LOVE INSPIRED

K-9 Alaskan Defence Sarah Varland
Uncovering The Truth Carol J. Post

Larger Print

....

 LOVE INSPIRED

Defending The Child Sharon Dunn
Lethal Wilderness Trap Susan Furlong

....

 LOVE INSPIRED

Cold Case Mountain Murder Rhonda Starnes
Christmas In The Crosshairs Deena Alexander

Keep reading for an excerpt of a new title
from the Intrigue series,
TRACKING DOWN THE LAWMAN'S SON
by Delores Fossen

Chapter One

Deputy Luca Vanetti ran through the ER doors the moment they slid open, and he made a beeline to the reception desk. The nurse on duty saw him coming and got to her feet. Luca figured the concern on her face was a drop in the bucket compared to his.

He tried to tamp down the worry and fear that were firing through him. Tried not to jump to any bad conclusions, but Bree and his baby boy could be hurt.

Or worse.

No, Luca couldn't deal with *worse* right now.

He just needed to see Bree McCullough and his two-month-old son, Gabriel, and then try to get to the bottom of what'd happened. Bree and he might barely be on speaking terms, but they both loved Gabriel, and Bree would know what a gut punch it was for Luca to get a report that she'd been in a serious car accident.

"Where are they?" Luca demanded before he even reached the reception desk.

The nurse, Alisha Cameron, was someone he'd known his whole life. Something that could be said about most people in their small hometown of Saddle Ridge, Texas, where there weren't many degrees of separation.

Alisha motioned toward the hall. "The exam room on the right. Slater's already here."

Slater McCullough was not only a fellow deputy at the Saddle Ridge Sheriff's Office, but he was also Bree's older brother. Luca had expected him to be here since Slater was the responding officer who'd arrived on the scene of the single car accident, only to learn his sister was the driver.

"Gabriel wasn't in the vehicle with Bree," Slater said the moment he spotted Luca. "I just got off the phone with the nanny, and Gabriel's with her."

Some of the tightness eased up in Luca's chest. Some. His baby boy wasn't hurt. "And Bree?" Luca managed to ask.

"She's in with the doctor now," Slater said after he swallowed hard. "She has a head injury, and they're examining her."

"How bad?" Luca wanted to know.

Slater shook his head. "I'm not sure. When I arrived on scene, she was trying to get out of the car, but her seat belt was jammed, and she couldn't reach her phone. There was blood," he added. "Some scrapes and cuts, too, on her face, but I think most of those came from the airbag when it deployed."

"What happened?" Luca wanted to know. "Why did she crash?"

"I'm not sure what caused the accident." He paused, his gaze meeting Luca's. "Her car went off the road right before the Saddle Ridge Creek bridge, and she slammed into a tree. If she hadn't hit the tree, her car would have plunged into the creek."

Hell. That was where his parents had been killed, so Luca knew firsthand that a collision like that could have been fatal because the creek was more than twenty feet deep in spots. But crashing into a tree could have killed her, too.

Luca studied Slater's eyes that were a genetic copy of not

only Bree's but of Gabriel's. "Why did she go off the road?" he pressed.

Slater shook his head again. "I don't know. Like I said, she was woozy, and I arrived on scene only a minute or two before the ambulance got there. The EMTs loaded her right away and brought her here."

Because Luca knew Slater well, he could see that Slater was worried. And troubled. "You said Bree has a head injury. How bad?" Luca asked.

"I don't know," Slater repeated. He scrubbed his hands over his face. "Other than what I've told you, the only other thing I know is a delivery driver traveling on that road spotted Bree's car and called it in. There were tread marks nearby, but I have no idea if they were from her vehicle or not. The delivery driver didn't see any other vehicles around."

So, maybe she'd gotten distracted or something and had lost control of the car. That wasn't like Bree, though. She was usually ultra-focused. A skill set she needed for her job as legal consultant for the Texas Rangers. But she was also the mother of a two-month-old baby, and it was possible lack of sleep had played into this.

That possibility gave Luca another gut punch. Because he could see how this would have played out. Even if Bree had been exhausted, she wouldn't have asked him for help. In fact, he was probably the last person in Saddle Ridge she would have turned to. Ironic, since they had once been lovers.

Had.

That was definitely in the past, and as far as Bree was concerned, it wouldn't be repeated. Luca was learning to live with that even though they'd had an on-again, off-again thing since high school. The *off* had become permanent eleven months ago when they'd landed in bed after Bree's father had been murdered.

That brought on gut punch number three of the day.

Because Bree's late father, Sheriff Cliff McCullough, hadn't only been Luca's boss, he'd been his surrogate father after Luca's parents had died in a car crash when Luca had been just sixteen. Luca had been grieving and on shaky emotional ground following Cliff's murder. Bree had been, too, and they'd spent the night together.

The night when she'd gotten pregnant with Gabriel.

Bree hadn't told him that though until four months ago when she'd moved back home. Only then had Luca learned he was going to be a father. Luca hadn't quite managed to forgive Bree for shutting him out like that, but she apparently didn't want his forgiveness.

The door to the exam room opened, and Dr. Nathan Bagley stepped out. Another familiar face but not an especially friendly one. Well, not friendly toward Luca anyway. Luca knew Nathan had always seen him as a romantic rival. During Bree and Luca's off-again phases, Nathan and she had dated.

"How is she?" Luca immediately asked.

The doctor didn't get a chance to answer though. "I'm fine," Luca heard Bree say.

Nathan's sigh indicated he didn't quite agree with his patient, but he stepped back out of the doorway, and Luca saw another nurse who was in the process of washing her hands.

And Bree.

Her short dark brown hair was tangled and flecked with powder from the airbag. And she was pale. So pale. She was also getting up from the exam table. Not easily. She was wobbling a little, and Luca immediately went to her, took hold of her arm and steadied her.

There was blood on her cream-colored shirt. A few flecks

of dried blood, too, on her right cheek by her ear. That had no doubt come from the cut on her head that was now stitched up.

Bree dodged his gaze, but that was the norm for them these days. "Thanks," she muttered, and stepped out of his grip. "I'm fine," she repeated, her gaze pinned to Slater.

"You're sure about that?" Slater questioned. He went to her, gently cupped her chin, lifting it while he examined her.

"Sure," she insisted at the same moment that Nathan added his own comment.

"She doesn't appear to have a concussion, but I'd like to run some tests," the doctor said. "I'd also like to admit her for observation for the head injury."

All of that sounded reasonable to Luca, but Bree clearly wasn't on board with it. "I'm fine. I want to go home and check on Gabriel."

"Gabriel's okay," Slater assured her. "I called the nanny just a couple of minutes ago."

Now it was Bree's turn to study her brother's face, and it seemed to Luca that she was making sure he was telling her the truth.

What the heck was going on?

Slater and Bree were close, and Slater wouldn't have lied to her. Well, not under these circumstances anyway. And not about Gabriel. Slater might have downplayed the truth though if Bree had been in serious condition, but that wasn't the case.

"I need to go home," Bree repeated. "Can you give me a ride?" she asked, and then moved away from Slater. She went to the small counter where the nurse was now standing and picked up her purse.

"Hold on a second." Slater stepped in front of her to stop her from heading for the door. "What happened? Why did you wreck?"

Her pause only lasted a couple of seconds, but it was

enough to make Luca even more concerned about her. "A deer ran out on the road in front of me," Bree said. "I swerved to miss it and lost control."

There were indeed plenty of deer and other wildlife in the woods around the creek, and drivers did hit them from time to time. But something about this still felt, well, off.

"Why were you on that road?" Luca asked. It wasn't anywhere near Bree's place. Her house was one she'd inherited from her grandparents when she'd turned twenty-one, and it was on the outskirts of the other side of town.

"I was going to Austin for a business meeting," she said.

That didn't seem off. Bree was a lawyer who did legal consultations for the Texas Rangers and some state agencies. Most days, she worked from home, but she sometimes had meetings in nearby San Antonio or Austin.

"I thought I was going to end up in the creek," she added in a mutter.

Now she looked at Luca. Or rather glanced at him, and he saw the apology in her eyes. She no doubt knew it always hit him hard to be reminded of his parents' deaths.

"A deer," Slater muttered, a question in his tone.

"Yes," she verified, and Bree suddenly sounded a whole lot stronger. She didn't look it though. She still seemed plenty unsteady to Luca. "And now I need to go home and see my baby."

This time, it was Nathan who maneuvered in front of her. "You hit your head. You really should stay here for observation. You need to have medical supervision."

"I can get someone in my family to stay with me," Bree insisted right back. "I need to check on Gabriel."

Nathan huffed and turned to Slater to plead his case. "Head injuries can be dangerous. She shouldn't be alone."

A muscle flickered in Slater's jaw, and he volleyed glances

at both his sister and the doctor. Slater must have seen the determination on Bree's face because he sighed.

"She won't be alone," Slater told Nathan. "I'll make sure someone is with her for the next twenty-four hours."

Nathan repeated his huff, but his obvious objection didn't stop Bree. "I'll phone in a script for pain meds," he called out as Bree headed for the door. Slater and Luca were right behind her.

"Where are you parked?" she asked without looking back at them.

"By the ambulances," Slater provided. It wasn't far, but Luca's cruiser was closer.

"I'm right by the ER door," Luca said. He'd left his cruiser there when he'd been in a near panic to check on Bree and their son.

"Your cruiser then," Bree said, and her glance was just long enough for Luca to confirm she was talking to him.

She was obviously shaken to the core so Luca understood her urgent need to see Gabriel. The baby would likely steady her nerves. Again though, it seemed like more than that.

"Slater, why don't you ride with us, and I can give you a statement about the accident?" Bree asked when they stepped outside. She fired glances around as if looking for something.

Or someone.

"Sure," Slater said, sounding as concerned and skeptical as Luca was. He opened the passenger's side door to help Bree in, and he slid into the back seat.

"Drive," Bree insisted the moment Luca got behind the wheel.

Luca didn't press her to explain what the heck was going on. He pulled out of the hospital parking lot while he, too, glanced around.

"All right, what's wrong?" Slater demanded once they were on the way.

Bree dragged in a quick breath and squeezed her eyes shut for a moment. "Someone ran me off the road." Her voice cracked. "I think someone tried to kill me."

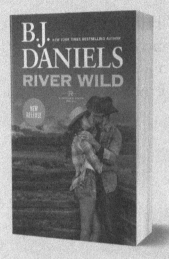

Subscribe and fall in love with a Mills & Boon series today!

You'll be among the first to read stories delivered to your door monthly and enjoy great savings.

WE SIMPLY LOVE ROMANCE

MILLS & BOON

—— JOIN US ——

Sign up to our newsletter to stay up to date with...

- Exclusive member discount codes
- Competitions
- New release book information
- All the latest news on your favourite authors

Plus...
get $10 off your first order.
What's not to love?

Sign up at **millsandboon.com.au/newsletter**